Beatrice Hitchman was born in London in 1980. She read English and French at Edinburgh University and then took an MA in Comparative Literature. After a year living in Paris, she moved back to the UK and worked in television as a documentary video editor; she has also written and directed short films. In 2009, she completed the Bath Spa MA in Creative Writing, and won the Greene & Heaton Prize for *Petite Mort*, which is her first novel.

PETITE MORT

Beatrice Hitchman

A complete catalogue record for this book can be obtained
from the British Library on request

The right of Beatrice Hitchman to be identified as the author of this work has been
asserted by her in accordance with the Copyright, Designs and Patents Act 1988

First published in 2013 by Serpent's Tail,
an imprint of Profile Books Ltd
3A Exmouth House
Pine Street
London EC1R 0JH
website: www.serpentstail.com

ISBN 978 1 84668 906 2 (hardback)
ISBN 978 1 84668 950 5 (trade paperback)
eISBN 978 1 84765 868 5

Designed and typeset by sue@lambledesign.demon.co.uk

Printed by Clays, Bungay, Suffolk

10 9 8 7 6 5 4 3 2 1

Thanks to: Antony Topping and Rebecca Gray for their brilliance, generosity and tact; to Anna-Marie Fitzgerald, Ruthie Petrie, Serpent's Tail, Greene & Heaton; Tricia Wastvedt, Clare Wallace, Bath Spa comrades and tutors; Clare George and the SW Writers.

To Richard Abel, Ginette Vincendeau, Rebecca Feasey, Kathrina Glitre, Luke McKernan, Paul Sargent, Catherine Elliott for their help — inventions, inaccuracies or flights of fancy are mine alone. The line *Who Doesn't Come Through the Door to Get Home* is an excerpt from 'Song' by Cynthia Zarin.

To Danny Palluel, Jo Hennessey, Churnjeet Mahn, Vin Bondah, Jen and Lucy, Tim and Ed, Pete and Lee, Anna Rutherford, Lou Trimby, Alison Coombe and LEBC, John and Lesley Hodson, the Sear-Webbs; Frank Hitchman, Bruce Ritchie, Richard and Jay Hitchman, Ellie Hitchman; my much-missed grandmother, Betty Allfree. And most of all, to Trish Hodson with love.

for T.

Le Monde, 2. juin 1967

MYSTERE!

PARIS, Tuesday – Film technicians examining a recently rediscovered silent film print, *Petite Mort,* have found that a segment of the film is missing.

A fifty-year-old revenant

Though it was shot in 1914, the film had never before been viewed.

An inferno at the Pathé factory destroyed the film's source material before it could be distributed.

The film was not re-shot because of the involvement of the star, Adèle Roux, in a murder trial later that year – and *Petite Mort* passed into cinematic legend.

Last month, a housewife from Vincennes brought a film reel in to the Cinémathèque for assessment. She had found it during a clear-out of her basement.

The whereabouts of the missing sequence, however, remains a mystery.

Juliette BLANC
News Team
Paris

THE ASP

1909

LIGHT IN A LIGHT-BOX, light in your beloved's eyes, is not as light as the morning sun filtering through leaves. Light in the south moves differently; everything takes its time.

Today, it moves like treacle and so do we. I and my only sister, Camille – a bright-eyed, sly duplicate of myself – are lounging on the riverbank.

For once, we're allies. 'We don't have to go back,' I say to her, trailing my fingers in the shallow water, 'he can't make us. She should do her work properly. We can't do everything.' We pause, picturing our mother straightening her back after sweeping the kitchen. Out of spite, I don't tell Camille what I've come to suspect: that our mother's ballooning knuckles make even the smallest movements painful.

'Where will we go?' Camille asks, turning the idea over to catch the light.

'Oh, I don't know,' I answer, settling back and shutting my eyes, 'we'll find jobs as maids in some large house. We've had the practice.'

Not for the first time, I fight down the feeling that she is buttering me up: Camille should not be, at eleven, as sharp or as secretive as she is. She isn't remotely interested in my cast-off clothes, or in dolls, or reading, or in religion; nobody seems to know what Camille is interested in. I so wanted a younger sister to admire me and to confide in, and still she simply gives the impression of biding her time.

They aren't there, and then they are: ten boys from the

village, a gang, round-shouldered and low-browed, skirting the fringes of being men. They rise in clumps from the scrub around the stream. The largest is Eluard, the stableman's son, a boy who promises to be handsome, who knows how to charm, but whom we avoid, because everyone knows there is something wrong with Eluard. He doesn't go to the village school any more, although the little girl lived. Her family couldn't afford to move more than a few hundred yards up the hill away from Eluard's family home.

'What do you want?' I ask, Camille standing behind me, her breath ragged. Eluard doesn't even bother to study his nails. 'A little kiss,' he whispers, and makes a grab at my wrist, which slips through his grasp. The other boys step closer. Their faces look as though they've been melted down and clumsily pressed back together, as though someone had tried to mould them into what-is-presentable. As I step back to get away from them, the curve of a tree-trunk bumps my spine. The nearest house is a mile away.

Eluard smiles, as though it doesn't matter that his first attempt has failed. He knows he has us cornered, and it will only please him more that there are two of us, one to be played with and one to watch the show. He stands, rocking back and forth on his heels, hands in pockets in an exaggerated display of nonchalance. As he tilts back and forth, *rock, rock*, I think about pushing him over and running. In my mind's eye, I see myself streak up the hill, making a furrow in the corn, my mother opening the door to safety; I imagine Camille, left behind as the boys close in.

Eluard lays his palm under his mouth, puckers his lips and releases them. The sound hisses to us, an arrow finding its mark. 'What if I don't want to?' I say, feeling Camille start to climb the tree behind us. Eluard shrugs and the boys move a step closer in, laughing at her attempts to get away. Camille's boot scrapes a peeling off the bark by my ear. Eluard merely stands watching her, and when I can hear she is out of reach I steal a glance up. She sits atop the tree, a strange bird, black skirt buffeted by a wind that has come from nowhere. Eluard snatches at me again and this time his grip is firm, so I bite till I feel my teeth scrape bone and he yells and I jump for the lowest branch and pull myself up.

The lower branches snap as they try to swarm up the tree after me; not one of them is light enough, and each tumbles to the ground. 'Help me up,' I say, and Camille looks blankly at me. Then her hand wraps around mine and we sit together on the highest branch. Eluard prowls at the foot of the shelter, crying over the pointed wounds on his wrist.

'We can wait,' he says, and he points to the lowering sun, mouth still wrapped round his wrist. One by one they all sit down cross-legged around the tree, and all faces turn to his as he produces a stick and starts to whittle it, whistling. The sculpture is half-finished, a totem like a mandrake root, pin-head perched on voluminous breasts. Eluard flicks shavings off the wood swiftly and indiscriminately. Camille stares at the knife. 'I promise nothing will happen to you,' I say to her quietly, 'someone will come.' She shakes her head.

The story is an old one, and it goes like this: in the Middle Ages, our local city was under siege from the Saracens, and the people had all but starved to death. So the aldermen fattened up their one remaining animal and sent it out as a gift to the invading forces. Deducing from this gesture that the inhabitants of the city were healthy and well-stocked with food, the Saracens gave up the fight, and as they retreated, the bells of the city rang out in gratitude – *carcas sona*. But perched atop the sapling, ridiculous and terrified, Camille and I have nothing to offer the boys but ourselves.

After a while, the light changes, speeds up; the wind whips up clouds and a gentle rain begins to patter down. The boys grumble and kick stones, but they don't dare to disobey their ringleader, and Camille hunches trembling into my shoulders as the rain finds a way down the back of our necks. Eluard is standing now, kicking the base of the tree savagely, his boot slipping on the wet bark. 'When I get down,' I whisper, 'run for the house. It's me they want.' As I say this Camille studies me oddly, as though offended – *how can you be so sure* – but in the short silence that follows, she nods.

'I'm coming down,' I shout, starting to lower myself down the central branch. Away across the valley the thin wail of the evening bells begins, calling the handful of faithful, the old and the sick, to worship; Eluard smiles, just as the lanky figure of Père Simon, our priest, breaks cover from the nearby scrub and pauses, his thin legs stepping high in the long grass. 'Adèle,' he calls, voice full of concern, 'whatever are you doing up that tree?'

I slither down the trunk before the world can change its mind. Camille grips my hand as we stand at the foot of the tree, while Père Simon looks at each of the boys in turn, his face blank. 'I think this is a good enough spot for my washing,' he says, and sits down on a rock by the edge of the river. He settles, arms folded, watching Eluard. Camille and I start up the path towards the house. When I turn, further up the hill, Père Simon is still cross-armed on the rock, and the boys are sidling off in sullen dribs and drabs.

'He didn't have any washing, eh, Adèle,' Camille repeats over and over, tugging my hand all the way home.

1911

THE IRONY OF THE *CARCAS SONA* STORY is that church bells never meant anything to us. Around Carcassonne, we remembered another faith: cultish, medieval, heretical, and in our village, the bells were melted for scrap the year after my rescue from the treetops. We all wondered what Père Simon, who always seemed so studious and calm, could have done so wrong that he was banished by the bishops to our desolate region. Shortly afterwards, we – or rather, I – found out.

'It's here,' says my eldest brother, bursting over the threshold, pigeon-chested. My father turns back to his soup, and we shift impatiently, waiting for his verdict. Eventually he nods, and we scud, Camille and I, out of the door and clatter down the hill towards the church. In the twilight, I can just make out my brothers' silhouettes threading their way, slow and steady, down from the upper fields.

By the time we arrive, the entire village is already huddled together on the broken-down pews. At the back, I recognise Eluard and his surly, faithful followers; and at the front stands Père Simon, folding and re-folding his hands in amazement at the size of the congregation before him. The church is open to the elements, but a white sheet hangs down from the rafters, held by twin pegs and rippling in the evening breeze. Behind Eluard's gang there is a mechanical contraption propped up on a table. A man I don't recognise stands with one hand on a large wheel attached to the machine, watching Père Simon. A cigarette droops from one corner of his mouth, smoke trails heavenwards and, as I watch, Père Simon points at him with one trembling hand, the man begins to turn the wheel, and images begin to pour out of the white sheet.

Next to me, Camille breathes an almost silent *oh*. My superstitious aunt shrieks; in the front row a fully grown man kicks out his legs and snorts like a frightened horse. A woman has appeared on the sheet, sitting on a garden bench, one hand across her brow. OH! says white writing on a black background, WHO WILL RESCUE ME FROM MY PLIGHT? The woman turns to face us. She is so real, more real than anyone I know. I put my hand out in front of my face and compare it to her: she wins. Now another figure has appeared on the sheet: a man with eyebrows like upside-down Vs. He moves stealthily towards her: she cringes away from him. HELP! says the writing, I FEAR FOR MY VIRTUE! By now half the village are on their feet. The men shake their fists as the vicious baron advances, uttering words I was told I should never have to hear. And then, in a puff of smoke, grimacing wildly, the baron snaps his fingers and vanishes. The audience looks around the church, astonished. Père Simon stands up and pleads for calm; his palms try to flatten out the uproar, but Eluard is on his feet, trying to wrestle the machine out of the operator's hands. It takes several men to drag them apart.

When the film comes back on, the woman in white is wearing a veil, standing next to a handsome moustached man. AND SO THEY WERE MARRIED says the writing. The woman turns to look at her new husband, as from one corner of the frame the vicious baron capers and grips the bars of his cage. Her look says everything: I don't need the rest of the story to tell me how happy they will be. After the sheet goes blank, the others get up and mill about, re-enacting the story in hoarse leaps and shouts. I continue watching, desperately hoping the woman's face will reappear.

The neighbours beg the machine-operator to tell us another

story, but he snorts and shows us the damage Eluard has already inflicted on his projecting device. 'Twelve sous,' is all he says, holding out a calloused palm.

The following afternoon I shrug off my chores and trot down the hill to Père Simon's house. Up close, it doesn't seem as clean: paint peels and flutters from the door as it creaks open. And close to, Père Simon's skin looks white and fragile, like parchment. I had always thought of him as a young man, but now I wonder how old he really is.

'You've come about last night,' he says, following me into the one main room. My mother has taught me that a lady always sits, so I take the only chair and press my knees together. Père Simon remains standing, fingers laced behind his back.

As I speak, I feel ashamed of myself and of what he must see: a girl with her hair in disarray, eyes large and pleading in a thin face. I ask him what the name of the woman is, where she lives. I ask him who was responsible for last night's story, whether there will ever be any more like it.

He stoops and folds his hands round mine.

'The woman's name is Terpsichore,' he says. 'She has her own particular magic, Adèle, a quality all her own: one of the greats. At her first premiere, in Paris, of *La Dame aux Roses*, the audience was moved to tears.'

I ask him how he knows that. He pauses. 'Because I was one of them.'

Père Simon watches me for a moment, then moves to the fireplace. He moves jerkily, just like the woman in the film, half-eager, half-held back, leading me to it: what I didn't see before, which is that the wall above the mantel is covered, to the ceiling, in photographs of people. They are laid half over each other in a jumble, hundreds of them.

I have only ever seen one photograph before: a daguerreo-type of my grandparents, who had left us the money that my father drank, and the farm we lived on. My father's father sat; my father's mother stood, her hand on his shoulder. Neither of them was smiling. But these: these were a thing apart – each one was a young man or a woman with a dazzling grin and gleaming hair, staring out directly at me as if it was me making them laugh.

I cross the room to look more closely.

Père Simon says softly: 'Promotional postcards. The studios, who make the films, hand them out in advance of the films' release.'

She is right in the centre of the display: unlike the others, she isn't smiling, just staring back at me, her huge eyes rimed with kohl, the rest of her body stretched out on a chaise longue. There is a scribble in the corner – I can just make out the words, *Best wishes* – and before I can stop myself I have reached out and snatched the card from the wall.

I imagine the spells I would need to transform myself into her. In my mind's eye I see myself in a dress that shimmers like fish-scales, my face heart-shaped, all my gestures graceful, surrounded by people who love me.

Père Simon is standing with me. He sees how shocked I am, and gives a bitter little laugh and a shrug. How must it have felt for him: the young priest, stepping out from his seminary one evening, wandering the Paris streets, perhaps visiting a cinema of attractions on a whim, and leaving an hour later with his carefully constructed world a world away.

And that was how I got religion: my parents watched in amazement as I walked dutifully down the hill to visit the priest every single Wednesday. Père Simon bought a second chair, and under his careful tutelage, I studied the dramatic monologues of the great playwrights until I was word-perfect. We nursed my ambition as Cleopatra nursed the asp, letting it grow over the years.

Juliette Blanc and Adèle Roux
1967

Adèle Roux fixes me over the rim of her coffee cup: all bird bones, black sleeves flapping around the wrists. Fine silver hair in a bun at the nape of her neck and one concession to couture, a miniature hat, perched at an angle and secured with vicious-looking pins. Perhaps it's the cup, obscuring everything below the nose; perhaps it's the way the waiter passes behind us, whistling, or reflecting light over us with his silver tray: but suddenly I can see it. And, seeing it, can't see how anyone can have missed it.

Watching me, she smiles. 'You are thinking,' she says, 'that the cheekbones are the one thing which never changes.'

'I did wonder if you'd ever been recognised.'

'Never.'

'It was such a famous trial—'

'Famous in 1914. People forget.'

'But you've been living in Paris all this time...'

Her smile widens: becomes wicked. 'You've read *The Art of Living Invisibly*?'

'No.'

'No? The ancient Chinese text by the philosopher, Sun Tzu? It's a later book. Perhaps you are familiar with his more famous companion work, *The Art of War*?'

'No.'

She raises her eyebrows; then waves it away. 'A surprising number of lessons we can apply to 20th-century Paris. You'll have heard how, struck by the way a panda-bear fades into the

13

forest of bamboo, Sun Tzu invented camouflage. But to my mind, the most important advice he gives to those seeking anonymity is the simplest: *be eccentric, but not too eccentric.*'

She nods as I think about it. 'Take my hat. A relic. People look at it and think: *poor thing. Clinging to her youth.* They give me one swift glance and move on.'

I nod. Look down at my tape-recorder, because she really has embarrassed me this time.

She beams at me. 'One other thing: Sun Tzu recommends particularly – I quote directly from the text – *in the quest for invisible living, do not offend your concierge. You'll come home and find her going through your underwear.*'

'They had concierges in ancient China?'

'Oh, yes,' she says. 'They're a universal plague.'

She holds my gaze for a moment longer. I feel myself go suddenly red.

Her eyes sparkle. 'Admit it. The panda was a good touch.'

I don't know where to look.

She says: 'But how could I resist you? Such faith in the world.'

At 2 p.m. today, I was at my desk at *Le Monde* when the telephone rang.

'A woman for you,' said the switchboard operator – bored, Friday afternoonish. 'Calling about your article. Says she has some new information.'

I was still scribbling on my yellow pad; a four o'clock deadline loomed.

'Put her through.'

A hiss on the line; a crackle, and then the crisp voice, sounding as if it was coming from miles away: 'Is this Juliette Blanc? The author of the article in last week's paper, about the recent rediscovery of *Petite Mort*?'

'That's me.'

A breathy pause: high whining, ghost-voices brushing past.

'This is Mme Roux, whom you mentioned in your piece.'

The phone clamped to my ear, some instinct forewarned me: *don't gush. Don't say: I thought you'd be dead. Say what's on your mind.*

I said: 'This is a surprise.'

A chuckle. Then she said: 'Mlle Blanc, I wish to engage a person of vigour and conviction to write my memoirs. All about the film, and everything before and after. If this sounds like an assignment for you, please meet me at the Café Conti at five o'clock tonight. Café Conti, Place St André-des-Arts, 6ème. We will treat this first meeting as an informal interview of sorts. To see if we *get on*.'

She pronounced *get on* like an illness. I reached for a pen and paper, scribbled the address, and was about to ask any one of a hundred questions, when I realised the line had already gone dead.

25. janvier 1913

CAMILLE'S BREATHING stays steady. She is lying on her front: early light is creeping over her outstretched hand.

The mattress of my twin bed creaks as I pull out the little wallet from beneath it. *Enough to get you started,* Père Simon had said, dropping it into my satchel. *You'll want to address yourself to Studios Gaumont in the 19th arrondissement. Ask for M. Feuillade.*

When I tiptoe to the door and look back, there is a gleam underneath Camille's eyelids.

'You're running away,' she says.

Then she just looks at me: long and solemn like when she was small.

PARIS!

2. février 1913

TO THE NORTH, the tip of Notre Dame's spire rises, cut out against a dirty gold sky. The plume of Agathe's cigarette smoke lifts next to it, a signal; it drifts away from the windowsill and curls out over rue Boissonnade, hanging in the space between our attic apartment and the roofs across the street. A premature sun is winking and struggling over the rooftops opposite, and in one of these gleams the smoke is lit orange for a moment, then vanishes.

Beside me, Agathe lets out a hiss of a sigh. She squints as she removes the cigarette stub from her mouth. She doesn't offer me a final pull, but presses the stub delicately out on the window ledge – the broken sill leans, slack as a jaw and pock-marked from this morning ritual. And then, as it does every morning, the camaraderie of the shared cigarette vanishes, and hostilities resume. The sill jumps as Agathe lifts her meaty forearms from it, jolting my elbows; she turns and lumbers back into the salon.

A nasal sound comes from the kitchen: it is Mathilde, our landlady, singing as she prepares breakfast for us. Agathe readjusts her dressing gown as she reaches the one plush chair in the tiny salon; she sits and snaps open *Le Temps*. I take my seat at the table, Mathilde's song reaches a climax, and our meal arrives: thin porridge, borne aloft by Mathilde, like a waiter at a fashionable restaurant. '*Et voilà!!*' she trills. The newspaper crumples as Agathe lays it aside; she lumbers over to the table; *chink* goes the bowl, set down on the table-top, and Agathe's spoon is already ploughing a furrow through the food, ladling an enormous portion onto her own plate. As usual, she starts to eat straightaway.

Mathilde smiles apologetically at me, and whispers *bon appétit*. I dip my spoon into the porridge and try a few bites. Only once she is satisfied that I've started eating will Mathilde begin her own meal, stringy wrist lifting and lowering mechanically. Her gaze flickers between Agathe and me as she watches for the first sign of trouble.

Agathe's hatred for me sprang out fully formed on my very first day at 14 rue Boissonnade. The three of us sat in the salon, starchy with formality; I squinted into a patch of afternoon light, my valise propped next to my ankles, as Mathilde's hands writhed over each other in her lap.

'We are constrained by circumstance, Mademoiselle Roux,' she said, 'to invite another lodger into our little family.'

Agathe sat looking out of the window, ignoring us, her face wreathed in smoke. It was six o'clock in the evening; her scarlet silk peignoir was stretched tight across her stomach, her face painted into doll-like lines.

With a little jolt I realised what she was.

Mathilde leapt to her feet: 'Let me show you your new room!'

Though it was low-ceilinged, dusty, and filled with drab things, I exclaimed over its quaint charm. After years of sharing with Camille, I truly was a little excited at the prospect of my own territory; and I had little choice – my small fund would not stretch to anything better.

In the salon, I bent out of the window to admire the view; I did not notice how thin and grey the curtains fluttered in the evening breeze. I admired the room's one ornament, a fine miniature on the mantelpiece. 'My dear mother,' Mathilde sighed, pressing a hand to her breastbone, 'from whom I inherited the apartment.' Agathe snorted, and I wondered whether we were thinking the same thing: that Mathilde had also inherited the beaky nose and querulous expression.

'And what are you here to do?' Agathe asked, turning to look at me for the first time.

'I am going to look for an acting role, in the moving pictures,' I told her proudly.

Agathe's cigarette end glowed orange in the shadows.

'And how are you proposing to do that?' she asked.

The afternoon after my arrival at rue Boissonnade, I smoothed my best dress down in front of the rust-spotted mirror, stepped out into the waiting city and took the Metro to the 19th arrondissement.

At first I thought I had the wrong address: the north end of rue des Alouettes was a street like any other, with apartment blocks rising high on either side, cafés, even a greengrocer's. But as I walked along the buildings gradually gave way to tall grey walls, constructed in the modern style with cement brickwork. If I stood on tiptoe it was just possible to see the roof of a glass structure, like an enormous greenhouse – that must be the studio Père Simon had told me about – and next to it a factory chimney, puffing smoke into the crisp morning air.

If it was not what I had expected, then I supposed that every river had its source; I walked confidently along the edge of the wall until an opening presented itself – a wrought-iron gate flanked by what seemed to be one-storey cottages.

In my mind's eye, there had been bustle and buzz. This place seemed deserted. Moving closer, I noticed a sign fixed to the door of the left-hand cottage that read CONCIERGERIE. I marched up to the door and rapped on it.

A slip of a man in a stained shirt and pince-nez opened it. Through the half-open door I saw a cluster of desks with men and women sitting at them; a woman pecked at an odd sort of machine with her fingertips, and the men lolled about, smoking and chatting.

I told him I had come to see M. Feuillade.

The man put his hand out, palm up. 'Is he expecting you?'

I shook my head – perhaps I hadn't been clear – and told him I had come to ask M. Feuillade for a part in whatever film they were making.

The man pinched the blood from the bridge of his nose. 'Perhaps you can explain this to me, Mademoiselle: how is it men and women train for years at the Conservatoire to become actors, and yet everyone who's seen a two-reel at the funfair thinks she's the next Bernhardt?'

In the room behind him, one of the men had lowered his newspaper and was staring at me over the top of it.

'I've practised,' I said quickly, 'memorised the roles of Célimène and Phèdre and I am working on Lady Macbeth de M. Shakespeare—'

'*Bravo*,' he said, and made to shut the door. It closed, and closed some more; his beady eyes still wide and staring at me as the gap tightened – I put the toe of my boot between the door and the frame.

I said: 'You don't know what I can do.'

His face was startled; he chewed his lip. Suddenly the air fell out of him. 'Mademoiselle, this isn't the line of work for you.' The mocking light had gone from his eyes; they were sad.

I pulled my toe back; drew myself up. 'I want to see someone in charge,' I said. 'I want Feuillade.'

'You're talking to him.' He slammed the door before I could do my trick with the toe again.

I waited for a moment; leant my knuckles against the door, rapped on it, a continuous hammering like a woodpecker's.

'Do you know where I can find the right people to help me?' I shouted. Inside the room, there was just the sound of the woman typing, drowning me out.

~

Who could I ask for help? Père Simon? I couldn't bear it. His poor, eager face, reading my letter of bad news.

To buy thinking-time, I walked along the quai de la Tournelle. It was early evening: barges were gliding downriver towards the dark struts of the cathedral, their captains perched on their roofs, still as the boats themselves. I crossed the bridge and wandered towards the Boulevard St Michel. The book-sellers were closing the green doors of their boxes; I caught a flash as I passed of a series of postcards of Max Linder's grinning face, along with other stars. As I lingered, the bookseller caught my eye. 'Beautiful shot of Max?' he asked, and when I shook my head, he plucked a newspaper from his rack and rattled it at me, 'Max Linder, Mademoiselle! His new film is reviewed today in *Le Temps*! Two for one, let's make that pretty face smile…'

I shook my head and walked smartly past: but at the next corner kiosk, I bought a copy of *Le Temps*, then ink, envelopes and stamps from the stationer on the Boulevard Montparnasse; hurried to my room, ignoring Mathilde's piping voice offering a little restorative, and began to turn the pages. The articles about film were hidden at the back underneath the theatre reviews.

So that, in the early days, was my routine. Every morning I went out to buy *Le Temps*, and every afternoon, I directed a volley of enquiring letters to cinema stars, care of the relevant studio, congratulating them on their recent success and enquiring about roles in their next film; I planted a kiss on the back of each envelope and pushed it into the postbox on the corner of rue Boissonnade. At night, I lay awake, listening to the bored cries from Agathe's bedroom and the heavy tread of gentlemen's boots.

Two weeks passed and not a single reply. My anxiety grew: please let me not have to confront another studio face-to-face. The postman's pitter-patter steps passed our apartment every morning; jealously, I heard him ring the buzzer of Madame Moreau's apartment across the corridor.

The third week came and went. Over tea, I told Mathilde that I would pay her double-rent the following week. Though I tried to sound nonchalant, my cheeks coloured, giving me away.

Mathilde tilted her head to one side and looked at me brightly. Then she dropped her embroidery in her lap, put her hand onto my shoulder and squeezed it. Her grip was firm – quite unlike her usual quavering hands. I shrank back; surely she was measuring the flesh on my bones.

The day came when my fifth week's rent was due, and still there had been no response to my missives. At four o'clock in the afternoon, I leapt out of bed, convinced I had heard the postman's step on the stairs. I ran into the hall just in time to see that I had made a mistake: what I had heard was the door just shutting, and beyond it I caught a glimpse of Agathe's bulk, her empty string bag whisking round the corner. Her heavy steps plodded down the stairwell. She must have got up early to go shopping.

I stood in the hall for a moment, willing a letter to appear. As I turned, disconsolate, I noticed that Agathe's bedroom door had been left ajar.

A mere push with the tips of my fingers and it creaked wide open.

The room smelled of stale cigarette smoke. Cracks of light filtered through the shutters and laddered the chenille cover on a double bed. This was so vast it almost filled the room, leaving only enough space for me to stand at its foot. Beside my feet was an ancient blanket-box. I placed my fingers experimentally on the bed cover and pushed the springs, which protested. Then nothing: just the silence and the smoky smell. There was an ashtray on the bedside table, spilling over with old cigarette ends and fine grey dust.

I stroked the ceramic of the ashtray, but it was the bed that drew my attention back. I patted the pillow, then slid my hand underneath it and felt stiff fabric; drew out an enormous brassiere. Old sweat caked the material around the armpits; flaring my nostrils, I dropped it and slid my hand down underneath the pillow again.

Letters – a bundle of them, tied up with a faded red ribbon; but carefully, bound together twice over. I sank to my haunches and listened; hearing nobody, I slipped the knot and bent over the topmost sheet of paper.

It was just a few lines. The handwriting was ill-formed and masculine: all scratch marks and ink blobs. *Darling*, it began, *do not be downhearted. When you've made your name, and you have finished treading the boards of the Comédie Française, the wedding bells will sound in Domrémy again. Remember the little house behind the orchard?*

The date was from five years ago.

I thought how her slippers cut into her puffy ankles as she walked around the apartment.

A movement in the doorway: Mathilde stood watching me. She took in the letters, me.

'You mustn't think of it as a failure,' she said. 'We don't all have the talents we'd like.'

She stood there, the silence stretching around her—

She opened her mouth: her lips hovered around a smile. 'It isn't such a bad life, dear. Food on the table, good friends all around. We are all friends at rue Boissonnade, aren't we?'

The slap of an envelope onto the parquet in the hall.

Mathilde blinked, turned to look and was herself again. 'Oh,' she bleated, 'we so rarely get any post—'

This morning, over breakfast, there is no way to tell whether Mathilde has told Agathe about my searching through her room yesterday or not. Agathe is concentrating on her share of the baguette, which she breaks into tiny pieces and eats. There are particles of leftover sleep around her eyes.

'Here,' I say, 'take mine.'

She accepts it without even looking at me.

In my pocket is the letter that must take me away from all of this. This morning I could fly away, stepping off the windowsill and lifting, stretching my arms out to love the whole of Paris.

Something of this must show in my face, because Agathe leans in over the table. 'Will you be going out to look for work this morning,' she asks, 'or do you have a scrapbook to fill?'

'Actually, I have an appointment,' I say, trying to keep my voice light.

Mathilde drops her spoon and leans over towards me, her lips stretching into a smile, and takes my wrist. 'I have a feeling,' she confides, 'I have a feeling, Adèle, that this is going to be a very special day.'

Her touch makes my own fingers curl; I tug away, slip one hand into my pocket and feel the letter crackle reassuringly.

'Well, good day,' I say, rising from the table. As I walk towards the front door, I feel Mathilde's gaze on my back, taking in my smart dress, the sway of my hips.

I pelt down the stairs three at a time. Monsieur Z lies in his usual tangled heap at the bottom of the stairwell, filthy rags concealing clinking, empty bottles. He raises his head and shouts his familiar greeting – 'Trollop! Whore!' – as I vault over him – and then, as usual, he cringes, a vision of terrified penitence. His cries fade siren-like behind me as I rush into the street: *sorry, sorry, sorry.*

4. avril 1913

THE COLOURS FLICKED ON: sunshine flared through the grubby windows, and the train surfaced at Vincennes, hissing as it came to a halt. I stepped down onto the platform and was immediately caught in a group of other passengers. All were women, and all dressed the same: dark skirts, dark hat, dark gloves. 'Come on, Louise, it's five to nine, you can walk, can't you?' tutted one, as another bent to tie her shoelaces. Chastened, Louise straightened up and the group hurried on.

Guessing who they were, I followed in their slipstream. After the station exit, they marched straight ahead with an uncanny single purpose, geese strutting across a lawn, down the broad avenue; and as we swept past an omnibus stop, more women stepped off and swelled the group, all wearing the same uniform of dark clothes. They exchanged a few demure greetings and then the flock moved forward again: the sound of a hundred heels rapping smartly on the pavement.

Suddenly the women swung to the left, and there was the Pathé factory.

My first impression was of unfriendliness. It looked like the barracks I had once passed by at home: a collection of buildings running continuously the length of a block, but with no windows at ground-floor level, at least not on the outside; they only began on the second floor and stretched upwards to the height of a city block. It was as though nobody could be allowed to peer in, only to peer out. The buildings were faced with white stone of a startling cleanliness: a palace ruled by some fastidious, self-regarding creature.

Then there was the smell, already seeping into me: shoe polish and fireworks. I pressed my handkerchief to my watering eyes. None of the others seemed to notice it: bored, they moved on. An entrance to the mystical kingdom came into view up ahead: a gleaming pair of tall, spike-topped gates stood, swung open, with a crowd before it waiting to shuffle through: 'Hélène! Late again!' called one of the women suddenly to a girl standing near the back of the crowd. The girl grinned back, then rolled her eyes as the crush of bodies began to push her forward.

None of the women made any comment as I was carried along with them into a wide courtyard. A shadow fell across our faces – directly in front of me were three towering industrial chimneys, belching steam upwards, and on the central stack was a giant clock, fat and white above the crowd. As I watched, the huge second hand tocked heavily to one minute to nine and a siren started somewhere very close by; I jumped, the hairs lifting on my arm, but the workers around me only murmured their irritation and began to hurry. With a creaking sound, the gates swung shut behind us, pushing us into a crush as the workers bunched together.

The siren wailed to a halt – a baby that had cried itself out.

As we came close to the chimneys, the stream of workers diverted – they called their goodbyes to each other and marched smartly to left and right, disappearing along the avenues between the factory buildings, until nothing was left but the ringing sound of boots in the distance.

Then it was quiet, and I was alone, and stood clutching my invitation. In every direction were buildings whose shining windows gave nothing away.

'Mademoiselle? Can I help you?'

A young man trotted towards me across the courtyard. A wide, anxious face peered at me from beneath a fringe of carroty hair; the buttons on his guardsman's uniform were carefully polished.

I showed him my note. He peered at it. 'The *Fée Verte* audition? You want the *Société Cinématographique* studio. That glass one there.'

I thanked him with my warmest smile, just to watch the colour flood up from his neck and drown his face in pink.

'I'm Paul,' he said, to nobody, as I walked away.

I had expected glamour – a taste of my future – in my surroundings, but the audition waiting room looked unloved: dusty, with seats arranged around the walls, and just one small window giving onto the courtyard. The only sound came from the rustling of notes and play texts; five other women sat around the room, their heads bent in nervous last-minute study.

My hand went to my hair, and I sat down next to the window, and opened my play text at Lady Macbeth's famous soliloquy.

The door to the audition room opened, and a man's head appeared in the gap. Everyone's head snapped up. 'Lemesurier, Bérénice!' the man said. A woman on the other side of the room got to her feet, smoothing her skirts nervously, and followed him through.

It grew stuffy in the little room. I turned my face to the window behind me and let the breeze dance across it. The sun was high in the sky, which was a faint, creamy blue. In the distance I thought I heard, carried to me on the wind, the sounds of the city: catcalls, the hum of traffic.

I recited my audition speech under my breath to myself one more time.

Five minutes later the door to the audition room opened, and Bérénice Lemesurier walked across the antechamber without hesitating. At the exit she paused and turned to face the room.

'Good luck, everyone,' she said, and left.

The morning progressed. One by one the women went silently in, came out just as quietly, and left. At last there was just me and one other; a thick-waisted woman in her thirties with a bright, expectant look on her face. She was obviously too old, and her features too coarse, to hope to succeed; but even so, when the door opened and her name was called, and she turned to smile bravely at me, I wished she wouldn't go.

A siren wailed, very close this time. There came a patter of feet on flagstones, and a gaggle of dark-uniformed women crossed the courtyard outside, laughing to each other. Behind them came three young men, jumping and whooping. *Of course she will marry you!* cried one man to another; *of course!* and one of the girls turned round and beamed at him. The sun lowered itself another notch, and the door burst open, and the woman hurried out, head down, not looking at me; a man's voice called my name.

Three men sat behind a table at the far end of the room. The windows were small and high on the walls and gave little light.

The men looked at me with interest. One narrowed his eyes and drew on his cigarette, then puffed the smoke from the side of his mouth thoughtfully; the second, a large man in an embroidered waistcoat, looked up from doodling on the notepad in front of him.

It was the third man who caught my attention. He sat very still, with his hands loose on the table in front of him. His hair was dark and curly, worn too long, I thought, for a man in his thirties; his chin was a point as sharp as a weapon.

'Mademoiselle Roux, Adèle,' the cigarette man said, drawing out the *e* in my name. He frowned at a piece of paper on the table. 'You wrote a letter, is that right? To M. Durand here?'

He indicated the curly-haired man, who inclined his head

and smiled as though a private joke had been made.

'*I am of no little beauty,*' the cigarette-man read out loud, '*and have memorised the principal roles of the theatrical oeuvre.*'

He sat back and folded his arms. My hair stuck damp to my forehead.

'Shall I start?' I asked, finally.

The fat man put his fist to his throat and cleared it, a loud, amused *harrumph*: 'Please do, Mademoiselle.'

Halfway through my speech, the audition room had faded into a castle shuddering in high winds, its walls spongy with moss. Crows tottered on the battlements; ambitious servants whispered behind cupped hands. The curly-haired man was the one I had chosen to fix upon as my nerveless husband; he watched me back, but with an expression that I couldn't read.

I shuddered to a close.

The curly-haired man had sat back away from the light so that his face was invisible. The thin man stubbed his cigarette indifferently into a saucer. The fat man's face was stretched in a yawn. 'No,' he said. The material of his waistcoat strained as he sat forward to the table. 'No, André,' he said to the curly-haired man, 'it won't do. What was all this business with the hands?'

He moved his arms in a grotesque windmill, and swivelled to stare at me crossly. 'Don't tell me you can see her playing the Absinthe Fairy.'

None of the other men spoke.

'Our old faces do us perfectly well,' he said, drawing a line in ink on his notes – which could only be my name, being crossed off a list – 'no need for any new ones.'

I made a twitching movement towards the door, and nobody tried to stop me.

The sky was speckled with early stars; when I reached the exit I laid my forehead on the stones of Pathé's gatepost and thought of Mathilde's thin smile.

It was only vaguely that I heard the sound of purposeful steps coming towards me, and my eye caught the flicker of a coat-tail; then the curly-headed man was leaning against the wall next to me.

His eyes were very fine: amused, smoky-grey, with pupils which extended far into the iris.

He smiled widely. 'I am André Durand and, as I think we have established, you wrote me a letter.'

I tossed my head. Had he come to humiliate me further?

'You may know we have just set up a department of seam-stresses for our larger productions. We need a costumière for the *Fée Verte* film.'

There was a twang in his accent – *kos-toom-iaire* – a tiny imperfection that gave him away: not French.

'Steady work with prospects,' he said. His gaze travelled brazenly up over my best dress as far as my throat. 'Anyone can see you are interested in couture.' (*Koo-toor.*)

My one chance had slipped through my fingers, and now this man was offering me a job handling cloth. Was it mockery?

But André gave me the gentlest of reassuring nods.

5. avril 1913

ALL THAT NIGHT I thought about him; about the point of his chin and the way his voice sandpapered over its vowels.

The very next morning, I appeared at the Pathé gates, a quivering vision in my best shawl, certain that André would be waiting for me, craning my neck to look for him as I was bumped along by the waiting crowd; listening in rising irritation to the creak of the gates and the complaining siren. He would appear out of nowhere, take my elbow and smile an apology: *Yesterday was a travesty. Chances like you don't come up very often;* then usher me into my own dressing room, the pressure of his fingertips warm on my forearm.

But when the crowd cleared, instead of André a lumpen young woman stood in the courtyard, her hands folded officiously over her apron. Where her flesh met her blue uniform it stuck in great damp patches; her waist was thickish, her feet flat. When she saw me she attempted a smile: a crooked thing, more than half dislike.

'I'm Elodie, the head costumière. M. Durand sent me to show you where we work.'

I returned the smile in the spirit it had been given. She turned on her heel and crossed the courtyard, turning left into an alleyway between buildings.

In a minute or so, we came to a long, low block at the end of the alley. A number was painted in white on the side facing us.

'Building Number One,' Elodie said, 'where Charles Pathé

has his offices,' but I was unable to comment, for a cloud of flies had materialised in front of us: I spat several into my handkerchief. Elodie laughed. 'The chemicals from the filmstrip building bring them. You'll get used to it.'

Eyes streaming, too proud to complain, I pressed my handkerchief to my nose, and was glad when we walked up the steps and in through the front entrance of Building I; corridors flashed past; soon we were in the bowels of the building. I craned my neck round every corner, hoping to hear a confident laugh, or catch a glimpse of André's immaculate torso and curly hair.

'In here,' Elodie said, pushing open a heavy door.

The room's single humming light bulb showed me an Aladdin's Cave of garments: racks of clothes, rubbing shoulders gorgeously, stretching away into felty darkness.

Nearest the door was a set of tables with sewing machines upon them, and a set of women to go with it.

'Solange,' Elodie said, pointing at a pale woman in her fifties, who blinked at me from behind enormous spectacles. 'Georgette,' – barely fourteen years old, with wrists like twigs; 'Annick,' a woman with pale ginger hair that sparked under the electric lights. All the women were sewing costumes made of green velvet.

Elodie indicated a sewing machine on a vacant table near the entrance. 'We'll get you a uniform sorted out tomorrow. It's costumes for that absinthe film today. A hundred forest fairies, we need. Patterns are on the cards in front of you.'

I stared at the machine.

'You do know how to work one of these?' she said.

Two hours later my foot ached from operating the pedal; my fingers were rubbed raw and pricked full of tiny holes, and my first fairy uniform lay mangled in front of me. The other women appeared to notice nothing; their faces were bent over their work. The hammering of the needles rang in my ears.

My nails sank viciously into the velveteen flesh of the fairy costume. Why had he buried me alive in here if he wanted nothing from me?

Pathé as a studio, of course, was never empty, the great production line worked twenty-four hours a day, would have worked more if it was possible; but in our small department we always went home on time.

At five o'clock on my first day my quota of costumes was nowhere near ready; I announced that I would stay until I had finished. The other women nodded indifferently and, one by one, vanished. Only Elodie paused in the doorway, looking at me suspiciously; thinking, I suppose, that I was plotting to usurp her role as chief costumière. During our midday break she had told us about her son, Charles-Edouard, to whom she longed to rush home each night; now she was caught between her affection for him and her own ambition. She had shown us a photograph of the child: a jowly baby and a younger Elodie, posed ridiculously in front of a painted seaside backdrop. I had eyed her scornfully, but was forced to admit that, once upon a time, she might have been attractive. Attractive enough, at any rate – I found out later that Charles-Edouard's father was a minor aristocrat whose occasional cheques were never quite enough.

At last, with a worried smile, Elodie picked up her purse and straightened her hat on her head, and left. The door closed on her and I was alone; I stopped pressing the pedal, stretched and got to my feet, jubilant. I had never really intended to do any more work. On my own I could explore the studio further; perhaps seek out where André's offices were, the better to bump into him as if by accident on some subsequent day.

In fact, I never left the costume department. Is there anything more gorgeous than a place of work without workers? Loneliness hung on the air; from the corridors outside I heard nothing. I went first to the racks of old costumes behind our desks, and buried my face in their mothy scent. *It doesn't matter*, I told the clothes, *I still love you*; their arms waved helplessly in reply.

Let's be clear: it was not the word 'love' which summoned him; but there he was anyway, lounging in the doorway.

'Evidently you are enjoying your first day.'

I dropped the dress which I had been holding up to my cheek in an asinine fashion.

'You are an unusual person, Mlle Roux.'

'Why is that?' I asked.

'Beautiful people do not usually feel the pain of inanimate objects.'

It was all I needed him to say. I surprised myself with my boldness in stepping up to him, and raising my chin so that it almost met his, asking for a kiss. He looked at me – eyes grey as the Pas de Calais – and we stood for a while. I placed hot palms on his chest; he laughed again, and then he did kiss me.

The kiss said, *look at you, a snake with your prey*. It said, *do you suppose this will secure you an acting role?*

And mine said, *yes*.

I went home. Agathe, sensing a change, turned in her chair and looked at me for ten seconds or so. She rolled me a cigarette and we smoked it together. Far off, the pinnacle of the Bastille was pointing at the moon; that evening, the weight of her arm next to mine was not an intrusion but a comfort.

One other thing: I leant back after the act, gasping as women are supposed to gasp, and asked that hackneyed question: 'Where did you come from?'

And to my very great surprise, he told me. Not all in one go – and not everything – only a fool would suppose André Durand ever bared his soul to anyone – but a little each night, piece by piece. Just enough to keep me wanting more.

André, i.

Grosse Tete, Louisiana, July 1886, population 245: a few tin huts, eternally catching their balance on the crust of mud separating settlement from bayou. Beyond the Grosse Tete Convenience Store and the Grosse Tete Laughing Woman bar, a signpost extends its white finger –

NEW ORLEANS 85 MILES

– but that is 85 miles away; here, every log is a potential crocodile. The heat cracks wood and peels paint from doors.

The town has just one permanent fixture. The Orphanage stands at the Grosse Tete's edge, its windows gazing northwards: two storeys of incongruously imported marble, dotted with mica which dances in the ever-present sunshine. It is run by nuns, stern and secretive, virtuously hiding their faces from strangers; the building has been there for as long as the town's oldest inhabitant can remember.

Today is the first Sunday of the month, around midday, and shutters are slamming closed all around the village. Everyone knows it is Adoption Sunday: a monthly event when wealthy gentlemen seeking a new child visit the Orphanage, to take tea with the nuns and make their selection. There are few inhabitants who haven't at some time or other, when passing the Orphanage, seen a child's fingers spidered against an upstairs window – and in Grosse Tete, where superstitions outnumber residents, it is considered bad luck to witness the children being taken away.

Strange, thinks Auguste Durand, *to find the place so deserted.*

He peers from the curtained windows of his carriage, which rattles down Grosse Tete Main Street. His only audience are cats, sunning themselves, who leap to their feet in offence as the wheels spin gravel over them. *It is as though all the inhabitants have been spirited into the swamp overnight,* Auguste thinks – and it seems to him a plausible explanation. Don't they say that is what happened to Thibodaux, thirty years ago? That the town vanished, leaving only the spars of foundations sticking up out of the bayou?

A part of Auguste's fifty-four-year-old brain knows this cannot be true: Auguste has been a sugar-cane man, a plantation owner, all his life and his younger self would laugh at such fancifulness. But Auguste is not young. So, as he smoothes down his sober dark suit, and grips the Orphanage door knocker in his signet-ringed finger, his hand trembles: what if nobody answers, and his journey has been in vain? What will he tell his wife, waiting expectantly at home?

The nun who opens the door to Auguste sees a short man with faded blue eyes. From his clothes she would say he is a rich landowner, but his white beard is unkempt. She senses something: a halo of incipient madness. But a client is still a client, however eccentric, so she shakes hands in welcome.

Auguste doffs his hat and whispers his name to her. Once his relief has passed, he finds he is cowed by the schoolishness of the place – as though it is he who is on display, hoping to be picked, not the orphans.

The inside of the building is a shaded atrium; colonnades, festooned with thick ornamental swamp-creeper, run around the walls. The sun arches down into the central courtyard; Auguste blinks, dazzled; and realises that, directly in front of him, what he had taken for more columns are ten children, standing in a line, arranged from tallest to shortest.

The nun's smile tautens. 'M. Durand,' she says, 'if you would like to step this way—'

The children stand with their hands behind their backs, eyes fixed on a spot somewhere higher than his head: a mixture of boys and girls and – a little shock to Auguste's sense of propriety – races. They all wear the same grey serge uniform; faces are scrubbed clean, and the girls' hair is plaited where possible. The smallest is a toddler still, with a halo of nappy fuzz standing out from his head, and his finger hooked through the hand of the boy next to him. The oldest and tallest, a girl whose thin white hands seem to be all bone, looks to be about seventeen.

What will become of you, Auguste thinks, staring into her face, *when you get too old to live here any more?*

The nun clears her throat. In his scrutiny he has walked right up to the tall girl: she is leaning back away from him, nostrils flared, a sapling in wind.

Auguste steps back, embarrassed. These children are all too old; they already have pasts and histories to themselves. He looks around the room in despair and notices something, someone, else: a boy of about eight, standing watching from beside one of the columns. He is looking directly at Auguste.

The boy's eyes remind Auguste of the sea, which Auguste visited once as a child. The beach was disappointingly grey, and so was the water, not the blue of picture-book illustrations. Undaunted, Child-Auguste had run to the line where the water met the land; but dipping his fingers in the surf, the froth bubbled away to nothing.

The nun has noted Auguste's interest. Ideally he would take away one of the older children who has less time left to find a family, but she understands an inevitability when she sees it; she moves across and places a hand on the boy's shoulder – but gingerly.

'This is André,' she says. 'A fine strong boy, who loves his building blocks. He would be an asset, M. Durand – am I right in thinking you are in sugar?'

'Yes,' Auguste says, distracted.

'And as you and Madame Durand have not yet been blessed—'

The nun lets her voice trail off, intimating visions of the heirless future, the plantation burning, lighting up the night – Auguste pictures the stillborn boy, its full head of black hair, and shakes himself down. He ought to ask a question. He looks at the child's bewitching stare.

'Who were the boy's parents?'

The nun spreads her arms in a shrug. But Auguste's thoughts have already flitted into a great uprush of joy: he is going to be a father. Just as quickly his eagerness becomes paranoia: is the nun thinking him unsuitable? Will she snatch defeat from the jaws of victory?

'Yes,' Auguste barks, 'I'll take him.' With one arthritic hand he gestures to the boy to follow. André trots after the old man as he scuttles out to the waiting carriage. A curl of smoke drifts lazily upwards from the chimney of the Laughing Woman. Though Auguste turns, triumphant, to display the child to the waiting world, there is nobody to see them go.

The sun is an unforgiving white disc; a fine house comes into view as the carriage rattles on down the dusty trunk road, like something out of a painting: white and formal against the blue of the sky. The carriage sweeps through the valley below the house – a forest of rustling stalks, head-high. In between the stalks, heads lift. Plantation workers – the sons and daughters of sons and daughters of slaves – have paused in the cutting of sugar cane to see the carriage, with its precious cargo, sweep by.

The carriage rocks uphill, arriving at a verandah that extends to the front of the house. Auguste leaps out as the wheels stop rolling; his feet make the verandah's floorboards creak. André follows him, taking in the view with his arms laced behind his back, as the nuns taught him, indicating his politeness.

'Caroline,' Auguste calls, repeatedly and in mounting excitement.

A young woman steps from the dark oblong of the door. Caroline is all porcelain and gold and in her early twenties.

'This is André,' Auguste says, his voice quivering: it is his great moment.

She looks at André, looks at his poor serge suit. André's pose shifts and becomes genuine: he wants to please her, never having seen anyone like her.

But though she stares at him, he understands that she does not really see him.

She kisses Auguste's dry cheek and turns to go back inside.

Over the next few weeks, visitors come to pay their respects to the child. They perch on the horsehair settee and look at André, and he feels special, he feels somebody, in his new suit with the high white collar. He learns to rank them in importance based on how anxious Auguste becomes when greeting them. Caroline isn't upset at all, not by anyone: she sits, laughing at their jokes, when he can see she doesn't really mean it; when he turns to look at her, she quickly looks away, and coldly, as though he has been too bold.

One day a man with a handlebar moustache comes. He takes tea in the salon like the others, and the moustache twitches when he drinks and André longs to put his hands up to it and feel the bristle against the palm of his hand. This is Maître de la Houssaye, Auguste says, he is a lawyer come to help Papa with a dispute amongst the workers: would André like to come to the office and see?

André nods, one eye always on Caroline. He wants her to be the one to give permission.

'Kiss your mother goodbye, then, we'll be a while.'

The room hushes; André knows that this is a kind of test; and also that he isn't the only one being tested. He slips off his small chair and hurries across to Caroline. She bends down, awkwardly, and loops her arms round his neck. He understands from her stiffness that she is not used to this, that perhaps she doesn't hold people. It feels entirely strange.

'Come on, boy,' calls his father from the doorway. 'We haven't got all day.'

7. juillet 1913

SOMETIMES ANDRÉ WOULD pop his head round the door of the costume department during the day. With a very straight face he would say, 'Everything ticking over, ladies?' And I would bend my head to the sewing machine and beat my foot on the pedal, and his gaze swept over me and back. He would nod and retreat: the picture of the caring boss.

'Such a charming man,' my colleagues would sigh, touching their hands to their hair; and I would feel the secret warm me up.

The only person who remained immune to André's charms was Elodie; when he came in she bent her head more closely to her work and hunched her shoulders as though trying to disappear. I could see no reason for her dislike; but in the end, I did not have long to wait before the answer was revealed, some weeks after my first encounter with André. At the eleven o'clock pause Elodie handed round cups of coffee and we rested our aching wrists. Along with re-modellings for the *Fée Verte* picture, due to be filmed in a few days' time, we were making revolutionary outfits for the filming of Hugo's *Misérables*. A hundred extras were to storm an improvised barricade in the Pathé courtyard that afternoon; blue, white and red strips of fabric were scattered around the room.

André stepped into the room with his usual deference. 'Ah, the Uprising,' he said seriously, reaching for an abandoned tricorn hat. 'I must tell the other overseers to watch their step.' I thought he had never looked so handsome than when he positioned the hat on his curls.

My colleagues tittered like schoolgirls and he doffed the hat to us – I coloured as with its final flourish he met my eyes. Then he dropped the hat onto my desk, and stepped back out into the corridor again. As he closed the door, when nobody else was looking, he winked at me.

There was a contemplative silence, then: 'He looks tired,' said Annick, winding a strip of electric-ginger hair around her finger.

'Well, that's no surprise,' Elodie said, 'considering who he's married to.'

The other girls tittered, and I joined in, so as not to stand out. I had guessed from the start that André was spoken for. An air of well-fedness, of being adored – he did not have the lean look of a bachelor. But what other ties he might have had had little bearing on what I was asking from him. Night after night, I asked him to try me in a role.

The evening before, he had laid on his back next to me, drowsing; I had rolled into the crook of his arm to look up at him.

'Do I get the part?' I asked playfully.

He turned onto his elbow to look at me. 'You're certainly moving up the shortlist,' he said. I kissed him again, in triumph. He had almost said it: it was only a matter of waiting for the right opportunity.

So as Elodie chattered on, I was able to tap my foot on the pedal and listen calmly – I was naturally intrigued to find out the name of my rival. 'Of course he looks tired,' she continued. 'She keeps him busy enough, with all her carryings-on.'

'Poor hen-pecked man,' said Solange.

I tossed my hair back for my own benefit. André's wife was suddenly taking on a form that differed from my idea. Tantrums: that didn't fit, because he was such a connoisseur of women. Didn't he tell me, every evening, *you are a beautiful little thing? My mannequin – my doll?* She must be rich by birth, a patroness whom he'd married for her title. Liver-spotted hands chinking with rings.

Georgette said: 'They say she sleeps on a mattress made of peacock feathers.'

Annick said: 'I heard she employs a poison taster, and the last two died.'

Elodie stared at her work and said: 'They say she's a hermaphrodite.'

This met a blushing silence.

Georgette ran her needle along a line of cloth and sighed: 'But the talent goes with the temperament, doesn't it? And she can move an audience to tears.'

My stomach plummeted, my needle stabbed my finger; I pulled it away, sucking the blood off the tip. I felt the others staring: Elodie's quick, bitter glance and Annick, her mouth hanging slightly open, flushing to clash with her hair. Only Georgette failed to notice. She prattled happily on: 'At her *Dame aux Roses*, the crowd went quite wild! They say Sarah Bernhardt wept with jealousy!' She giggled; and then, interpreting the sudden quiet, her face froze and she looked at Annick, Solange, Elodie: me.

'What's her name?' I asked her.

'Terpsichore,' she said.

Juliette and Adèle
1967

I say: 'So that was how you discovered they were married?'

'Yes. Through their pity.'

'Pity?'

Adèle narrows her eyes. 'Of course! The girls were trying to help me. They had kept quiet about his wife, out of tact, for months. But when they decided it had gone too far – when they could see me pale before them, becoming absent-minded, losing myself to an impossible conundrum – then they told me who she was.'

'They planned it?'

'No. But it was an attempted rescue, just the same. I ran outside and stood against the wall of the factory building, where nobody could see me.'

She takes a demure sip from her coffee cup. 'Kindness is so often mixed with other things. It can be hard to see it when it comes.'

André, ii.

André was fifteen years old when his gift was discovered.

It was harvest season, an October day; he was idling in the salon, long legs lolling as he sketched on thin paper at the table, when Caroline, threading a needle through embroidery, raised her head, the perfect skin between her brows puckering into a frown. Through the salon window the small dot that had caught her attention was getting closer: Auguste's head and flyaway white hair, running towards them along the rows of cane. Following his progress, other heads were bobbing up from the cane on either side: indentured workers, sensing trouble.

Caroline laid down her embroidery and waited.

A minute later Auguste burst into the room. 'All wrong,' he said, 'no good,' and put his hat down on a horsehair chair. On his face was the kind of look that once, she might have wanted to comfort. 'What is?' she asked.

'The engine in the mill. Stopped.' He tried to smile and ended up grimacing instead. 'Can't fathom it. Just stopped.'

The steam engine they used for grinding cane was twenty years old, and a friend to Auguste. He still remembered setting the donkeys free from the old horse-powered mill; opening the new mill, his first wife cutting the ribbon, already frail but smiling at the childishness of the task. But it was also the *sine qua non* of his business. Merchants in New Orleans were tapping their watches even now, waiting for him to deliver cargo. What nobody knew but Auguste: how perilously the whole enterprise tottered on the edge of disaster. His friends had all made the switch into other crops when the slaves were set free, and laughed at Auguste for keeping going. He had shaken his head and smiled at them, not understanding how anyone being set free could be a cause of loss.

'What do the engineers say?' Caroline asked.

Auguste reddened. 'How should I know? I don't understand a damn word.'

He put a hand to his eyes; took it away, and sat slowly and gingerly on the arm of a chair. 'I don't know,' he said again. 'I don't know.'

'It will be all right,' Caroline said, and when he looked at her, child-like, she nodded once, encouragingly, and waited for him to get to his feet again, and put on his hat and walk to the verandah door. 'Best go and see,' he said, and ducked his head sheepishly under the lintel.

It wasn't fixed. Auguste reappeared once more, an hour later, to curse and slump on the arm of the horsehair chair; soothed by Caroline, he departed for the mill again. The light began to fail: an orange Louisiana sunset, twinklings in the cabins of the workers, and Caroline finally closed the door.

'Tidy away now,' she told André, 'we'll have supper, just us,' and she clicked her fingers for the maid.

The soft chink of cutlery, neither of them looking at the other; and it was not until the dessert course that Auguste walked into the dining room, his face so thunderous as to preclude any conversation.

'Don't ask me,' he said shortly, and then immediately began to tell them, talking as if to himself. 'It's not the crankshaft, and it's not that a cog is missing,' he said. 'What the devil do I pay them for?'

André said, stabbing at his dessert, 'If it's heated beyond endurance it will fissure. Perhaps that's it.'

Auguste's fascinated face; Caroline's frown. André got up

from his seat and walked back into the salon. After a moment Auguste and Caroline followed, to find him standing over his sketches. André indicated a spot on a delicate drawing of the interior of a steam engine and said: 'Here is your weakest point.'

That night, Auguste undressed thoughtfully.

'He needs proper tuition,' he told his wife.

Caroline put her book aside. 'I can give him lessons,' she said, 'more advanced than what he gets from the governess. Until we can find someone more suitable.'

Auguste nodded; nodded faster. It had always been a source of great pride to Auguste, the son of a farmer: his wife's urbanity, the unusual lightness of her mind. She could teach him things a tutor couldn't, all the accoutrements of a gentleman. Wasn't that what Auguste wanted for his son, at the end of it all? Hadn't they seen, this afternoon, the proof that André could be not just a good person, but a great one?

So it was decided: they would convert the fifth bedroom into a schoolroom. Auguste clambered into bed; out of the dark bloomed the thoughts he kept for bedtime. The thoughts had started the first time he had seen André, but he dared not confide them to Caroline; they required careful handling in case they be disbelieved. Auguste might be the only one to see it for the time being, but it was clear that André's grey eyes were growing to look more like Auguste's blue ones every day. The boy's lengthy stride was becoming shorter, to match the famous Durand bandy knees. Auguste tried not to breathe too fast, so as not to wake Caroline. It would be a wonderful surprise for her, when the time came. The boy he had brought home had turned out to be theirs, after all. It would help her be a mother to him: there had been, from the start, a sort of coolness towards the boy. He would wait until the evidence could no longer be ignored. He would wait until he could see signs of suspicion on Caroline's face: and then he would break the great news to her.

Outside the bedroom window the cicada song became a buzz. He let his drowsiness gather momentum. It made perfect sense to Auguste that the child had found its way back. There was no reason why all those lost years should stay lost for ever.

Two days later, Auguste left for Thibodaux-Nouveau before it got light. Caroline went downstairs with him and clasped his shoulders as she kissed him goodbye. The carriage stood waiting, the horses whinnying their discomfort at the cold air. Auguste was more distracted than usual, his eyes darting to left and right but never finding her face.

'Give my regards to Maître de la Houssaye,' she said to him, pressing her cold lips to his cheek.

'Certainly,' Auguste said, then hurried to rectify his mistake. 'You wanted the blue silk, didn't you? Or would you prefer muslin? I have it written down here somewhere.'

Caroline smiled. 'I don't mind. It doesn't matter, does it?'

Auguste fumbled with the reins; guiltily he geed up the horses and was away.

But Caroline did mind. Over the past six months she had seen the depredations of senility on her husband: she'd seen the way Auguste watched André – a fascination that bordered on the awestruck; she had listened to Auguste's excited breathing at night, and heard his elaborate, circumlocutive mutterings when he thought he was alone. His trip to town today was not to buy cloth for her Christmas dresses but to see the lawyer and change his will in his son's favour. Now that André was grown, and apparently a prodigy, why delay?

When her husband died – and Caroline thought he must die soon, because how could his softening brain withstand everyday pressure for much longer? – she would not inherit.

Caroline had not been forced into marriage, but she had been pushed. She would have nothing to show for all the long dry years – André would acquire everything: the roof over her head, the clothes on her body.

But was he not also a commodity of sorts, something to be acquired in turn?

Auguste was not expected back from town till late. At two o'clock in the afternoon she summoned André to the schoolroom.

While she waited for him she arranged herself underneath her own portrait, which had been commissioned by Auguste shortly after their marriage. She was painted alone, wearing her white high-necked costume, the cane-fields swaying behind her. Her knees were pressed together and turned slightly to the right, sensuously outlined beneath the flowing white fabric in the painter's one concession to the feelings she gave rise to. Her eyes met the painter's; her hands rested on a sketchbook which lay open at a drawing of the whole scene in miniature, complete with green cane and tiny white figure.

Caroline looked up and saw André; smiled and patted the chair beside her with a white-gloved palm.

He stayed where he was, uncertain; but also something else.

As she crossed the room to him, she registered his tallness, and wondered who the boy's father had been, to have given him such long legs. She reached him, put her arms around his neck and leant the whole of her weight against him.

7. juillet 1913

THAT EVENING, I didn't stay late for André. I left early with the others, and Paris was drowning: rain fell in sluices, pooling in the courtyards and battering our umbrellas as we giggled and hopped our way out towards the street. The Metro steamed with the closeness of our bodies pressed together. Further down the carriage, a man smiled shyly at Annick; she smiled sweetly back and then, turning to us, she crossed her eyes and stuck her tongue out; we burst out laughing and the man looked down at his feet.

Annick and Georgette were the last to get out, arm looped in arm. The train moved off: for the final ten minutes of the journey I stood alone, looking at the pitch-black of the tunnel walls. *Let him wonder.*

The train surfaced and I left the station and crossed the Boulevard Montparnasse with its array of winking red lights, and turned into rue Boissonnade. The surface of the cobbles shone with water; the rain had stopped, washing everything clean.

From the salon came an unmistakable clicking sound. Mathilde was sitting in her shawl, hunched over the flicker of her hands. When she saw me, she paused in her knitting and brought her lorgnette up to her eye.

'There you are,' she said, 'working hard as usual.'

She paused, as though picking words. I rushed to forestall it: 'I get paid at the end of the month,' I said. 'I can give you all of it, I promise.'

'No, dear, it isn't that,' said Mathilde.

She paused again, as though trying to find how to say a delicate truth. Then she said: 'A young lady came asking for you, who says she is your sister. I told her there must be some mistake because your family were all dead. But she insisted.'

Camille is sitting on my bed, facing the window. On the coverlet next to her is an envelope which I recognise as one of my own. It belongs to the letter I sent to Père Simon; the return address is scribbled on the flap. Inwardly I flinch, as I recall the closing phrase: ...*almost certain that I shall be engaged as the lead in M. Durand's* Fée Verte. *And we both know, my dear friend, to whom the first invitation for the premiere shall be sent!*

Camille doesn't turn straightaway.

'I like your dress,' I say.

She twists to look at me. With a jolt I see that the months since I last saw her have transformed her: the childish scarecrow has been replaced by poise. She plays with the hem of her calico – *this old thing?*

'Pa gave it to me as a leaving present,' she says. Already she is lying to me; our father would never have allowed her to come of her own free will. She looks up at me, a trick I know well because I use it myself, the slow lifting of the gaze, making me feel the force of her eyes.

'You can stay for a week,' I say, at the same time as Camille says 'I thought I could stay here for a while.'

The impasse stretches out into a silence that feels like falling. I let myself drift – how can I do otherwise: it comes to me suddenly that wherever I go, it will never be far enough. Seeing my face, Camille peels down the sleeve of her dress, revealing a series of vicious welts across her shoulder.

Putting my forefinger over them I can feel how the skin is raised to the touch: the stripe of a willow cane like the one my father used. And there are others, none of them very old, forming a complex knot of scars intertwined.

Did I already know this, at the back of my mind? That when I left home our father would look for someone else to beat?

'I can find work as soon as they've healed,' she mumbles into my shoulder. I have pulled her into an embrace so tight that neither of us can speak.

Camille half-woke at three o'clock in the morning.

'It's so loud here,' she complained groggily. I listened, and heard only ordinary sounds – the clink of Monsieur Z's bottles in the stairwell, the carolling from the all-night restaurants on Boulevard Montparnasse.

I brushed the hair off her forehead to soothe her, and within a few moments she was asleep.

The noise from below faded; there was just the rustle of an old newspaper crackling on the pavement, and then the room was silent. But still I couldn't sleep.

The street cleaners sluicing water over cobbles woke me at half past five and I lay watching the pale light filter in through the shutters until it was time to get up.

Camille turned over just when I thought I had reached the door without waking her. She propped herself on one elbow, and my heart sank as I recognised the expression on her face: matchless cunning that was not cunning enough to hide itself. It was as though the previous evening's reunion had dropped away.

'Are you off to work with Durand?' she asked.

I was immediately on guard. 'How did you know?' I asked, trying to keep the strain from my voice.

'Your letter, silly.' She yawned. 'Père Simon was so impressed. *A senior producer*, he said, *I always knew it*, he said, *always*, like this.' She made her voice fluting, and clasped her hands piously to her chest, eyelids batting, expecting me to join in the joke.

Then her eyes narrowed.

'You're wearing your smart dress,' she said. 'There's a boyfriend. You didn't write about that.' Her eyes glittered with joy of the discovery.

What tic of the mouth could I employ to convince her of my truthfulness, when my mouth was the same as hers?

'It's just an ordinary dress,' I said.

She studied me for a few seconds, then her mouth twisted into a smile. 'When you see Durand, you can tell him about me,' she said. 'Tell him I'll come and work with him too. Tell him I've got a *skill*.'

She nodded proudly to her valise, still standing by the bed. For the first time I noticed it was new – square and black, more like an artist's paint-box than a suitcase.

'What *skill*?' I asked.

Camille bit her lower lip between her front teeth, and shook her head at me. 'Tell you tonight,' she said. She flopped back down onto the bed and closed her eyes.

Of course I did not take her seriously. What skill could she possibly have to rival my own?

On my way out of the apartment it occurred to me that I did not even consider telling Camille the truth.

It would have been a relief. *There is someone*, I could have told her, drawing innocent patterns on the bedspread with one finger. She might have folded me up in her skinny arms; it might have wakened the impulse I had longed to see in her; that she might want to take care of me a little, too. But even now I can remember the precise way her lip curled as she laughed at me; the prideful way she pointed out her valise.

I do not know why they say that the present draws a veil over the past, when it is only later that one sees things as they really were. Now I understand that I could not have done otherwise, because the jaws of the trap had sprung shut when we were children. I told myself, as I set out for work, that my secrets were mine to keep.

That day, my mind was so full of Camille that I barely paid attention at work. The others read my mood: Elodie watched me from behind the safety of the sewing machine. 'Something on your mind?' she asked, and I shook my head.

At five I hurried away; when I got home I found Camille sitting on my bed, perusing my scrapbook of newspaper cuttings.

'They're mine,' I said, and she glanced up, lost in the stories, brow furrowed – a child. 'But of course you may borrow them,' I added, and felt idiotic. I would never learn; she would always unseat me.

She stared at me for a moment, glanced at the clock on the wall and then hopped off the bed. 'I'm going to take tea with Agathe now,' she said.

'You'll have to be quick,' was all I could think of to say to this, 'don't let her eat all the biscuits.'

Camille ignored me and skipped away down the corridor.

I called after her: 'Have you seen Mme Moreau about that cleaning position?'

Camille looked at me blankly. I knew what she was seeing: a fussy ten-year-old, trying to make her tidy her half of the room. She shook her head and pushed the door of Agathe's room open. When I turned back to my bed I noticed that she had taken the scrapbook with her.

André, iii.

She taught him to hold himself back until she was ready; taught him to be quiet and stealthy. More than once they paused, Caroline's hand plastered over André's terrified mouth, as Auguste called out merrily that he was home. André would scrabble for his shirt: she would draw him round, place her hands on him and soothe him: they had a few more minutes, at least. He was such a great joy to look at: his long limbs, his cheekbones, the skin like milk.

An afternoon, six weeks after the first time: early November. The autumn had cooled the earth outside, but Caroline lay on the bare floorboards of the schoolroom floor, her white dress beside her, in a pile with André's blue trousers; and on the other side, arms and legs spread-eagled as though he had fallen from a great height, was André.

Caroline played with the curls on his forehead. Everything was peaceful. The house slumbered around them, basking in the sun. She felt him squirm, and sit up. They smiled at each other as they began to dress.

A curious thing happened: André turned away from her as he knotted his cravat, and when he had finished, he turned back and his cheeks were scarlet – startling Caroline, who thought he must have succumbed to a sudden illness. Then she saw it, and wondered why she had not seen it before: the boy had fallen in love with her in the way that is indeed a sickness. The display of passion frightened her: she sat down on her chair to think what to do.

André knelt before her. His fingers pressed into her waist as he said what she'd feared: 'We must go away somewhere together.'

But the house, the sugar-fields, the lace collar on my finest dress… she shook her head. 'Where would we go?' she said, with a touch of temper.

His face was mutinous.

Why, she asked, when they had everything they needed here.

He's my father, André said. *I don't want to be dishonest any more.*

She almost laughed. Honesty: the preserve of rich men.

'Let's talk about it later,' she said, and began to stroke with one hand the fork of his trousers. André pursed his lips and turned his face away.

The door slammed; later, she heard him stalking up and down in his room. She stood at the classroom window and bit her nails, one by one, down to the pink.

As they had never known when André's real birthday was, it had always been celebrated on the same day as Auguste's – the twenty-first of November – with a special meal. 'A pack of blessings,' Auguste liked to say each year, rubbing his hands, 'we shall be spoiled, shan't we? I plan to eat until I cannot move!'

When Caroline woke on André's birthday morning, she found Auguste with his back to her, standing out on the balcony which adjoined their room. His hands were spread on the railing; as she watched he took a theatrical breath in.

She padded over to him. It was indeed a glorious winter sunrise, hazy and gold as a bitten coin.

'Sixteen today. Can you believe it?'

It wasn't a question; as always, it was a statement to which Caroline was only expected to murmur her assent.

'All this,' said Auguste, and instead of finishing his sentence, he waved an arm over the rich brown sea of the plantation; small dots of cane-workers trussing and tying the husks of cane for winter.

Suddenly he was clutching her hand. 'You've been happy, haven't you? We've been happy, the two of us?'

His face was so strange: so earnest and terrified, she took fright.

'Of course we have.' She searched wildly for safe ground, and found it by showing him the plantation. 'Look what you've achieved.'

'Yes,' he said, 'I suppose so.' To her relief, he rallied. 'It's a great day today, isn't it?' He clapped his mottled hands together and walked to the door, where he paused and blew her a kiss.

Caroline dressed carefully and went downstairs to eat breakfast. André was out there working in the field: she could feel him, picture him listening to the overseer with all that respectful, youthful attention.

After she had eaten, she went to the reception room and read until it was time for the note to be sent. She wrote: *Your birthday present will be waiting for you at four o'clock in the library*, rang for a servant and told her to take it to André. The servant bobbed and hurried away. Crossing to the window, Caroline saw her running down the paths between the corn until there in the distance was André. Squinting, Caroline could just make him out receiving the note; then he looked up towards the house and raised one arm: *yes*. She could not see if he was smiling or not.

Caroline's heart pressed on her ribcage as she sat down at the little walnut bureau and wrote out the second note. *Auguste — forgot to tell you, have ordered birthday cake for A. A birthday tea, quarter past four in the library? Say you'll be there. Love as always, C.*

She looked at her handiwork. It was beautiful: glistening black ink on the white paper.

It was time to decide what to do. Another stroke and she would no longer be able to see the land.

She smoothed it out, sprinkled sand, folded it and beckoned to the servant.

Caroline sat, read, stood, sat again to table but couldn't eat; thought the servant's gaze on her was speculative as she waved away her plate; sat again, this time in the salon, folding her hands first one way then the other.

She could stop if she chose, at this point *now*, or this one; or this new second, the tock of the clock's longest hand slotting into the next, then the next. But she didn't move; she sat, hands in her lap, looking at nothing. And then, at five to four, she stood and went out of the reception room and down the corridor to the library.

A Southern belle to her core, Caroline's body gave her advance warning of barometric changes: she could feel the oncoming rain in little damp pinpricks up and down her forearm; as she took her seat in the library, dry-throated, rain began to scatter against the French windows which led out to the plantation.

A few moments later André appeared at the French doors, his face swimming in the wash of water on the glass; she unlatched the doors to let him in; and then left them carefully ajar. She scanned his face for evidence of a change for the better, and saw none: André looked like a boy dying for love. As he smoothed the rain out of his hair his movements were quick, jerky and doll-like, his pallor extreme.

Since that day in the classroom, they had barely spoken, still less been alone together; Caroline's heart fluttered. It was important to play the game perfectly. She bent her head, as if in apology, waiting for his next move.

André looked not at her but up at the books, a smooth skin of leather covering all the walls. He looked at the furniture; over at the door, swallowing; anywhere but at her.

She took his hand. 'I want us to go away,' she said, and he looked back at her, astonished. She smiled. 'We'll get somewhere far away and start again.'

He reached for her as she'd known he would. She let herself be pulled in but with one eye on the clock – it was getting late, almost ten past – so she held him away from her as he tried to lead her to the door. 'Here,' she said, pointing to Auguste's reading armchair. 'Please,' making her mouth open, her eyes glaze as she knew they did when she was possessed by feeling.

André picked her up and settled her on his hips, where she could feel he was hard; now it was all simple. They half-walked, half-fell towards the chair. He knelt in front of her and reached under her dress; she squirmed against his hand, tilted her head to check the time, and reached for the fastening on his trousers.

How silky he was, already pearling with excitement. He raised himself on his toes and pushed himself into her; she gasped – it hurt a little – and as André scrabbled for purchase on the parquet, knuckles bulging on the arms of the chair, the French doors opened inwards and Auguste stood in the room. In his right hand was a poorly wrapped package; André's birthday present.

Do it now.

Caroline filled her lungs with air and screamed to Auguste to help her, flailing at André with her hands; André turned and shouted out in shock, then pulled away from her and knelt, covering his shame.

Caroline made her eyes wide and pleading, she looked up at her husband. 'The shame of it! He forced me,' she whispered, 'as though possessed…'

Seeing Auguste's face turn purple, she thought: *He will send the boy away. He will cut him out of the will. I have done it.*

But: 'My love,' Auguste said to Caroline, and then he toppled. The servants ran into the room and took him by the shoulders and ankles; one of them ran screaming for horses, to fetch the doctor.

They found André's present afterwards, skidded under a chair. It was a book: a fine new edition of a new book. The inscription read: *To my son, who I always knew would come back*, and the spine said: Thomas Edison's *PRINCIPLES OF MOTION TELEGRAPHY.*

Juliette, i.

The Pathé archivist unrolls the promotional poster lovingly, smoothing the edges with her white cotton gloves.

'This was made in preparation for the release of the *Petite Mort*,' she says. 'It's all we have in terms of promotional material. Everything else was lost in the fire.'

The poster isn't as large as the modern ones I'm used to seeing – only a bit bigger than typewriter paper.

At the top of the page, in curvaceous black type, is the title – **LA PETITE MORT.** Underneath, down the right-hand side, is a drawing of a slender woman in a floor-length black dress. Her posture is elegant and composed apart from her face, held between her cupped hands as she stares directly at me. Her lips are pulled back from her teeth as she screams at something we can't see. In the background, there is a slit window and bare stone walls, and in the corner of the room, a full-length mirror.

The left-hand side has text on it. In the same bold font, it reads:

**A TALE OF MYSTERY AND SUSPENSE!
FEATURING A NEVER-SEEN-BEFORE
DOPPELGÄNGER TRICK BY ANDRE DURAND!**
PATHE FRERES

I signal to the archivist, who comes over to stand beside the desk.

'They told me the Doppelgänger trick is what's missing from the print that's turned up?'

'Yes, that's correct.'

'Do we know what the trick consisted of? Aren't there any papers?'

She shakes her head apologetically. 'All we know is the studio gossip. It was supposed to be a great coup, a hitherto unseen trick, and everyone was excited about the film's release. Only then, there was the fire.'

I look at the poster for a minute longer, as if there might be some hidden detail somewhere, but there is nothing: just the girl, and the mirror, and the castle room.

'Don't you have a script somewhere? Couldn't we get an idea from that?'

She touches the tips of her gloved fingers to each other in turn: 'No. I'm sorry. We looked all through the archive when the film print was found, but there was nothing.'

The girl's eyes in the poster are dark blots in a pale face.

9. juillet 1913

THE FOLLOWING DAY, something happened which eclipsed even Camille's arrival.

When I got to the costumery at ten past eight Elodie was already there, holding something up to the light for inspection.

'Is that the Absinthe Fairy's costume?' I asked.

It was venom-green: the seed pearls on the bodice were winking at me.

'That's it,' Elodie said, admiring it. 'Her assistant's coming to pick it up in a minute. They're filming today.'

Terpsichore was somewhere close by; perhaps in the very next building, putting on her make-up in front of a mirror, being fussed around by executives and flattered by the director.

I sat at my station and started my machine, trying not to steal glances at the costume. Five minutes later, we heard a clattering of boots in the corridor, and a girl about my own age appeared in the doorway.

She wasn't wearing a uniform: instead she had a smart dress on, which had been well-tailored, and her boots were polished to a bright black shine.

She stepped into the room as if she owned it; I felt the collective hackles rise. 'Is this it?' she asked, and when nobody answered, picked up the green dress and swept away, nose in the air.

~

As I remember it, that morning was full of gossip: enough to distract me totally from the problem of my sister. An ageing wolf had escaped from the zoological film section of the factory and was at large in the Bois de Vincennes; it was not proposed to retrieve him, on the basis that a lifetime of being fed treats had made his teeth too soft to bite. Another rumour: they were going to divert the course of the river to run through the Pathé lot in order to film the story of Moses. Moses was to be played by Charles Pathé's grandson, widely considered an ugly baby – but of course everyone was too afraid to object.

At half past eleven, we heard running feet again. The door opened and a runner stood there, excitement all over his face. 'You've got to see this.'

We all looked at Elodie, but she was already half out of her seat.

At the joining of the corridors we met a crowd of other workers – the secretaries and producers from the first floor – the whole of Block One was emptying in front of us.

We spilled out onto the building's top step and into the back of a crowd made up of the other workers. The sky was a mutinous grey, and fat drops of rain bounced up from the paving stones. Across the courtyard, workers were crammed into every crevice of the doorways of the other buildings.

'There,' murmured Elodie, pointing to the centre of the courtyard, where a few people stood huddled. A low-slung studio car was waiting there, and next to it was a group of men in the expensive suits of high-ranking employees, talking to André. The men had their arms crossed. The rain had damped André's curls to his forehead. It was clear from his gestures that he was losing the argument.

And standing next to André was a person who must be Terpsichore. She was wrapped in a fur coat, holding an umbrella tilted against the rain.

I whispered to Annick: 'What's happening?'

'They're saying she threw a glass vase at her assistant.'

'Why?'

'Apparently the costume didn't fit right.'

'Is she all right? The assistant?'

'She'll live, but it's not the first time. They're putting her on leave of absence,' Georgette whispered.

The tall figure turned towards us, bending to open the car door. She shut her umbrella with a shower of raindrops; the door clicked open and she bent to get in.

'She's beautiful, isn't she?' said Georgette.

Then the door closed, and all I could see was a shadowy profile, sitting quite still and unconcerned in the cab. André leant in to speak to the driver, their heads bent close together, then stood back from the car. The engine fired, and the car purred away down the narrow alleyway between the buildings.

André, iv.

Three o'clock in the afternoon, the day after Auguste's stroke. Rain drums on the roof, but the sick-room itself is quiet. Caroline sits beside Auguste's bed, brushing the creamy edges of the coverlet with her fingers.

The doctors have said that Auguste won't survive. His breathing is slow and gurgling, like a person drowning. Caroline remembers how apologetic he was on their wedding night and how scornful and impatient she must have seemed to him. She recalls the way Auguste patted her knee after her miscarriage; how he held her hand as she cried herself to sleep.

The door shuts quietly, and André is standing just inside the room.

She knows why he has come: because the carriage is outside waiting, because he is leaving. His face has changed: all the pallor and the passion is gone. Caroline has one weapon remaining, a final effort dispensed through gritted teeth.

If you'll only wait for the will.

Perhaps if André knows about the money he will be persuaded to stay; perhaps in time he'll understand why she had to trick him.

Last night's scenes come back to her. André, wild and hysterical: *You wanted him to find us together*, he said. *You wanted him to send me away.*

She had moved towards him, and the shock on his face vanished so quickly, replaced by arctic cold.

Now, standing in the sick-room doorway, André shakes his

head as though shaking off a fly. *I don't care about the money. I'm going now. I want to be someone to make him proud.*

Caroline crosses to watch his departure from the sick–room window. Perhaps now he will remember her crooked smile in the schoolroom; perhaps now he will recall the night–sweats and fevers and her thumb on his jaw. But André steps through the puddles and into the waiting carriage without looking up at her. She stays watching at the window anyway, even when the carriage has vanished. The clock ticks softly on.

When she turns back to the bed she sees that Auguste's chest has stopped rising and falling.

She is fascinated by the change in him: in death his face is fixed and molten at the same time, like wax.

Then André dips out of view for a while. There were sightings in a brothel in New Orleans; reports of a young man in blue serge hiding out in a railroad car. Tramps along the Montana line, presented with a sketched likeness, shook their heads and could not swear to it.

It was easy to lose him because nobody really wanted to find him. Auguste's family lawyers made a cursory investigation and then recalled their agents. There had been rumours of an unfortunate entanglement at the plantation, the details of which were vague but damning; better, they thought, that André make his peace with himself in his own time.

On January 3rd 1897, André presented himself at the offices of Mr Thomas Edison in New York.

The office door was opened by Edison himself – now in middle age, with tufty grey hair and a lean, narrow-eyed cast to his face. He saw a gangly teenager with grey eyes and a careworn shirt in expensive material. André in turn took in the view through the half-open door: three foreign-looking gentlemen were sitting in the offices. One gentleman's hand rested protectively on a machine which André immediately recognised: a projector. With Edison distracted at the door, the gentleman leant across to his colleague and André heard him say, in French: *Let's not sell for less than a million.*

Edison saw André peering round the edge of the door. 'Are you the interpreter?' he grunted.

The French gentleman wore a fur stole and a monocle and spoke very quickly, in a Parisian accent; André, translating, struggled to keep up. The man accorded his salutations to Mr Edison; it was his pleasure to present the new Visiscope, his very latest invention, a revolutionary projecting machine that could show images to an ever-larger audience. He patted the projector's casing, extolled its many virtues – *Think of the profits, sir!* – and sat back with folded arms, waiting for Edison to make an offer.

André was bewitched. Auguste had taken him to a nickelodeon once in Baton Rouge, and he had seen illustrations, but never the apparatus of such a thing before. When the inventor opened the casing to demonstrate the mechanism, André leant closer and looked at the loving, ingenious armatures, savouring the hiss of the machinery. When the Visiscope started, and shapes leapt to life on the blank wall of the office, Edison was transfixed; but André did not glance at the wall once. He looked only at the way the film unspooled, smooth as water, inside the projector.

Edison hemmed and hawed and twirled his moustaches. He hated to lose money on a deal, but feared still more that he would lose to one of his competitors. The inventor waited politely, with a smile like ice. Finally Edison sighed, crossed his arms behind his head and said to André: 'Damn patent's worth a million. Tell them I'll pay it.'

Though he did not understand English, the inventor leant forward, sensing victory.

'I wouldn't do that,' André said to Edison.

Edison coloured instantly. He was the inventor of the light bulb, of X-rays; it was years since anyone had contradicted him. 'What the devil do you mean?'

'The mechanism that holds the film in place could be improved. If we were to introduce a simple loop here, you would reduce the pressure on the film as it passes through. It would be safer. And sufficiently different to qualify for a new patent. We wouldn't have to buy theirs.'

Edison peered into the body of the projector and saw the boy was right.

The inventor's eyes darted from one face to the other.

Edison sat back, the Visiscope forgotten, and stared at André.

The year 1897 was a busy one at the New York State Patents Office. There were ten patent applications for new cinematic equipment. And, though they ranged enormously in technology – projectors and cameras and primitive sound-cylinders – eight of those patents bear the same blocky and youthful signature. Beneath the first signature was the confident flourish that the patent office knew so well – Thomas Edison – which signified joint ownership.

In the year that followed, the patents continued to flow thick and fast, all with the same scribble and confident employer's countersigning. It is only in 1899 that the rate of invention tails off: it peters out in a series of applications for licences. One for a 'folding mirror device' and another, a 'handle-operated smoke-producing machine'.

These were the traditional paraphernalia of the fairground attraction, with minor modifications. They were not countersigned by Edison, and not original enough to be considered seriously. They were rejected by the Patent Officer out of hand.

~

Electricity was Edison's business. He understood that a current will not always run smoothly: instead, it may leap erratically from point to point, arriving at its destination through the route that suits it best. And, though he never shared his view with anyone, Edison believed that people worked like electricity – coursing for the most part drone-like through life, but sometimes throwing up an anomaly. He, who had been expelled from school as mentally deficient, when all the time he was studying the flight patterns of the birds through the window, was his own proof.

Therefore – knowing that brilliance, physical or metaphysical, might flare in unexpected ways – Edison gave André a long leash. Along with the rest of his engineers, the boy was set up on a decent salary and given workshops on Edison's lot. By and large he was left to his own devices, to tinker in whatever way he chose. And for almost two years Edison's policy bore fruit.

Nevertheless, by the summer of 1899, André's erratic ideas could no longer be ignored. All spring, the guards had come running to Edison with reports of men in fur coats drawing up to André's offices late at night; peering through the window, the guards saw the room lit up by zoetropes in action, by mirrors laid out in odd formations on the floor. They saw André's pensive face as he poured hard liquor for the men, listening to them give away their fairground secrets one by one.

Was this some kind of fad? Edison told himself that he was angry because André was inviting dubious characters onto the site, and called André to his office.

The young man stood before his desk. Edison made him wait a full minute before looking up from the papers he was signing.

'What is this I hear about inviting trick-film merchants in?' he asked.

André had known it was only a matter of time.

'The mechanisms are ingenious—' he began, but Edison held up a palm.

'Charlatans and misfits: it must stop.' He didn't want reasoning; he wanted contrition. Why didn't the boy make it easy for himself?

André knew he could not convince Edison to see the world the way he did. Edison looked down at his papers, dismissing him. 'Don't be careless with your future,' he said, more sternly than he felt; his faith in his electric metaphor was undimmed. André might fizz and crackle, but he would eventually find his way home.

André packed the same night. He bore Edison no personal grudge; his decision was calculated on the basis purely of profit and loss. Nobody saw him slip out of the compound. He stayed the night in a hotel by the docks, and boarded a ship the following morning.

9. juillet 1913

ALL THAT MORNING, the studio talked of nothing else. The vase had been crystal, and had lodged in shining splinters in the assistant's face. The assistant had found a lawyer; the assistant had been paid off handsomely.

'It's the Absinthe Fairy producers I feel sorry for,' Georgette piped. 'Having to replace Terpsichore at the last moment.'

The others shook their heads. I stared at her, dazed by a new idea. Unsettled, Georgette gave her shoulders a mutinous little shake and said, 'Poor M. Durand. All his film in tatters, and his wife too.'

There was general assent, and gradually the subject died away. But I was listening only to myself. I was overdue this, wasn't I? With Terpsichore gone, who would replace her in the role, if not me? Somewhere in the building across the courtyard, André would be persuading the casting directors. *Let's give the Roux girl a chance*, he was saying. And one by one the others would be slowly nodding: *Let's*.

There was no sign of him in the early afternoon; three o'clock and four o'clock came and went. By the end of the day I was cross, taking it out on the others with needling little asides; Annick flushed once or twice and bit her lip; I had almost made her cry.

It was only at ten to five that a runner came to the door. 'Message for Mlle Roux,' he said, 'M. Durand wants to see you in his offices immediately.'

Elodie looked up, surprised.

I beamed as I rose, smoothing the cloth of my skirt.

'This way,' the runner said, and I followed him up to the second floor of the building, where the upper echelons of staff had their offices.

There was a corridor with just one door at the end of it. The runner knocked, and André's voice called out: 'Come in!'

I opened the door to a long, low-ceilinged room. At one end was a green baize desk. Two of the walls were lined with bookshelves, and stuck to the third was a mass of paper – sketches and geometric drawings.

Where was André? I heard a clock ticking – no, not a clock – and there, making its waddling way towards me, was a monstrosity. A clanking figure made of metal, the size of a child. Someone had painted a crude face on it: red for the lips, blue for the eyes, though the paint had run on the mouth before it had dried, and it was this that made me squeak.

André's laugh rang out, and he stepped forward. 'Do you like her?'

I watched the automaton come towards me. It was nothing to be afraid of – stage-magicians used them. But this one was unfinished: though its legs marched smartly, its arms were mismatched pieces of metal and hung by its side. It wheezed up to me, fell over onto its side and froze, fixing me with its blue eyes.

André peered down into its face. 'Back to the drawing board,' he said.

'Did you make it?' I asked. 'What for?'

'Work,' he answered, and for some reason, the room felt flat and irritable.

'I was sorry to hear about your wife,' I prompted.

He looked at me. 'Adèle, she's not dead. She just needs a rest.'

I decided to press my advantage, and crossed to him, placing my palms on his chest. 'You have something to tell me, don't you? That's why you sent for me.'

His hand slid under my breast.

'No,' I said, pushing him away, 'tell me what you want me for.'

He sighed. 'Very well,' he said. 'It is an offer of some importance, after all.' He was looking at me strangely, I thought, his lips twitching. 'You will make a wonderful new assistant for my wife,' he said.

In the corner, the automaton convulsed and then was still. 'Are you—?' I said. 'Are you joking?'

Smiling, he shook his head.

From the stairwell outside the apartment, I heard an entirely new sound. High, yet girlish: it sounded like Mathilde laughing.

Shuffling from the ground floor caught my attention. I peered down through the banisters, and saw Monsieur Z rustling on his newspapery bed; he looked up at me and grinned, revealing pink and toothless gums. 'Happy,' he cackled, and indicated upstairs with his chin.

I opened the front door and stepped inside. The hall was in darkness, but a wavering, flickering light – candles – came from the salon. I hesitated, listening – and heard low chatter: Camille's voice, as though telling an anecdote. And then again, Mathilde's giggling.

I peered round the corner so that I could see into the salon.

The first thing I saw was that the furniture had been rearranged. The dining table had been dragged to sit cross-wise in front of the fireplace, and the large mirror from over the fireplace placed on top of the table, so that the mirror's back was supported by the mantelpiece. Mathilde's family miniatures lay piled carelessly just inside the door. The room was lit by two candles, one on either side of the mirror; and on the dining table were scattered an array of pots of powder and kohl.

Mathilde was sitting up to the table, facing the mirror, expectant and child-like; Camille was to her right, leaning in to dab at Mathilde's eyes with a finger greased with Vaseline. Agathe stood behind Mathilde, watching the proceedings. Even she was smiling, enchanted at Mathilde's transformation.

When she saw my movement out of the corner of her eye, Mathilde swivelled to look at me. She was painted chalky white, with black swirling details on her cheeks, and one black tear-drop eye: a pierrot.

Camille stood back, smiling. Her glance flickered to the corner of the room, where I saw the squat black valise she had arrived with. *A skill,* she had said the night she arrived: *I've got a skill.*

'You weren't the only one who was clever,' Camille said. 'I've taught myself. I used to practise on the little ones after school.'

'You never told me,' I said.

Camille tossed her head, which meant, *you never asked.*

'Isn't it wonderful?' Mathilde said, 'Isn't it exciting – you can find her employment at Pathé! Surely some of the directors could make use of Camille?'

'The actors do their own,' I said coldly. 'Most of them,' I corrected. For what did I know about the individual habits of the stars?

Camille had waited patiently for Mathilde to stop speaking, and now bent gently to dust powder over her cheeks: I suddenly saw, as she moved into the candles' range, that she had made herself up. It was no more than a touch of rouge and the lightest shading around the eyes, but she looked *finished.*

'So I'm afraid there are no opportunities at present,' I said.

Mathilde turned to look at me, bewildered.

Camille said smoothly: 'But you could have a word, couldn't you, Adèle? I thought you and M. Durand were close.'

I fled to my room, curled up in bed, and held onto my own toes for comfort. The rain continued whispering at the window late into the night, and still the laughter came from the salon, and Camille did not come to bed.

I thought back to that afternoon. *What on earth were you thinking?* André had asked, grabbing my wrists after I had reached up to try to slap him. *An established actress will take over the Absinthe role. What did you expect?*

He had let me struggle, turning my head away from him.

'Think about it,' he had said, 'just think,' over my tears. 'Don't you know how often the assistant becomes the understudy?'

I had sniffed and hiccuped, caught out.

'Besides, you'd come and live with us. My wife finds it preferable to have someone there all the time. She and I each have our own quarters. You will be in the room just above mine.'

André smiled and gave my shoulders a little shake, till I began to smile in turn.

'Really?' I asked. 'Really?'

'You will have your pick of gowns. All the advantages of knowing the studio people. And me, of course. As much of me as you like.'

I thought of myself, whisking a costume away from my own assistant: *You have not sewn the hem correctly. Take it back, please.* Would I say please?

André looked at me with narrowed eyes.

'I don't want to be a costumière for ever,' I said, trying out the words.

In the early hours, Camille came to bed. She turned away from me, and soon I heard her breathing steady and slow. Her nightgown fell below her shoulder blade, exposing the new skin growing over her scars. They were healing on their own, without any help from me.

André had said: 'I'll send my driver for you tomorrow evening. Of course you will have to be vetted by my wife. My car will take you to our house in the Bois de Boulogne. All you have to do is be there to meet it.'

André, v.

A rainy November evening in 1904: five years after André stepped off the boat from New York to Paris, and into his proper life.

As usual, he was in the Pathé building long after everyone else had left, reclining and doodling on his sketch pad. He had nothing to do apart from be perfectly himself: there was an invitation, of course, to a gallery opening later in the evening, but he was not obliged to attend. He loved above all things the long hours after dark, when the hum of the human factory workers had subsided. He had his best ideas at night, because it was then that he was left alone with the noises he loved: the clanking of the stage-machinery pistons, the hiss of water in the pipes above his head, on its way to douse down the film-strip laboratory floor.

Then, mixed with the mechanical sounds, André heard something that should not have been there: footsteps, approaching his door. He frowned: a little flare of temper, and dropped his sketch pad as the knock at the door came.

'Come in,' he barked. The door opened a crack, and one of the runners poked his head into the space. 'This came for you, M. Durand,' he piped, holding out a flat, oblong parcel in trembling fingers.

André snatched the parcel, tossed it onto the table, and tried to get back to his thoughts. He locked his fingers behind his head and closed his eyes. The pitter-patter of the runner's feet receded, and he sighed and inhaled the factory sounds.

But the parcel had made a dent in the weave: an oblong silence where there should have been noise. It lay staring up at him.

André swore. Who had sent him a film idea at this time of night? What could possibly be so urgent? But he would get no rest until he had, at least, looked at it.

One quick peek – and then it would go where ninety-nine per cent of the ideas he received went. Giving in, he tore the manilla envelope that was used for inter-departmental traffic, and found, as he had expected, a note from Charles Pathé:

This came from a friend. Of interest. Difficult trick. C.

André smiled. Declaring something *difficult* was a lure of Charles's, designed to pique André's interest: but it was a phrase without bite because they both knew that André never found camera tricks difficult. His films were the talk of Europe: his speciality was the illusion; films which made the audience cover their face with their hands; and he did it all with a shrug and a smile, finding it easy. Inevitably he would stride into Charles's office the following morning and toss the script onto his desk, along with the sketch book containing the solution. *Not so difficult then*, Charles Pathé would smile, and André would answer: *Apparently not.*

He turned the paper over:

LA PETITE MORT
A drama of a haunting

André's lip curled. Charles was losing his touch: when had there been a ghost which André could not conjure? Mercifully, the script was just a few pages long, and well formatted – not like some of the scribbles he got nowadays. He quickly found the scene which would require his attention:

The Doppelgänger, enraged, steps out of the mirror.

Intertitle:

HOW DARE YOU CONJURE ME WITHOUT MY PERMISSION?

The Doppelgänger wraps its hands round the girl's throat.

The sluicing of the pipes overhead faded out and was replaced by the tingle in his elbow that signified an idea.

André tossed the script aside, and reached for his pencil and sketchbook. Designs ran down his arms and fingers and onto the page. He drew a stage model of the standard set-up for Pepper's Ghost, the illusion which had so amazed London three seasons ago. The action ran as usual on the stage: but a sheet of glass was added during the interval, running invisibly stage left to right. Via a series of projections, the reflection of an actor in the wings was thrown onto the sheet of glass: and a ghost appeared to walk back and forth on stage.

In the silence of his room, André furrowed his brow. It was easy enough to duplicate a person in the same shot. One simply filmed the same scene in two passes, confining the action to one side of the shot only on each pass, and then laid the two sections of film over each other to get the full picture in the finished print. Or a better option might be to block off a part of the camera lens, and expose one side of the film – have the girl step towards the mirror – and then rewind the film, block off the other half of the lens, and shoot the other side – have the same girl play herself stepping out of the mirror.

But in this type of trick, the doubles usually stayed firmly on their respective sides of the set, and never touched each other. The contact of nebulous hands on living throat: that was more difficult.

Half an hour passed; the clock struck eight, and André tore the sheets from his pad and ripped them into strips. He flung the script into a drawer.

As he stared at his desk, unseeing, the invitation to the

gallery opening swam into focus. Suddenly he did not want to be alone in his office any more.

He locked the drawer with its shameful contents before he left, locked his office, smiled at the night porter on his way out, and hailed a cab which took him to Montmartre, and to a rainy pavement outside a gallery lit by electricity and champagne.

Juliette and Adèle
1967

I say: 'But he did work out a method by the winter of 1913.'
　'Yes.'
　'How was it done?'
　Adèle shrugs. 'I don't know exactly.'
　'Why not? You were there.'
　She leans forward: 'Have you ever stood under cinema lights? After two minutes, you smell your own hair burning. I was alone, faint and dazzled, being told what gestures to make, one by one. I do remember there was a mirror, and that the director became very irate, and kept moving me around, saying I wasn't hitting my marks. But apart from that – a blank.'
　'I can't believe it,' I say. 'There must be something.'

A hiss of steam from the coffee machine; someone comes into the café, and Adèle Roux is looking at me.
　'I've got you wrong, haven't I?' she says. 'I thought you were a person who let things happen to them, but you're not. You have to find things out. You won't rest until you know.'
　It's the best summary of myself I have yet heard.
　She passes her hand in front of her mouth as if hiding a smile. 'But when we come to the part about the film,' she says, 'you will see why I wasn't concentrating.'

10. juillet 1913

THROUGH THE GLASS PARTITION, André's driver tells me about his daughters. 'Our eldest, we hope, may be a doctor one day.' His eyes crinkle. 'Why not? It's changing everywhere, isn't it?' Failing that, he says, a doctor's wife. 'She's turned out good-looking. A bit like you.' He winks: complimentary rather than lascivious, but I've turned my face away.

Outside the car, the city has gone away without anything to go on. It seems one moment a white-aproned waiter inclines over a lady in furs, frozen in the act of obsequiousness; the next, the avenue is white dust and lined with poplars – neat façades behind high walls – countryside, but pruned and arranged for the rich, speeding along too fast, pressing me into the sides of the car as we corner. I fold my hands over my valise and wish he'd watch the road.

'First time in an automobile?' the driver says.

'No,' I say, and then: 'When I was little there was a horse and trap; we hired it to take us on picnics. Only the pony was used to deliver milk the rest of the time, so it kept trying to stop in at every house on the way.'

He laughs out loud, confident hands on the wheel, and I feel a little better.

The house radiates wealth: gold stone, its shutters beaming wide, its windows blue in the summer evening. The mansard roof is slate and the lawn trimmed a perfect poison-green. In a spin of gravel, the car swings round a turning circle in the drive and stops outside wide steps leading up to the front door.

The driver hops off the cab and clicks the car door open for me. He touches his cap: 'Hubert, Mademoiselle,' he says. 'I look forward to being of more service to you in the future,' and smiling, he steps away.

Inside, led by the butler, Thomas, the house isn't what I expected: a smell of camphor and the old stone of the marble floor. The hall is dark apart from the yellow pool of a lamp, standing on a marble occasional table: as we move through, a wash of colour from a stained-glass window dapples my feet. Further back, a glimpse of a snail's shell staircase, drifting up into the floor above.

Thomas stands for a moment listening outside a door halfway down the corridor, his hand in readiness on the door knob; he raps with his other knuckle and without waiting for an answer, goes in.

She is sitting on a sofa under the large front window, head bent over a book; as we enter, she puts it down on her lap.

'Mlle Roux, Madame,' Thomas says.

She says: 'Oh – the new assistant!' as if she has never heard of such a thing; Thomas withdraws, closing the door behind him.

She looks down, produces a bookmark and inserts it, marking the page. Makes a business of it; smoothing the covers and closing it and putting it down again, this time beside her; and then we look at each other.

You always ask yourself: how much of what I remember is real, and how much of it is detail that I have embellished afterwards? In my mind's eye, she makes a quick movement, as if she is hesitating to speak, and we stay like that for I don't know how long – but when I try to square that trembling image with what I know of her now, I can't imagine her doing it.

I felt, in those couple of seconds, that I'd known her for a long time. I thought, as she finally started to smile, and her teeth appeared, I saw her recognise me too. Perhaps that was what she had been going to say, but stopped herself: *Don't I know you?*

'My husband tells me you have aspirations in the cinema.'

Now she has fixed her eyes on the window behind me, with a slight frown, as if momentarily distracted by someone passing by, and I'm glad of the interruption, because her voice is a disappointment. Unremarkable: the accent aristocratic but not Parisian. Not the rich chocolate I'd imagined.

'Yes,' I say, 'I am extremely keen to learn.'

'And can you read?'

'Fluently.'

'Good. And you know the duties involved in being my assistant? Clerical, as well as the social aspect? You'll answer my correspondence and help me keep my paperwork in order. And you don't mind about the money? You will have your own rooms, your own suite, and you can eat your meals with us if you like. I expect M. Durand explained.'

I nod, thinking that I'll have to be careful not to use his first name.

'Are you able to start immediately? We can send for your things. There isn't anyone at home waiting for you?'

'No.'

'Then I'll ask Thomas to show you to your room.'

The smile broadens until all her teeth appear, and above them, her eyes, wide and amused.

Three days later I returned to rue Boissonnade one last time, to collect my things.

I went in the last hours of the night so that nobody would see me. Wisps of mist hung in the street and wreathed themselves about the hall door; I crept past Monsieur Z and up the creaking staircase and turned my key in the lock of the apartment.

From Agathe's room came the sound of snores. I moved on, past the salon door, which was propped open. In the dead light the furniture looked august and almost expensive; Mathilde's family were frozen on the mantel, glinting in their silver frames.

The door to my old bedroom creaked under my hand.

The room was warm with sleep. Camille lay in my bed, huddled over on herself like a small animal, the blankets clutched between her legs. On the tiny desk, she had laid out the tools of her trade – the half-used pots of rouge, the eyelash curlers, the hand mirror.

As quietly as I could, I stole my best dress from the cupboard and then I fled into the street.

Two days later, the letter would have arrived.

It was a Sunday – Agathe's day off, and so she would have been up early – it would have been Agathe who found it and tore it open, never mind that it was addressed to Mathilde, greedy hands ripping the paper in case there was something personal inside. Levering herself into a chair, she would have read André's brief note explaining where I had gone and why. *Post as secretary. Hope this will cover unpaid rent. Expenses. Thank you for your kind understanding. Do not hesitate. Yours, &c.*

And then it would have dawned on her that money was in the envelope – she would have held it upside down and the notes would have fluttered out and lain on the parquet, twitching in the breeze from the open window. One hundred, two hundred, three hundred. Agathe's fingers flexing; her piggy-eyes glinting, for André, with his rich man's lack of understanding, had more than bought off my deposit and my three months' notice; the three hundred francs was a sum the like of which Agathe could not have earned in several months.

She would have made a rapid calculation, and folded the

notes quick as winking into her pocket, and the letter – the letter she would have burnt, letting the fragments sprinkle into the breeze, as she stood at the window where we always used to smoke together. She would have spread herself with a grunt into the place I used to occupy, and thought no more about it.

Mathilde would have continued hoping for a word from me to explain my sudden absence. 'Do you think we should alert the police?' she would have asked, and flinched at Agathe's snort. And then, what would she have said? *We run an honest little boarding-house, officer, visited only by a few discerning gentlemen...*

Nevertheless, she would have waited for a note or a letter. Late at night, thinking she heard a light step on the stairwell, she would have paused in her needlework and listened.

'You shouldn't be surprised,' Agathe would have said, flicking her cigarette end high over the rooftops and watching it fall in a firefly, ember-tipped arc, 'she was always flighty.'

Juliette and Adèle
1967

'So you just left without saying goodbye? Without leaving an address?'

'Imagine if she'd followed me to the house. It was my big opportunity.'

She looks out of the window, and I don't interrupt her: I'm getting used to these pauses.

Eventually she says: 'Did you say you were going to see the film tonight?'

'Yes.'

'Then you'll see what I was like as a girl. I was beautiful.'

She still has that absent expression. I wait.

She says: 'One day, five years ago, I went to see a plastic surgeon, a man with fine hands and an office behind the Palais-Royal. He took my face like so, pinching the skin here, and smoothing it here, and he never once looked me in the eyes. At the end of the examination he said: *Good news, Madame. We can nip here, tuck here. I can give you back what you've lost.*'

She draws herself up, indignant at the memory. 'What do you think I told him?' she says.

I think about it. Realise I know the answer.

'Nobody can give another person what they've lost?' I say.

She looks at me, faintly surprised. Then she levels her finger, like the barrel of a gun, right between my eyes. 'Very good, Mlle Blanc.'

Juliette, ii.

In the dark of the viewing room, a flickering light, and then the picture forms.

An intertitle:

LA PETITE MORT
OUR TALE BEGINS IN BOHEMIA, A LAND ROAMED
BY FELL BEASTS AND BANDITS...

The screen changes: a jagged landscape, triangular mountains and floating cardboard clouds, and in the background, a tiny turreted manor house.

IN THE CASTLE BISMARCK, THE BARON IS
PLANNING THE WEDDING OF HIS YOUNGEST
DAUGHTER...

A room at the top – cut-out stars and moon visible through a window. A middle-aged man appears, gesticulating and striding up and down. Sitting stage right is a young woman with her face in her hands.

As the actress takes her hands away I feel – not recognition, because I don't think anybody could see Adèle Roux, the person I know, in this frightened, hungry face.

I WILL NOT MARRY FOR MONEY!

The Baron shakes his finger at her:

THE COUNT IS A MAN OF WEALTH AND
DISTINCTION!

BUT I LOVE ANOTHER!
WE LEAVE FOR THE CHURCH AT DAWN
TOMORROW!

Adèle runs to the door, sobs against it, slithers to the ground;
flings herself onto her bed. Cries; then lifts herself on one elbow
and, after a moment's thought, leaps from the bed, runs to a
bookshelf near the door and pulls a large book from it.

MY LOVE FOR MAURICE WILL NOT BE SULLIED.
I WILL CREATE ANOTHER WHO WILL GO FORTH
AND DO MY BIDDING.

Her hands lift:

WATCH ME AS I CAST MY SPELL—

...

...

Lightning across the film – but not part of the film – and
without warning the scene changes completely.

'That's where the missing bit was,' the technician says.

The castle tower is gone – now an Alpine field, strewn
with tiny wild flowers. In the background there is a card-
board-looking church, and hundreds of guests milling about
in front. They have the unmistakeable air of amateur extras,
over-excited and unsure of themselves: one young man sneaks a
glance direct at camera, looks away, then looks back and stands,
mouth open, until the woman next to him tugs him away. The
film technician chuckles.

A man in a velvet tunic runs to and fro across the screen, his
hands clutching at his scalp.

The intertitle reads:

THE NEXT MORNING, BEFORE THE WEDDING,
MAURICE SEARCHES FOR HIS BRIDE...

The technician cuts the motor and smiles apologetically.

'We'll never know,' he says, unspooling the film from the reel. Holds it up to the light. 'Here.'

I hold the silky filmstrip, and together we look at the part where the two scenes meet. One minute mirror; next church.

'Was it found in two halves? Did you stick it back together yourselves?'

'No, it was like this when we got it. That's editing cement. They use it to splice pieces of film together. Whoever cut the scene out must have glued it back together again after they'd removed it.'

I run my thumb over the roughness of the join.

A LITTLE DEATH

10. juillet 1913

'SO,' ANDRÉ SAYS, slipping his shirt back over his head, 'what did you think of my wife?'

There hasn't been time for talking, in the first tumble on my own feather bed. The room is moonlit grey; the ormolu clock on the mantelpiece of my new room ticks quietly. He sits on the edge of the covers, his hand still resting on my thigh, smooth under the rich person's sheets.

I arrange my face into the malicious smile he will expect. He smiles back, reassured; always fastidious, he clears his throat and buttons up his trousers. 'No doubt you thought yourself more attractive and more talented,' he says.

'She's what I expected,' I say airily, and he nods and shrugs, happy with the diplomacy of the answer. 'Same time tomorrow night?'

I plump up the coverlet under my fingers. What he will expect me to do: look triumphant.

Thomas had been the one to show me to my room earlier that evening; up, up and round the great spiral staircase, my valise handle sticking to my palm. The walls were papered in cool silk, embossed with fleur-de-lys. Above us there was a cupola, a disc of indigo: an eye peering through the roof.

Each member of the household had their own floor. Terpsichore's was the first and smelled of nothing: the walls of the corridor were draped in pale yellow silk. André's, the second floor, smelled of the factory: cordite and business sense.

And then, knowing, expecting a reaction, Thomas said: 'This is for you.'

He had opened the first door in the third-floor corridor and stood aside to let me pass. I didn't go to the bed or the wardrobe in chocolate mahogany or the cold china vase on the dressing-table or any one of the hundred other beautiful things the room contained; I didn't exclaim girlishly – I was too proud, in front of Thomas. Instead, I crossed to the window and leant out from the waist, squinting into the sun. Directly below was a flagstoned terrace, with a balustrade, and two mossy stone lions for sentinels; it was lit with lanterns, just starting to show in the fading sun. Beyond it, the lawn stretched away for half a mile or so, until it met the fringe of the Bois de Boulogne.

I said, keeping my voice level: 'This is very nice.' A great wash of happiness: *Look, look where I had got to.*

'The Durands take the evening meal at eight. You will hear the dinner bell chime.'

When the time came, I hovered on the upstairs landing, waiting to hear them go down; not wanting to be the first to arrive. As soon as I heard doors opening and shutting I ran downstairs.

When I entered the dining room, I noticed a change in her straightaway: where in our interview she had been calm, now it was as if she was surrounded by a heat haze of energy. She was taking snails from their shells with a miniature fork, her other cutlery laid out before her like a butcher's implements: knife, scoop, tweezers. Not timid: cheerfully pulling at them until they gave way.

A chandelier hung twinkling from the ceiling; servants stood blending into the walls, waiting to serve food from the sideboard. The polished table gleamed my own ghostly image at me; she was seated near the door and André sat at the far end, his back to the French window. He looked up at me and I felt, as clearly as if he had really done it, his finger trace my cheek: *pretty little devil.*

'Do you find your quarters to your liking?' he asked.

'They are extremely comfortable. Thank you.'

He had risen into a reverential half-bow; now he sat back in his seat, his smile in the corners of his mouth.

I looked down at the finicky morsels of food: *amuse-bouches*, a miniature egg perched on a salad, and the snails and dish of sauce – toy dinner – and hovered over the cutlery until I could be sure what each was for.

'Mlle Roux saved my life today,' Terpsichore said.

André pressed his thumb into his wine glass: miniature pink lines sprang to life along the stem.

'Yes, it happened like this: I was re-reading *Thérèse Raquin* by M. Zola, which as you know,' – she paused to press her napkin to her mouth – 'is a great tragedy of disappointed hopes and loveless loves.' Her eyes were busy on the table as she spoke, and her hands swept the snails' shells fussily back into their silver dish. 'I had come to the final paragraph, so desperately sad, where Laurent and Thérèse take the poison and collapse into each others' arms, unable to bear the weight of their guilt.' She lifted her wine glass; her eyes twinkled over the top of it. 'And I sat on my sofa and thought, nothing can surpass *Thérèse Raquin* – I have known it for some time in my heart of hearts. M. Zola is a towering inferno of genius who will never again pass amongst us, so what use is it, then, to stay alive?'

André smiled indulgently.

'So I thought then: *What will it be? Knife, rope or drowning?* My resolve was fixed; I had only to determine the *modus operandi* – I barely heard the door, nor did I hear Thomas escorting Mlle Roux into the room, but unquestionably she rescued me from certain death by my own hand.'

André snorted and smoothed his cutlery, repositioning it on the tablecloth; then looked up as the fish course was brought.

'How do we know that it was not Mlle Roux, performing voodoo in the back of our automobile, who put such thoughts into your mind in the first place?'

She levelled her knife at him down the table. 'We don't. Mlle Roux is therefore a rescuer or a bird of ill omen, depending on your point of view.' She smiled her bright, interested smile. 'In any case, the great work of saving me from myself begins tomorrow. Mlle Roux must always be on hand with matches, to set alight any book which might distress me; to remove tempting nooses, to whisk sharp objects out of my reach.'

André dipped his eyes to his food, smiling and prodding the fish with his fork. I looked up at her, and found she had absented herself, lifting her wine glass and staring at a point in the dark window past André's head. Her neck drooped slightly, in the way that tall people's sometimes do.

I dissected my sole into smaller and even smaller pieces, irritated by what she'd said. She expected me to be at her shoulder with the matches, always on hand to shelter the corners of furniture. It was as if I was a negative person – someone she would only notice through the things I removed.

The shutters in my bedroom window creak in the night air. At the doorway, André pauses: 'The two of you don't have to be enemies.'

'You'd prefer it if we were.'

He grins, and is gone. His light footsteps patter down the stairs to his rooms one floor below, and there is the sound of his door gently shutting.

11. juillet 1913

THE NEXT MORNING I woke up naturally for the first time in years. It was wonderful: listening to the sounds of other people having to work; scratching at André's leftover papery scales with my thumbnail.

The house was all small sounds: the clatter of pans in the kitchen, the sweep, sweep of the housemaids scrubbing down the terrace outside; the regular tread of Thomas carrying food trays to the different occupants of the house's three floors. What there wasn't: polite conversation between Mathilde and Madame Moreau, comparing last night's prices on the landing; Monsieur Z's whining sea shanties echoing up from the street. I'd write to Camille later.

Finally the footsteps came outside my door, and there was a discreet knock and the rattle of a breakfast tray being set down. 'Madame expects you in her study at nine-thirty,' Thomas whispered, and then his soft pad away down the stairs again.

I hopped out of bed and dragged the tray into the room; examined the meal. They had gone to the other extreme from last night's picky nothings: now there was fried kidneys and coffee thick as oil. I pushed the tray out of the room again with one toe, unable to stomach it; and then, because it was still before nine o'clock, dressed and went to explore my domain.

The corridor was warm and sunlit: to the right of my bedroom, doors ran away along a corridor to a picture window at the end, beyond which a tree moved soundlessly, its leaves quivering in a light wind.

I stepped across the carpet runner to the door almost opposite my room, and tested the handle. By daylight, the paintwork in the hall had a bleached-out, dusty look of disuse; the door knob rattled uselessly in my hand. Pursing my lips, I walked to the next door – another set of weary paintwork – and gently turned the handle. Nothing. The same for the next door, and the next, by the window. The leaves outside ruffled, discontented; I tried the rooms on the other side of the corridor, but they were locked right the way back up the passageway to my own room.

I stood outside my bedroom with my hand on the door frame. *This floor is yours,* Thomas had said, beaming at me. But he had not even given me keys to my own room, let alone to the rest of my miniature empire.

Just then, from inside, the clock on the mantelpiece chimed nine-thirty. I pulled the door shut and crossed to the top of the stairs.

When I reach Terpsichore's floor I don't know which is her study so I listen, and sure enough, there is the rasp of a page being turned, behind the door at the far end of the passage.

I knock at the door and hear her clear her throat. 'Come in!'

She has laid the novel on the sofa beside her and now her hands are clasped together. She isn't the only one posing: the room is long and light, with bookcases lining two walls. It reminds me a little of Père Simon's front room, but these books are all new, and if dust spirals in the shaft of light from the windows, it is only showing off. On her left, propped against a cushion, is her discarded breakfast tray: a brioche bleeding a dab of jam.

'Just in time,' she says, and casts her eyes at the novel splayed on the seat beside her, 'I was almost at the poison scene again.'

I'm confused. 'Didn't you read that last night?'

'I needed to look at it more closely.'

'Why?'

She smiles a wicked-fairy smile. 'I wish to understand the best method of poisoning someone.'

'Who?'

'My husband. I'm running away.'

I don't know the rules of this game, so I go quiet.

'So my routine,' she says, 'until the studio comes to its senses: I read in the morning, scripts or studio business, and the afternoons are for exercise and social calls. Does that sound amenable?'

'Yes.'

'Good.'

She looks at me, eyes slightly narrowed, thinking me over.

'You may begin by answering some of my correspondence,' she says, and gestures to the desk under the window, where a stack of handwritten letters is waiting. 'Just write a brief note of acknowledgement to each.'

I don't need a second invitation to sit to something straightforward, and besides, I want to show her what I can do; I pick up the topmost letter, dip the pen in ink, and bend my head. For a while the only sound is the scratching of my nib on the paper, and the soft turning of the pages of her novel. Sneaking a look, I can see that she has started again at the beginning.

The letters are very mixed. They range from the romantic to the pornographic in tone, but are always fervent in their enthusiasm. Five contain the phrase: *You are the greatest actress of your generation.* Two are semi-religious: *A living star come from our Lord to save us.* Ten or more are fiercely competitive, as if she was an army to be laid bets on: *My brother and I have fifty francs that you will be more famous than Max Linder in half a year.* All of them, without exception, write as if they know her; seven ask for her advice on matters of the heart. *Should I marry the man my parents require, for his farmland? But he bores me to tears. And his fingers are so square, the backs of his hands so wiry-haired, and besides,*

I always wanted tall children. And then answer themselves: *I know you would tell me to marry for love, but where will I find a loveable stranger of reasonable height?*

An hour or so passes and my writing hand starts to get tired. She looks up, though I have not spoken, only begun to massage the knuckles.

'Do you need to stop?'

'No.'

She bends her head to her novel again. Her eyebrows are drawn together in concentration, as if someone has put a stitch through them.

At midday the pile of outgoing letters is much higher than the incoming, neatly stacked instead of the tottering mess I had first found on the desk.

As the clock finishes chiming she closes the novel and looks up, smiling.

'Quite the little worker,' she says. 'The previous—'

She clicks her tongue and looks at her feet; she was going to say, *The previous assistant.* 'Not fair,' she says.

I fuss with the composed letters, for something to do. I like the feeling of almost having been in on a secret.

In the afternoon, she shows me the garden behind the house.

There is a high wind which blows our hats half off our heads, and makes us walk at an angle.

After twenty paces she stops, and with a catch of a laugh says: 'May I take your arm?'

For a moment I go blank, then I realise it is to steady her, and hold it out for her to take. She curls her arm round the crook of my elbow, and rests the palm on my wrist, a steady pressure but not too tight. The backs of her hands are very smooth, but unexpectedly covered in a mass of freckles.

She laughs as she catches me staring. 'My whole arms are like that,' she says, too loud because of the wind. 'When we made *La Dame aux Roses*, the amount of Leichner No. 2 to cover it, you wouldn't believe.'

We walk on in silence for a few moments, and then she pauses, and looks around her, the mistress surveying her terrain, and says: 'Where you're from, is it like this, or something else?'

I pretend to be looking at the green lawn and the white blooms in the rose beds, and manage to think of a longish thing to say. 'Not much like this. It's hotter, and the plants are different. But there isn't much, just a few houses, and occasionally people pass through on their way to somewhere else.'

She laughs. 'Bandits and caravanserai, how exotic.'

'No,' I say, 'just deserted.'

She frowns as she reaches for a white petal, bruising it between forefinger and thumb. 'But you got out.'

I don't say anything.

She pulls the petal off, taking a scattering of others with it, scurrying away on the wind.

We walk on for a while. Suddenly she stops, puts her hand palm up to the sky and tuts. 'Rain,' she says, and turns to direct us towards the house.

'Thank you for your company,' she says, when we are back in the salon. 'See you at dinner.'

Then she bends to pick up *Thérèse Raquin* again.

All round the garden I've been thinking about whether I dare say it, and I do: 'I'd use the poison from *Romeo and Juliet* by William Shakespeare, to put him to sleep, and then make my escape. That way nobody has to die.'

'Very good,' she says. She looks into my face, frowning; then the gaze wavers down my body to my feet, and all the way back up again. She looks down at the book, and turns one page, then another, as I leave the room.

The next day, the silence between us, as she reads, and I work, is peaceable; drowsy, even, as the weather is warming, the chill spring winds having faded away.

Later that morning, I look up from my work and see how she frowns at the book she is reading, as if the text is upside down or in another language: her concentration is extraordinary. Her lips are puckered; occasionally they pull back into a sneer, and then purse again.

She looks up suddenly and smiles, crinkling her eyes and lifting the book to show me the new title. 'I've moved on,' she says. 'No more poisoning.'

'Any good?'

'Yes.'

I want to ask something else, but she has dipped her head to the page again. She looks as abstracted as two nights before, when she stared out of the dining-room window; she lifts her thumbnail to her mouth, chewing on the skin there as she reads.

That night, I am propped on my elbows and André is kissing his way down my stomach. 'Are you learning much to your professional advantage?'

'Yes,' I say, shutting my eyes.

'You don't sound sure.'

'I am.'

'Not just answering her letters?'

'No,' I say, 'why?'

'No reason.'

He draws a line with his tongue and I drop back onto the pillow. 'There's nothing wrong with correspondence,' he says. His tongue reaches its destination and I sit back up to watch.

Five minutes later he says it again: 'Correspondence makes the world go round.' His curls bounce on his forehead, perfectly in place. *One of these days*, I think, *I'll tear one out, just to see the look on his face.*

17. juillet 1913

As I walk into the salon she throws her novel down.

'I thought we might pay a visit to my great friend Robert Peyssac. The studio gossip is that he has a film in the preparatory stages, and I want to talk to him about a role before the news gets out.'

Without waiting for my answer she leans across to pull the bell.

Hubert punches the horn despairingly as we rumble over the Pont-Neuf onto the Ile St Louis: horses and carts bombard the automobile, an omnibus trundles past, two rows of blank-faced passengers crammed in, their hat brims touching. At the end of the bridge a bread delivery-woman steps off the kerb, stops dead in the road and stares in at us, her hands gripping the arms of her cart; she mumbles her lip, and then proceeds slowly across the road, threading between the stopped vehicles. Hubert leans out towards her, tapping the side of his head.

'Leave us here,' Terpsichore says, as we turn onto the little central street of the island, 'his house is just next door.' Hubert rides the car up onto the pavement and hops down from the driver's seat to let us out.

The air is sweet with lunchtime cooking smells from restaurants on the island: cassoulet and crêpes. The river flashes unexpectedly at us down an alleyway next to the block, barges drifting in the sunshine, tethered to the quays.

At the front door she turns to me. 'How do I look?'

She is wearing a blouse and skirt in a cobwebby grey; the sleeves of the blouse taper where the freckles start to emerge at her wrists. In the strong light from the river I can make out the down on her cheeks and the flecks of her irises.

'You look the part,' I say.

Looking down at me from her great height, she smiles.

'Now, Peyssac was used to my old assistant. He likes his women quiet; doesn't like to be interrupted.' She leans in to press the buzzer. Far inside the house there comes an answering ghost ring. 'So let me do the talking. He liked Huguette, she was a paragon, quiet all over; her mouth moved but there was no sound.'

I hesitate, then turn my face casually away and say: 'Is that why you hit her?'

'It was a projectile. Not *mano a mano*. And besides, she recovered, for which we are all extremely grateful.'

'You don't seem grateful.'

Her smile is enormous. 'So sharp, Mlle Roux, I could use you to peel an orange.'

I suddenly find I am hot all over: under my collar and on my cheeks, damp-palmed, and glad, because she is distracted: the door has opened, a retainer bows low. We step inside.

In the central courtyard of the big house there is a cobbled square of sunlight, scattered with pots of geraniums.

'Please wait here,' the retainer whispers, and vanishes through a doorway on the far side. Less than a minute later he reappears: 'M. Peyssac will see you now.'

Terpsichore tosses her head and follows him back through the doorway. She has forgotten me now, sweeping down the corridor. I scurry after her, a solo duckling; up some stairs and into Peyssac's parlour.

A grey stuffed gull glowers down at us from a glass case; in the corner, a column of *immortelles* ascends the striped wallpaper, silhouetted lips parted in expectation of the hereafter. And in an armchair in the corner is a little man past the point of middle age, with an immaculate white goatee. He is framed in the light: I can imagine him adjusting his chair fussily as we were announced.

'My dear!' Peyssac cries, bouncing to his feet, all the while looking over her shoulder, his gaze darting everywhere, sliding off me. 'How wonderful! And you are looking so well!' He reaches up to hold her shoulders and look into her face.

'Robert, it's wonderful to see you again,' she says, bending to put the *bises* on his soft cheek. 'May I present Mlle Roux, my new assistant?'

I bob my head. Of course he is too polite to ask about Huguette.

'Charmed,' he says. 'I am Peyssac.'

I nod mutely; from the corner of my eye, Terpsichore's lips twist into a smile.

'Charmed,' he says again, nodding approval at the straightness of my spine. He snaps his fingers to the butler standing in the doorway: 'Tea? Coffee! Cake!' To us: 'Well – sit,' and waves to two wing chairs. I am careful to perch on the very edge of mine.

Terpsichore: 'It's so nice to see you again, Robert. How are the children?'

Peyssac waves away the question, chortling: 'Manon is so high, every time I see her she's shot up another foot. Micheline does the most astonishing sketches: a real little talent!'

'And Marguerite?'

'The same. Perpetually exasperated with my long hours, but she says she still loves me. What more can one expect?'

Terpsichore nods and laughs, as if charmed by his witticism. The sunlight slants down to a point in the middle of the Turkish rug, and suddenly the conversation has grown strained. She and Peyssac smile at each other, and he says: 'To what do I owe the pleasure of this visit, Luce?'

I flush, and hope nobody notices. Had I thought Terpsichore was her real name?

'They say you are making a new film. A sort of revenge fantasia, featuring a ghost?'

'As to that! We are at the mercy of Charles Pathé for the money. But surely you know all about *Petite Mort* from André? We are relying upon him to work his tricks for the ghost scene. Surely he has mentioned it?'

Shouts from the bargemen float through the open window, filling the thunderstruck silence. I sneak a glance at her: her throat is mottled red, but she laughs, and if her voice is not quite ordinary then maybe it is close enough: 'Robert, if I listened to one-fifth of what my husband tells me—'

Peyssac slaps his thigh. 'Quite so! Oh, very good! I must remember to tell Marguerite.'

Whilst he is wiping his eyes, Terpsichore rises to her feet. 'We must dash.' She crosses the room and bends over him so that he can plant a full Judas kiss on either cheek.

She straightens. 'Our best to Marguerite and the girls, and good luck for the film.'

'*Au revoir*, Mlle Roux,' says Peyssac miserably as I pass.

But she cannot resist. My chest aches; I want to tell her not to – as we reach the door, she turns and points at Peyssac, smiling. 'If there's a role, Robert, think of me?'

He freezes, a child with his fingers in the jam pot. Her face freezes too; she turns and marches away from him down the corridor, with me trailing in her wake.

We do not stop on the pavement; she marches us to where the car is waiting and stands, white-faced, as Hubert fumbles with the handle.

He hums as we pull away from the kerb; I watch the wheel spin in his capable hands. We drive back over the river and along the rue de Rivoli with its crowds of tourists and shoppers.

'You see, Mlle Roux,' she says, smiling but not really, 'one is

only as good as one's last good role.' She turns her face to the
window.

She is quiet again until we are back on the Left Bank,
and then she puts her hand over her mouth; her voice comes
through her fingers.

'They are piss-weak. Men! Let themselves be pushed and
prodded—'

Her great eyes staring out of the window. She says: 'Even
when I was the toast of the Comédie Française, it was always
doublespeak! Even when the Crown Prince of Russia waited
outside my dressing-room every night – even then, parts came,
parts went, and we never knew which of us actresses would be
favoured next. I didn't come to Paris to be rotated on a spit, and
kept in the dark, and played against my friends. Do you know
what he said to me, the Tsarevich, staring down his imperial
nose? *In Russia we would never treat our artists so.*'

She's too bright to be looked at, and yet it is impossible not
to look at her: the flared nostrils, the flush on her neck.

'Peyssac will have asked Eve Bray,' she says, biting the tip of
her thumb, 'or Lily Lemoine, or Vivienne! She couldn't act her
way out of a sack—'

I search frantically for something to distract her: 'How did
you come to be an actress? How did you come to Paris?'

She stares at me; for a long, awful moment it seems she will
reach for something, anything to throw at me; then her outline
softens.

Luce, i.

Luce's family were Norman, but Luce is not a Norman name. It has echoes of the Mediterranean, and Luce's parents, minor aristocrats, felt sheepish at the christening. Nothing could be further from the south: the wind howled around the abbey church, and mist swept in from the Channel. A maiden aunt stifled her cackles in the third pew – just outside of those reserved for proper family – and remembered the time she and a young cousin had tried to bottle light in a jam-jar during a seaside trip. It was to this sound – high unrepentant laughter – that Luce was given her name.

She was a tiny baby, with such odd-shaped eyes that the midwife's first thought was of those children one sometimes heard of with the beginnings of second heads sprouting from their necks, or webbed feet, as though they were born for being underwater. The midwife had only once seen something of the kind, amongst a poor country family who had welcomed the baby just the same, whisking it away from her so quickly that she barely had time to believe what her eyes were showing her: the stump of a tail, still translucent in newborn frog-skin. It could be hidden under fashionable dresses, but the midwife wondered what happened to these children, all the same. When she handed Luce to the nursemaid, who handed her to her mother, it was with a downcast look, almost an apology.

There was no need. Luce's mother, who at thirty-five fully intended this to be her last child, thought she had never seen anything so perfect.

'She's the picture of you,' she said, holding up the baby to her husband.

As she grew, Luce was enthroned in her similarity to her parents.

She was younger than her brothers and sisters by six years, the only baby in the house, and visitors quickly understood she was the favourite, and took care to toe the line, exclaiming how like her father, how like her mother, she was. She was set apart from the other children by treats, presents, and time spent dandled on her mother's lap; by kisses dropped on the down of her head. Where the older children had been brought into their parents' company only a couple of times a week, to greet each other solemnly and perhaps recite a morsel of verse, Luce was in the great salon with them almost every afternoon.

The nursemaids pursed their lips, and muttered behind their hands – but the Marquis and Marquise ignored them. It was 1880: in America, Thomas Edison was founding his landmark magazine, *Science*. In Germany, Cologne Cathedral was finished, a mere six hundred years after construction was initiated. In Normandy, the neighbouring Duc de Polignac had married a Canadian steel magnate's daughter for a dowry of seven million dollars – and he was still invited to every social function. The Marquis and Marquise, gazing fondly at their daughter, felt a daring thrill at treating her differently from the others; this warmth and proximity, the way they could brush the fine hairs on the child's fontanelle whenever they chose, and hold her up to the window to see the horses being led out to pasture. Perhaps this was what it felt like, being modern.

What Luce's brother would have said about Luce, aged five: she is an oddity. She won't play games. When we try to trick her into playing hide and seek in a far-flung attic, she ends up back at the beginning, watching us run after her. And then, when she can hear an adult is near, she cries, and when they ask her why she's crying, she points the finger at me.

On Luce's sixth birthday, the Marquis and Marquise organised a party for her, five times as lavish as for any previous child. A juggler and a puppet theatre, a collation for the villagers and servants served on the lawn. The older siblings were offered pony rides, and grew frantic with sugar; the afternoon took on a hazy logic of its own, and Luce, wanting a pony ride too, threw a tantrum.

She ground her fists into her eyes and turned puce: the Marquise held her, but she was inconsolable. As she howled, her brothers and sisters' faces turned stony. Servants' eyes narrowed, too; but her parents were distressed by her distress.

The Marquise snapped her fingers to have her own mare fetched from the stables, and to hoist herself side-saddle and have Luce hoisted up beside her.

The Marquis stepped forward. 'Is she big enough?'

The Marquise smiled, and shrugged, and held the child closer. 'Just a canter,' she said, 'just a run to the boundary and back.'

'Take me riding, Mama,' Luce said, imperious.

The Marquis's instinct to protect vied with the enchanting picture before him – Madonna and child on horseback.

'What harm can it do?' he said.

It was only established afterwards, from a logical regression of the sequence of events, what had happened. The manservant who rode out in search of the Marquise two hours later found the mare, rolled on its side and white-eyed, and the Marquise a few feet away. They were on the other side of a hedge which the horse had failed to clear.

Predictable confusion. The manservant picked up the Marquise's body and rode with it back to the house; the Marquis, who had sat waiting, his hands folded in premonition, came out to meet him and collapsed. A second trip was needed to go out and look for Luce. It was dark by that time; the sweep of the lamps found her lying quietly just ten feet from the dead horse, with an open fracture where her femur protruded through the skin.

The wound healed gradually, leaving a patch of shiny skin where the bone had come through. In her attic room, Luce practised walking with two sticks, then one, then none. She was discouraged from spending time downstairs by the maids who looked after her.

The Marquis had become a person glimpsed, in his dark suit, through half-open doors.

A few months after the accident, he made the trip to Luce's room.

'Pack her things,' he said to the maid, 'she is going to Paris tomorrow, to live with my sister there. It is all arranged. It is high time she went to a real school.'

There was nothing; no hesitation. The maid stayed in her curtsy position until she could be sure that he was really gone.

17. juillet 1913

IT WAS CHILDISH TO IMAGINE I could make it better –
and I wanted to be anything but childish: so I said, 'It's sad.'

Her face was turned away from me, to look out of the
window at the green–gold light dappling through the trees; we
were almost home. 'I suppose it is sad,' she said. 'I suppose it did
happen to me.'

She half-shut her eyes and leant her neck against the back of
the seat. The length of her throat was white against the leath-
erette seats.

The car drove in at the gates and rattled up the gravel drive;
Hubert held the door open for us.

She seemed almost to have forgotten I was there; she set off
up the stairs and I followed. She walked so fast it was difficult
to keep up with her. It was only when we reached the door to
her study that she turned and said: 'I won't have anything for
you this afternoon. You may sit with me and read, or sew, or
you may retire, I don't mind.'

I said quickly: 'I'll sit with you.'

She nodded, neither approving nor disapproving, and we
went into the salon. She picked up a paperback. There were
no letters, so instead I took a copy of *Comoedia* from the side
table, and moved shyly to the sofa opposite her; she did not
protest, and I sat demurely with the book propped upright on
my knees, pretending to read.

My chest felt tight, and my arms and legs too big. But she
had said I could join her; I was not intruding, was I? We sat in

silence for ten minutes, and then I stole a glance at her. She had flattened the novel on her lap; her face was turned to the empty grate. As I watched, her features grew pinched. It was like one of those chemical substances I had heard about at Pathé, which hardens on contact with air.

She looked, I realised with a little jolt, her age. In the light from the window, fine strands of silver led down like electric wires from her parting to her chignon.

It was not hard to guess what she was thinking about. So we sat like that, with just the quiet sounds a house will make around us, and all that time she did not move, just went on staring at the place where the fire should have been.

At seven-thirty I left her to go and change for dinner; stood looking at my own reflection, my cheap dress, for a long time, and when I went downstairs at eight, I found both André and Terpsichore already in position.

Precise sounds of crustaceans being broken into; the crack of the spines of the langoustines. André tore off pieces of bread and popped them into his mouth one by one, staring at a spot on the wall.

She will say, *Today we went to Peyssac's*, I thought – or even, *Do you know, Peyssac is getting up a little film, he says you are involved, and I said, it cannot be true because how would my husband not have told me?* All with a peal of laughter and her fingers pincering the stem of her wine glass. I looked at her, half-expecting because I had thought the words, that she'd say them; but her head was bowed and she ate with her usual elegant movements, not seeming to notice anyone else in the room. André continued to put the food into his mouth apparently without pleasure, and then pushed the plate away, stretched back in his chair, and threw his napkin onto the polished table. It flopped, meeting its own white reflection.

He could say: *I was going to tell you, of course I was. Or I thought we should rest you from Pathé, let the dust about Huguette settle.*

The main course came. Now Terpsichore did reach for the stem of her wine glass, and turn it between forefinger and thumb, making a scraping noise on the surface; André attacked his food with knife and fork, and *scrape, scrape,* went her wine glass on the table, the red liquid swirling and splashing inside.

After dinner, I went to my room to wait for him. It was only half past nine; ages until he would come, so I pushed the windows and the shutters open to look across the park. The lawn had faded to grey. I could smell jasmine and, from somewhere above and to my left, came the ruffling sound of wings being folded for the night.

At times like this the house itself seemed to listen; each joist and timber straining to catch the conversation.

I tilted my head, sure I had heard something – but not from the window side, from nearer the door. My first, erratic thought was: it is her, coming up to my room, she wishes to discuss Peyssac and form a strategy. *She will sit cross-legged on my bed with me, and we'll talk –* my chest seemed to tighten in anticipation, staring in a panic at the coverlet as if she was already there; and then I realised the sound was not footsteps. I padded over to the door, easing it open. Then tiptoed across the landing and, seeing as it was fully dark and where was the harm, down the stairs to the landing of the second floor.

But here was her perfume suddenly, floating towards me, a little piece of her; and here too, it was possible to understand the sounds, peering over the banister to the ground floor and the living-room door ajar: their voices.

The gulp of her sobbing – André, low and vehement – and then her, repeating the same two words, over and over: *humiliate me.* I stood, shocked by the sound of her crying, staring into the darkness; and then the door opened – and André stood in the light spilling out into the hall. His fingers were curled in on themselves. After a moment he marched towards the stairs.

I had barely reached my room and jumped into the bed when the door opened and he came straight across to me; in a few seconds I felt the whole weight of him on top of me, straining against the sheets.

His hands were cold and he worked up to his own release quickly.

Afterwards he lay on his back with his arm under my neck, staring at the ceiling.

'Why didn't you?' I asked. 'Tell her about the film?'

His eyes gleamed savagely.

'Because it's your business now?' he said. 'Whose side are you on?'

Juliette and Adèle
1967

I am just about to pack up my things, when Adèle leans across the table and says: 'And the boyfriend? What does he do?'

'I don't have a boyfriend.'

She widens her eyes. 'It's 1967!'

I say: 'I don't have time.'

'No? But there was someone. Recently.'

'How did you know?'

'How could you not have somebody?'

I feel the blush starting. 'It doesn't matter, does it?' I say, shovelling my pens and notepad into my bag.

She watches me, her face alive with interest.

'And the film?' she says. 'You saw *Petite Mort*? Was it illuminating?'

I stand. She looks up at me, the picture of innocence. 'It was,' I say. 'Same time tomorrow?'

Her eyes sparkle. 'We do keep our cards close to our chest, don't we,' she says merrily, to herself, as I leave.

18. juillet 1913

THE NEXT MORNING, when I go to the study, she is sitting at the writing desk in the window; curved over her correspondence like a child, a strip of her hair loose, hanging over the page.

'Shit,' she says, holding up the half-finished letter – ink has smeared a fan across the words – and then, seeing me, 'I'm writing to Linder and Feuillade, the same letter to both, telling each that I've been engaged by the other.'

'Why?'

'Don't you want a thing more, if you're told you can't have it?' She shakes sand from a pot onto the ink stain, and then folds the paper and pours the sand off again. I watch her hands move as she reaches for an envelope, slips the letter in and licks the gummed surface. 'Peyssac's finished, anyway. He hasn't had a new idea since 1905.'

'What about M. Durand?'

She stares at me. 'What about him?'

She seals the envelope, turns away to drop the letters onto a tray on the table, then dusts her skirt down, as if searching for what to say next.

Finally she goes to the window, and studies the view, determined, fists on hips. The sky is a flawless blue. 'Let's go out,' she says.

The Allée des Acacias is a long, wide strip of white-dust road running through the Bois de Boulogne. And today it is full of people: some being driven along slowly in automobiles, some in pony traps, but the majority strolling in twos and threes.

'Let us out here,' Terpsichore says at last, rapping on the glass; and the motor cuts, and Hubert hops out and opens the car doors for us.

The other ladies, strolling with husbands and children, notice her: the way she stands, and extends her parasol. And the men, passing by, jog their hands in their pockets and look brazenly at her face.

We begin to walk down the side of the road, following the slow march of the crowd. She doesn't seem to want to talk; she frowns, as she looks at the people walking past. 'Young love,' she says, at last.

I sneak a glance sidelong at her – the straightness of her profile, the way her lower lip is jutting out in thought – and then quickly away.

'And you?' she says, her voice very light. 'Is there a young man waiting for you at home?'

My thoughts turn inescapably to André; I feel my face go hot. 'No,' I say.

She's frowning. 'Nobody at all?'

I keep my eyes on the hat of the lady walking ahead of us.

She looks away and laughs: quick and bitter, and the silence descends again. After a while she says: 'You are an enigma, Mlle Roux.'

And it is in that moment that someone close by says: 'Luce!'

The woman is dressed in grey, with a ruffle at the throat of her blouse: but underneath her skirt I see the toes of riding boots. Her face is long and lean, like a horse's, brown-grey hair pulled sharply back, but the eyes are twinkling, and the skin of her face is leathery, as if she spends a lot of time outdoors.

Terpsichore is grinning; they lean forward for the *bises*; the woman looks at me over Terpsichore's shoulder. Then she takes my hand and shakes it, like a man.

Terpsichore says: 'Mademoiselle Roux, may I present

Madame Vercors, wife of Louis Vercors, former Minister of the Interior.'

'Aurélie,' says the woman. 'Call me Aurélie.'

'*Enchantée*,' I say.

'In the flesh,' Aurélie says, staring at Terpsichore, 'an actual sighting. The girls will be *so* jealous.'

Terpsichore smiles. 'I'm sorry. It's this business with the studio. I've been distracted—'

'I can see that,' Aurélie says, and then says to me: 'We never see her any more.'

When I don't respond, Aurélie turns her scrutiny back to Terpsichore. 'In a month it will be forgotten.'

Terpsichore lifts her chin, her throat moving; to my horror, she suddenly looks as if she is going to cry.

Aurélie says: 'Come on. It doesn't mean a thing.'

Terpsichore gives her head a little shake.

'That's better,' Aurélie says. 'Now, ask me what I've been doing.'

'What have you been doing?'

'Did you know my husband has been corresponding with the anarchists? Oh yes, the actual remnants of the Bonnot gang. *They have some interesting ideas*, he says, *of course I used my personal letterhead, why shouldn't I?*'

Terpsichore smiles fondly at this someone I don't know. 'Oh Louis,' she says.

Aurélie slaps her gloves on her thigh. 'I must go, he's worse than an infant, who knows if the house will still be standing when I get back?' She narrows her eyes. 'Anyway, he's having a little *soirée*. Next weekend. I'll die of boredom if you don't come.'

Terpsichore lifts her head and smiles.

Aurélie winks at me, leans in and pecks Terpsichore on the cheek. Then she waves, and turns and walks away. She isn't like the other women – drifting aimlessly; she has purpose. She disappears into the crowd.

I turn to find Terpsichore watching me.

'So that was the wife of the Ex-Minister,' she says.

I make a non-committal sound and she arches an eyebrow and laughs at me: a surprised laugh, as if she has found something out about me.

'I liked her,' I say.

She smiles; shakes her head, more at herself than me. 'Your mouth gives you away every time.'

Luce, ii.

Luce's Aunt Berthe sits in the waiting room, seeing the spectre of her past flit across the sunlit wall opposite. She is tense with irritation, holding her gloves and purse taut on her knees, smoothing the fabric into submission. She strains her ears but cannot hear anything but the low murmur of voices from behind the audition room door.

On a chair on the other side of the room, next to the door into the other audition room, a lean woman with a Roman nose sits, watching Berthe, who tosses her head, aware of and disliking the scrutiny. Besides her impertinence, the woman is common-looking and poorly tailored. She looks like she knows all about Berthe, though they have not exchanged a word.

'Your daughter, in there?'

Berthe shakes her head and looks haughtily away. 'My niece.'

'The acting competition?'

'Yes.' Berthe suddenly wishes to confide everything, *How ridiculous it is, because this isn't what our family does, we have tried to dissuade her, but she would not be told. How like her mother she is.* The woman opposite is saying: 'My daughter wants to dance. It's better to try the acting, though, because you have a longer career. Ten years is all you get as a ballerina, and she is already fifteen. Have you been to the Conservatoire before?'

Berthe's nostrils flare. 'Never,' she lies. The waiting room looked exactly the same thirty years before; she recognises it all, down to the peeling paint of the ceiling and the little piece of glass missing from the high window.

125

The door to the dance room opens and Aurélie exits, high-stepping like a pony at dressage. 'I've been accepted,' she says, and her mother clasps her hands in front of her face. 'My darling,' she says, 'you must work hard, you must strive. I am quite overcome! My daughter, the ballerina!'

She looks, astonished, at Berthe, who forces a smile; at the same time, the door to the acting audition room opens and Luce appears.

Luce says nothing to Berthe, who doesn't ask, but simply thinks, *Lord be praised, now we can get on with making her respectable,* and gathers up the child's scarf, still smiling tightly at Aurélie's mother, who is holding Aurélie's coat up for her to put on.

'Did you get in?' Aurélie asks, her arms held out behind her to find the sleeves. 'You look like you did.'

Luce nods, intimidated by the older girl, and obediently wraps her scarf round her own neck.

In the dormitory, it is thought appropriate to have the younger children shepherded by the elder ones, and to mix disciplines, so that dangerous rivalries are discouraged. Aurélie and Luce start at opposite ends of the dormitory and conspire: swapping their way with hair ribbons and sweets down the rows until they are next to each other.

Aurélie teaches her ballet exercises to help her with her stage movements. 'Pretend you are an oak tree,' she says, pressing down on her shoulder.

Late at night, they confide their secret fears. 'I'll only ever be *corps de ballet,*' Aurélie says, matter-of-fact and too loud, so that other girls in the long line of beds rustle. She whispers: 'I don't have it in me, the way some do.'

She looks speculatively at Luce. 'They say you do.'

Luce thinks for a minute. 'They say a lot of things, about how my aunt only takes me home in the holidays because otherwise I'd be a ward of the State and that's common.'

It is a long speech for her, and has Luce's characteristic way of closing off the subject at the end of the phrase. Aurélie settles the sheets about her ears and does a horizontal shrug; she knows different.

Luce takes her first role as a maid in a Scandinavian tragedy in a little theatre in the Faubourg St Honoré, and Aurélie sits in the front row on the first night. Aurélie's face will always be too long and her expression too knowing, but the gentlemen see her nonetheless: rising from their seats and nodding to let her pass to the middle row seat, noting the ballerina's long legs and her hands – even they are muscular – as they grip the stole about her throat.

The lights go down; the play starts. Luce, taken by a violent attack of nerves, looks out to the audience where possible, and at last spots her friend; she relaxes, and the rest of the first act goes better. Aurélie sits with a smile on her face, knowing that Luce has seen her.

The papers are full of it: '*The newcomer Mlle de Jumièges betrays her noble stock, speaking her part with a zest worthy of a much older actress. Her grace and poise are that of a dancer.*' Those critics who have not yet come to the play flock to see her; the sound of frantic scribbling is all that disturbs the reverential silence. It only takes a couple of days before the stage name – Terpsichore, the muse of dance – is coined, which will follow her wherever she goes. Throughout the next year, Aurélie comes to all Luce's engagements, sitting in the front row where possible, once taking an overnight train back from Marseille, where she is playing Odile, so she can attend a premiere.

Juliette, iii.

'See,' says the editor, lifting the strip of film up to the light –
delicately, gingerly, with his long pianist's fingers.

'Hand splice,' he says, indicating the section of *Petite Mort*
where the missing scene goes, 'uneven, bad workmanship, almost
certainly amateur, and now look at the other splices, done in
the course of the assembly.' His fingertip brushes a point further
down the print, where a thin line joins two frames. 'These were
made with a splicing machine, of course, by the film's editor.'

Then he says: 'And you were right about the cement. It's all
the same stuff they used in the 1910s. Acetane and dioxane.'

I say: 'So the person who cut up *Petite Mort* was a different
person from the editor who made the rest of the joins? And
our person couldn't use a splicing machine? But could lay their
hands on cement?'

'Yes.'

'That could be anybody.'

The editor has turned his back to me, storing the film strip
in its box. 'No,' he says. 'It would be somebody who had access
to the materials, and who was familiar enough with the theory
to attempt to cut and repair the film by hand. But who lacked
the expertise to do it properly.'

He waits. Then, seeing that I have no further questions, he
lifts the *Petite Mort* reel into its canister again.

As he is leaving, he stops, fingers on the door frame. 'You
said it was found in somebody's basement.'

'That's right.'

'This isn't the safety film stock we use today – it's the old stuff – nitrate cellulose. Highly flammable. If it's stored above twenty-one degrees centigrade for any length of time, it degrades. If you don't handle it right, it may even catch fire.'

I frown. 'What are you saying?'

'Talk to the person who handed it in.'

21. juillet 1913

WE WAITED FOR AN ANSWER to one of the two letters that Terpsichore had written.

The weather had turned dreary; the window panes were spattered with sudden bursts of rain. Terpsichore set me to classifying household bills at the writing desk while she fidgeted and read; when I looked up, I would often catch her staring out of the window, or picking at the lunch tray that Thomas brought, her face pale and thoughtful.

She rarely asked me what I was doing, or told me what she was reading. She just sat there, neck drooping, saying nothing and chewing her lip, for hours at a time.

Dinner times, since the Day of Peyssac, were strained. André always started the meal confidently, talking about the studio and his plans for the next season's films, but finished by speaking almost exclusively to me, as Terpsichore stared over his head to the garden beyond, making the minimum possible response.

At the end of the week, suddenly, over supper, Terpsichore spoke. 'I don't suppose you want to go to Aurélie's party?'

He looked up. 'To what?'

'The salon.'

The crystal sparkled, holding its breath, and he frowned as if trying to remember having discussed it. 'No, but you go.' He made a long arm for a copy of *Le Temps* that was lying on the sideboard.

'Take Adèle,' he said, sheltering behind the news, 'if you need company.'

I didn't dare to look at her, in case I saw disappointment on her face.

But instead she looked neutral. 'Yes,' she said, 'I might do that.'

He cleared his throat, closing the subject.

'There you are,' she says when she greets me the next morning. The air is different in the room: tinged with anticipation. All around her on the settee are copies of *La Femme Moderne* and *La Mode Parisienne*, flipped through and discarded, as if she were looking for something but the thing she wanted has not come to hand.

'I think,' she says, not looking at me, her voice too light, 'I think what we need is to go shopping. I have a violent urge to spend my husband's money.'

Rue de Rivoli is streaming with people; Hubert drops us on the corner of the place du Louvre, swearing under his breath at the hurrying crowd: 'Madame, it's the closest I can get without murdering somebody.'

'We'll only be an hour,' Terpsichore says, and climbs slowly down from her side of the car; I follow, jostling her through the people standing open-mouthed in front of the window displays. The great sign of the department store, LES GALERIES ST. PAUL, twinkles overhead, gold against the grey colonnaded façade; all around me are *oohs* and *ahhs* at the clockwork soldier in the window beating a wooden drum.

She leads me past the shop, and down a side road, and we come to a halt at a front door halfway down the street, next to which a discreet plaque reads: WALLACE MONGE, MAISON DE COUTURE.

The door opens before we knock. A slender man with brilliantined hair stands in the doorway, and holds out his arms with an expression of goodwill. He embraces Terpsichore silently, and holds out a hand to me. 'Wallace Monge,' he says, and I nod, pretending I know the name; 'Come in, come in,' he says, and leads us inside.

I want to look everywhere at once. The walls of the tiny room are papered with designs – elegant female silhouettes. There are orchids in pots, and a miniature palm tree, and a table, behind which a girl my own age is sewing a hem by hand. A row of silk turbans in ascending sizes march along a shelf above her head.

'I have just the thing,' he is saying to Terpsichore, 'let me find it—' and he disappears behind a screen.

The girl looks up from her sewing and smiles at us. I return the smile as best I can, feeling awkward; but she doesn't seem to mind that I am a customer.

'Here,' says the man, reappearing with a sketchbook, which he flips to the back page and holds up for her, so that only the two of them can see.

'Yes,' she says, critical at first, then convinced. 'But can it be ready for tomorrow night?'

They discuss measurements and delivery times; my eyes wander. Gowns hang from hooks on the wall: steel-grey, watermelon, butterscotch. But the dress which catches me out is on a mannequin at the far end: red silk with a wide skirt, the whole embroidered with tiny flowers.

'And for Mademoiselle?' asks Wallace Monge, smiling at me.

Terpsichore says: 'I think she has decided what she wants.'

Wallace snaps his fingers, and the girl who was sewing jumps up and bustles to unpin the red dress from the mannequin. Then he leans in and pecks Terpsichore on the cheek. 'Can I leave you with Denise?'

She waves him away with a smile, and he squeezes my elbow and turns to go.

Terpsichore is watching me, smiling as if from a long way away.

Wallace Monge's foosteps disappear up the rickety staircase.

'You can't,' I say, mortified.

She is trailing a fingertip along the neckline of another dress on another dummy. 'Why? Don't you deserve it?'

In the corner of the room there is a booth with a curtain on iron rings. The girl ushers me inside. She turns away modestly, pretending to fiddle with her tape measure, and when I am in my underthings, she kneels in front of me and begins to palpate, running the measure from my ankle to my hip. When she stands in front of me to pull the tape round my breasts, she whispers: 'Is it her? Is it Terpsichore?'

'Yes.'

She beams. 'They said she had an account. Isn't she lovely, though. Even more beautiful in the flesh!'

I hold my arms out to the sides, like a martyr in an old painting, and look at my face in the mirror over the girl's bobbing head.

She makes notations in a tiny notebook with a pencil so worn down it is barely a stub, and snaps it shut. 'There!' she says, 'we'll barely have to alter it, now let's just see it on—'

She helps me drop the dress over my head. It whispers past my hips, hanging just so, a sheen catching the light.

'Shall we show Madame?' the girl asks, sitting back on her haunches.

'No, don't,' I say, but it is too late, she is jerking the curtain back, and I turn and there she is.

Behind her, the drawings on the wall replicate her to infinity; each of which could be her, the tall silhouettes in their many dresses. But she doesn't say anything, only stands with a strange, blank expression. Her eyelashes sweep her cheek as she blinks once, twice.

It is awful to have her look at me like this: as if she's a stranger. I bob a self-conscious little curtsy to her, trying to make it all right.

Still she says nothing; she lifts one hand, the palm cupping her cheek.

Eventually she says: 'A little narrow in the shoulders.'

The assistant is putting pins in her mouth one by one like cigarettes, and saying through them: 'Yes, of course. Now, shall we change her back?'

Terpsichore turns away, and the girl sighs happily, and rattles the curtain closed again.

When I emerge, smoothing my damp palms against my old skirt, Terpsichore smiles vaguely at me again and we move towards the till.

'I don't have to have it,' I burst out.

'Yes, you do,' she says, taking the pen from the girl, and signing her name with a flourish. The girl blushes at the contact of their hands.

The dress arrives just after dinner. It is spread out on my bed waiting for me when I come back upstairs, and it is still lying there when André arrives.

'Nice,' he says, fingering the substance. 'How much did it cost me?'

He runs his hands rapidly over the fabric, looking for a tag or a receipt; finding none, he gives up.

'Very nice,' he says, standing back. 'I wonder if I should change my mind about the party?'

I bend low over the dress and start to fold it: 'Perhaps tomorrow night, afterwards, I'll keep it on for you.'

'Why not try it on now?'

I push back my hair. 'I just don't feel like it, that's all.'

I can feel him smiling in the dark room. He puts his cold lips to my neck.

24. juillet 1913

MY REFLECTION IN THE MIRROR in my room is fretful. I have smoothed my hair as best I can, but I'm ashamed of the small hairs that spring up on my temples which look so Mediterranean; of the tan of my skin, when everyone else will be pale. The only good thing is the dress, and when I look at it, I feel confused: it whispers to me as I move.

Walking nervously down the stairs, I am met by Terpsichore's upturned face; but all she says is, 'Very nice,' and then turns to the mirror above the console to smooth her hair.

I thought she would look like a stranger to me in her new clothes – a dress in silvery silk, with wide sleeves, like a kimono – but she only looks more like herself. In the mirror, she stretches her lips into an oval and inspects the colour on her mouth, then bats her eyelids: light moves in bands over her hair.

The car rolls along the Quai d'Orsay; stern government buildings rise into the summer evening. A late starling sings from the shelter of the plane trees on the quais as we turn onto Avenue Bosquet; she leans forward to rap on the glass separating us from Hubert, and the car slows and stops outside a white stone apartment block.

A uniformed footman stands outside the large outer door, hands neatly folded. 'Madame Durand, how nice to see you again,' he says, inclining his head. He doesn't acknowledge me; just holds the door open politely for us, and leads us inside.

We step into the tiny lift, upper arms touching, and as my

stomach drops and we ascend, I turn to find her watching me. 'Nervous?'

'A little.'

The footman is shuttling back the iron grille. She leans in and whispers: 'I have a tip for you. Picture them in bed.'

She winks and, as I turn back to face forwards, my face raging red, a door is opening and a roar of voices fills the hall. Aurélie stands in the doorway, wearing a long blue dress and a tiny hat that fits close to her head, hiding her hair.

'Look at you!' she shouts over the din, exchanging kisses with Terpsichore. 'Can that be a Wallace Monge?' she asks, and pushes Terpsichore in a little twirl, holding her hand above her head. Then she half turns and calls: 'Louis! It's Luce! And,' – her eyes find mine, and she smiles thinly – 'is it Mlle Roux?'

A tall, lugubrious man with a walrus moustache appears by Aurélie's shoulder, and bends to kiss Terpsichore's hand, and then mine. 'So charmed,' he says, 'I am Louis Vercors, ex-Minister of the Interior,' and draws himself up impressively. Behind him, Aurélie rolls her eyes and says: 'Can the Ex-Minister find Mlle Roux a drink?'

Aware of Terpsichore's eyes on me: 'Adèle,' I say, 'it's Adèle.'

'So charmed,' Aurélie says, and taking Terpsichore's arm, she leads her away into the room. Terpsichore looks back at me over her shoulder: a little shrug and a smile that's like a promise.

The room is full of all kinds of people, flushed red faces, cigarette smoke and laughter. A chandelier sparkles overhead, but the rest of the furniture in this wide room is modern, all clean lines and angular shapes; a baby grand piano gleams in the corner. The Ex-Minister snaps his fingers and a servant appears, and pours me a glass of champagne.

'Your apartment is very chic,' I say to Louis Vercors, who is standing mute at my elbow.

He puffs up again. 'It is our official residence; I am granted it in perpetuity in my capacity as a former Minister. On your right, you can see my portrait, painted during my second year in office—'

I swivel obediently, and my eyes travel the room to see where Terpsichore is, and glimpse her glossy head, and her teeth bared in laughter. Aurélie is huddled next to her, their heads close together, pointing out someone else in the room.

I look away. A few feet from us is a strange object: a camera, but a fifth of the normal size, on a correspondingly miniature tripod. Guests are milling around: one reaches out to touch it, and draws her hand back, laughing.

'What's that?' I ask the Ex-Minister, who pauses, irritated at the interruption. 'That is our Pathé Baby camera, a gift of our dear friend André Durand, a device for recording film in the home, for recreational purposes. Aurélie proposes to make records of our *soirées* for posterity. In fact, we used it only last week, at the ceremony of my investiture into the Collège de France in my capacity as…'

I half-turn, desperate; this time Terpsichore sees me, nudges Aurélie and excuses herself, laughing and trailing a hand away from her. 'Please, I think my mistress need me,' I say to Louis Vercors, who nods, sad-eyed – people must be for ever leaving him like this – and go to meet her in the middle of the room.

'Have you tried my suggestion?' she asks.

'I forgot,' – and she is smiling down at me, and the light seems very bright from above, when there is the sound of someone clapping for silence; we turn; it is Aurélie. 'Guests! Take a seat, or if you can't find one, choose the lap of the neighbour who seems most to your taste,' – she grins, appreciative of the laughter – 'we will now hear a *lied* by Schubert from our most esteemed guest, M. Leydermann.'

A murmur, and the guests begin to mill about, picking their positions next to friends. An elderly woman in black begins to flutter her fan; a slender young man in a velvet waistcoat perches on the edge of his seat and shuts his eyes in anticipation.

'Here is as good as any.' Terpsichore pulls two chairs towards us, and we sit.

A few moments later, the hubbub dies down. Someone has closed the window, and the heat in the room begins to mount; a fair-haired young man gets to his feet and moves to lean on the piano. A burst of applause; he bows, all seriousness, and stands, smiling in a glazed fashion at the audience, gathering himself.

We wait, watching him close his eyes and open them again – he is sweating, beads lining his forehead – suddenly he crosses to Aurélie's seat and whispers something. She leaps to her feet, a marionette, clapping her hands together. 'I quite forgot – M. Leydermann's usual accompanist cannot join us, but I told him that someone here would be glad to play.'

A silence; five or six people are looking fixedly at the floor, but not out of modesty; there is the hot, yearning silence of wanting to be selected.

Aurélie is looking directly at us. 'Will you help?' For a horrible moment I think she means me; then I realise she means Terpsichore. Surprise in the room, but immediately there is a buzz of nodding and encouragement; the wish not to be seen to be ungracious, but also a certain ungenerous interest: *Let us see if her playing matches her acting.*

Terpsichore smiles fixedly. 'I suppose I can try,' she says, and there is muted clapping and laughter.

As she gets to her feet, she flashes me a smile – then she walks over and sits at the piano, hands resting gently on the keys, waiting. Behind the audience, Aurélie stoops to put her eye to the camera.

The tenor laces his hands behind his back. 'The Erlking,' he says.

A silent signal passes between them: how it works I don't understand, but they have decided when to begin, her hands hammering, forcing the notes out; a moment later the singer leans forward and follows her.

Who rides, so late, through night and wind?
It is the father with his child.
He has the boy close in his arms
He holds him safely, he keeps him warm.

Her fingers, so precise, so menacing, branches stinging the face of the riders; the child shrinking away from a pale face hovering, keeping pace with them.

My father, my father, don't you hear
What the Erlking is quietly promising me?
Be calm, stay calm, my child;
The wind is rustling through withered leaves.

It is as if she draws all the light in the room towards her; the notes flowing out, an unceasing stream. The tenor leans forward, his face a gargoyle:

I love you, your beautiful form entices me;
And if you're not willing, I shall use force.

Suddenly, slowing and quiet. The horse stands still, high-stepping, eyes rolling back; a light goes on in the farmhouse ahead.

In his arms, the child was dead.

You can hear the servants clearing away glasses in a room beyond; the elderly woman's fan is motionless before her face.

The tenor gives a tense little bow. Terpsichore closes the piano lid, and everyone is on their feet, clapping.

I expect her to get up from the stool to receive the applause, but instead she is pale and pinched. Just as I am starting to worry, she recovers herself, looks towards the audience, and smiles.

~

A tired-looking young man stands and recites some of his poetry, which has been composed entirely without the use of the letter A; then a thin-voiced woman sings a bawdy boulevard song, hands clasped before her, and everyone murmurs that it's charming: but it can't equal what has gone before; the crowd are restless and thirsty, and soon people begin to slip away to continue the evening elsewhere. The Ex-Minister has snared another victim and is showing her a medal case fixed to the wall. I feel Terpsichore's hand close on my elbow, and she jerks her head towards the door.

Since the music I can barely look at her, so I nod. Aurélie comes across the room and enfolds her in her arms, resting her chin on her shoulder blade: 'It was a fabulous rescue; if I were a poet I'd write you an ode,' she says, and then steps towards me and says crisply: 'We'll see each other again.'

I give a little curtsy. 'I'll look forward to it.'

For a few minutes, driving along with the river oily and shining on our right, we say nothing.

'I didn't know you could play.' My voice sounds odd even to my own ears; I hope the darkness in the car will disguise it.

'What surprises you? That I can play, or that you didn't know?'

'That you could play like that, and that nobody knew.'

'Lots of people play.'

I stare out of the window. I want to say, *But people should only have one great talent, not more. People shouldn't be so—*

'Anyway,' she says, 'Aurélie is far more accomplished than I am. She was just being modest.'

I have made a mean little sound before I can stop myself; she turns her head, and I can hear that she has caught it.

It seems as if she may say something, when suddenly the

statue of St Jeanne slides past, lit up from beneath; at its foot, a pair of tramps swing a bottle and sing to each other; one of them raises the bottle to us as we pass, and Terpsichore's face opens into a smile. She leans forward and cranks the window down: '*Vive la France!*'

'*Vive la France!*' they reply, arms looped around each other's necks, midnight friends for life.

She settles back into the corner, against the swaying wall of the car. In the gloom there is just the lustre of her eyes, gleaming like an animal. I suspect, but cannot prove, that she is looking at me.

The car rolls up outside the house; in the now-familiar routine, Hubert hops out and holds the door open for her first, then me.

The hour being late, there is only one table lamp on in the hallway, turned low. When we reach the door, Thomas looms up in front of us, ready to receive our coats. We shrug them off and he hangs them up, and asks Terpsichore if she requires anything else.

'No, thank you,' she says, and he leaves us, his footsteps padding away down the hall.

She waves towards the staircase. A faint silvery light shows us the swoop of the spiral and the landing up above. 'After you, Adèle.'

There are things to say, but what? I do a little spasm, forward and back at the same time; decide on forward, if it's what she wants: 'Thank you, Madame.'

Her laugh, high and not quite right. 'Now we've been to a party together, I think you should call me Luce.' She pauses; the sound of the sea swells and booms in my ears. 'I think it's time, don't you?'

I turn back to her, wanting to offer her something but not knowing what.

She leans in towards me and kisses my cheek. 'Goodnight.'
She pulls back slowly, keeping her eyes fixed on mine: the pupils large.

I turn and flee up the stairs, taking them two at a time, not stopping till I reach the corridor outside my bedroom, where I pause for breath. On my face, the cool pressure of her lips, now fading, like the touch of a ghost.

Caroline Durand, i.

Two days after Auguste Durand died, Caroline Durand went to Thibodaux-Nouveau to be fitted for her mourning clothes.

As he wound the black crêpe around her, the tailor pushed his pins firmly into her flesh. The pins did not hurt much but she was surprised: only two days, and already the gossip must have begun.

As she stepped out of the tailor's, she felt the townspeople watching from doorways without speaking.

Caroline lifted her chin and turned in at the lawyer's offices.

'Mme Durand,' – the attorney pressed her palm between both his – 'so sad – but if you'll follow me—'

In the inner office, she sat motionless as the lawyer opened the envelope and drew out the précis of Auguste's will.

'M. Durand left his estate to your adopted son,' he said. There was no way to disguise the bald truth of it; he passed an embarrassed hand over his forehead. But Caroline merely nodded – it was as she had expected – and got up to leave.

'Wait,' the lawyer said, 'there is something else. A painting – a painting of you?'

Caroline nodded.

'Your husband specified that you be allowed to keep it.'

Caroline nodded again.

For three months she kept up appearances, writing letters, answering condolence cards, eating less, snuffing candles out earlier, letting the servants go one by one. Of André there came no news.

One day, a gentleman caller came, professing himself an old friend of Auguste's paying his respects. Caroline guessed the man was one of those itinerant collectors who went from town to town enquiring after the recent widows, but she let him in anyway. The man accepted tea and made polite conversation: and as he did so, his eyes roved over the teak and the mahogany furniture and settled on her portrait.

He looked at it for a moment, then looked away, but too late: Caroline had seen his interest flick its tail.

As he left he passed her his business card.

Another month went by. One day Caroline looked in the mirror and saw the delicate point of her wrist emerging from the sleeve of her black dress.

She wrote a letter. A day later the collector sent his apprentice, a scrawny youth whose hands shook as he worked, to wrap up the portrait, and a banker's draft was made out. It was enough for a passage to Canada, where she could be anyone she chose.

When the picture was packed and tied with string and carried out of the door Caroline went to her room and lay in the dark for several hours.

The following day she caught the train north.

She loaded her small valise onto the rack herself, sat slowly blinking in her seat. Outside, green turned into distant blue: mountains unrolled, whose tops she couldn't even see, forests of trees that weren't gummy-leaved or trailing. The gradually lowering temperature left goose pimples along her arm.

Juliette and Adèle
1967

'The painting meant that much to her? That she'd starve herself to keep it?'

Adèle leans forward. 'But it wasn't just a portrait.'

'How do you mean?'

'It was herself, at her best, in a time where everything seemed possible.'

Her eyes sparkle. She says: 'Oh yes, Juliette. An object can be a soul.'

Luce and André, i.

A gallery opening in Montmartre, six years later. The low-ceilinged room is crammed with the rich and the modish, making it difficult to see the pictures on display: but nobody is there for that. The artists huddle resentfully in the corners, smoking; and in another corner, with a private table and a private bottle of champagne, two young women sit, their heads bent close in conversation.

Aurélie has brought Luce to the opening to cheer her up. Success has come at the price of exhaustion; a matinée and an evening show to perform every day for the past three months, leaving Luce wan and on the verge of tears, questioning her career. 'I can't remember the lines,' she will say, distraught in front of the mirror, and Aurélie, never at a loss, has a constant stream of events up her sleeve – shows, galleries, intimate parties – with which to distract her friend.

While Aurélie gets up to fetch more champagne, Luce leans forward in her seat, looking at the room. Without thinking about it, she finds herself studying one picture that is already attracting quite a bit of attention amongst the gallery-goers. Luce feels singled out by the woman subject's gaze, which seems to be directed at her.

It takes her a while to get across the gallery floor, ignoring the curious stares, but eventually she stands directly in front of the picture. The brass plate says *Unknown Woman in Louisiana*, and there is a guide price for the following day's auction, hanging on a little paper tag.

146

Luce notices the woman's expression: covetous, confident to the point of arrogance, but unfulfilled. There is something missing from the subject, she is certain, and she is so busy wondering what it might be that she does not notice a young man with dark hair cut in a fashionable style entering the gallery, turning the heads of the artists, who know a born model when they see one. He appears to know a few people, but not to want to talk. Then, abruptly, he stops in his tracks, cranes his neck, and heads for the same painting as Luce. The way he elbows his way through the crowd is barely polite. Art lovers edge away from him; a woman whispers to her neighbour that the strange young man looks on the verge of some kind of fit.

André reaches the portrait, and stands next to Luce without appearing to see her, though she notices him; his mouth has opened and his face is grey; he manages to stand for a moment, then teeters.

It is the first time Luce, never a sportswoman, has ever caught anything. To her astonishment the young man is not heavy: his lungs and upper body seem to be made of nothing but the air they hold, and she supports him easily on her forearms, her weight thrown forward over him.

But the pose is too painterly, too perfect, to last, and even as the room's artists are admiring the late romanticism of the tableau, Luce begins to shake. They hold onto each other for dear life, but the collapse is statuesque.

Aurélie comes forward from the back of the room, the stems of two champagne flutes clutched in one hand.

André and Luce bought the painting of Caroline Durand together that very same evening, as soon as André had come round from his faint. They paid half the money that was expected for the portrait – each haggling with all their charm, breaking down the alarmed dealer's resistance – then split the price, paying half each, and signed their names next to each other. They left together, with their first joint purchase held awkwardly between them.

STAGE SIREN ABSCONDS WITH EFFECTS WIZARD: it was all over Paris within the week. Debutantes wept and mothers cursed at André's unexpected removal from the market.

Luce's Aunt Berthe returned home that same evening to a venomous little note about the catastrophe from her closest friend. Rushing upstairs, she verified that Luce's room was indeed empty, and covered her powdered face with her hands.

Towards dawn, Berthe lay staring up at the corniced ceiling of her bedroom; water hissed and boiled overhead, circulating around the pipes of her apartment, and she clenched her fists and boiled too; inside her hair-net, each strand had transformed into an individual snake. There was nothing for it: she rose early and summoned the carriage.

She was forced to admit that the Bois de Boulogne neighbourhood was better than expected. This Durand must have some money. The carriage turned up a long drive and swept to a halt in the turning circle outside the front door. Nevertheless, Berthe tossed her head as she alighted from the carriage, and reached up to knock on the door.

Thirty seconds passed – then a minute. Where were the servants? Berthe had never been ignored on a doorstep before. Then the door opened, and André stood there.

'Yes?' he said.

Berthe was fascinated. The man was in his nightshirt.

'I am Berthe de Jumièges,' she told him in her woman-about-town voice, and smiled. Usually the name was enough.

André shook his head, smiled and shrugged.

The voice had been designed to reassure: *We are people of the world together*, it said unctuously, *if there is an arrangement, we will be sure to arrive at it, you and I.* Now Berthe felt her courage failing; the nightshirt's edge twitched in the breeze. What she had come to tell him seemed far away and improbable now, but she steeled herself and said it anyway: 'Her aunt. I've come to take her home.'

André shrugged again, and smiled.

'I don't think she wants to go,' he said.

A burst of laughter, far back in the shadows of the hallway; and Berthe, peering, saw Luce sitting on the bottom step of the stairs, wrapped only in a sheet.

Berthe tried one final line. 'Her father is unwell. I have done my best to keep the newspapers out of his reach but there are limits to what I can do, and if he finds out, the scandal will be the death of him.'

André's expression cooled. 'It comes to us all in the end.'

Berthe gathered herself. 'Then I think, I know, I can speak for the family, I can honestly say we wash our hands of her.'

Luce's stare said: *You did that a long time ago.*

25. juillet 1913

THE MORNING AFTER THE SOIRÉE, my eyes snap open, recalling what happened. What did happen? We went out for the evening. That's all.

The red dress is hanging on the back of the door, where I tore it off last night: I take it to the cupboard and push it behind the other dresses, so that it can't be seen when I open the door. I get dressed quickly, but go downstairs slowly. I will make some breezy remark: *Quite an evening last night! Does your head ache like mine?*

But when I get to the study, she is sitting at her desk again, holding a letter up to the light. Her fingers are glowing red where the morning sun shines through them, and what I had planned to say, I forget.

She jumps when she sees me and her hand flies to her hair: 'Adèle!' and for a too long, appalling moment I think she is going to say, *About last night…* but she doesn't; she looks away quickly, back at the letter.

'Feuillade wants to see me,' she says. 'It seems he has something in mind for me, and wants me to visit him this morning and read a piece of my choosing.'

She folds the letter thoughtfully; then darts a quick glance and a small smile at me. 'Good news, isn't it?'

'Yes,' I say, and then: 'I could come with you.'

She looks at me for a moment; her hand goes to the back of her neck. 'Oh no, you stay here in the cool. I'll be back before you know it.' She looks around the room hurriedly, and her gaze falls on a stack of correspondence by the sofa. 'Could you send the money to the manicurist? And sort out the order for my hats?'

Then she gets up and begins to bustle, looking for the things she will take with her to the audition, her back turned.

I watch her go from the study window, the top of her head bobbing. Hubert smiles as he holds the car door open. The angle lets me see her sitting in the cab, grey behind the glass, her hands folded in her lap.

She will be going up the steps to Feuillade's office, she will be sitting, he will be steepling his fingers and earnestly outlining the proposal; she will be nodding and smiling, a real smile, like the one last night, over her shoulder, as Aurélie dragged her away.

I close my eyes, tired – last night the Erlking galloped white-faced through my dreams – and when I open them, the sun in the room is so strong that it dazzles me; in the shaft of light and the flutter of the drapes I imagine Agathe standing there.

She smirks: *One would say certain things.*

Nonsense.

You have the signs.

It's nothing.

So last night?

What about last night? It was a soirée between friends.

Agathe studies her bitten nails. *Friends.* The curtain twitches in the hot breeze and she is gone.

The clatter of the front door, and excited laughter; feet on the stairs and she walks into the room, with Thomas carrying her coat. 'Imagine!' she says, 'he has engaged me as a highway-woman in a big film called *Dick Turpin*! And the best thing, the best thing is that if it's successful, I am to tour America with it!'

She looks at me, flushed and beaming. 'America!' she says.

I am thinking of her far away in a city of electric light. 'Wouldn't you have to speak English?' I have said before I can stop myself.

Her face closes. 'They will use an interpreter,' she says. 'Feuillade said it won't matter.'

She moves to the desk in the window and rearranges the corners of the stack of read scripts. She has her back to me.

'What about M. Durand?'

She waves a hand. 'It might be best to keep it under our hat until the contract is signed.'

The booming silence is back between us.

'It'll be our secret,' she says. Then, when I don't say anything, she blushes. 'Why don't you take the car? Go into the city for the afternoon.'

'If you want,' I say.

She doesn't look at me. She has turned away again, back to the desk.

All that week, I presented myself to her in the study, only to find her hand on the nape of her neck; she was distracted, absorbed in paperwork. 'You could visit the Jardin des Plantes, and see the leopard,' she would say, with a smile that seemed wide and flat, like a painting, while she fussed with her hair; or 'You could fetch my novels from the shop in rue des Ecoles.'

At the earliest possible point, she'd look away, as if I was an embarrassment. I'd turn, go down to the automobile and ask Hubert to drive me into Paris.

Faces were just faces, seen through the car window; or they were grotesques, staring at me as if they knew me, then turning away. In the Jardin des Plantes, I walked to the leopard's enclosure and found it asleep in the heat, half concealed by the foliage in its cage. The bookshop owner passed me the packet of new detective novels, and it seemed to me that he wouldn't look at me, and that he withdrew his hand too quickly from the parcel.

The evenings were the worst. André seemed in a high good humour, cracking his knuckles and eating enormous portions; Luce seemed hectic, brittle, keeping up a constant stream of society chatter to which he listened, for once, with keen interest. 'This sun will drive us all mad,' he'd say cheerfully, when she related some idiotic, scandalous tidbit for him.

If I sometimes caught her cool gaze on me, when André was distracted by the butler, I tossed my head, miserable, and would not look at her. *I'll keep your secret*, I thought, *but that is all*, and hated the quickening feeling in my belly, and hated even more the misery when I looked up and she had looked away.

One night, waiting for André in my room, I heard the roiling slam of thunder and the drumming of water on the leads.

I got up and crossed to the window, throwing it and the shutters wide; a gust of warm rain blew in my face. The sky was a sickened yellow; wind chased a stray newspaper across the terrace, and in the far distance, I could just make out the tree line, bending in the rising gale.

The weather seemed all the more savage in the manicured landscape: I had a satisfying vision of rose petals being strewn across the garden.

'What a night!' André was suddenly there, rubbing his hands idiotically as if the weather was his department. 'Shut the window.'

'Not yet.' I wanted to be out in the storm, not in here with him.

'I said close the shutters.'

'No.'

He crossed the room and caught at my arm, pulling me

away from the window, stinging my wrist; he leant out and slammed the shutters.

Immediately the room was watchful; too small and hot. He brushed his hair out of his eyes and turned away, tight-lipped, and began to unbutton his shirt, as he did every other night of the week.

I found I was trembling as I watched him. 'You have got me here under false pretences. You have brought me here as your concubine.'

He turned to face me, smirking, fingers still unbuttoning. 'You talk like a girl in a romance novel.'

'You said there would be professional advancement, opportunities—'

He tried charm, striding towards me. 'And haven't there been chances? Peyssac, he's famous—'

'She barely talks to me, she won't even look at me!'

'Adèle—' He took my shoulders and stroked his thumbs down them; I shrugged him off, and he grabbed me again and this time he shook me: my teeth chattered. 'We've taken you in, we've clothed you—'

I twisted away from him, spitting out the first words that came into my head: 'You're wicked. You're a wicked man.'

His lips tautened: he shook me again, harder this time.

I stared back at him, just wanting him out of my room; he looked at me, scouring my face, and then abruptly gave it up.

'Leave, or do what you want,' he said in disgust, dropping me back onto the bed; he crossed to pick up his shirt and stalked out of the room, slamming the door.

1. août 1913

THE NEXT MORNING I lay in bed, feeling sick.

Finally, at nearly midday, I got dressed and went to stare out of the window of my bedroom. Puddles had formed in the uneven slabs of the terrace, reflecting the blue and gold of the sky. In the far distance, a gardener nipped at the roses with secateurs.

The clock on the mantelpiece ticked the minutes into hours. Several times, I thought I heard Thomas on the stairs, only to find it was just the housemaids sweeping the terrace.

I was suddenly appallingly homesick. I sat on the bed and drew writing paper towards me; even as I dipped the pen to the creamy surface, it quivered with things to say, but as it made contact, the words faded away.

Dear Camille

Dear Camille

The pen hovered. *Dear Camille.*

I tore the paper into thin strips and then across again, so that only little squares were left, and those I dropped into the washstand and watched them turn into pulp.

As I turned away, my eye snagged on the carpet near the window, the spot of the struggle between André and me. There was something there.

I walked over and bent down to pick it up between forefinger and thumb. A key, finicky and lovely like everything else belonging to the house: cool and slender ceramic body, gold filigree head. It was as long as my little finger; it must have fallen out of André's pocket last night.

I put it to my lips, tasting the metal, wondering. But then Thomas's knock came at the door, startling me: I fumbled to hide the key in my pocket.

'Come to M. Durand's study in five minutes.'

André's corridor was dark, and smelled of his pomade. A cough came from behind the door at the end, directly below Luce's study, so that was the one I chose.

There were two tall windows but the shutters were still closed. André sat behind an enormous desk in the centre of the room, his elbows resting on its green leather top. The surface was strewn with sketches and diagrams.

Over the mantelpiece was a portrait: a woman in a flowing white dress against a green and beige background. It was too dim to see more, but I had the odd impression that she was waiting for me to speak.

André was busy writing. 'I'm going away for a while,' he said, without looking up. Now that my eyes were accustomed, I could see the tower of paper by his right elbow was money: tottering stacks of notes.

'Where?' I couldn't take my eyes off the bills.

'To Marseille. There's an inventor who may have the answer to something I've been looking at. So I wanted to ask what you had decided.'

'About what?'

His eyes clouded with confusion. 'Last night, I asked you if you were staying or going.' He looked down at his blotter again, then his hands moved independently, counting notes. 'Because if you are going, we'll find someone else.'

In another age, you would have said he was simple: his literal-mindedness; his ability to catalogue even things said in anger. I thought of how it had been at Pathé: how I'd loved his curly hair.

I said: 'I'm staying.'

'Fine.' He threw the bigger denominations onto a separate pile. Nothing in his face to show we had ever been intimate at all.

André left the following afternoon at five. Alone in my quarters, I listened to the rap of feet in the hallway below, his cheerful shout *goodbye*, and some muttered conversation with Thomas – doubtless telling him to keep an eye on me. A warm summer rain fell; Hubert dashed through the puddles from the car to the front door, umbrella flaring.

You never know how much noise a person makes, how much their presence counts, until they are gone. Very soon there was absolute quiet – that absence which allows you to hear your blood in your ears. The carpets rustled in the minute air currents crossing the floor. Mice scurried about their secret business in the wainscoting.

I sat, ruminating. At last, the dinner bell rang.

I crossed to the wardrobe and opened it, and looked at the red dress hanging there.

Why not? I thought. It was mine, after all.

I climbed angrily into it, not caring if the material snagged, and then stood at the mirror and patted my cheeks red, licked spit into my eyelashes, smoothed my brow.

She turns to look at me as I come into the dining room, her mouth slightly open. I have a sudden, aching glimpse of her as a child: in the back row of a classroom, suddenly picked on by the teacher for an answer.

André's chair is empty, his place unlaid. Thomas hovers for a moment, out of habit, just to the right of the spot where André's shoulder would have been, then moves on to serve the first course to me.

At first everything seems as I have come to expect it. After asking me how my day was, and after my stiff response, she retreats, becoming a faintly smiling statuette; I stab at my meal.

But it is not quite normal; not quite. She says: 'I was going to ask how you have been filling your time, since I have been so occupied with Feuillade.' Her hand briefly touches her collarbone. 'Was there anything worth reading in my correspondence?'

I think for a moment, then say: 'I found a letter from one of your fans. He wishes to know why you didn't keep to the secret rendezvous you had arranged.'

When I look up at her, she has turned pink, staring at me. 'I know of no secret rendezvous.'

I shrug: 'He seemed very sure.'

She stares, flushes deeper. 'I've never heard of him. Truly, Adèle.'

'He said you communicate via a private telepathy which allows you to signal to him your secret desires.'

Her eyes now clearing as she understands; a strand of her hair free and floating by her cheekbone.

'You are teasing me,' she says.

I smirk. 'Admit it… the telepathy was a good touch.'

She has regained some composure; still smiling, now privately, she has swept the strand of hair back into place. 'And what did you reply?'

'I told him you'd meet him outside his house at midnight tonight, holding a white camellia.'

She snorts with nervous laughter, the most unladylike sound, and brings her napkin to her mouth to cover it.

The silence fills the room, making it warmer. She snaps her fingers for Thomas to open the glass doors to the garden; the evening air rolls in. She has a high red spot on each cheek.

She says suddenly: 'I am sorry to have left you to your own devices so much recently. It was work – unavoidable. But I hope that now things are settled we may spend our days together again.'

She pauses, lips still parted as if there is more to say, then looks at me to see my response.

'Yes,' I say. 'I'd like that.'

'Good.' She beams. The silence descends again, thick and nervous. She fusses, making a play of finishing her dessert, and we don't speak. The red spots have expanded to her throat, which is blotchy.

At last she says: 'Best go up,' hitching her skirt to step free of the chair.

For a moment it seems she hesitates, as if she might say something else; then with a smile, she walks to the door.

I listen to her small, precise steps as she goes upstairs.

In bed that night, I touch myself for the first time. My hand creeps to where André used to press with his tongue, and rubs.

The sheets gather damp around my thighs. I imagine crying out to her, her laying her hands on me. *Is this what my husband does? Or this?*

I clamp my other hand to my mouth, in case I have made a sound.

7. août 1913

THE HEAT GATHERS ITS SKIRTS: the temperature rises hour by hour, wilting flowers, the sun huge in the sky. From Paris, the news comes of young women hurling themselves into the Seine in an attempt to cool off. They say it's a curse, that there is a Jonah in the city – *It's the Russians, the poets, the English, the gypsies, the anarchists, the wickedness of cinema, the vengeful ghost of Josephine Bonaparte, your cousin. Your mother. Not my mother!* – fights break out; the hospitals open their doors to get air: hysterics escape en masse from the Salpêtrière, whooping naked through the streets of the city.

One morning, Luce opens a note from Feuillade, reads it through and pouts. 'His daughter is ill. They are going to Switzerland for a cure.'

She refolds it. 'He won't be back for months. I won't have to spend time at the studio after all.'

She says it lightly, tossing the card back onto the pile of unopened correspondence. 'I'll just have to stay here and annoy you.' She looks directly at me.

I am careful to keep my eyes on my book, but it's too much – I have spoken, been incautious: 'You don't annoy me.'

Her eyes on me, cool and thoughtful. 'What a little gentleman.'

I turn a page, hoping she won't notice how my lip trembles.

Later, when it is too much to bear, being in the same room, I turn my head into that hanged-man posture and pretend to be asleep. Under my eyelids I watch her move to the desk and write a letter: no doubt to Feuillade, sending him condolences on his daughter's illness. I look at every line of her, from the curve of her neck to the straightness of her fingers.

When I wake with a start, she is watching me: motionless at the desk, her pen in her hand.

'You sleep like a child,' she says.

The following morning, I smooth my damp palms on my skirt and go to the salon; push the door inwards, and find it empty.

I am agonised: where has she gone? Then I hear laughter through the open window, cross to it, and lean out to see her sitting in a wicker chair on the terrace below. She shades her eyes and beckons me down.

A package of books and papers has arrived – M. Leroux's *The Yellow Room* and other detective novels. She fidgets, fluttering an Oriental fan; beads of perspiration trickling down her temple, reading fast, scanning the page, occasionally drawing in her breath if something surprises her, and then her eyes lift to meet mine: 'The detective has discovered that the person who was impersonating the duchess is in fact an insane priest on the run from the mad-house,' or 'Apparently the murderer escaped the locked room by means of a special hatch in the ceiling, disguised as a monkey.'

Each time she laughs at the expression on my face. 'The monkey was a good touch.'

I rarely smile back, and I never laugh. She must be able to see it all over my face.

At midday she settles her head back, folds her hands in her lap and shuts her eyes.

Searching for distraction, I pick up the *Revue Satirique* and flip through to the caricatures.

I stare at the page for a good ten seconds.

The caricature is a scene from a tearoom: a person sitting at a table in the foreground – a woman, by the swell of her bosom – dressed in a man's suit and hat. She is leaning across, with her arm looped round the waist of a blushing girl sitting next to her, pulling her closer.

The woman is saying to the girl: *Trousers! Practical, not just for bicycling!* Underneath, there is a legend: *Teatime in Montmartre: unnatural love in its natural habitat…*

I look at the bow ties again, my heart thumping in my chest, the trousers the woman is wearing; at the face of the young girl shying away.

'That's better,' Luce says, opening her eyes and pushing herself up in the chair a little. 'Adèle? Are you all right?'

'Yes.' I put the magazine down hurriedly and try to shoo it underneath my chair.

She shades her eyes. 'Something in the news? Something to do with home?'

'Nothing.' The magazine rustles against my bare feet.

She watches me for a moment longer.

Then she settles back in her chair and closes her eyes, her legs stretched out in front. Her pale skin will burn; I worry about how pink it turns, how quickly.

I practised saying it all last night, till the words sounded like nothing. She twitches, getting comfortable, and for a moment I think I almost have told her it.

But her eyes don't snap open, outraged.

Worse: she'd be kind. *I don't understand,* and then, *you mean, like the ladies in the papers? But you know I am not like that. You know I'm married.*

That night, I imagined what she would look like on the pillow next to me, her hair spread out like a fan. Turning to look at me: the slow blink of her eyes.

As I lay there, I heard a sound. It was like the throb of a bee against the window; I thought the insect must have got into my room during the day, so I hopped out of bed and went to open the shutters, only to find there was nothing there. The panes were clear and grey in the light of an enormous moon.

Now the noise had moved, humming away down the corridor outside my room. I went to the door, opened it and listened. Definitely, the sound came from the right-hand end of the passageway – I tiptoed out and stole along, pausing halfway to listen, and laid my ear to the waxy surface of the last door. Very faint now, there was just a trilling sound somewhere beyond.

I knew all the rooms were locked, so it was no surprise when I rattled the handle and pushed to no avail. I leant my cheek on the door – *I wonder* – and then turned and scampered back to my room, to fetch André's ceramic key.

It gleamed cool in the faint light; slipping it into the lock, it turned smoothly and the door swung inward.

A small bird was there, brown and indistinct except for the yellow of its eyes. A trail of broken glass led across the dusty floorboards to where it sat, shuffling and terrified; air rushed through the broken windowpane.

I went to it, cupped my hands around it and shushed it; holding it to my breast I crossed to the window and tried to push the sash up with my other hand. It was locked, the glass grimy with disuse. The bird turned its sharp beak into my skin and beat its wings; at least it meant there was nothing broken. I left the room and went to the corridor window instead, rattled it open and put the bird on the sill outside. It moved to the end of the sill without hesitation: a moment later I saw it swoop away.

Thinking of André, his punctiliousness, I went back to close and lock the door, pausing to peer inside as I did so. The room was in disuse and looked to have been for many years: there was an open fireplace in one corner, and several dust-sheeted items of furniture: a chest of drawers, a standing lamp, an old-fashioned crib. There was nothing that I could see of value; nothing remarkable enough to warrant the locking of the room or the keeping of the key about his person.

On the way back up the corridor I tried the key in the other rooms. It didn't fit any. I tapped it against my teeth, thinking; opened the door to my own room again, and almost shouted out. There was someone in the bed, hunched over on their right-hand side, away from me; it was her.

My agonised squeak died away. There was no one in the bed. It was the sheets, mussed where I had flung them off, that looked like someone's body.

Juliette and Adèle
1967

'My grandmother used to say a bird trapped in a room was an omen.'

Adèle says: 'No, the locked room itself was the omen.'

She leans inwards. Then she says: 'But you still haven't told me about Phantom Boyfriend.'

I feel my lips pursing.

'Let me guess,' she says, 'he was from a rich family, and he wanted you to settle down, and when you said you wanted to carry on working, have your career, he cooled it off.'

I say: 'He wasn't from a rich family. We met at university. We were involved in student politics together.'

'*Politics*,' she says, 'and what was his name?'

'Is this relevant?'

'Oh, because you're the one interviewing me?' She leans back, arms folded.

I tell her how he left my apartment in the middle of my deadline without saying goodbye, took his coat, and never came back. How I'd seen him at the cinema last week with another girl, who was wearing a cashmere sweater.

Adèle listens intently.

When I've finished, I find I'm looking down at my notepad, blinking. Tears of embarrassment, mostly.

She watches me for a moment. Then she leans forward and says: 'Why are you crying? It can't be because you think he is worth crying over.'

I shake my head, my lips pressed together.

She says: 'But there's not a thing wrong with you. Nothing at all.'

Juliette, iv.

The weather clears into bright sunlight. To the north-east, the city is being replaced by another version of itself: gleaming geometric blocks in creams and pinks, instead of grey stone, row upon row of faceless windows; a nest of cranes, their angular necks drooping with the weight of the concrete they carry.

I turn the car down the slip road, and into Vincennes.

Dilapidated and sooty tenement blocks; a café missing several letters from its name. At the end of the street, the Square Jean-Jaurès has been colonised by a couple of cardboard shelters leant up against the wall. The cardboard drips the last of the rain and vibrates in the breeze, but its residents are nowhere to be seen.

Anne Ruillaux's house is a square grey block tacked on to the end of the row of apartment buildings. Once, it might have been genteel: the home of a factory overseer, proud of his second storey. Now, the façade is crumbling off in chunks, and net curtains hang limp in the windows; the house next door has been demolished and lies in a pile of half-cleared rubble.

I lift the door knocker and let it drop.

In the street behind me, a group of small boys has materialised out of nowhere, kicking a lamp-post and staring.

A dog-walker appears at the corner of the street, cap pulled down against the drizzle. The dog whines and strains towards me; its owner pulls at the leash — *Shush, Pitouf, heel* — and walks past, ignoring its yelps.

Something is nagging, something about the timbre of the dog-walker's voice; I look back at the figure walking briskly down the street.

'Anne?' I say. 'Madame Ruillaux? May we speak?'

She turns. The dog watches too, its tongue lolling.

'Can I ask about the film you found?'

She reaches down and unclips the dog's lead – *Go on, Pitouf* – and the dog dashes forward, to stand at the front door, dancing.

A dog-lover's room, not refurbished since the war: ratty wallpaper, an ancient wooden table with chewed legs, a series of black and white photographs on the mantel. In the corner, a wheelchair is folded in on itself, like a stick insect.

Anne has fading red hair, badly cut into a bob, weathered skin, and can't be more than fifty-five: despite the wheelchair, she seems to walk normally. She sits opposite me but says nothing, one hand on Pitouf's neck, scratching his ears.

'You said you found the film in your basement,' I prompt. 'How did you come to discover it?'

When she speaks, it's in a monotone. 'I was having a clear-out. I came across the reel in amongst some other junk. I decided to see if it was worth anything.'

'When was this?'

'A month or so ago.'

'And you didn't recognise it? You don't know how long it had been there?'

She shakes her head to both questions. The same flat gaze.

I ask: 'How long have you owned the house?'

'Twenty years. We bought it when we married.'

'We?'

'My late husband and I.'

'And was the film there when you bought it?'

She thinks about it, shakes her head. 'I'm not sure. I know

there was a lot of junk in the basement.'

'Could the previous owners have left it?'

'My husband was in charge of moving all the furniture in. But he never mentioned the film.'

I say: 'The thing is, Mme Ruillaux, that film seems to have been kept very carefully, somewhere relatively cool. Otherwise it would have degraded much more, or possibly even been destroyed.'

Pitouf whines as she tugs too hard. 'My late husband used to have his workshop in the basement. He ran to hot, so he liked it cool down there. Maybe that's why.'

'Was your husband in films?'

'No. He worked in the supermarket with me.'

'So he never mentioned the Pathé factory, or knew anybody in that industry?'

'No. We met at the supermarket. We always worked there.'

'Did he like the cinema?'

'We used to go once a year, at Christmas. What he really liked was model aeroplanes.'

She shifts her weight in the chair. 'We aren't fancy people. Weren't.'

'When did he die?'

She nods to the wheelchair in the corner. 'A year ago.'

I say: 'Do you have any idea who owned the house before you?'

'No. I don't want any more questions.'

A thin crease has appeared on her forehead, her glance flitting everywhere but my face. It's time to leave.

'Thank you very much for your help.'

She shows me out. The door slams; the small boys across the street stop their game of hoopla to watch me walk to the car.

15. août 1913

THAT DAY, TWO PIECES of post arrive. We have moved back inside; the weather has cooled enough to be tolerable. Thomas brings the salver and deposits it on a footstool in front of the sofa.

She slits the first envelope, pulls out a gold-edged invitation, and frowns. 'Aurélie. She's sent us two tickets to the *Rite of Spring* premiere at the Champs-Elysées. That new ballet.'

I look up from my book.

'Sweet of her,' she says, frowning.

She opens the second letter. Then her hand flattens to her throat, fingers drumming her collarbone.

She clears her throat – 'From my husband. He expects to return on the overnight train and be back with us by eleven o'clock tomorrow morning,' – puts the letter back in the envelope and says brightly: 'That is sooner than expected, isn't it? He must have had some success with his inventions.'

It feels like falling backwards. 'That's good, I suppose.'

'Yes, I suppose so,' she says.

Somewhere in the house, Thomas's voice is low and malevolent; matched by the high chime of a housemaid, being taken to task for bad cleaning; but in the study there is no noise. André coming home early when he could have stayed away. André whistling as he jogs into the house, flinging his hat at the hat stand.

She says: 'It's curious. These past few days, I have had the impression of time standing still, and of the house—' she stops,

170

looking for the right word, 'knowing there was someone missing. As if there was an absence, but not — that it wasn't something to regret. That the house seemed more alive. There was more fun to be had here, within these walls, than anywhere.'

She waits. 'A strange thing, being married. I have woken up each morning, since he went, to the most joyful feeling, the most contentment, since we met. In fact, you could almost say I didn't miss my husband at all.'

Time is a chord trembling. Her skin, too pink anyway from the sun, is pinker still: tender as a newborn baby's.

She says gently: 'Do you understand what I am telling you?'

I sit frozen. *Those women, in their tweeds.*

At long last she drops her gaze to her feet; she seems to gather herself, and says: 'All this talking! Now, will you fetch me my novel? I left it by the doors in from the terrace.'

When I reach the door and look back, she has stiffened, staring at a spot on the rug near my feet, and when she speaks her voice sounds like someone else's: 'We'll still go to the ballet together? We must have a wonderful time, mustn't we?'

I nod, feeling the words recede back down my throat, and close the door softly behind me as I leave.

In the corridor, when I'm safely away from the door, all the crying comes out in a succession of gulping sobs. I run down the corridor, terrified she'll hear.

'There.' She levers my chair round to look at the mirror.

My face: I put two fingers near my mouth, where she has drawn on lipstick, near my eyelashes where she bent, applying kohl, her breath hot on my face.

I am a miserable stranger.

Standing behind me, she says: 'You look like a film star.' Her voice is proud and sad; her eyes meet mine briefly in the mirror, then sheer away.

~

In the dark of the car, I can watch without seeming to. She sits very straight, with her hands folded in her lap, gazing out at the passing houses: lit window after lit window. I enumerate her tiny imperfections: the furrow on her forehead, the patch of dry skin at her throat, scratched red over the weeks, now healing.

'The ballet, Madame?' Hubert says as he opens the cab door for us opposite the shiny concrete block of the Théâtre des Champs-Elysées. 'I don't have to come in, do I?'

She rolls her eyes; he grins. As we cross the street I look back and see him settling into the driver's seat with a cigarette and a newspaper, and wish I could join him. What if I say the wrong thing in front of her? What if she is embarrassed by me, turning away tight-lipped into the crowd?

On the steps ahead is a gaggle of people, all talking loudly to one another; most of them middle-aged and beyond, the men in top hats and the women with their hair piled on top of their heads and ostrich feathers in the set wave. As we make our way up towards the entrance, I catch a glimpse of a familiar figure right in the heart of the throng, his little eyes glinting with amusement, nodding vigorously at someone else's joke. He half turns, sees me, and his face glazes over.

'Adèle?' Luce says, frowning, trying to get my attention; then follows my look to where Peyssac stands. Her eyes narrow but she laughs, and raises one arm.

'Robert!' she calls, loud enough to stop all other conversation. 'Wonderful to see you here!'

Peyssac stares, and the crowd swivels to look at her; and he is caught, he has been seen. 'Yes,' he bleats, 'marvellous!' and like a minnow he turns and slips away.

The crowd murmurs, beginning to piece the gossip together, and conversation starts up again; turning back, she laughs at my expression. 'The old rogue,' she says, to no one in particular, and we carry on into the foyer.

Our seats are in the middle of the stalls. We shuffle past the patrons who have arrived early, two elderly women with haughty, lined faces, and a gentleman with a monocle. 'After you,' she says, all politeness, placing her hand in the small of my back. She levers herself into the seat next to me, her arm lying on the armrest between us.

Her head comes next to mine, too, dizzyingly close. 'There's the Duc de Guise,' she murmurs, 'two rows in front, the one with the weak chin. That's the Duchesse next to him.'

A thoughtful pause. Then she says: 'They say the Duchesse is actually a man, and is frightened to be seen in full light in case her stubble shows.'

'Who says that?' I ask.

'The Duc de Guise's mother, for one. She claims to have come upon her daughter-in-law during her music lesson, singing Berlioz in a pleasing baritone.'

I lift myself in my seat and peer over the tops of the audience's heads till I can see the person: she has half turned to look up into the boxes, and it's true, she is glancing around anxiously, with her shawl pulled up around her ears.

'She does have quite a strong jaw,' I say doubtfully, reporting my findings, and Luce turns back to sit staring at the stage, and laughs.

'What?'

'The Duchesse de Guise is one of my oldest friends. I'll have to tell her she needs a better cosmetician.'

This isn't funny any more. I am blinking back tears, turning my face away so she won't see.

'The Berlioz was a good touch,' she says, and puts her hand on my forearm. The fingers don't retreat.

The lights dim.

A diminutive man struts across the front of the orchestra

pit and, stepping up onto his podium, raises his arms in appreciation of our applause. He turns and raises his baton; I steal a glance at Luce. Her eyes gleam as she waits for it to fall.

A watchful bassoon, swelling to sweep away houses, joined by a clarinet. Dry leaves, lifting and rustling: the audience, whispering behind their hands; two people getting to their feet, threading their way out, with the flushed faces of early leavers. A ripple of laughter courses round the auditorium; the orchestra plays on, frowning with the concentration of sliding up the scales. I glance at Luce: her lips are slightly parted, caught halfway between a smirk and amazement.

When I had asked Luce, in a moment of boldness, *What should I expect, I've never been to a ballet before*, she hadn't even looked up from her magazine. She had flipped the pages and said, *Tulle, expect lots of tulle.*

The curtain rolls back, revealing a stage full of people in costumes of coarse yellow and brown, against a painted backdrop, the swell of a hillside. Immediately behind me, a young rake says loudly: 'It looks like an arse,' and the laughter gets louder. Onstage, the dancers begin to whirl and stomp, throwing themselves into angular shapes: I look at Luce for reassurance – where are the pinks and the ivories, the chiffons and tutus? Someone shouts from a box: 'Nijinsky has found his ballerinas in the asylum!' But it isn't an asylum they make me think of: rather, the animals in the fields at home; rhythmic, undulating, arching their backs. The elderly gentleman at the end of the row has half-risen from his seat, frowning, his tongue running over his gums. He shouts: 'For shame! Filth!' The cry is taken up further forward in the stalls, men and women swaying on their feet; someone else stands up and yells at his neighbour: 'Sit down, imbecile!' and suddenly a fist flies, a white streak, and two men are tussling in the aisle.

A woman next to me stands up, eyes alive with delight at the ruckus. Two more men pile into the fray, and now it seems the whole audience are on their feet, screaming their insults. The orchestra plays on and I clamp my hands to my ears, jostled by the swaying of the crowd on either side. A knot of spectators is leaping the barrier to the orchestra pit and advancing on the conductor: the timpani boom a warning.

Luce's hand touches mine. 'Let's go.' A high sound may be a police whistle or a piccolo. Her glossy head has bobbed away and disappeared; she dips and surfaces, a flash of her frown, her face turned towards me, and she's gone again. I am fighting my way towards the end of the row: there is no way out, just a mass of bodies, and real screams now, blocking my way.

I whip round to escape the other way and see Luce, standing firm against the people pushing against her – her hand extended to me – I reach for her fingertips, catch at them, and she brings her other arm around and hauls me by the waist towards her, until I am pressed up against her, the din whirling in our ears.

I am conscious of my heart hammering, and of how she must feel it; of her right hand in my hair and her left on my waist, their gentle pressure. The noise is all around us; she shifts and her thigh is against mine, and although we are standing in the same way we are not standing in the same way. I look up at her; her eyes are drowsy and speculative; she's saying something.

'What?' I can't hear her over the din.

She keeps looking down at me, lips pursed; then she turns, gripping my hand and pulling me after her as she fights her way towards the exit.

In the foyer, the theatre manager hovers, trying helplessly to staunch the flow of patrons flying out into the street. On the steps, a portly man in a top hat is saying to all who pass: 'An abomination, I will personally bring this to the attention of Monsieur the Minister tomorrow. Assuming tomorrow comes.'

It has been raining; the cobbles are shining wet. Hubert is standing next to the car across the street, looking around in amazement; seeing us, he puts two fingers to his mouth and whistles.

In the car, she leans her head back against the seat and closes her eyes – but she still hasn't let go of my hand.

When we reach the house, Hubert lets us out of the car and says goodnight, and we go inside. It is totally silent. The sky is curiously light: as if it is already anticipating the day ahead.

We walk up the stairs, our fingers laced together, as if it was the most natural thing in the world. At the first landing – her floor – we pause for a moment, the door to her room a hovering outline; she turns to look at me and I look back. Whatever it is she needs to see, she sees it; she turns the door handle, and we walk inside.

A double bed comes clear; thin silvery light through the window. I stand there drinking in all the things that up until now I've never seen: what is private and hers.

Now, as if taken by a sudden shyness, she walks away from me. She crosses to the window and looks out, holding her arms across her body, as if she's cold.

She is standing there, looking out: just her silhouette, the slender, dizzying height of her. She's further away from me than she has been before: and I know – seem to have known for a long time – what I have to do to bring her back.

It will be easier to say it like this, with her facing away.

'There's something I have to tell you,' I say. 'About your husband.'

It feels like a failure; an abomination. There is a humming in my ears.

The clock on the mantelpiece ticks away another second, and another.

She turns to face me. Pale and tall. 'It doesn't matter. Does it?'

I stand rigid where I am.

'It doesn't matter,' she says again.

She walks across the room, slowly and deliberately and stands in front of me; centimetres away. Close enough to see her chest rise and fall in the half-light.

She puts her fingertips to my face and says my name.

Dawn: bruised light. Book spines, arranged on the mantel, came gradually clear; she lay on her side away from me, with her arm flung out.

As I watched her, she opened her eyes – sharply, as if she wasn't sure who she expected to see – and turning, reached for me.

When the first household noises began, we tiptoed up the stairs, her little finger laced in mine, without speaking.

She walked me up to the third floor landing, and there we stopped and looked at each other.

'I can make sure André doesn't come to your room any more,' she says. 'If that's what you want.'

'It's what I want,' I say.

Under her eyes, the shadows were violet. Standing there, she kissed me for a long time, until we heard the servants' voices, very faint, downstairs.

16. août 1913

I SLEPT FOR A FEW HOURS. At half past ten I heard André's cheerful shout hello, and then his footsteps going up to his study; and then nothing, just a long silence and the breeze in the trees.

At half past one I got up and went to her salon. She was sitting upright on the sofa, straight-backed, reading.

Her face softened.

Thomas's footsteps, up and down the corridor.

She bent back over her novel; a high red spot on either cheekbone.

For distraction, I crossed to sit at the desk, arranged myself, picked up a letter. *I have never met you but I love you*, wrote a man from Normandy.

At four o'clock I went to my room. There was nothing to do but wait. I looked out of the window, at the high, white, unreal sky, and wondered how she would dissuade him. What she could be planning, and if it could work. We'd fallen out, André and I, but I was still living in his house: there for the taking.

I went down for dinner at eight. He was there, lounging in his seat, tanned from his trip, but otherwise the same. Looking at him, I wondered how I had ever mistaken his silken waistcoats for sincerity.

He looked up at me, a quick glance under his eyelids. 'You look well.'

'Do I?'

'Very.' He reached casually for bread. I folded my hands in my lap and stared at them. She hadn't said anything yet, or the plan hadn't worked.

Luce said: 'So your trip—'

André tipped his chair back and laced his fingers behind his head, all his teeth on show. 'You should have seen his workshop. He has an automaton so realistic it could be sitting where Adèle is right now. She could *be* the automaton.'

'I think we'd recognise the real one.'

André lifted his wine glass and swirled it. Then he asked: 'Anything exciting happen while I was gone?'

Luce took a sip of wine – the muscles of her throat moved as she swallowed – and shook her head.

At the end of the meal, André sat swilling the dregs in his glass, staring at the wall; she was perfectly composed, opposite him. Eventually she turned her gaze on me.

'Goodnight,' I said, getting to my feet.

As I left the room, she rose too. For a delirious moment I thought she was coming after me. But she followed me to the door and put her hand on the handle.

I stood in the hall, staring back at her.

'Goodnight,' she said. On her face was a fierce look I had not seen before. She pulled the door closed.

I went upstairs to my room and sat in my nightgown, propped up against the pillows, to wait.

I thought about the last time with André. I could hardly remember it: I just had the impression of conserved energies, and no noise, as if noise were an expense he didn't want with me.

After a while I heard the dining-room door open and close.

Her softer steps and his quicker ones going up the stairs: no voices.

I heard him walk up the second flight, clearing his throat. A pause, and his footsteps kept on coming, up the last flight of stairs to my floor.

I pulled my knees up to my chin and shut my eyes; then I reached for the stem of the lamp beside my bed. I lifted it an inch, to test its weight.

The footsteps had stopped; I breathed, and listened harder.

There was a creak of floorboards just outside my door. He was shifting his weight onto his other leg.

We waited, on either side of the door, in silence, for more than a minute.

Abruptly, there was a squeak as he spun on his heel – and then his footsteps jogging back down the stairs.

I waited half an hour, letting the sweat on my body cool, then slipped out of my room and stole down the stairs.

At his floor I paused, but of course there was nobody there.

I continued to Luce's floor. Stood for a moment outside her room; brushed the door with my knuckles.

There was no answer. I pushed it open.

The shutters were faint silvery outlines. I couldn't hear breathing, so she was not asleep; and sure enough, after a few seconds, her shape came clear. She was sitting up in bed.

I walked to the bed. Still no sound.

I climbed onto the bed, knelt over her and kissed her.

Her lips were cold under mine; barely moving.

She let me push back the covers. Her nakedness: a white slender body. The nipples dark circles. I reached out for one—

She held my head in place, and put her hands in my hair.

She pulled my nightgown over my head. The air in the room was summery warm, a gentle draught from somewhere.

As I was bending to kiss her again, she put a hand up to stop me; ran a finger down my jaw. The fingernail dug in.

She pushed me gently onto the bed and rolled towards me; put her hands on my thighs and spread them wide apart.

Looking at her expression, I understood that there was a price, after all.

'He wasn't even—' I tried to tell her. 'He never even—'

She covered my mouth with her hand; then, without checking whether I was ready, she pushed four fingers into me.

'Am I anything like him?'

It hurt: a good pain, but shocking.

'Did he do this? Or this?'

Each movement a separate sound from my mouth. Her eyes, half-shut, watching me.

I took her hand away from my mouth, rolled over and straddled her; took her wrist and pushed her further into me. Bent down and kissed her; told her that if this was how the account would be settled, I'd pay.

Much later, I woke to find her still asleep. Pale light was just beginning to show in the cracks of the shutters.

She slept with one arm curved above her head, protective. I watched her for a long time, then put my hand on her stomach.

Her eyes flew open. She stared at the ceiling; then at me.

'What did you say to him?' I asked. 'To stop him?'

'It doesn't matter,' she said.

I went on watching her. Her nostrils flared.

She said: 'He won't come to your room any more. Isn't that enough?'

She closed her eyes again. Her hand came crabbing over the coverlet and seized mine convulsively: gripping my fingers so tightly they turned red, then white, changing position every thirty seconds or so, finding a new hold.

22. août 1913

IN THE SALON, DURING THE DAY, we did everything we could not to meet each other's eyes.

Sometimes we caught each other out. She straightened her back, arching her neck to release the tension from reading, rubbing the nape with one palm, and in the course of looking at the ceiling, her eyes wandered to mine.

On those occasions time slowed and stopped. Her hand stayed where it was; a smile hovered on her face; the hand rubbed gently, ruefully over her neck, forward and back. The moment would lengthen out until one of the many sounds that made us jump, made us jump: a clatter of pots and pans from the kitchen, or Thomas's step on the stair.

At supper, the sharp pain of watching her speaking to André. In the first days after his return, he had seemed quiet, almost wary of her. But night by night he became more boisterous: drinking more wine than before, making tasteless jokes, watching her with a flushed attention that I could not look at. And at the other end of the table, she laughed where appropriate, exchanging gossip: only a little pallor to show anything was wrong at all. And when he wasn't looking, she would glance at me, warning me to smile, laugh and make conversation: to pretend.

At night, I'd undress for her: a slow tease, the garments falling one by one. She'd lie propped on one elbow, smiling crookedly; and when I was naked, she'd look at me. From ankles to eyelashes. 'You're beautiful,' she'd say. 'Come here.'

Juliette and Adèle
1967

The last of the lunchtime crowd is dissipating; bars of dusty sunlight across our table.

I say: 'Didn't you worry about being discovered?'

Adèle smiles. 'Of course. But then again, not.'

Her fingers hover in front of her mouth: 'I had this fantasy: being caught out. The five short minutes to get dressed; the servants lining the hall. André ejecting us from the house. Our suitcases being flung down the steps behind us. To be alone with her on the drive, with all her ghosts streaming out ahead of us, evaporating on the morning air.'

25. août 1913

IN BED, SHE MADE ME WAIT, trailing a fingertip over me till I almost cried; she turned me into someone I wasn't: I barely recognised the sounds from my own mouth.

But when I tried to return the favour, most often, she'd smile, and shift me gently onto the bed beside her, and turn away from me, onto her other side.

One day, we took a picnic to the Bois de Boulogne.

Hubert dropped us on the side of the main road through to Paris; leaning into the cab, she arranged to have him pick us up at five. She carried the picnic hamper and I took a blanket, and we walked away from the path towards where the trees grew a little thicker. It was a fine afternoon: the leaves and grass buzzed with activity, but as it was a week-day, other visitors were few and far between. We picked our way between the patches of tufty grass and the tree roots, and finally found a spot where there was just one other couple visible in the distance.

We ate in reflective silence, and cleared the plates away into the basket; then she piled her coat behind her head and lay down, shading her eyes with her hand.

I watched her, found myself smiling.

'What?' she said, laughing.

'Nothing,' I said. I'd been thinking how I'd come to the house hoping to take her place. But now there was no longer anything outside her or around her – no films, no future.

She squinted up at me under her fingers, still smiling.

'I'd swear you're taller,' she said.

I looked down at myself.

'Yes, you are. You're only seventeen. You're still growing.'

We smiled at each other again.

'Seventeen,' she said, uncertain. 'An ingénue.'

There was a pause. She laughed, but the laugh faded quickly away.

I suddenly thought I understood. I sat down beside her.

'Is that it?' I asked. 'Is that why? Because I'm young?'

She blinked, lowered her eyes. 'Is what why?'

I bent over and kissed her.

'Adèle,' she said, in her old commanding voice, 'if somebody comes—'

'They won't.'

The sun in her eyelashes; the sound of the birds in the trees, oddly magnified.

When I moved my hand between her legs she caught at my fingers. I took her hand and flattened it on the grass and left it there.

'Do you think I care that you're older? Do you think I'm too young to know my own mind?'

Her face fell.

I slipped my hand under her petticoats. This time she didn't try to stop me.

She turned her head to one side, frowning.

Oh, she said. Turned her head to the other side. I cradled it with the crook of my arm, protecting it each time she turned, again and again, fighting to escape.

And then she was unrecognisable. Laughing and crying together. Her tears slid into my mouth.

Over supper that same evening, André lifted his wine glass and stared at her over the top of it.

'You look healthy,' he said to her. 'Glowing.'

'It must be the fresh air,' she said, cutting demurely into her food.

20. septembre 1913

ONE DAY SHE LOOKED OUT OF the salon window and said: 'I think this is the last fine day. What shall we do with it?'

I shrugged. It was true: the light had that slanted quality that meant autumn. I had no particular needs, now, apart from being with her, so it didn't matter to me if we went out – but I wanted her to have what she wanted.

She turned, clicked her fingers. 'The boating lake,' she said.

In the car, she held my hand loosely, under cover of our coats, and pointed out the fashions of the ladies walking along the Allée des Acacias.

'Do you remember when we met Aurélie by accident here?' she said. 'I thought you were going to knock her out.'

I smiled at the memory, but didn't comment, because it seemed like another person. How small my aims had been then: grasping after fame. I never thought about acting any more.

'My knight in shining armour,' she said contentedly, snuggling down amongst the coats.

Hubert parked the car on a stretch of grassland. She told him to wait, and we walked towards the lake. There was a small boathouse, and a wizened old man hiring rowing boats. Luce picked her way towards him; I saw her flash a smile, and coins changing hands.

When she came back, she was triumphant. 'He wanted five francs,' she said, 'but I beat him down to three.'

I rolled my eyes.

'It was the principle,' she said vaguely, already shading her eyes and pointing at the rowing boats drawn up on the bank. 'That one, don't you think?'

We crossed to the boat and hauled it down to the water. There was the business with setting it upright, and testing its water safety, and finding the oars; all of which I loved.

'What are you thinking?' she said.

I'd been looking at her shoulders: how she pulled the oar handles back, tight, then the release. The shower of tiny droplets scattering back into the water.

The lake was not busy – it was too cold for that. There was just one other couple in a rowing boat: a young girl and her beau. The girl clutched her hat and screamed as it tried to blow away.

'Your shoulders,' I said.

She smiled at me, and shook her head in mock disapproval.

I watched her face. That puckered frown she occasionally had, that I remembered from before, pulling her eyebrows tight.

The girl in the other boat finally lost her hat; it blew away from her, skimming across the lake. She shrieked, and stood up. The young man stood, too, to balance the boat. They teetered, for a moment, and then tipped into the shallows; laughing, they stood, the water running off their faces. Then he held up his hand to her and escorted her to shore. She stepped onto the grass as proud as a queen.

Luce had let the oars drift; her eyes had narrowed with enjoyment at the scene.

She turned her face away. Eventually she said: 'What would happen if we just kept going?'

'Where?'

'If this lake had a tributary, a stream, leading off somewhere.'

The oars creaked in their rowlocks. A breeze made the boat tremble in the water.

'Out to sea?'

'Just as far as one of those dilapidated resorts. Those places people go to die. We could stay there for a while. Take a hotel.'

The idea of being alone in a hotel with her was so painfully beguiling that my mind tied the thought off. An image came to me of her on a pebbled beach, dissecting the fashions of the provincial ladies.

'You'd last about five minutes,' I said.

She smirked – 'Perhaps' – and looked down. Then up again, uncertain, and this time, she held my gaze. Her smile was the shyest, most gorgeous thing I'd ever seen.

7. octobre 1913

ONE NIGHT, OVER DINNER, André announced the party. 'We haven't entertained in months,' he said. 'I'm ready to be seen.'

He struck a pose. I turned my face away. I could barely see him these days without wanting to wind my plait round his neck. Just when it seemed he ought to recede into the distance, he was more present than ever: haunting the corridors of the house, always whistling just out of sight.

Luce said, slowly and to my surprise: 'Yes. It's an idea.'

André looked surprised too. 'Saturday?' he said.

'Yes. Why not?' She pressed her handkerchief to her mouth. 'One condition: no Peyssac.'

André grinned. 'In that case: no Ex-Minister.'

'Then none of your stupid trick-film has-beens.'

'None of your twittering fashion-obsessed friends.'

She took a long sip from her wine glass, enjoying, I could only suppose, this idiotic game of bargaining.

I looked from one to the other, trying to see beyond their faces, and failing.

'Fine,' she said, smirking. 'Then we'll have a party.'

The following morning, seeing my expression, she said: 'Is that why you didn't come last night?'

She looked drawn and tired, but in her hand was a caterer's order book.

'It's just a party, Adèle,' she said.

'I wish you wouldn't plan things with him,' I said. I could hear my own voice and hated it. 'Why are you so excited about it?'

She lifted the order book, flapped it helplessly, and shrugged. 'I'm not. These are the things we have to do.'

'I heard you last night. You were flirting with him.'

She passed her hand across her mouth: for an awful moment I thought she was laughing, but the hand came away grim. She was too clever to say the dangerous thing that hovered between us. Her fingers tightened on the book. 'Have you considered the fact that I am doing this for us? For appearances?'

Her colour was high; the long autumn light slanted through the window.

She sighed – a small, unhappy sound – and picked at the cover of the order book. 'This is what people do, my love. They are seen.'

I hated this vision of myself. Didn't I want her to have whatever she wanted? So instead, I said as bravely as I could. 'Let's be seen.'

Her face cleared – relief – sun moving over a landscape; her face twisted into an uncertain smile.

'Our first argument,' she said, and smiled until at last I smiled back. She put the book away, and did not mention the party for two days.

On the third day, the wife of the Ex-Minister visited. She didn't send up a card and wait, she simply followed Thomas up to the salon and walked straight across to plant a firm kiss on Luce's cheeks. She didn't look at me.

'It's the talk of the town,' she said, eyes sparkling, 'your invitations arrived this morning. By ten o'clock I had a dozen phone calls asking me what you were going to wear.' She sat down on a pouffe, her eyes never leaving Luce's face. 'So what are you going to wear?'

Luce tried to laugh this off. 'I hadn't thought,' she said.

Aurélie crowed, and then turned to me: '*I hadn't thought!* Whatever are we to do with her, Mlle Roux? My love, all the young directors are coming. Everyone who has a film in prep will be there.'

She sat back, for effect. Luce turned white, then red. 'Really?' she said, as though disbelieving. 'Everyone?'

Aurélie leant forward, took her fingers in her knuckly hands. 'Everyone. So let's make a plan. Let's make you seductive.'

I held my breath until I could be calm again.

Later, I sat flipping through one of the fashion magazines she'd left; Luce was reading, with every appearance of tranquillity.

Without lifting her head, she said: 'She's only trying to help.'

When I didn't answer, she put her fingertips to her eyes. 'She thinks she's helping me, by inviting all these directors.'

'Isn't she?'

She lifted her head and stared at me. She had flushed bright red.

'I don't know what you mean,' she said.

'She's always helping you, isn't she?'

She stared at me.

'Adèle,' she said, 'she's my friend.'

I took a deep, shivering breath in; we looked at each other.

'It's just a party. Let's just get it out of the way,' she said, 'please.'

She kissed me there on the sofa without a thought for the servants. Then she laughed, bent me backwards and pushed up my skirts. 'You don't have anything to worry about,' she said.

14. octobre 1913

SHE INVITED ME to her room to prepare.

I changed quickly so that I could watch her put her make-up on; sat on the bed and pulled my knees up to my chin, savouring the moment.

She powdered her face with big, aggressive strokes; stared at her own reflection, eyes narrowed.

She smiled at me in the mirror.

'Welcome,' André said, walking forwards to the salon door with his hands wide. Standing next to me, Luce repressed a tremor of laughter; the first guest was the Duchesse de Guise.

As Luce did two kisses, the Duchesse's hawky eyes scanned the room. 'Charming,' she murmured, looking at the sparkling gold of the lights placed on every available surface, the sheen on the silk sofas and the obsidian gloss of the windows.

'You look well,' she said to Luce. 'What are you feeding her, André?'

André bowed his head. 'The finest foie gras.'

The Duchesse sniffed. 'The finest foie gras is from my estate in the Cévennes. Luce, your father never writes to me any more.'

André slugged back his champagne and excused himself. Luce said: 'May I present Mlle Roux?'

The Duchesse looked over my shoulder at the arriving guests. 'Oh! It's Aurélie Vercors.'

Luce looked at me, and dipped her eyes, left me and walked over to Aurélie.

The Duchesse peered at the Ex-Minister. 'Of course, he was in trade—'

I was watching Aurélie and Luce embrace, their torsos entwined from the breast upwards. 'Darling,' Aurélie said, pushing Luce away to search her face, 'you look delicious.' Luce gave her a small, brave smile that turned my stomach; put her hand on Aurélie's arm and led her away into the room.

'—ghastly little *arriviste*,' the Duchesse finished, with a last swallow of her champagne, and turning away from me, vanished into the swelling crowd.

People milled around me, talking. I looked around for André, but he was half in the hallway, welcoming guests.

A laugh made me look up. Aurélie and Luce were sitting on the window seat, facing each other, Aurélie telling a story, using her hands, and Luce had thrown her head back, tears of merriment in her eyes. Wiping them, she turned her head and looked at me, sprinkled her fingers to me – *come over*.

Next to her, Aurélie smiled thinly and without encouragement.

Flushed, I drained my champagne glass and looked at my feet. Luce's face turned blank – *please yourself* – and Aurélie leant forward to begin another anecdote.

Heads around me turned towards the door; there was an anxious murmuring. I craned to see who the new guest was, and saw Peyssac. But he didn't appear to have come unannounced: André was gravely shaking his hand, and Peyssac's eyes were darting around the room, settling on Luce and sliding away. The guests around them put their heads together and whispered behind their hands. André said something into Peyssac's ear; and with a final clap to his shoulder, he propelled Peyssac into the room and stood back, his face showing nothing.

Luce was sitting upright, her expression cold. Aurélie stopped talking and turned, put her fingers to Luce's arms and rested them there. I turned my face away.

A cough by my shoulder. Peyssac was there, his goatee bobbing anxiously. 'Mlle Roux. Might I have a private word?'

Luce's eyes on a point between my shoulder blades.

I said: 'Will the hallway be private enough?'

The noise level in the hall was softened, the light a yellow slit under the door. Peyssac stood, pulling at the rings on his fingers with his other hand. 'Mlle Roux, I have an indelicate request.'

I couldn't think what he meant: what was he doing, making a proposition in the hallway of someone else's house?

Peyssac looked at me, evidently discouraged by my stare, then said: 'I am afraid you will think the worse of me; but it is an idea that has been growing and growing in me since I first saw you at my apartments in the summer.'

I glanced at the light under the door. 'I don't know to what you're referring,' I said coldly, 'but please excuse me. I have to find someone.'

Peyssac stepped forward and took my hands in his, just hard enough to make them impossible to retract. I recoiled and he held on tighter.

'Forgive my clumsiness,' he said. 'You have, Mlle Roux, such an open quality: I cannot now consider anyone else in the role.'

Cold air on the back of my neck.

'You will think me despicable,' he said, rubbing his thumbs into my palms. 'I have you in mind for the heroine of *Petite Mort*. Oh, yes, you are quite right to look at me like that: the same part that your mistress wanted.'

With a last rub he released my hands. He was looking at me with an expression of pained eagerness.

'I haven't got any experience,' I said.

'You have the right look, and a natural elegance.'

Peyssac watched my face. He said: 'My girls go on to such wonderful things. To America, some of them, to Italy. My good friend Lily Lemoine, who started out in my pictures, has me to visit every year in her house on Como. She has other houses, of course, on the coast, in the south, where I believe you're from?'

Somewhere in the house a door opened and closed.

'I can't,' I said.

Peyssac's eyes glittered. 'I understand,' he said. 'But in the service of art, we are all compelled to be unscrupulous, are we not?'

He produced a card from his waistcoat, slipping it into my palm. 'Should you reconsider.'

With a gracious nod he insinuated himself back into the salon.

After a minute I was composed enough to go back to the party. When I opened the door, it seemed to me a hush had fallen. André was engaged in laughing conversation with some studio bosses.

For a good thirty seconds I pushed mindlessly through the crowd, looked anywhere but at her, and then gave in. She slithered off the seat and walked towards me; when she reached me, she took my arm and pulled me towards the door.

She marched me out into the hall and towards the stairs.

At the first landing she paused, but a giggling burst from behind one of the doors – some guests had evidently broken away from the main party. We walked on, up and up, until we were alone and everything around us was quiet.

She threw my wrist away from her and turned away, putting her hands up to cover her cheeks. 'What are you doing? In front of everybody.' Her eyes were huge in her face. 'Everybody was laughing at me! In my own house.'

Anger made me cold. 'I thought you didn't care about directors. So what if I talked to Peyssac? You didn't even notice I was gone!'

She stared at me through her fingers. 'She's my friend!'

'She wants you for herself! And you encourage her…'

She shook her head; I crossed to where she was, but she took me by the shoulders.

'What did Peyssac want?' she said.

'Nothing,' I said. A void had opened in my chest: I felt as if I'd crack in two.

She narrowed her eyes. 'What?' she said, giving me a little shake.

I shouted: 'Whatever he'd asked, I would have said no!'

I reached up and caught hold of her hands and did not let go.

Then she made a small sound, of abandonment and surrender: I pressed her against the wall of the corridor and kissed her.

I reached down and lifted her skirts around her waist. She was wet through the material of her petticoats.

I slipped my fingers inside her.

The sounds of her breathing, higher and higher—

All of her muscles tensed, poised on the brink, eyelids fluttering—

I knew immediately whose the footstep was, coming quietly up the stairs.

The top of André's head was visible on the landing beneath. If he looked up, he would see the hems of our skirts.

Not my room: he would check there, and how would we explain it?

Her eyes were wide; frozen open, fixed pleadingly on mine. I took her by the waist and half-dragged, half-walked her down the corridor. We reached the end of the passageway and I fished in my pocket for the ceramic key, and slotted it into the keyhole of the door by the window.

I pushed Luce through it and closed it as softly as I could

behind us, turned the key in the lock, and pressed my ear to the wood to listen.

André walked up the corridor as far as my room. I heard that door open; then it was closed softly.

There was absolute quiet for thirty seconds – I counted them. Behind me in the darkness, Luce held my fingers.

André's voice calling to her.

I tried not to breathe. Another eternity passed; my fingers convulsed on the door handle.

Eventually, there was the squeak of his hand running down the banister, and his feet jogging downstairs.

I turned to Luce: 'We'll say you needed a pin for your dress—' but stopped at the look on her face.

Through the window, there was a faint light from the lamps in the courtyard outside, and the objects I had seen when I visited the room before glowed grey: the lamp, tall as a wading bird; a couple of half-unpacked cartons, the crib.

This is the direction of her gaze: the wicker, hooded object, with its pale mattress leaking stuffing onto the floor. Her hands are clutching at themselves; she does not seem to really be in the room at all, and when I call to her she turns to look at me as if I were a stranger with bad news.

She falls without warning and without cushioning herself: her elbow hits a chest of drawers behind her with a crack, and she lies, knees bent, at my feet.

Then I am pulling her bodily into the corridor, as far towards the stairs as I can. I am looking at her eyes rolled up under the lids; calling for Thomas and seeing André's shocked face as he comes running up the stairs.

The door to Luce's room closed in my face, so I stood outside and leant on the banister to wait.

It wasn't possible to hear any detail – just low voices. Then a silence followed by a sharp cry. I started forward and hesitated, my knuckles poised to rap on the door – and then more talking.

Another silence. The door opened.

'What is it?'

André held the door open for the doctor. 'We've set her arm,' he said. 'She'll need to rest. But there'll be no lasting damage.'

15. octobre 1913

I TAPPED ON HER BEDROOM DOOR and opened it.

Wintry sunlight. Two pillows were propped behind her head, her hair spread on her shoulders; her arm in a sling.

I crossed to sit beside her; bent to kiss her. She put her arm up around my neck; we didn't speak for a long time.

Then she dried her eyes and said: 'They tell me I ruined the party.'

I pulled back. 'Don't you remember it?'

'No. I just remember waking up and being here, with the doctor. I've always been prone to fainting. And I can never remember what I've missed.'

She talked on and on; the words tumbled out, she lost her thread and found it again, watching for my reaction, all the time clutching my hand.

I stared at her, not recognising her.

I said: 'We were in the room at the end of the corridor. Something happened that startled you, and you fell.'

She looked fixedly at the window. At first I thought she was thinking. Then I saw that she was trying not to cry, the tears spilling out at the corner of each eye anyway.

'Tell me what it was,' I said.

Luce, iii.

For months, nobody saw the newlyweds. Autumn turned to winter; Paris expected its first glimpse of them at the Christmas balls, or skating on the Seine, and was disappointed. The house remained a blank gold façade; André sent his notes and ideas to Pathé by post.

In the spring came the news that took everyone by surprise: Luce was going to star in André's next film.

At first it was not believed. Was she not cheapening herself by dabbling in the fly-by-night art of circuses and fairgrounds?

For a few months everything went quiet. It was said, with a wink, that she had reconsidered. The city settled down again: she would turn her hand to tending roses and breeding horses, as every aristocratic wife did, and that would be the end of it.

Posters of *La Dame aux Roses* began to appear on the city walls and outside cinemas. The critics chewed their nails; but when the film print was finally released, it was clear that the venture was anything but foolish, and so everyone pretended to have known all along. *She dignifies the medium. She brings a finery to the coarseness of cinema. She is a star.*

She began to act, not just for André, but for Peyssac, Feuillade, Blaché. The months ran by, turning into three years of relentless happiness: riches, professional success, plenty. And then Luce found out they were going to have a baby.

It is five months into the pregnancy – June, 1908 – and she

is walking in the gardens behind the house. She is alone and exhausted by the extra weight she carries.

She has given up work because the bump was getting too hard to disguise. André wanted to tell everyone, but she would not allow it. So the journalists report that she is struggling with her childhood injury and has taken a leave of absence to recuperate. Nobody knows she is pregnant: not their friends, not their enemies – not even Aunt Berthe, who is a regular visitor now that Luce is famous.

André thinks she fears a miscarriage. Luce has let it slip that her mother suffered several, and so naturally he assumes she does not want anyone to know until she is almost to term. This is not the real reason for her secrecy.

Though it is still early summer, the day is very hot; the air is filled with the overpowering scent of flowers; she feels light-headed. So she walks to the fringe of the Bois and ducks under the branches. There is an old path here, blissfully shady; she follows it, pushing the branches aside with her fingers as she goes.

After half an hour the path ends at the last thing she expected: a wide pond, twenty metres across. She has never come this far into the woods before; she had no idea the pond was here.

She almost laughs because the water is dark and glossy; she is looking at the exact twin of a lake on her parents' estate in Normandy, which she had sat beside as a child.

How deep is the water here? She dips her toe; her shoe sinks through the water, to the ankle, to the calf, without touching the bottom.

How can she tell André the real reason she wants to keep the pregnancy a secret? How can she say *I'm worried I won't love the child*? She cannot. She cannot say, *Give me more time, lots more time before it's born, and I will be equal to it*, because she knows she will never be equal to it. It is like a dream from which she can't wake; and with each passing day, she feels the thing inside her grow closer.

She could easily slip here, on the mud of the bank; her belly might bump against the pond floor, or she might swallow enough water to bring about an accident.

She stands, tempted and indecisive. *For shame*, she thinks, but distantly: she could have her career back, her old life; everything will be as it was before. She could crawl back to the house, weed draped in her hair, and nobody need ever know the fall into the water was deliberate.

And the child isn't a child yet, is it?

Protesting, the baby kicks hard against her belly: the first time it has moved.

She pulls back from the lip of the pond and waits, fascinated, counting. Sure enough, ten seconds later, still reproachful but fainter, another kick.

As the baby kicks a third time, she finds herself flooded with the last thing she expects – not guilt, not irritation at this demand for attention, but worry for the child. Is it normal for it to kick so much? She puts her hands to her stomach and curves them around it protectively. The skin between her and the womb feels thin under her fingers. Who can she ask if this is normal?

Sadness and irony make her smile. Most women would ask their mothers. She turns and walks back to the house.

That night, André notices that the sparkle is back in her eyes. She goes to bed earlier than usual, kissing him chastely on the lips. He watches her go, relieved. He loves her, but recently he has not known how to help her; now he sees that whatever personal storm she was weathering has blown out to sea and away.

For the rest of the pregnancy Luce is covetous of each kick and murmur. She spends her days on the chaise longue, reading and resting as avidly as some people exercise, eating everything she is meant to eat; she passes the time imagining the baby. Now it is asleep in its permanent night, thumb jammed into its proto-mouth; now it is rotating, stub-fingers pressing the amniotic sac almost to breaking-point. *What will you be*, she wonders, *a man of money and ambition like your father? Or will you be like me?*

André is in his office when the note comes, in Dr Langlois's precise hand: *Labour commenced an hour ago*. He flings down his pen and whirls his coat round his shoulders. The guards watch him go, astonished: though he has wanted to crow the news from the rooftops since he first heard, André has still not told anybody at Pathé that he is about to be a father.

He feels the change as soon as he sets foot in his house. The servants are keeping downstairs, out of harm's way, and everything is very still. He runs up the stairs three at a time, up, up to the attic floor, where Thomas stands, holding a fresh bowl of water, outside the door of the confinement room.

The door is half open; André steps forward, suddenly unsure of himself, even on his own turf. Being an orphan, he has no map for this event: aren't fathers supposed to stay outside?

When he peeps round the open door, he sees Luce stretched – but really stretched, not just lying, every tendon arching in pain – out on the bed. The room smells of exertion. At the foot of the bed stands grey-haired Dr Langlois, peering into his wife, exhorting her with gentle murmurs, over which she screams and screams.

Dr Langlois sees André standing appalled on the threshold, and Luce's head turns to follow the doctor's look, so he receives both looks at the same time: the doctor smiling his reassurance and Luce baring her teeth. He does not know which to believe, but 'Perhaps you'll wait outside?' the doctor says, still encouraging and kind; so he does. Time passes slowly but at least it passes; the screams become weaker. 'That's a good sign,' he says to Thomas, 'she is in less pain, the baby's coming.'

They hear Dr Langlois' voice slightly raised, as though he is telling Luce off. Then the screams become fainter. André nods vigorously – they are almost there now. He does not care if it is a boy or a girl, doesn't care whether it is tall or small or gifted or plain, as long as it's theirs. The day is not quite gone; a pale streak lines the sky above the horizon but that is all.

The sound of crying, quickly stifled; but not a child's crying. Dr Langlois appears in the doorway, wiping blood into a cloth; not his blood.

'I'm sorry,' he says, still kindly, 'she's conscious, and she'll recover, but she has lost the baby.'

André smiles, polite and uncomprehending.

'Stillborn,' Dr Langlois says, shaking his head. He reaches out and puts one palm on André's shoulder, steadying him; the palm is damp.

André pushes past him and into the room. He won't believe a trick until he sees its outcome.

The thing is laid out on a chair, swaddled in its swaddling clothes up to the neck. Its features are all there – the mouth half open, the eyelids fat and closed – but an object more than a human. He expects it to burst into life and take a breath at any moment, but it persists in its silence and its stillness.

'It may have stopped growing a couple of months ago,' Dr Langlois tells him. André shakes his head to say, *But we were so careful*, thinking of Luce sitting beautifully on her couch; and then shakes his head again. He can't see anything of himself or of her in this tiny half-amphibian.

Luce watches André from the bed. She knows what has happened; tears ooze from under her eyelids. When they try to tell her some things about the baby – sex, size – she lets her face go blank, and doesn't hear them. Two days later André arranges a small funeral in the grounds of the house, which she does not attend.

But it isn't over, not yet. They tie her to the bed in the attic, and she forgets things: she forgets who André is and when he comes to sit beside her, she thinks it is a stranger, unpardonable in his rudeness, gripping her hand. *How dare you*, she hisses, and hearing how much like a stranger she has become herself, she laughs.

To try to make it clear to her, they move the empty crib they had bought for the baby into her room. Every day a doctor comes and asks her: *Do you know what this is? Do you remember what it was meant to be for?* Sometimes she thinks she has become an animal: a cat or a wolf or an owl, staring at her own sleeping form on the bed from the other side of the window. She learns to slip the knots around her wrists, and goes wandering through the attics, chafing the skin of her hands to warm the joints, she walks up and down the corridor, thinking she has heard the baby calling for her. But when Thomas comes to fetch her he tells her it is only an owl hooting, and there it is − bluish and terrifyingly large in the moonlight − perched on the windowsill, looking in at her. *I did hear the baby*, she hears herself insisting. Deferential, with a bob of the head, the owl slips off the sill and takes flight; Thomas smiles − *Madame, take your medicine* − and she watches fascinated: the owl's wings move mechanically, a stage prop flying away.

When they escort her downstairs, she is surprised to see that it is still autumn, or autumn again. André's hand is on her arm, guiding her; at her questioning look, he nods: yes, a year has passed.

Everything looks frail but familiar. The chaise longue is as it was, but wafer thin in the pale afternoon light; the desks, chairs are watery and sly; even the books on the shelves seem to be holding their secrets away from her.

From this she deduces that she is still not quite well.

André is in the room, in another chair, but she doesn't know what to say to him. A year!

She knows the stillbirth was her fault, because she had once thought of killing it, and someone, somehow, knew.

It is time André was made aware; it is carrying this secret which has kept her chained to the bed. She opens her mouth to tell André, but feels his hand laid over her own, a warning to keep quiet.

The silence runs down from their joined hands and over them and spreads out over the carpet, blending with the sunset, which is unexpectedly fiery and distinct. They sit like statuary of a king and a queen, saying nothing to each other. Eventually the silence fills the whole house.

Juliette, v.

The man from public records sighs; it's his lunch hour.

He says: 'The cottage that is currently owned by Mme Ruillaux was built in 1930.'

I scribble 1930 on my pad; prop the telephone in the crook of my shoulder and ask: 'By whom?'

Another sigh. 'A M. Undin. But he never lived there; he was an absentee landlord. According to this, it was occupied on a short-term basis until 1945, when M. Undin was killed. Mme Ruillaux bought it at auction.'

I ask: 'How short-term?'

'The tenants changed every year or two.'

'Can you see anything about their occupations?'

He sounds affronted. 'Of course. This is Public Records.'

'Is there anyone who worked at the Pathé factory?'

I imagine him running his finger down a list of names. 'I'm sorry. There's nothing here that I can see.'

'There's no connection? No wife or husband or other tenants?'

'I'm sorry. No.'

I say: 'Can you send me the list of names anyway?'

16. novembre 1913

WHILE HER ARM HEALED, she stayed in bed, and I went to read to her every afternoon.

But she was not quite herself. I chose passages from Zola, to which she listened with a kind of pained attention, as if she were trying to tether herself to the room.

Sometimes, out of nowhere, her breathing became raucous, as if she was drowning in front of me. 'Is it because of the child?' I'd ask; and she'd nod. She would clutch at my hand; I would scream for Thomas, and he'd come running, bringing wet cloths, and smelling salts.

Afterwards we would sit in silence. If I tried to talk to her, about the baby, she would shake her head, squeeze her eyes tight shut, and the tears would come so quickly that I gave it up; pressed her hand and shushed her.

Once, I climbed into the bed beside her. We made love quickly, and afterwards she slept.

In early November she came downstairs.

She stood in the middle of the salon, held her arms out in front of her and smiled. 'I'm so thin,' she said.

I told her the truth, which was that she looked luminous.

She smiled shyly, as if she didn't know whether or not to believe me.

Visitors came. Aurélie, every couple of days, once with a bouquet of flowers so enormous it obscured her face; the

Duchesse de Guise, to sit poker-straight and bemoan the passing of moral rectitude; other women, actresses and friends, whom I had never met before.

André stayed at home. When I passed him in the corridor, he would blow theatrically on his hands and say 'It's too cold to go to the studio.' Nevertheless, he always seemed to be on the way to his study, so I had no doubt he was working on something; besides which, he too had visitors, workmen holding their caps and looking at the fine plasterwork, and Pathé bosses, clearing their throats and waiting for Thomas to take their umbrellas, almost every day, sometimes spending long hours in the study with him, and often staying for supper with us.

He talked openly about *Petite Mort* at the dinner table – the process of arranging the sets, selecting the actors, finding a reliable cameraman – his guests nodding with rapt attention.

Luce ate quietly, seeming indifferent to everything that was said.

At night, it was like a door opening: she spoke to me more. She told me what she was feeling; told me things from her past without my asking; in bed, she told me what she liked and didn't like, in a constant, hoarse whisper, as if we were not the only ones in the room, and she was rough: not with me, with herself. Intermingled with her words were reckless terms of endearment: *My only one. My right hand.*

One night, she took my fingers and curled them into a fist; I pulled away.

I had promised myself I wouldn't cry as long as she was like this. But suddenly I couldn't help it. 'I can't do this,' I said. 'I don't understand what's wrong with you. It's like you don't even see me.'

She had lain down on her back again; now her head turned towards me. Her breathing slowed; not the panicked whispering I'd grown used to.

'I do see you,' she said.

I reached for her hands. 'We have to go away. You'll be all right if you're not in this house.'

She squeezed my fingers in hers: listening.

'Somewhere nobody would know us,' I said.

She took a breath. 'What would we do for money?'

'Spend yours.'

She said: 'It's in André's name.'

'I'll work. I'll make costumes, or clean. I don't care.'

She looked at me critically. 'You don't care at all?'

'Anything.'

She laughed. 'Then it's easy, isn't it?'

The laugh she gave was wild, but I didn't hear that. I heard her saying yes.

Aurélie visited again, and more often, and spent as much as an hour with Luce, sitting, holding her hand and talking in low voices. I welcomed her warmly and offered to make myself scarce, because I had a secret. Even André's whistling and constant presence could not touch my mood: I smiled at him over supper, and laughed at his jokes – laughed for the two of us.

In bed at night, I closed my eyes and gave myself over to calculation. Nearing Christmas, the house was awash with money: gold brocade hung from the banisters, and boxes of expensive fancies arrived every day in preparation for the Ice Ball which they held every New Year. But none of it was cash. Luce and I spent our afternoons making paper chains, whilst I wondered out loud, turning our problem over and over.

She still had sudden fits of panic. She would clutch my hands and shut her eyes tight; but when I asked her what was wrong, she only pressed her lips into a line and shook her head.

'We will really go away,' she said.

'Of course,' I said. 'Of course,' and smiled back at her, happy to see her face clear. 'Now let me think.'

I closed my eyes and let the winter sunlight play over my eyelids, making shapes like a child's kaleidoscope. And in time the plan unfurled as if it had always been dormant in my mind, only wanting an opportunity to be exercised.

31. décembre 1913

NEW YEAR'S EVE: the coldest in living memory. It was too cold for wind, for clouds; the trees rocked silently in the cradle of their roots. Birds fell from the sky in the icy Paris night and, of course, it was the day Aleksandr Romanov died. The ageing Russian princeling was found frozen to death in a gutter in the Latin Quarter, his fingers curled around a bottle of vodka, wearing nothing but a top hat and a happy grin.

In the house, every lamp was lit from eight o'clock in the morning; for warmth, and because there was the Ice Ball to prepare for. Though the guests were not due to arrive till seven, lanterns must be strung to light the path to the lake; refreshments must be prepared and carried out, tray by painstaking tray. A car arrived from Paris with a hundred pairs of ice skates; servants flew to and fro; I flattened myself against the wall on the stairs as Thomas and André supervised the carrying down of a trestle from the upper floors.

Hoping for a moment alone with Luce, I looked for her, and found her by the French windows leading out onto the lawn. She stood, eyes wide, hands clasped at her front, giving directions to a pack of maids.

There was nothing to be done; the maids looked at me too, pink-cheeked and expectant. 'Carry on,' I said, and she turned gratefully back.

It didn't matter. Today was for biding my time.

At five o'clock the sun fell from the sky. Inky blue on the

horizon, then black; I watched from the window seat of my room. A solitary maid worked her away along the string of lanterns leading out across the lawn, lighting each one.

Just before seven, the slam of carriage doors; shouts of laughter; hail-fellow-well-mets from the front of the house. Then the sounds were sucked down the central corridor and with an *Isn't this charming*, the first guests emerged onto the terrace at the back of the house, underneath my bedroom window.

It *was* charming. The terrace was flooded gold with torch-light. With a surge, the lawn was suddenly filled with people: shadows walking towards the wood. The going was picky: a woman-silhouette leant on her husband's shoulder, cackling, as she struggled along in her delicate shoes.

Then came the knock I had been waiting for.

'M. et Mme Durand are making their way to the lake now,' Thomas said.

'Thank you.' I smiled at him for the first time in months. He shut the door. I turned back to the window, and sure enough, there they were: André, with Luce on his arm.

He was sleek in his black overcoat. She was wearing furs, under which shone a white dress that I had never seen before. The bodice glittered with tiny jewels.

I slipped down from the window seat, crept down the stairs and along the corridor to André's study. A piece of luck: the door was unlocked. I had brought a candle, so that nobody would see the electric light and wonder who was in the room; I crossed to his desk and started pulling at the drawers, looking for the stack of money, or something like it, that I had seen him count out before. The first drawer opened without resistance. It was empty.

Then the second drawer; a spare pen and ink-pot rattled, and a third item. I held it up to the light: tiny and golden.

I stood in the darkness, turning the little key over and over in my fingers, wondering what it could unlock. All I knew about theft came from films, where the burglar would tiptoe into the house, pause to peer greedily at the sleeping demoiselle, then creep into the library and find a safe located behind some exquisite painting.

I moved about the room, thinking; and my eye fell on the portait hanging over the mantelpiece. I raised the candle: green swamp, gold sky – and wondered how I could have missed it the first time. That knowing smirk belonged to Caroline Durand: the portrait was the portrait from the story.

Could it be that simple? I thought how André might like to hollow out Caroline as she had hollowed him out. I slipped my hand behind the frame, looking for a catch or a lock; and with a flick of one finger the painting swung away from the wall. I laughed under my breath as I slotted the little key into the metal locker set into the plaster and opened the safe door.

A sheaf of papers at the front. I pulled out the tottering stack and held the leaves up to the light one by one. Deeds to the house; the purchase of an automobile; a marriage certificate, which I considered burning, then put back in place.

At the back of the safe, my fingers felt wafery paper; I pulled out a tightly bound bundle and found it was not money, but what looked like a will. I scrabbled with my fingers at the back of the safe: there was no cash in there.

I went to slam the locker door shut, piqued, when my fingers brushed another object: cold metal, which I had first thought was part of the inside of the safe.

I drew the revolver out into the light and studied its snub nose, its brutal little tongue. For a moment I considered taking it, for its workmanship, strictly to the purpose and nothing more, struck me as beautiful – but then I reconsidered. It would be better for André not to notice anything was missing. Laying it back in its place, I shut the safe door, blew out the candle and crept from the room.

~

The cold was edged: my breath froze into a cloud before my face as I joined the last of the guests heading for the lake.

I was the only person walking on their own – all the rest were couples, and nobody spoke to or looked at me. After twenty aching minutes, we were suddenly at the fringe of the Bois. The lanterns showed us how the path straggled in under the eaves of the woods; there were giggles and fallings-over, as the ladies of the party grappled with the uneven ground. Then the track broadened out, and suddenly we were on the edge of a white clearing.

From behind me I heard a chorus of well-bred *oohs* and *aahs*. The lake's frozen surface was perfect, violet from the moonlight and streaked gold from the lanterns strung in the branches overhanging the banks; the trees closed in on every side. The ice was already covered in skaters, zipping adroitly here and there, insects to flowers. A long table for refreshments was stationed on the far bank: steam rose from a vat and behind the table I could just make out Thomas standing watching the scene. Set a little further back was a bonfire, just beginning to take; a couple of ladies had already retreated nearby, holding their hands out to warm them.

I looked around for Luce, and saw her standing with André in the very centre of the lake, in a knot of admirers. She was laughing at a joke or an aside; her hand still resting on André's wrist. As I watched, André leant forward to add a bon mot and she, along with the other guests, threw her head back in laughter. She turned to watch André tell the rest of his anecdote, her face shining, her fingers gripping his arm, her lips rouged.

It was strange: like going back in time to before her illness.

As I wondered what to do, how to approach her, a footman tapped me on the shoulder. 'Skates, Mademoiselle?'

I said yes, and stared as he put a pair of white boots in my hands; the blades were clean but hungry-looking. But the only way to Luce was across the lake, so I bent and struggled into them, and placed one tentative foot on the ice.

Immediately the world tilted. *Steady*, laughed a man as he whooshed past me. I put another foot down, and stood, wobbly-legged, on the ice; tried to advance, picking up each boot as though walking. *Careful*, another man said impatiently – I glimpsed his flashing eyes as he whirled away, arms laced behind his back.

Why hadn't I been born rich, so that winter sports were second nature? I gazed at Luce, willing her to turn and see me. *Darling*: but she was talking now, engaged in a story, her gloved hands moving in the air.

The inevitable happened. A lady shrieked as she cannoned into my sprawled body; her skates missed my outstretched fingers by half an inch.

Firm hands gripped me under the arms and hauled me upright; clever eyes staring at me from a lean, weather-lined face.

'All right?' said Aurélie Vercors. 'No bones broken? Back on the horse,' and, her fingers tightening on my forearm, she pulled me after her. 'That's it,' she said, as, despite myself, my ugly-duckling stumble drew out into smooth strokes, 'just let yourself go.'

'I have to speak to Luce,' I said.

'Not until you can put one foot in front of the other,' she said brightly. She was wearing a fur-trimmed grey dress, her hair drawn back into a tight bun.

My skates made a sound like scissors as we moved over the ice.

'Good,' Aurélie said. 'You're a natural.'

She moved with absolute ease. On our second circle, she jerked her chin at Louis, standing alone on the bank, watching us nervously, still wearing shoes. 'He doesn't skate. Too much thin ice in politics as it is.'

I didn't even smile. Luce was still invisible behind the knot of guests.

'What is your plan, Mlle Roux? Are you going to storm over there, and fall as you reach her, and give André the satisfaction?' Bright eyes watched me from above her Roman nose. 'A scene is never worth one's time. We will stay back, like this, and choose your opportunity with caution.'

I could not think of a single intelligent thing to say to this. We skated on.

'Refreshments,' Aurélie said. We had reached the drinks table. She snapped her fingers to Thomas, who passed her two cups of mulled wine. 'Now come and sit with me on the bank.'

She tugged me over to the firm ground and helped me climb a way up the bank. I wrapped my hands gratefully round the mug and peered through the steam.

'Come in under the eaves, the view's better,' she said, and without waiting for an answer she grabbed my hand and led me a little way under the tree line.

There was nobody else about; the trees extended into the darkness behind me. Aurélie was right: we were afforded an excellent vantage point. From here it was possible to see the entire canvas, the way the whirling lights and shadows combined. I had never thought of Aurélie as someone who could appreciate the form of things.

'So,' she said, 'here you are alone, when by rights every person with eyes in their head should be asking you to skate.' She spoke without pity: merely outlining a problem.

'How did you – did she—' I asked.

'She didn't have to tell me. It was obvious, if you know her as well as I.'

There was a little pause. I turned back to the problem at hand.

'She has to be her social self tonight,' I said uncertainly. I wished I could believe that was all it was: just camouflage.

'Oh, no doubt.' Aurélie swirled her wine and looked out

over the frozen lake; laughed as a large woman in furs fell over, arse in the air and her red round face angry, and began shouting at her husband.

'It never ceases to amaze me how people who are born rich carry on,' she said. 'It's as if the world should be perpetually to their liking.'

'I thought—'

She watched me over the rim of her cup, dark eyes twinkling. 'My parents were grocers in Orléans.'

'And now?'

'Now I'm married to a bore. But I have security, my books, my stables and I find that I can watch those people out on the lake and not mind if they hardly see me.'

'She's different,' I said. 'She isn't herself. She hasn't been for a few weeks.'

'And why do you think that is?'

'I don't know. I can't think how to help her.' It was surprisingly easy to talk to her, sitting here away from the rest of the world.

'Here,' she said, taking off her stole and reaching across to wrap it snugly round my shoulder.

'It's been since the faint,' I said. 'I can't seem to get her to listen. Sometimes she's there and sometimes she's not. And then, things like tonight—'

'She seems to pick and choose who she is.'

'Yes.' I blushed. But there was a warm feeling, too, the spice of the disloyalty.

'So what are you going to do about it?'

'I don't know.' I thought unhappily of the empty safe. The plan seemed stupid – out of reach and childish. I turned to look at Luce. She was talking to someone else now: as animated as I had ever seen her.

'In the meantime, what about you?'

The wine had made my cheeks hot; I pressed my palms to them to cool down.

She murmured: 'It seems there are a lot of things you're not sure of.'

She reached for my hands, and folded them in hers, and gave them a squeeze. 'That big house, and André so very present all the time,' she said. 'I suppose you must ask yourself: *How long am I prepared to wait?*'

'I don't know,' I said again. She was still holding my hands loosely in hers. It was more for something to say, than anything else: I felt dull, and tired. It was as if the wine had drawn a curtain between us and the rest of the party, skating in endless loops.

She drew a pattern on the back of my hand with her thumb. 'One must wonder how many other opportunities one may miss along the way?'

Her look was lowered; at first I didn't understand. Then she looked up, and the old Aurélie was clearly visible in the cast of the lips.

I pulled my hands away. She knew then that she had miscalculated; she licked her lips. 'But wouldn't you agree, we only regret the chances we didn't take?'

I stepped back, away from her clutching hands, towards the ice.

She smiled her lemon-slice smile, followed me forward and gripped my wrist, and we stood like that, in tension, running away impossible.

Her voice was a low murmur: 'She'll wring you out and run back to what she knows – it's how she is built.'

'You don't know anything about us. She loves me.'

There was something like tenderness on her face. At the same moment, the crowd parted and I saw Luce, laughing and talking, not ten feet away, a circle of admiring, fashionable women around her.

'Come now,' Aurélie said. 'Did you really think you were her first?'

~

I stepped off the bank and half-skated, half-staggered as fast as I could across the ice. From the corner of my eye, Luce turning, confused, to watch me go.

On the other side of the lake, I took my skates off and started back down the path towards the house.

I had reached the lawn before I heard her footsteps behind me, looked around and found her close enough to touch.

She moved round till we were facing each other; stood watching me, her chest rising and falling. She looked like the person I had thought was mine, the person I had met in the salon all those months ago: her face lovely with exercise, her eyes sparkling from all the fine conversation and clever jokes.

'Why didn't you tell me about Aurélie?'

Her eyes widened. I saw it clearly now, how she darted here and there, looking for the right thing to say.

'It was a long time ago. Nothing.' Her eyes cut downwards. 'Why, what did she say?'

'That you use people up and let them go. Is that what you did to her? Were you in love with her? Are you still together now?'

'No,' she said. 'No, it wasn't like that.'

I shake my head. 'What haven't you told me? What's going on now, that you won't tell me about?'

She closed her eyes, tight: but not before I had seen something flicker in them.

I slapped her. A casual, arcing blow, but hard, because it made the small bones of my hand hum.

Her head snapped sideways; she put her hand to her cheek to test for blood; finding it, she put her fingertip experimentally to her tongue, and was her old self again; all the way back, wiping out everything, to the person I had seen being expelled from Pathé, eyes narrowed and glittering. In the distance, the pop and fizz of New Year fireworks bursting over Paris.

Juliette and Adèle
1967

Adèle looks out of the window, watching something else.

At last, she takes a sharp breath in. 'But you said you had something to ask me,' she says.

I slide the list of names the man from Public Records had sent me across the table. She reaches for her handbag, extracts a pair of reading glasses, and perches them on the end of her nose.

'What am I looking at?' she asks.

'These are all the people who lived in Anne Ruillaux's house before her.'

'Anne Ruillaux being the lady who handed in the film canister?'

I say: 'Correct. Can you tell me if you recognise any of them? The man from Public Records said they had no connection with Pathé, but I just thought one of them might be familiar.'

She studies the sheet. Slides it back across the table.

She says: 'No. I'm sorry. I don't recognise anyone.'

She watches me for a few seconds. 'When I have a problem, I turn the telescope around. Look at it from the reverse angle. Start again from the beginning, or recommence at the end. Might that be of some assistance here?'

I put my fingers to my temples and press inwards. 'I'm not sure.'

'What is the beginning of the mystery? When was the last time anyone saw the film?'

'During the fire at the Pathé factory,' I say. And look up at her.

Juliette, vi.

The Pathé archivist beams when she catches sight of me, her pointed face opening.

She walks towards me, carrying a box-file, and puts it on my desk.

'The Pathé fire of 1914,' she says. 'This is everything.'

'Thanks.' I pull the box towards me and lift the lid.

She hovers. 'Is this to do with the missing film?'

I am leafing through the newspaper articles about the fire — *Inferno at Pathé factory* — *Workers evacuated* — *No fatalities*…

'They started the fire,' I say. 'The person who stole the print set the factory on fire to cover up the theft. I'm sure of it.'

The archivist frowns. 'But the papers all said the fire was an accident.'

'It's the only way the thief could be sure nobody would know the film had been stolen. This way, everyone would assume it had just been destroyed along with everything else. It wouldn't even be missed, and nobody would come looking for him. And you have the records, don't you?'

The archivist stares. 'But nitrate cellulose is so flammable. The reaction generates its own oxygen, so it just burns and burns. When a film reel caught fire at the Paris Bazaar in 1897, the fire continued for days. A hundred people died.'

I say: 'You mean whoever started the fire couldn't be sure the firemen would be able to put it out? Without loss of life?'

'Yes. Whoever it was must have been really desperate.'

She looks down with distaste at the papers arranged in a fan on my desk.

'He's in there somewhere,' she says. 'Your ruthless person.'

5. janvier 1914

I'D DREAMED OF HOW this would feel; the cosmetician asking me to bend my head a little to the right, and with deferential flicks of her wrist she dusted my right cheek with powder. Then she invited me to offer a pretend kiss to the mirror, and painted my lips, and then put kohl just underneath my eyes, which wavered away from their own reflected gaze.

'All done,' she said, starting to replace her pots and unguents in her make-up case with precision and fastidiousness. Everything in its proper place.

I wanted to ask her to stay with me until it was time to go to the stage, but she kept her back to me. I heard the snap of the clasps fastening her bag, and she left the room without saying anything else.

The dressing room is quiet apart from the ticking of the pipes overhead. I put my palms on my knees and listen to my own breathing.

A knock at the door: the camera assistant. 'It's time.'

It had taken me a few attempts to get through to Peyssac on André's study telephone; a few tries to understand how the dialling worked, and which end one picked up. And then I had to choose my moment, before the household was properly awake and I could be interrupted.

Peyssac's early-morning-peevish voice came through on the crackling line: 'Yes? Who is it, please?'

'It's Adèle Roux.'

I thought: *Perhaps he won't remember me.*

A hush, as he considered. 'How wonderful to hear your voice again.' The delicacy of the pause. 'And do you have good news for me?'

'Yes.'

'Delightful. So pleased.'

Another pause. What do you say to a co-conspirator?

'Can you be free in two days' time, say, at nine in the morning? We will arrange for a car. And – given your situation – yes, I think we can complete your scenes in a single day. Nobody need know until such time as you choose to tell them.'

'Thank you.'

I was about to hang up when I thought of the money; I'd need it if I was going to live independently again. 'I will want to be paid,' I said.

Miles away, Peyssac spluttered. 'Of course! Your wages will be available to be collected at the Pathé offices, the day after filming, as is customary.'

I replaced the receiver without saying goodbye.

The night before the filming, I packed my valise and slid it under the bed. Straightening up, I hesitated, listening.

Then shook my head: of course that sound was not footsteps, coming to my room. It was only the floorboards complaining as the house tacked into the wind.

'That is our final shot. Thank you, everyone.' Peyssac bounces forward, hands clasped. 'Mlle Roux. Words cannot express – it has been an honour. I do most fervently hope we will work together again.'

The cameraman is turning away, collapsing the tripod. Extras mill about, chatting, getting out cigarettes. The light coming through the studio roof is tinged with pink.

In the dressing room, I am left alone to remove my make-up:

the Vaseline in long, greasy smears; the kohl, picking at it with watery cloths to get it out of the creases under my eyes.

At the factory gates I get into the car Peyssac has provided: the latest model, its engine builds to a roar before we purr away.

The streets unribbon. At a greengrocer's, I see Mathilde. Her spidery fingers are engaged in examination of fruit – she holds a plump apple up, inspecting it for bruises, then drops it satisfied into her string bag and looks up, scanning about her for the next thing.

I raise my fingers to wave to her: she sees me, her head turning as the car passes; her face too unlined, her dress too fine – it cannot be her after all. Not-Mathilde: not someone I knew. The woman turns away, crossly, as if I have offended her.

When I get home there is a fluttering sound: looking up into the curve of the stairwell, hundreds of sheets of paper are floating down towards me with a sound like wings.

A silk slipper is discarded on the lowest step; its fellow has been hurled further, and lies on its side under the console table.

Thomas comes hurrying down, his carefully professional face disarranged. 'Come quickly,' he says, loops round and starts to run back up, with me in his wake.

I hop over a pair of silver-backed hairbrushes balancing on the steps. At the visible destruction something in my chest has begun to flutter inconveniently: by the top of the stairwell, the walls are lurching. *Can it be*, they ask, *that with your stubbornness you have finally made her candid?*

'Your valise had gone, so naturally she feared you had gone with it,' Thomas says. He pushes at his brilliantined hair as he stands outside the salon door. 'She will expect you to explain.'

Without waiting for me to tell him that the valise was only pushed out of sight, he opens the door inwards for me to go in.

The twin vases from the mantel have smashed, eggshell on the floor; books have been torn from the shelves and had their spines viciously broken. The writing table where I used to sit is an insect on its back with the legs snapped off. The only intact object in the room is the sofa where I used to sit, and this is where Luce is.

She doesn't hear me come in: she is rubbing her face as though she wants the top layer of skin gone.

When she removes her hands, she forgets to be angry: her eyes fill up with grateful tears, and then she remembers, composing her face.

'I'm so tired of being tired,' she says.

Above her cheekbone there is still a bruise the colour of parchment.

She says: 'With Aurélie, I had something, very briefly, a few years ago. I wasn't myself, and I got better, and then it wasn't important – at least, not to me. We carried on as before, and I tried to make it all right with her; but she's never let me forget it, and now I don't know if we're even friends. I think I knew, unless I was careful, she would bring me trouble in the end. And now she has.' A breath in. 'I should have told you.'

Trees sway silently outside the window. It's my chance to tell her where I have been. I want to say everything. How abandoned I felt when the make-up went on, sitting alone in the dressing room; how I could only think of how she would do this gesture, look in that mirror. Of how in another world she would be proud of me, playing this part.

I will say it. But before I can open my mouth, she says: 'I think it's time, isn't it? I really think we ought to go away.'

Silently, from one fraction of a second to the next, in the great wash of relief, I let the chance of a confession pass. I will tell her when we are right away from here. Sitting on a beach, her knees bent under her, massaging a grey pebble as we look out across the Pas de Calais, she will pre-empt: *Did you think I didn't know you'd been to the studios? It never mattered.*

She is looking up at me. 'Or have I burned my bridges?'

I poke at a shard of smashed vase with my toe. 'You seem to have been burgled.'

She looks at me, dazed and miserable.

I say: 'When we live together, we'll get better locks.'

She looks at her feet and smiles, private at first, then wide open.

Then she says: 'As soon as we can. Tomorrow, if possible. Is it possible?'

The last thing I expect, and the thing I most want: the sooner the better, for the less chance for the gossip to leak out of Pathé. Nevertheless, I'm so surprised by my good luck that I don't quite know what to say. Was Aurélie right? Will she always pull her fingers back at the last minute and run to what she knows?

But look, look at the broken things all around us.

'There is a small sum of money which is due to me,' – this is the best I can do with the Pathé wage office – 'that can be withdrawn tomorrow morning.'

She starts to laugh and cry, wiping impatiently at her eyes.

That night, in her room, we plan.

'We'll get right away at first,' she says, 'until the dust has settled and' – she takes a shivering breath in – 'we can come back to Paris.'

She smiles; turns her face away. 'We need some out-of-the-way, unfashionable place.' She snaps her fingers and spins round. 'England!' she says. 'We can take the boat at Calais.'

'I don't have a passport.'

Her face falls. 'Calais, then.'

'We can't use Hubert to get to the station. Nobody must know where we've gone.'

She bites the ragged skin at the corner of her thumbnail.

'We'll hail a cab from the road.'
    'What about our suitcases? Won't Thomas see us leaving?'
    'I'll ask him to clear out the back bedrooms.'
    We stand facing each other.
    'Don't worry,' she says. 'This will work.'

6. janvier 1914

HOW THE GARDEN LOOKED from my window that morning: silvery mint-coloured, the blades of grass curled over under their coating of frost. I didn't feel it. What I yearned for was for the day to have already gone to plan.

I turned back to my valise and snapped the clasps shut. The sound was encouraging: definite and businesslike. I dusted my damp palms on my skirt and, going to my bedroom door, opened it a crack to listen, nudging my untouched breakfast tray out of the way with my toe.

The squeak of door hinges, the chatter of servants swelling and dimming as the door swung to. Luce and André must still be at breakfast. I waited; a minute, two minutes passed, and my neck began to twinge from the odd position; then I heard the scrape of a chair being pushed back and André's voice, saying something over his shoulder, and his steps up the stairs. I drew back; heard a door open and close – his study – and then footsteps going back down. In the hall, I heard the rustle of cold-weather clothes, him whistling, and the front door clunk open; the buzz of the car engine, the slam of the door, and he was gone.

I heard Luce calling; walked down the stairs to the second landing. She was standing on the landing below; her upturned face was worried.

'A visitor is coming to the house. He'll be here at half-past eleven.'

'But that doesn't matter. We can wait until he's gone.' André would not be back until the evening. 'We can still catch the two o'clock train. It doesn't matter, does it?' I said.

'Oh. Not at all.'

'Just don't let him to stay to lunch.'

She nodded.

We had been whispering, but a door closing somewhere on the ground floor made me suddenly mindful of standing out in the open. I blew her a kiss to encourage her; she gave a little shiver of nerves and a smile, turned and walked away down the stairs.

I waited till she was gone, then walked down the stairs to the ground floor. I heard Thomas in the salon, crossed the hall and rapped on the door. Pretend-confidence made my voice quiver as I asked him to fetch Hubert.

As he reached the door, worry made me add: 'Mme Durand wants me to fetch her scripts personally from the studio.'

I knew at once it was a misstep, giving so much needless information. But all he said was, 'Right away, Mademoiselle.'

I sat on one of the salon chairs, staring out of the window until the car slid past; Hubert's steps outside the door; I ran to meet him.

I thought at first that he looked surprised to see just me, and not Luce – and then shook myself down inside – he was only surprised to be called so early, and those were just toast crumbs he was wiping from his mouth. 'To Pathé, please,' I said demurely as he held the car door open.

As the car crunched down the gravel drive I turned and looked up at the windows, hoping perhaps she would be watching us go.

'Just you today?' Hubert said, his eyes big in the rear-view mirror.

'Just me.'

He nodded, and flexed his hands on the steering wheel.

~

It was clocking-in time when we got to the factory. I looked at the sea of workers milling about outside and wondered how I had ever thought they looked happy. They turned thin, unfriendly faces to peer into the car as Hubert fired the horn; I looked at my lap, fearful of seeing someone I knew.

'Here is fine.' I jumped down from the cab and crossed the courtyard to the tiny administrative lodge on the right-hand side.

Knocking and entering, I found four small desks in a cramped room piled high with all kinds of papers. A man in spectacles looked up.

'I have come to collect monies that M. Peyssac left me. Adèle Roux.'

He peered at me. His hand hovered over a stack of ledgers on his overcrowded desk and he finally picked one up and, licking his finger, leafed through it. 'Now, now, let's see—' He looked through; turned the volume the other way up, squinted, and returned it to its original direction. 'When would the entry be for?'

'It was only yesterday.'

'Oh, *yesterday*.' He dropped the ledger; picked up a second, sighed heavily and began to leaf through. 'My colleague was here yesterday, not me. Let's have a look.'

More hemming and hawing. I thought of Hubert, leaning against the car bonnet, smoking; of André, very close perhaps, maybe even on his way to the studio from his office in Building I.

'This is most irregular,' the old man was saying, 'normally we don't release any wages until the filming is completed. Adèle Roux, Adèle Roux, I don't see it here.'

I could have closed my hands around his scrawny throat. Trying to keep my voice calm, I said: 'M. Durand is my employer and he requires it.'

The man looked up under his eyebrows. 'But in that case,

he would have countersigned the request.'

Another worker, a woman, looked up from her desk at me. I said: 'Find him. Ask him.'

The muscles in my throat tightened: what if he did really find André? What then?

The man pursed his lips. The woman looked down at her correspondence.

'On this occasion,' he said. He remained tight-lipped as he picked his way across the room to a box-safe in the corner. With agonising slowness he unlocked, counted out notes, recounted and fumbled about for an envelope. The clock on the wall read ten past ten; eleven past; twelve past, until at last he passed the envelope to me.

I counted it in front of him. 'Thank you,' I said, as crisp as the notes I held, and left the office.

Coming towards me across the courtyard was a redhead: Paul the security guard. I turned away, but it was too late: he was raising his hand and calling out to me. He broke into a jog and reached me as I reached the car.

'Congratulations!' he said. 'I heard about *Petite Mort*. Does that mean you'll be back more often now? As an actress?'

His face was all eagerness and goodwill.

I got into the car without a word.

I knew something was wrong as soon as we turned into the drive. Parked up in front of the house were two cars: an unfamiliar Daimler – this must belong to Luce's guest – and then André's studio car and his regular chauffeur, standing by the bonnet, squinting up into the winter sun in his dark uniform, the plume of his cigarette streaming skywards; he waved silently to Hubert, who saluted back, and drew our car round in a wide circle to park next to it.

'Why is M. Durand here?' I asked, leaning forward. 'Whose is the other car?'

'How should I know? Perhaps he's come home early.'
Hubert walked round to open the door for me.

Silence in the hall. I took the steps two at a time. There was
nobody in the first-floor corridor, so I ran lightly down towards
the salon door, which was closed. As I approached, I heard
voices from the inside of the room: I laid my ear to the panels
very gently. A stern, authoritative voice, holding forth about
something, the words impossible to make out: then André – I
jumped at how close he was, only a few feet from the other side
of the door – asking a question, then Luce, irritably countering
something; then the first voice again, making peace.

Something about the voice was familiar but I could not place
it: and finally, realising the discussion could go on for hours, I
drew away from the door and considered what to do next.

It must be almost twelve o'clock; the meeting would be
over soon, the visitor would leave and André would go back
to the studios.

I exhaled, looking up at the cupola, a startling blue.

Five minutes passed. The voices went on and on, behind the
door; downstairs, the grandfather clock chimed twelve.

Ten minutes became fifteen. I ran up to my room, took my
valise from the bed and stood with it in my hand, with some
idea of being prepared.

Five more minutes ticked by. Could we wait? But the news
had already broken from Pathé. By tonight, she would know
what I'd done.

As I stood there, indecisive, I heard the opening of the salon
door, André saying something hearty but indistinct, and the
party moved downstairs.

I waited, holding my breath, for the purr of a car engine –
and finally it came. But then also André's voice, cheerful, from
the hall.

Why was he still here?

I hovered in my room, paralysed with indecision.

Then I heard footsteps coming up the stairs to my floor. Hers.

She burst into my room, staring, her hair wild. 'I only have a moment,' she said, 'André isn't going back to the studio, he's staying, he wants me to have lunch with him and then he is having meetings here all afternoon. He's invited some people round for supper.'

I stared at her, aghast.

'I have to go,' she said, hovering and agonised.

'We'll go out the back,' I said. 'There's still time. Meet me by the lake. We can go through the woods and get a cab on the Boulogne road.'

She nodded. Put a trembling hand to her temple. Nodded again.

'Who was the visitor?' I asked.

'Nobody,' she said, and shut the door.

When she had gone, I took my suitcase and crept down the stairs.

Through the half-open dining-room door I saw her sitting at the table, doing her best to smile and laugh; the strain showing around her eyes.

I went through the back doors and out onto the terrace, and when it was safe to run, I did so, my feet thudding on the damp earth, the valise banging painfully against my knees.

For too long I seemed to make no progress: each time I turned the house was just as big as before, and then suddenly the woods were there, only fifty metres away; and then with a shiver of rain on cold leaves I was under the canopy.

I pushed onwards until the branches broke free and I was on the pebble path; five minutes' walk and it tapered; the lake appeared up ahead.

It was not frozen any more, but black and studded with tiny

green jewels of algae. I chose a position near the path, and slid down against a tree trunk to watch and wait.

I calculated two o'clock. The meal would be finished; a cold kiss on the cheek for André. She would be collecting her coat, slipping downstairs and out by the French doors.

I calculated five past two. She would be on her way across the lawn, the grass crunching underfoot, her eyes trained on the distant woods.

Twenty past. A willow trailed its fingers in the lake and whispered, *She isn't coming.*

A branch shook, somewhere in my line of vision: the barest quiver, and then another bramble spray was moved out of the way by a slender hand; her sleeve, her grey dress, her arm and brave face.

She was smiling; she had already seen me and was stepping off the path.

I ran to her. She burst into tears and clung to me.

'I see you brought your wardrobe,' I said, nodding at her valise. She held me, and turned her head to look at it. 'Silly of me,' she said. 'I won't need any of it where we're going.'

She wiped her eyes; I tugged her hand. 'Which way?'

'Over there,' she said, indicating a path through the trees; and smiled.

A rustling behind us: the branches moved aside again and André stepped through the gap. In his right hand, he held a revolver – the one from his safe – idly, as one might jingle a set of keys.

'Taking your suitcases for a walk?' he said.

I glanced at Luce, who had turned white and still.

'Am I to understand that, in spite of everything we talked about, you have made promises to this young person?'

What he'd said repeated in my ears, meaningless. I grasped the essential – that somehow he had found out about us

– without grasping any of the implications.

'She has made promises,' I said, 'we're going away.'

André lifted the gun and tapped his chin with it, thoughtful. 'Where exactly were you going to go?'

I looked at Luce. She had opened her mouth but said nothing. She was white and blank with shock.

'A little cottage in Provence?' he asked. 'Somewhere you wouldn't be recognised? The problem with being an actress, darling, is that everybody knows your face.'

He prodded her suitcase with his toe, toppling it; the gesture seemed to wake her out of her daze.

I said: 'She isn't coming back to the house. She's coming with me.'

'Sure about that?' he said.

I didn't understand. She had fixed her eyes on him, pleading. The revolver twirled in his hand.

He said: 'You haven't told her.'

'What haven't you told me?' I said.

Luce started to cry.

'What?' I asked again.

She put one palm to her stomach and rested it there and looked at me, a look of such liquid misery that at first I didn't understand.

Then I remembered the voice in the salon that morning.

'Dr Langlois,' I said.

André nodded, arching an eyebrow, impressed.

I said: 'When?'

'Five months. Just before I went to Marseille.'

My throat made its own sounds, like an old person.

The ideas flew: keys slotting into one lock after another: 'That night, at the party, the faint – you found out when the doctor visited, when he was examining you. That's when he told you. That's why they made you rest up, because of what happened before. You let me think that you were ill. You let me think you were fragile, and dance attendance on you.'

'I was going to tell you—' she said.

'—when? What did you think would happen?'

She looked skywards. André looked at her with an air of vicious interest.

She said: 'I thought you might understand it was an accident. If you loved me, you might love the child.'

'But it would be half him!'

'And half me. And then, in time, maybe half you as well.'

I covered my face with my hands, not because she was wrong, but because she was right. I would love anything that was part of her.

'Don't cry,' she said, 'it isn't broken.'

How would we know if it was broken? Such things needed time to determine. I looked at her eyes, enormous in her face, the lashes softened by tears.

André slapped his free hand against his thigh, mocking applause.

He said: 'Did you know she took your part? When you were putting yourself in a state because you thought she'd left, she was filming *Petite Mort* with Peyssac?'

Luce's throat worked; her eyes swivelled to look at me.

'It isn't the same,' I said, 'I only did it because I was angry with you, I regretted it as soon as I got there. I was going to tell you.'

André said: 'Come back to the house.'

I spoke faster: 'I was going to tell you, once we were away. I want you to listen. I want—'

André lifted the gun.

'Please,' I said.

Luce looked at me.

She took my hands in hers, gave them a gentle squeeze and then dropped them.

'I, I, I,' she said.

She turned her back on me and took a few steps to André;

stood apart from him, very straight, and looked at me.

André smiled, as if at a private joke; he lowered the gun a little, and said: 'You could take an apartment nearby. If it keeps her happy. What do you say?'

I couldn't say anything. Images came to me in a long cascade. Things that hadn't happened yet: her arm linked through mine, the boom of surf on a pebble beach. The child.

She had raised her chin a fraction: its point angled to me.

I looked at her, really looked at her, and understood I had lost.

'I'll ruin you,' I said. 'I can tell it all over Paris.'

'You won't,' André said.

Luce glanced at him. He had lifted the gun again: not levelled it, but raised it in his right hand, hefting it.

I said: 'I will get a lawyer. Who knows what they might find in your past, if they go digging?'

Then I looked for something that might just kill him with words: 'Your child will be taken away from you. It won't know you.'

The gun lifted a notch. The hole at the end of its barrel pointed at my chest. André ground his hand into his eye socket; then, suddenly, he laughed, as if at the situation, and drew back slightly. The trees around us ruffled their feathers: it seemed as though we might, after all, reconcile. Weren't we a household, after all?

The gun was shaking in his hand.

I heard a loud bang, an explosion: my skin and bone were the explosion, and that was how I died my little death.

Luce and Adèle, i.

One day, just after André has left for the south, a note comes to the salon. It says that Feuillade wants her most particularly to rehearse over the next two weeks. If possible she must come into the city and take an hotel, so that they may work intensively.

She folds the note carefully. The clock on the mantel ticks her decision.

'It is Feuillade. His daughter is ill. They are going to Switzerland for a cure. What bad luck.'

Adèle doesn't say anything. She has her studious face bent to the paperback on her knees. One would hardly know she was listening at all.

'I shall just have to hang about here, annoying you.'

Still nothing. A blink, then the crisp sound of a page turning. 'You never annoy me.'

The first time she has said *you* and *I* in the same sentence: so little, it shouldn't be enough, but it is.

Later, when Adèle's head has fallen sideways in a doze, one watchful thumb still marking the page, she scrawls a reply to Feuillade: *...inconvenience you. Sadly no longer able. May I suggest as a replacement my former colleague Nelly Sinclair, an adept horsewoman...*

With love, L. DURAND. She presses the nib into the page and looks at the sleeping girl, whose eyelids flutter and jerk with the violence of her dream.

THE DOPPELGÄNGER, ENRAGED, STEPS OUT OF THE MIRROR

Testimony of Grégoire MOREAU, Sergeant,
Gendarmerie de l'Ile St Louis

Q. Describe what happened on the morning of 8. janvier.

A. At about nine o'clock I was on desk duty looking after
the waiting room when the doors opened and I looked up,
expecting it to be Mme de Courcet again about her poodle,
but instead there was a girl.

Q. Can you describe her?

A. Her sleeve up to her elbow was dark brown and her dress
was torn. The hem was in ribbons; the whole had been cut
about and she looked, in short, very badly treated.

Q. Proceed.

A. Well, then she got close to the desk and asked 'Can you
help me?' and I said 'Your arm, Mademoiselle!' and she looked
at it: 'Oh this! I cannot feel it now at all!' Then a man waiting
said: 'Stop staring, can't you see she is about to fall?' […]

6. janvier 1914

SOMEONE LAUGHING became geese crossing an indigo sky.

Some time later I opened my eyes again. A weeping willow, stippling my forehead with insect-thin branches, drifting in the water around me. I began to panic and kick my heels for purchase. They met resistance: a light sucking sound and they touched mud, and the back of my head bumped against it too: I was floating in only a couple of inches of water, my hips resting on the bottom. I looked up and around, spitting out the cold water, and saw that I was only a foot or so from the bank; tried to push myself up but my left arm folded back in on itself.

A minute later I tried again, and this time managed to drag myself over the lip of the lake onto the bank and scramble backwards to lean against a tree.

I sat cradling my left elbow in my right hand, my fingers playing with the torn sleeve of my dress, then exploring higher. When I found the hole I drew my fingers away just as quick as I'd touched it. I was not brave enough to try again for a long time, but when I was, I found a ragged cylinder between my breastbone and my shoulder, into which it was possible to probe with the tip of one finger.

When I woke again, it was dark. I shivered, looking at the placid surface of the lake. There should have been scuttlings, the brittle noise of leaves drifting over each other, but there was no sound apart from my own breathing.

My shoulder flared, and with the pain came the memory. Three figures stood by the lake, one much beloved, another holding a gun, and the third was me. Luce's fingers straying to cover her stomach and then the muffled explosion.

When the pain had subsided enough, I reached up and felt the weeds laced through my still-damp hair. I saw myself, as if I was someone else again, pushed backwards by the force of the shot and falling into the shallows; Luce and André watching me from the bank. André leading her back to the house, concerned above everything else for the baby: who knew what a shock like this would bring about?

The memory played over and over, now forwards, and now backwards: the cold water hitting my face as I fell, the explosion a horse's kick to the arm, sighting down the hole at the end of the gun barrel and André's trigger finger, a pink blur.

I swung my right arm sideways and tested my weight on it; managed to lever myself onto my knees and a second later, found that I could stand. I held my soaking skirts in my hands for a moment, weighing them; stood there, confused.

How could you think I'd let him do that, she will say. *How could you? I was in the house all the time. And look, it is not serious: just a scratch. Come here.*

One step forward – two, more confident now – and I began to walk slowly back towards the path.

In the open, the wind met me, welcome and cold on my hot face; there was the house, black on the horizon, with its ground-floor windows twinkling yellow.

I went slowly in order not to jog my arm, my footsteps crunching across the grey lawn, but it was unavoidable: every few paces the pain would come. Each time it was too much I stretched my lips and showed my teeth, and in time the pain faded.

Now I began to feel serene: even if André were suddenly to leap out at me, there was nothing more that could be done; he would fade helplessly back into the darkness of the garden and I would keep moving on towards her. As I walked, I grasped for understanding of the situation – something was nagging at me – but my thoughts slid over the essential and found her. She would pull back the curtain and see me; her hand would fly to her mouth, her eyes round with shock. *Your poor arm. Bring it here: we'll call for help.*

Ahead of me was the balustrade of the terrace which led onto the lawn, coming clear; beyond it were the French windows of the dining room, the drapes half-drawn. A blur of movement through the gap: the gleam on the mahogany table, the flash of the footman's white shirt as he bent low, placing cutlery, ready for dinner guests.

When I was almost at the lip of the terrace, I heard a noise and froze. The French windows had clicked open, there was a rush of warm air into my face, and neat footsteps came out onto the patio. Thomas' craggy face flared briefly as he lit the lantern on the left-hand side of the dining-room doors. I waited; heard shuffling movements as he fiddled with the taper on the first lantern and moved to the other side of the door.

What had I been thinking? I couldn't be seen by him, or by the staff: I must not be seen by anyone but Luce. I waited for him to glance out into the garden, agonised: but his gloved hands moved deftly, closing the catch on the glass door of the second lantern; he turned away. The doors clicked shut again.

I looked down at myself; I was standing in the half-shadows at the edge of the pool of light thrown by the lamps. Then, inside the dining room, I saw the door open: five dinner guests, men and women smartly done up, were now bustling into the room. Their lips were opened in laughter and the polite, pleasurable confusion over who should sit where; unable to decide, they milled about, cheeks flushed with drink, and their chatter a muted thrum behind the glass.

Before I could decide what to do, a woman in a fuchsia dress broke away from the table and moved towards the window from inside. She was middle-aged and quick-eyed; she carried a fan which she beat very fast against her chest.

I was not five feet away – just the glass between us.

Charming, I saw her mouth say, looking past me at the view.

I gazed, fascinated, at the plump hand with the fluttering fan.

Come over here, Luce, and look at the lamps.

Luce moved slowly towards the window. She was wearing the dress she had worn for Aurélie's soirée, and her hair in a chignon, and everything was just as it had been, except that two tired lines drew down the sides of her mouth.

I raised my hand to spider it against the glass; her eyes widened. I fought an instinct to turn and look over my shoulder to see what had frightened her: she was looking right at me. I saw her mouth open, her hand go to her throat and then heard, very faint behind the glass, a scream.

Panic broke out in the dining room. The scream went on and on. Luce covered her mouth, then her eyes, and then her mouth with her hands; amidst the scrambling guests André came running into the room, his legs very lithe and his murderer's hands poised to grip somebody.

I saw André's clutching fingers, felt the sharp cold on my neck and face, turned and ran away over the terrace and down the steps. I stumbled over the grass to the left; then changed direction and made instead for the side of the house.

Behind, I heard the alarm being given: men's footsteps spilling onto the terrace to search for the prowler, and a woman's well-bred voice – not hers – repeating over and over: *There was nobody there...*

I stumbled onwards, listening to the voices grow faint behind me, my arm jogging helplessly against my ribs as I ran. At last I reached the corner of the house and slid round it; the soft stone crumbled against my back and the fingers of my spread hands.

7. janvier 1914

I KNEW I WAS GOING towards Paris because every half-hour
or so, the lights of a car would dazzle me, shining through
the trees on either side of the road; and then the car would
crawl, low-slung, past me. Sometimes I would catch a glimpse
of the driver's speculative eyes – but those in the back, the rich
men returning home from their parties and dinners, remained
hidden.

Once a car slowed almost to a halt; a man's face peered out
from the rear window, assessing, then caught sight of my dress
and the state of my arm and hurriedly gave the signal to drive
on.

At last I came to an open stretch of parkland. There were tufts
of bushes dotted over the turf – a clear plain half a mile long,
leading away to trees, and then the trees dropped away, and
beyond it was Paris.

The air was stale and cold: a thousand mansard roofs were
just turning into slate, a hint of blue on the dawn. The sun was a
rim on the horizon: as I watched, the Seine appeared, winking
gold as it snaked towards me, and pinpricks of window lights
near and far wavered off.

The 16th must be directly ahead; a flash near the horizon
might be the rose-tinted windows of Notre-Dame. I thought
I had the Boulevard St Michel and tried to follow it down to
the 14th but lost the trail before rue Boissonnade came clear.
Each time I tried my effort was poorer, and the lines of the

streets blurred into one another and petered out in unlikely endings. The closest I could get was the Panthéon: in one of those windows a mile to the south of its white dome – or perhaps those over to the right – Agathe was turning over in bed, mouth sagging open; and in another, Camille would be sleeping, her thin arms stretched out above her head.

Trees becoming roads: a breeze, leaves shaking themselves at me.

A woman on the other side of the road, wheeling a covered barrow from which rose the smell of fresh bread. Her look, quick and suspicious. The smart tap of her footsteps and the squeak of the wheels going away from me.

Exotic birds in greens and purples. One saying, hands on hips: *It's a wonder you get any trade, looking like that.* Then they scattered in a twirling of parasols and a shimmer of laughter.

Then the sun was higher than I had realised, and achingly bright; the streets were narrower, and emptier, but I had no idea which district I was in. Passing faces were blurs, looming in at me and vanishing.

Someone buffeted into me: pain shot up my arm, and he said, 'Look out, can't you?'

I snatched at him. 'I don't recognise anything,' I said, 'where am I?' but it was like catching a phantom: he pulled his sleeve out of my grip.

'The 14th, of course,' he said, frowning, and walked away.

My gaze began to waver again, useless and desperate, over the stone façades of the apartment blocks – and suddenly I saw the fat face of the greengrocer at the bottom of rue Boissonnade, staring back at me. The coffee-and-stew smell from the restaurant next door, the pine-green newspaper kiosk on the corner, with the boy calling the day's news. A dusty slamming sound: overhead there were even the two familiar women whose names I had never learned, gossiping as they beat their rugs over their balconettes.

I hobbled across the street towards him.

'Mademoiselle Roux!' he said. 'How did you escape?'

I knew, even in my feverish state, that this could not be right.

'Was I misinformed?' he said. 'The police said nobody got out.'

I stared back at him.

'This morning,' he said, and then again: 'Was I misinformed?'

His eyes travelled past me, over the street towards number fourteen.

There was a police officer standing at the entrance to the apartment block, arms behind his back, watching the street.

I walked across the street to the policeman and stood a few metres away, looking at a kicked-in hole in the door. The officer shifted on his feet and looked more closely at me.

'Can I help, Mademoiselle?' he asked.

I cleared my throat. The sound was rusty and unreal. 'What happened?'

'There's been an incident. Three people were found shot in one of the apartments.'

'Which one?'

'Top floor. A landlady, one woman of dubious reputation and one other.'

'What happened to the young one? The girl?'

He frowned. 'I told you, nobody got out. How did you know she was young?'

I began to shake. He was staring at me as if he knew me from somewhere; turning, I walked away from him, and did not look back.

Who was it André knew? It didn't matter. He must have nodded and smiled at his guests as they chattered about the prowler over the remains of their supper – all the time playing with his cutlery and thinking: *What if?*

With brandy and cards passed out, he would excuse himself and run up to his study, and lift the telephone receiver from the cradle; give the rue Boissonnade address. He had written to Mathilde, once, and paid my rent up to date for me so that I could go to live with him. He knew that I knew nobody else in the city.

He would give a description – seventeen, thin, dark hair.

Then downstairs again to sit in the salon, listening to the talk. Waved the guests off in due course; watching them shrug their stoles around their shoulders as they got into their cars.

Much later, the shrilling of the telephone would wake him. They'd found a girl in one of the bedrooms who matched the description he'd given, and disposed of the others when they came shouting. And André would have said, *Yes, fine.* He had never known I had a sister.

I wandered away, towards the river, and went down the steps to the *quais*.

Under the bridge was a fire set alight in an old container, and men and women huddled round. I thought I saw Monsieur Z; I thought he waved; but I was too tired to do anything other than shoulder my way in and curl up amongst the other bodies.

When I opened my eyes it was dark. The moon was a full white coin, and Camille was lying next to me. Her face was as cool and smooth as a child's.

She pursed her lips when I put a finger to her face, and pulled back.

I asked: *Did the men leave a sign by which I can find them? I could go to the law.*

She shook her head.

Then how should we get revenge?

Her glance wavered down to fix on my shoulder; then back to my face.

We lay for a while opposite each other, listening to the shouts of a fight breaking out amongst the people further down the row. She shook her arm out as if it had given her pins and needles.

Where you are – what's it like?

She did a mock-shiver, drawing an invisible shawl around her ears.

Juliette, vii.

When I arrive at the archive, my things have been left out on my desk overnight, the papers arranged in exactly the same order.

There are three articles in the press about the fire; *Le Figaro*, *Le Temps* and *Le Petit Parisien*. They all agree that the fire started about seven o'clock in the morning, in Building J, which was used by certain of the editors. The fire spread rapidly to the surrounding buildings; within minutes the factory was evacuated. Apart from that there is nothing of interest. All of them attribute the blaze to an accident.

Then I turn to the folder marked 'Witness Statements' and a set of papers slip out. I scan them for the Préfecture de Police stamp, and don't see it; flip back to the front sheet and see writing in a tiny, crabbed hand: *Property of Internal Security – Pathé Factory. If found, please return to Building I.*

The typewriter ink on the first statement has faded to pale blue.

REY Edouard
Security Guard – Day Shift
At seven o'clock on 8 January, I was alerted to the fire by a member of my patrol and we went straight to Building J where we saw that the fire had only recently taken hold. We immediately gave the order to evacuate the entire factory.

The largest quantity of smoke issued from the south-west corner of the building, which an editor tells me is where he stores his completed masters, ready to be collected and sent off for duplication.

I did not see anyone in the immediate vicinity of the building.

PHILIBERT Marc
Guard – Night Shift
On my rounds at a quarter to seven I saw nothing out of the ordinary. I was unable to check the door because I had lent my key out the previous night to a director, but I observed that it was fastened and there was no evidence of disturbance.

I proceeded on my way, returning to my cabin at five minutes to seven, and was roused from my cabin by shouts, at which point I made my way to Building J to see a sheet of yellow flame.

In summary, I did not see anything unusual that day. I cannot think of anyone who would want to start the fire deliberately.

There are no more witness statements: just a folder marked 'Photographs'. But when I open the folder, only one print slips onto the desk.

Black and white grins: three lines of men formally posed, in front of the wall of a building. The front two rows are young men, lolling about in overalls and caps. Behind them is a row of five starchier looking, older men in dark suits and ties. Underneath is a date: *7. janvier 1914. Pathé directors and juniors enjoying a break at the factory.*

I press my thumbs to my eyelids until the shapes appear.

Testimony of M. le Docteur HARBLEU

Q. [...] you were the physician called by Sergeant Moreau to the gendarmerie on the afternoon of 8. janvier?
A. Correct.

Q. And your findings were?
A. I saw a young female of between fifteen and twenty years in age. Her records were not on file and she confirmed she came from a small parish near Toulouse where written certification was sparse. She gave her name as Adèle Roux, 17.

Q. The wound?
A. Was clean in appearance, from a small-calibre handgun, from a short distance. The victim had been extremely fortunate; the bullet had passed within an inch of the upper left lung, and exited behind the shoulder. The arm hung from its socket – that is to say, the arm's motor function was naturally impaired – but the victim was able to walk and talk. There was no sepsis. I would say the wound was a day or two old, at best. In short, if one had aimed the bullet precisely it would have been hard to do less permanent damage.

Q. What was your impression of Mlle Roux?
A. She let me look at her without fuss. If she felt pain on examination she did not show it.

Q. Did she say anything to you?

A. I asked her who had done it and she said 'M. Durand of Pathé; and his wife.' When I asked her what she meant, she became agitated, and asked for someone to fetch the police inspector [...]

André, vi.

Inspector Japy blows smoke at the façade of André Durand's house.

It is a fine morning, with an improbable seasonal change in the air: the turf underfoot feels springy for the first time in months; white strips of cloud hurry across the sky. In front of the house, a chauffeur is playing a hose over the bonnet of a grey Daimler.

Go careful, Japy's superior had begged, sweating in his over-hot office. *Just find out if the girl worked for them, then find out why she ran away, or whatever it was: end of story.* His boss had dusted his hands of an imaginary embarrassment.

Japy had smiled sleepily. He'd reached the door before his boss had cracked: *Japy! Absolutely no mesmerism! Understand?*

The chauffeur looks up at his approach, flat feet crunching over gravel, and frowns: 'Can I help?'

'Is M. Durand at home?'

The chauffeur blinks at Japy's stained grey overcoat. 'Can I help?'

'You could show me in.'

Japy senses some petty infraction in this man's past – his hands tremble as he drops the hosepipe on the ground.

'Of course,' the chauffeur says, overly keen to please, and leads him towards the great front door.

A tapestry which wants to be the Lady and the Unicorn hangs in the hallway, next to an ostentatious hat stand. Japy fingers the tapestry as he passes: cheap Flemish wool, coarse in its modernity.

The chauffeur is sending anxious little glances back at him, hovering a few paces ahead, calling for the butler. Japy looks at the stairway, vast and curled.

A tall man appears at the end of the corridor.

Japy smiles. 'M. Durand, please.'

The man isn't used to being bossed about; all the more reason to do it, so when he starts to say, 'Do you have an appointment?' Japy changes the tenor of his smile, just lowers the temperature fractionally, and says, 'No.'

'I'm afraid it won't be possible for you to see him today.'

No flies on this one: a past whiter than white, in a monastery possibly. The chauffeur is hanging back, on the edge of disappearing to safety.

'Inspector Japy,' Japy says, producing a crumpled visiting card.

The butler takes it; says: 'Your cigarette.'

'What?'

'Is dropping ash on the carpet.'

The butler goes upstairs. A minute passes. Japy grinds his cigarette stub into an imitation High Flemish ashtray and stands back on his heels to wait.

Another minute; then a door closes upstairs, and André Durand is loping down the stairs to meet him.

'Inspector Japy? Follow me,' and leads him into a salon, where he makes sure to pull out the best chair for his guest; sits on the sofa opposite, running his hand through his hair. 'So, what's this about?'

Japy nods to a vase on the mantel. 'Surely that's First Dynasty?'

'I believe so. It's from my wife's family.'

'In my spare time, I am something of an antiques enthusiast.

One always recognises quality.'

'A second string to your bow.'

'Oh, but I don't consider it a secondary pursuit. Are you familiar with the lectures given by Commander Darget on the topic of magnetic effluvia?'

Durand shifts his weight in his chair. 'I'm afraid not.'

'By which all objects emit – if you will – a sacred emanation, an ectoplasm indicating the history of their displacements? Imagine if a detective were able to interpret the secret signs of a gun used in a murder? Trace the path of the bullet, faintly glowing, through the air? Imagine what tales that vase would tell us if it could!' He pauses, hand held dramatically in front of him, for just long enough to see Durand's lip twitch at the corner. 'No, M. Durand, my interest in objects is of the order of the professional.'

Durand's whole body is relaxed, legs lolling apart at the knees; his voice, correspondingly, is a purr. 'And has this effluvia led you to many convictions?'

'Not yet, Monsieur,' Japy says, 'but one lives in hope. What can you tell me about a Mademoiselle Adèle Roux?'

'Mlle Roux was my wife's assistant, until a few days ago,' he says.

'It is only that Mlle Roux has made some allegations against you and your wife.'

'What sort of allegations?'

'She has been very badly hurt, and claims you are responsible.'

'But that's preposterous.' Durand gets to his feet. 'If anything, we are the injured party. Mlle Roux ran away a few days ago, leaving us in a fix for our domestic position. Not to mention the worry we naturally felt for her wellbeing.'

Japy thinks: *You have prepared even this little speech.*

'What has happened to her, then?' Durand asks.

'She has been shot through the arm. You understand the

position. We are bound over to investigate where possible.'

'Shot? Dear me,' Durand says. 'Are you sure? She was such a demure little person.' He pinches his own lip, thinking. 'A boyfriend, perhaps, someone we didn't know about.'

'She will recover.'

'So glad.' He sits on the sofa. 'But I must admit to feeling very poorly used in all this. To accuse us…!' One hand goes to shade his forehead.

Japy reaches inside his coat for a notepad. 'Would you mind telling me how she left?'

'It was two days ago. We simply came back and found her gone.'

'When you say, you found her gone…'

'Suitcase, clothes, everything. Nobody saw her leave.'

Japy raises his hands to heaven. 'My dear sir! A mesmerist's dream!'

'Pardon?'

'You have only to show me to the lady's chamber, and there I will concentrate my mind and observe the trails left by the missing objects. That will certainly give us a clue to the nature of the mystery.'

He stands, flipping the notepad shut, beaming. Durand starts, as if unsure if this is a joke. 'Is this a joke?' he says.

'I assure you it is quite real.'

Durand pushes the bedroom door open. Japy smiles politely, shoulders past him and looks at the second-rate furniture, the old paint on the shutters, which have been flung wide to air the room.

'Yes,' he says, 'oh yes, I can see we are going to have some success here.'

He stands in the centre of the room, pinches middle finger to thumb on each hand and lowers his head.

'Yes, it was this way,' he murmurs to himself, a moment later, walking swiftly to the door. 'The valise went this way. I can see it. And down towards the stairs, yes, like so.'

He crosses to the landing and starts to descend. Durand waits, arms folded, and then follows him.

Japy leads him all the way back to the ground floor, and hovers in the hallway. The butler has appeared at the sound of footsteps and stands disapproving at the back of the hall.

'Almost,' Japy says through clenched teeth. 'Almost...'

With a swift movement he runs to the great front door and yanks it open, and stands, sniffing the morning air.

Behind him, he hears a cough of laughter.

'Almost...' he says again, seems to deflate, then rallies, turning to his audience, which by now includes the chauffeur and a footman he hasn't seen before.

'No?' Durand says.

'I can sense, definitely so, that she came this way carrying her valise. She left the house, as you told us, through the front door. Everything happened just as you said, Monsieur.'

Durand's nostrils flare. 'You will go back to your superiors and they will, they will give your report the credit it deserves?'

Japy: 'They take me very seriously indeed.'

Durand stretches out a hand. 'So pleased to have made your acquaintance, Inspector. I hope we meet again in better circumstances.'

Japy shakes the hand gravely. 'At your service, Monsieur.'

He waits until he is striding down the gravel path, has waved once, twice to Durand and his huddled staff; then turns back. 'One last thing.' He starts to walk back towards the house. 'Might I ask the privilege of seeing round behind, to admire the rear elevation? One never gets to see these fine old houses from the back.'

Durand smiles. There is nothing behind the smile except perhaps another smile, repeating ad infinitum into the distance. 'Of course,' he says.

Japy ducks his head appreciatively. 'And the girl's effects? They were taken with her?'

Confident: 'Yes.'

'You're quite sure she took everything?'

A flicker: 'Yes.'

'Thank you.' Japy turns and starts to walk around to the side of the house. There is the house wall on the left and then a narrow alley about four metres wide, then on the right a stone wall three metres high, which separates the house from the old stables next door. The space is not much used: nettles and high grass. At the end, sunlight, and a glimpse of a manicured lawn.

He must work fast now: he picks his way over the uneven ground, scanning the grass. The bonfire smell he first noted coming through the girl's bedroom window: is it stronger here, or here? Invisible trails hang in the air before him, leading him into the alley.

Halfway down, he destroys a dandelion clock with a single kick and squats to part the long grass. Sure enough, a cloud of little ash ribbons flies up at his face. On the ground in front of him are blackened chunks of suitcase leather; you can make out the remains of a handle, and brass studs, which of course did not ignite, lying in a little heap to one side.

He reaches for the handle, and turns it over. There is the silver back of a hairbrush, the bristles burnt away. And underneath that, a sodden lump of half-burnt paper is nestled in the grass. He picks it up, looks at the faded velvet ribbon tying the bottom half of the letters into their charred bundle. Holds them up to the light.

Only the top half of the page remains, written on with a crabbed, cramped hand, on paper so fine as to be almost transparent.

3. juin 1913. Dear Adèle…

At the other end of the alleyway, the light is suddenly

blocked. It's the butler: white-faced, sent to pre-empt the discovery, but too late.

Japy scoops the burnt offerings of the girl's suitcase into his handkerchief and pockets them.

The butler is still waiting. His lips quivering as if he wants to speak, but in the end there is nothing to say.

Juliette, viii.

PHILIBERT Marc
Guard – Night Shift

On my rounds at a quarter to seven I saw nothing out of
the ordinary. I was unable to check the door because I
had lent my key out the previous night to a director, but I
observed that it was fastened and there was no evidence of
disturbance.

The archivist threads her way between the filing cabinets and
bookshelves towards me. I point to Marc Philibert's statement.
'Would it have been normal for a security guard to lend a key
to a director?'

She peers. 'I wouldn't have thought so. Security was very
tight. They didn't want anyone stealing their ideas.'

I say: 'Edouard Rey, the day guard, says that there was no
break-in. So whoever got in must have had access. And Philibert
mentions that a director borrowed his key the night before.'

She frowns. 'That's interesting.'

'Something else. Isn't it strange that there are only a few
witness statements, and just this photo – no others? It's as if
someone's looked into the dossier already.'

We look together at the photograph. 'Do you know who
any of these people are? The directors, I mean? The ones in the
back row?'

She scans the print. 'No. We do have some material from the
bigger name directors, but I don't recognise any of them.'

She drums her fingers on the desk. 'But there's someone who might know. His name is Rinaldi. I think he was at Pathé back in the day. He's a professor of modern cinema now. He lives just outside Paris.'

4. avril 1914

THE HALL WAS LINED with eager faces in police uniform – every able-bodied man from colonel to private must have turned out to see the show – and from beyond the large, closed double doors to the gendarmerie came a sound like the baying of fairy-tale wolves.

My lawyer Denis Poperin – a thin, serious youth with a consumptive death rattle – took my forearms in his hands and looked at me.

'Ready?' he asked.

I nodded. He reached up and pulled the veil I was wearing down over my face.

He nodded to the youngest police officer, who removed the bar and opened the doors.

I saw the street crammed with people, all faces turned towards me. Half of them had notepads; one enterprising soul had set up a camera; a blinding flash of light caught me with my arm half across my face. The crowd surged forward and the police guard pushed them back. A car purred twenty metres down the street, surrounded by a ring of policemen.

'Did you invent your story? Did you make it up?' someone shouted as Denis manhandled me through the crowd. 'You should be ashamed!' cried a woman, and spat, though her aim was bad, and the gobbet landed on the man next to her.

Someone threw the first projectile as Denis tore open the cab door and bundled me in; it slithered down the glass of the window. 'All right? All in?' said the driver, his big, anxious face peering back at us through the partition, and Denis nodded, too breathless to speak. The car began to move. Disappointed faces followed us; the crowd howled louder and some began to run alongside. The police driver swore and shaded his eyes, as if trying to see a clear path.

I sat, listening to the crowd call my name. Denis said: 'Are you clear on your lines?' I nodded. 'But are you?' he asked. He looked out of the cab window, white-faced. We were rolling along the rue de Rivoli now, past the Galeries St Paul with gaggles of shoppers queuing outside.

The low walls of the Pont au Change seemed to fall away on either side, exposing the churning water beneath. Then we were on the Ile de la Cité, and the same noise, the baying, rolled towards us. Looking ahead, I saw the Boulevard du Palais blocked with people.

In the cab, the driver hunched over the wheel and slowed down, unable to make any headway; the crowd scattered on either side of the vehicle, their faces changing into sneers of recognition. Pointing, shouting: I watched the news spread. Up ahead, policemen lining the high railings of the Palais' forecourt moved towards the gates, and started to open them; swearing, our driver swung the car round.

'Come on,' muttered Denis, craning his neck to see what the delay was. I turned to my left and saw that it was another car, inching forward, arriving at the same time from the opposite direction. It was black and official-looking, with two figures sitting in the back seat.

The car swung round and drew level, competing with us for the front spot. The person looking back at me from the cab window, not three metres away, was Luce.

She was very changed; lines in the corners of her eyes and reaching down from her mouth had not been there a month before. I also saw that she was frightened, the muscles in her throat moving. The wide, dark eyes snapped shut and open, then stayed open, staring at me. I looked at her waist, just visible above the level of the window; it was as flat as when I had first met her.

She gave the ghost of a smile and shifted her shoulders sadly. I remembered her in the house last summer, inspecting a new dress that had been sent to her in the wrong size. *My, Adèle. What a pretty pass we are in!*

I felt myself want to smile back. Just then, our cab driver swore again, and the car lurched forward and gathered speed.

Juliette and Adèle
1967

'What happened to the baby?'

Adèle says: 'She'd given birth prematurely.'

'What happened to it?'

'She was in custody. Her family took it away with them.'

She looks at me and shrugs: a bitter smile. 'Rich people closing ranks.'

I say: 'What did you feel?'

Adèle looks at the back of her hands. 'The papers said that André took it hardest. He broke his cell, threatened guards, and made wild predictions about the end of the world.'

4. avril 1914

'GIVE ME YOUR HAND,' Denis said as we stepped out of the car. The noise hit us: from the line of people queuing for seats in the public gallery, which snaked round the courtyard, to the crowd stuck outside, gripping the bars. Some were screaming my name; some were screaming Luce's name, or André's. Denis's fingers closed round mine and he drew me onwards; a tight ring of policemen formed around us and ushered us through the tall doors and into the Vestibule d'Harlay.

'Wait here,' said the officer.

I stood looking up at the decorated ceiling, high overhead, and down at the red marble swirls of the floor, and I didn't feel anything very much.

'All right?' Denis asked. He gave me a sickly smile, pale to the gills, the hair plastered to his forehead. 'All right?' he said again. I nodded.

The officer reappeared. 'Please,' he said, 'we are to seat you before the crowd is let in, the judge says, to save a riot.' He ducked his head to invite us to follow him, and led us towards the doors at the end of the vestibule.

They opened onto an audience room seating about two hundred. At first it seemed a mass of fluted oak, but then the different levels asserted themselves: the judges' raised bench at the front, and the jury's to the left-hand side. Denis led us to a bench in front of the judges', and fussed about organising his papers. He shot me a look: 'You'll want to look nervous,' he said, as I folded my arms across my chest. 'Like we discussed.' He

272

fiddled with the collar on his red prosecutor's gown.

Just then there was the creak of a small door opening in the panelling on the right-hand side of the room; a police officer appeared, followed by André, then Luce; then by a walrus-moustached man dressed in the defending lawyer's black. Denis met his level stare, then cleared his throat and began to shuffle papers again.

The defendants were led straight to the dock and sat. Luce looked down at her hands. André looked up at me, his face blank. He stared, as if searching for something; from my eyes down to my hands and back up; he frowned. I looked back at him, until he too folded his arms and looked away.

A clatter at the back of the hall; the policeman had crossed to the main doors to open them, and a moment later the hall was flooding with people fighting past each other to secure the best seats in the gallery. They were all men, women not being allowed as spectators, and they were consequently unafraid to be seen staring. The front row of the seats came up to five feet behind my chair; I heard the whispering assessments of my dress, my shoulders and my waist. For the first time, I felt my stomach squirm, and looked to Denis; he saw my face and said: 'Not bad. If you could just be a little paler.'

The courtroom filled with people, moving crab-wise along the fixed wooden benches. Men were all but in each other's laps: a fight almost broke out near the door when one of the workers who had been saving a seat to sell changed his mind and wanted to keep it for himself. The policemen ran around the seats and back – sheepdogs penning in a flock – but still it took five minutes to calm the crowd enough to let in the judges.

I studied the presiding judge's face carefully as he walked in, flanked by his juniors, and made his way up to his lofty seat. He was a man of a certain age, bearded like the rest, but his beard was speckled with white. He moved with difficulty, lifting one leg after the other to mount the steps; and when he was there, he looked around the courtroom with infinite weariness, his gaze settling on me for a mere fraction of an instant before he said: 'Call the members of the jury.'

Had they a daughter? How old? Had their families ever been the victims of any violence? The jury members turned caps in hands, a soft rub-rub of cloth on skin, as they submitted to Denis's questioning. And then Maître Lazard's rich voice: *What were their opinions about the cinema? A fine profession? Had they any special feelings about people not born on these shores?* The audience behind me shuffled their feet and whistled, bored: the judge hammered on the bench for silence every five minutes. Denis returned to our seat to cough into his handkerchief in between bouts of questioning. A man at the back stood up, cupped his hands around his mouth and yelled: 'Pick me! I don't have any prejudices about women!' before a policeman put a hand to his collar and hauled him out. His laughter echoed from the marble walls of the Vestibule; his footsteps squeaked away across the floor.

'If I am correct,' the judge said, at the end of two temple-massaging hours, 'we have a jury now. Am I right?'

'Correct, Your Honour,' Maître Lazard smiled unctuously beneath his moustache. The jury members who had been selected stood up a little straighter, and looked around the courtroom with evident pride.

'Then I will call M. Durand to submit to my preliminary questions.'

André stood, head lowered, hands folded in front of him, and made his sober way to the witness stand. Catcalls from the gallery: he didn't react, just kept the same grave demeanour, the model of the earnest, caring boss. I cursed, inwardly, his face – that lying phsyiognomy which could appear to be anything it wanted.

Le Temps, *4. avril 1914*

NEWS FROM THE COURT
THE SENSATIONAL DURAND TRIAL'S FIRST DAY

[...] took the stand, dressed in a sober but elegant suit, and answered the presiding judge's questions with a countenance which, far from being nonchalant, showed how keenly he felt the seriousness of the charge.

M. le Juge: M. Durand, you and your wife stand accused of attempted murder and actual bodily harm. What do you have to say in the first instance?

M. Durand: That I regret it.

M. le Juge: Do you mean to say you admit wrongdoing?

M. Durand: On the contrary, I regret whatever circumstances have led our former employee to make such an accusation. She must have felt some slight or injury, unnoticed by myself and my wife; whatever we can have done to provoke such a response, I regret it wholeheartedly.

M. le Juge: Are you saying you provoked Mlle Roux's accusation?

M. Durand: Who knows what goes on in the mind of another? A refusal to furnish her a new wardrobe; to increase pay or prospects? Who knows which small slight may have become magnified, over time?

M. Durand, a self-made man, spoke at length about his upbringing in the Americas, and the path he had trodden rising to the heights of the film trade; a role which, he admitted, had sometimes led him to neglect his home life in the pursuit of excellence. He refuted utterly the imputation of any improper romance between himself and Mlle Roux, saying:

M. Durand: I am a man of simple habits, Monsieur. Cinema and my wife are my only pleasures.

M. le Juge: And you refuse Mlle Roux's claims of relations within the household and that when she threatened to disclose them you took action?

M. Durand: I do not dispute that Mlle Roux had romantic interests. But not with us.

M. le Juge: Your meaning being?

M. Durand: It is not for me to comment on what attachments she had. I believe M. le Docteur Harbleu will advise on this in due course.

The judge then called Mme Durand to the stand. Unlike her husband, Mme Durand, who wore an elegant black gown, gave only short answers.

M. le Juge: What do you respond to Mlle Roux's claim that you made advances on her?

Mme Durand: What did you call it?

M. le Juge: Advances, Madame.

Mme Durand: 'Advances'?

M. le Juge: Mme Durand, are you quite well?

At this point M. Durand stood and requested that his wife be allowed to rest, her recent troubles having left her under a strain, and this request was granted under special dispensation.

After the lunchtime recess, the judge chose to call Mlle Roux to answer his preliminary questions.

Mlle Roux, of small appearance, took the stand and looked

the judge directly in the eye as she told of her early youth in the Languedoc. She then answered questions on her time in the Durands' employ.

M. le Juge: At what point do you say you started relations with M. Durand?

Mlle Roux: Almost immediately. It was his suggestion that I come to the house.

M. le Juge: Rather than set you up in your own apartment like most men?

Mlle Roux: He wanted it to be convenient.

M. le Juge: And how did you plan to keep this a secret from Mme Durand?

Mlle Roux: He didn't care about that.

This elicited some laughter from the men in the gallery, who were doubtless imagining the reactions of their wives were they openly to install a concubine in the marital domicile. M. le Juge then asked about Mme Durand.

M. le Juge: In your statements you allege that there were relations between yourself and Mme Durand.

Mlle Roux: That is correct.

M. le Juge: Can you tell us about these relations?

Mlle Roux: There were various encounters.

M. le Juge: Encounters?

Mlle Roux: Various relations between us.

M. le Juge: But Mme Durand being a married woman…

Mlle Roux: M. Durand was a married man, but it didn't stop him.

At this point uproar broke out in the court so that M. le Juge was forced to eject certain members of the audience in the name of public order. Shouts of 'Liar!' and 'Perfidy!' rang out from every corner […]

4. avril 1914

'THIS IS VERY BAD,' Denis Poperin said, lifting his wine glass to his lips. His Adam's apple worked; he wiped the dregs from his mouth and looked at me. 'What were you thinking?'

We had retired to the gloomiest corner of a worker's café near Montparnasse, where we hoped nobody would recognise us. It was not far from Denis's home and my temporary, police-funded apartment; it was far enough away from the Palais de Justice. I looked away from him, at the accordionist playing to the assembled crowd. She was about the same age as me, but utterly lost to what she was doing: swaying on her feet, framed in the window, her fingers melting together on the keys and stops. Occasionally her eyelids would flutter, as if she were scanning the crowd for someone: then they would shut firmly again, blocking out the world.

'To admit to relations with Mme Durand. We agreed – didn't we – you were to play it down; imply she had made an unwelcome pass. Not that you went along with it without putting up the least resistance.' He sighed. 'I should fire you.'

The accordionist's tune lifted to its conclusion: she bowed and smiled, and her assistant, a small boy, produced a hat for coins. The customers raised their hands in applause and called 'Encore!'

'Why didn't you? Dissemble? You could have said she tried to force it. Nobody could have proved a thing. You could have said anything…'

Luce, her skirts in her hands, stumbling from room to attic

room. I shook my head at the boy, who had appeared at our table, jingling the hat. 'What will happen next?'

'It speaks!' said Denis, looking around the room with wide-eyed amazement. 'The judge has made up his mind already, but he will call other witnesses, though what use it'll do us, I have no idea…'

'But they found the gun. And the valise…'

The boy waited patiently, the hat held out in front of him.

'There are a thousand others like it! And no bullet! And the valise – the valise got us as far as a trial, I grant you, but it's not enough. I will make a brave attempt at a closing speech which will be minced by Maître Lazard's eloquence, and then you will tell me you can't pay me because you have not, have never had, a bean.'

He slumped further in his seat, fished about in his waistcoat pocket for his matches and attempted to light a cigarette.

'Please, Mademoiselle,' said the boy, 'my mistress says are you Adèle Roux of the Durand trial? Because if you are, she would like to sing a special song for you.'

Denis drew himself up in his seat, suddenly self-important: 'It is she,' he said, 'and I am her lawyer.'

A man by the bar had swivelled in his seat to scrutinise us, and now turned back to his comrades, head low between his shoulder blades; the news spread to the head waiter, polishing glasses, who moved along the bar to a cluster of men hunched over their drinks.

Amused glances, and caps being pushed back on foreheads; the beginnings of a leer.

'Let's go,' I said.

'I'll defend you,' Denis slurred.

I pulled on his sleeve, hauling him to his feet. Masculine laughter rang out from the walls as we staggered crab-wise to the door.

The red lights of Boulevard Raspail, advertising rooms by

the hour and basement-level nightclubs; a street cat yowled for cover as Denis lurched away, spinning across the pavement, finger raised for a last put-down.

'You think you can have it all your own way,' he began; tumbled over his own feet and folded up; teetered sideways into the foetal position, and was suddenly asleep.

His snores, after his voice, were gently wheezing and childlike.

I looked up at the sky and gritted my teeth.

The sound of the café door opening and closing behind me, and a musical exhalation: the accordionist was standing next to me, her instrument slung over her shoulders. It made whimpering sounds as she moved.

She, too, tottered; then, leaning her hand on my shoulder, she bent down to remove one shoe, and lifted the broken heel to the flickering café light.

She sighed, and threw the heel across the street; it rebounded off the night shutter of a shop and clattered away. Then she patted her pockets and a cigarette was suddenly between her lips, and a match flaring.

She had a shrewish, carefully made-up face; the crookedness of the smile, which I had dismissed before as uneven, now seemed her best asset. Her hair was dark, like mine, lifting in wisps away from her face.

'You look,' – she shook the match out and squinted through the smoke – 'just like I imagined. Not everybody does. Your lawyer, for example, cut quite a dash on the front page of the *Revue Moderne*, whereas—' She prodded Denis with her shoeless foot; the stockinged toes rasped on the material of his jacket, but he did not wake up. 'Whereas you look just like I thought.'

She held her elbow with her other hand, the cigarette aloft, threatening to set light to her curls.

'Difficult evening,' she said.

I nodded. She blew out smoke.

Neither of us said anything. The café door swung open and disgorged a group of three burly men, who called goodnight to each other and each set off in a different direction. The street grew quiet again.

A big smile inched across her face, crinkling her eyes and revealing a set of small white teeth. She stuck her foot out in front of her and wiggled the toes, then said: 'Chaperone me home.'

Later, I walked back to my rented apartment from gas lamp to gas lamp. It was that point of the night when everything had shut down. Cafés had been closed for hours, their signs extinguished, the revellers long since gone to bed.

As I walked past the wide, tree-lined junction of Raspail, I thought I heard a footstep in the street behind me, and turned, my mouth opening as if I was going to scream for help.

But it was only an old paper bag, which rose in front of me, crackled and wafted away across the cobbles and sank out of sight.

Juliette, ix.

It is late afternoon by the time I reach the address, fifty miles into the wooded country south of Paris. I miss the turn-off the first time; reverse perilously in the 2CV to make the turn. Sunlight dapples through the leaves of the plane trees that line the private drive. Beyond that a field of cows lift their heads to watch me pass; the car bounces from pothole to pothole.

Holding the door open is a small, elderly man in a tweed jacket. He smiles and beckons, beams as I shake his hand. Then he turns away into the hallway: 'Follow me.'

The corridor is lined with burgundy candy-stripe paper: after a few metres the space widens suddenly into a light and airy room, with open French windows leading out onto a lawn.

Rinaldi moves towards a sagging armchair next to the French windows and lowers himself, wincing, into its cushions. I choose the seat opposite.

'You've come all this way,' he says. 'It must be important.'

'I wanted to ask you about the Pathé fire.'

'Oh,' he says. 'That. Such a long time ago. I'd almost forgotten.'

'Were you there?'

'Not exactly,' he says, waving a hand. 'I was in the complex, working in accounts, as usual. A sad day. All those things destroyed, all that equipment. You could feel the heat of it right across the other side of the factory.'

I take the photograph from my bag and hold it out to him.

'I found this in the Pathé archive. Can you identify any of the back row?'

He smiles, reaches for spectacles on a thin chain and, levering himself forward, takes the picture. 'Oh, now, that is a thing,' he says. 'What memories. Thank you for bringing me this.'

He points to a figure on the far left: wrinkled forehead, receding hair. 'There I am,' he says. 'In my Sunday best.'

I say: 'I'm wondering whether one of these people might have started the fire. The witness statements imply that a director borrowed a key to get into the post-production building. And there was nothing in the dossier apart from this photo. It's as if it was left there for me to find.'

Outside, the sun is at its lowest point before vanishing: the light has thickened to burnt orange through the French windows.

M. Rinaldi places the photograph on the table.

'Well,' he says, 'aren't you thorough.'

He traces the photo with his fingertip. 'You're correct. There is someone in that photo who wishes they weren't there,' he says. 'The factory was always full of gossip. That's Basile, the Basque – dreadful accent. This was my friend Paul Leclerc, who went mad over a girl from the factory and tried to hang himself.'

'Adèle Roux knew him.'

Rinaldi nods briefly, uninterested. 'And this was the keeper of the menagerie they used for dramatic tableaux – Otto, from Bavaria.'

He hesitates, then his finger moves over the back row, skating over the smiling faces and coming to rest on a man a head shorter than the others; a pointed white goatee, a round face and blackcurrant eyes. Unlike the others, whose broad grins are full of lazy confidence, his smile is tentative.

'This is my friend Robert Peyssac.'

'Peyssac who made *Petite Mort*?'

Rinaldi puts his palms on his knees and sighs. 'The story

was that he used to meet young people, young workers, in empty buildings of an evening. He was fond of borrowing the keys from different security men each time, so as to cover his tracks.'

In the photograph, Peyssac's hand is resting lightly on the young Rinaldi's shoulder.

I ask: 'And what happened to him after the fire?'

Rinaldi sighs. 'He died.'

'How?'

'In the war. Like everyone else.'

'Wasn't he too old to fight?'

He says: 'Almost. For all the other directors, Charles Pathé obtained a dispensation to save them from the Front: he got permission for them to make patriotic films. But not for Peyssac.'

Somewhere on a floor overhead, a clock chimes softly, over and over again.

'That would explain why they didn't involve the police,' I say. 'They knew who it was and dealt with it on their own. And why the dossier is so slim. They only kept the pieces of evidence that proved the case.'

He nods.

I say: 'I don't understand. He was so excited about it. Why would Peyssac steal his own film?'

Rinaldi lifts his shoulders. 'Something that happened all the time: espionage. If he was in the pay of a rival studio, destroying the film could have earned him a substantial bonus.'

'But why? He was an artist…'

He says: 'But he liked money, too.'

I think about Peyssac's apartment on the Ile St Louis, the silk chairs that Adèle was not allowed to do more than perch on.

'But why would he cut out one of the scenes?'

Rinaldi shrugs. His finger brushes the photograph where Peyssac's hand falls on his younger shoulders. 'A memento?' he says.

Testimony of M. le Docteur HARBLEU, ii.
8. avril 1914

Q: Dr Harbleu, I understand you also work on psychological cases for the Hôpital Pitié-Salpétrière.

A: That is correct. I am considered an expert in the assessment of the psychological state of patients, specialising in hysteria.

Q: But you have said that Mlle Roux appeared quite calm when you met her.

A: That is true.

Q: And since? Have you had much contact?

A: I have been to visit her once or twice, at the behest of the Police Chief, in my role as attendant medical officer. It has been my business to check on Mlle Roux's wellbeing and fitness to give evidence.

Q: So you would say you have a fair grasp of her, how shall I put it, mentality?

A: I would.

Q: And what is your opinion?

A: At no point from the shooting onwards has she displayed any of the redeeming female emotions – no crying, or remorse, or agitation.

Q: And your thesis?

A: I can only go on a similar case some years back.

Q: To whit?

A: The case of Bertrande Iliot, chambermaid to a prominent civil servant, Aristide Perrin and his family, of Nîmes. Note the similarities instantly: a woman of the servant class, young, relatively attractive, living in the same house as a rich and powerful man.

Q: Go on.

A: Obsessed by Perrin to the point of illness, Bertrande Iliot took a kitchen knife and slashed at her forearms, then presented herself with these injuries to the local gendarmerie. She claimed that Perrin had inflicted the injuries. A classic obsessional fantasy of the ill-educated female mind.

Q: How does that relate to the gunshot wounds in the case of Mlle Roux? Surely not self-inflicted?

A: No, in that case, an accomplice. As M. Durand hinted previously, he suspected that Mlle Roux had a romantic liaison outside the house – some youth whom she persuaded to carry out her shooting.

Q: But that is grotesque!

A: True psychopathics are, when challenged, extremely frightening. They do not understand that you are telling them 'no'. I would not like to have to set my will against Mlle Roux's on any point at all.

Testimony of M. DURAND
8. avril 1914

Q: M. Durand, you have agreed to take the stand again to clear up some small points pertaining to the alleged valise discovered by M. l'Inspecteur Japy on your property.
A: Quite so.

Q: In his statement, M. l'Inspecteur says he found burnt pieces of Mlle Roux's suitcase in a side-passage by your house – Exhibit A, thank you, clerk. Now, in his statement he also says you were quite specific that Mlle Roux took the suitcase with her?
A: I was.

Q: And yet, here was the suitcase, burned!
A: Permit me to elucidate. Inspector Japy arrived unannounced, catching me quite unawares, and still perturbed by Mlle Roux's disappearance. He introduced himself, sir, as a Mesmerist.

Q: A Mesmerist!
A: He proceeded to sniff the air of Mlle Roux's room, and say with confidence that she had gone, I don't know, to the East or something.

Q: Really!
A: Your Honour, I ask you: which is the most preposterous? A grown man claiming to smell out the spectres of objects-gone-before, or a busy and preoccupied husband, forgetting

a small fact about someone else's suitcase? I realised later that Mlle Roux must not have taken her valise, and that it, along with the other sundry items she had abandoned, had been burned by my manservant.

8. avril 1914

AS ANDRÉ STEPPED DOWN from the witness stand he winked at me.

It was not the subtle half-droop of an eyelid you might expect from a man on trial. The audience laughed and nudged one another, liking to have caught the little dumb show.

Denis laid a hand on my forearm. I looked to my right, to where Luce sat; there was just the habitual stare straight ahead. If looks were gunshots, that one mahogany panel next to the high window would be bored right through. André reached the seat next to her, fluffed his coattails out behind him, sat and whispered something to her with a smirk; she nodded vaguely, her eyes never leaving that spot on the wall.

The judge pinched the bridge of his nose thoughtfully and said: 'Maître Poperin, have you any more witnesses to propose for the prosecution?'

'No, Your Honour.'

'Maître Lazard? For the defence?'

Lazard, reptilian eyes half-closed, shook his head.

'Then I cannot see how we can drag this out further. We'll proceed straight to the closing speech for the prosecution. Maître Poperin, are you prepared?'

'I am.'

'Then I suggest you gather your notes.'

These last words were said in a raised voice; I was vaguely aware of the sound of a door opening at the back of the courtroom; hushed voices; heads turning. The judge glanced up over his half-moons. 'And then, Maître Lazard, we shall proceed to your closing speech, if there's enough time in today's session.'

I turned to see what the commotion could be: it seemed someone had broken into the courtroom. The guards were holding onto the woman's dark coat by the elbows; a small boy, not more than five, hung from her hand.

'No women in court. You must come back later, Madame, if you wish to admire the frescoes.'

There was a current of laughter; the woman tugged herself free of the court officials and took a few steps down the central aisle, dragging the child with her.

At first I was not sure it was her. All the fight had gone out of her face, and the plump cheeks had sunken in. I could not fathom what she might be doing there, in her best hat and good coat and kid gloves.

'I must speak to the court,' she said. Now I knew it was really her: that you-and-your-fine-ways voice, hard and clear. 'I have new information about the case.'

Denis reacted first. 'Your Honour: for the defence or for the prosecution?'

The judge had taken off his half-moon glasses; he folded them away under his robe, frowning. 'Well, Madame?'

Her voice hardly wobbled. 'The prosecution.'

Out of the corner of my eye I saw André lean forward suddenly, his head close to Maître Lazard's; the judge frowned.

'What new information, Madame?'

Her voice turned belligerent. 'Swear me in, and I'll tell it before the court in the proper fashion. I know how these things ought to go.'

Maître Lazard was shaking his head; in André's fierce whisper it was not quite possible to make out the words. At last André sat back, but not fully – his hands gripped his knees.

The judge looked towards the window for inspiration, and

then said: 'Come up to the stand, Madame, and we will ask you to say your piece. Come now, you can leave your boy in the back there.'

While she was sworn in, André turned to look at Luce. She was looking at me, head tilted back, her eyes half-closed.

Testimony of Elodie KERNUAC
8. avril 1914

Q: *What do you have to tell us that's so important? What is your connection to the case?*

A: I work at the Pathé costumery, I'm the chief costumière there. Where Mlle Roux worked – we knew each other. Before she moved to the Durands'.

Q: *So?*

A: So I also knew M. Durand. He was our boss.

Q: *Come to the point, Madame.*

A: Please will someone stop up the ears of my boy, Charles-Edouard? I don't want him to understand what I am about to tell you.

Q: *Very well, Madame. See. Your son is outside.*

A: While I was there – when I had first started at Pathé, some five years ago – this is difficult for me to say, as a respectable woman – M. Durand made certain advances on me, which I did not repel.

Q: *To clarify: you were his lover?*

A: I would not call it love. We often used to meet in the basement where the costumières worked, after hours. I was flattered by his attentions. He was very dashing and handsome and attentive, and I was very young.

Q: *We are not disputing his charms, Madame. But where is the relevance?*

A: We had – relations – for some months. At the end of that time, he proposed that I should come to live with him and his wife, and serve as her assistant. He made me promises of things – with my career – that he would see I had advancement, and all I had to do was tolerate his wife.

Q: *So effectively, he made the same offer to you as he made to Mlle Roux?*

A: It seems so.

Q: *And you say that you were his mistress?*

A: I was.

Q: *You are aware that M. Durand has sworn before a court of law that he is a faithful husband? You know what a crime it is to give false testimony in the sight of the Law?*

A: What I am saying is, he is not an honest man, like you all think.

Q: *And did you agree? To the offer of a job?*

A: I had heard of Terpsichore's – pardon me, Mme Durand's – reputation around the studio as a hard task-mistress, and I didn't fancy it one bit.

So I told him that it was a 'no', and from then on we met less frequently. In time the visits stopped altogether, and I understood that he had – shall we say, he had moved on to pastures new.

Q: *But all this is in the past? Five years ago, you say?*

A: Four.

Q: *So you allege an affair with M. Durand in 1910. What does this have to do with the possible attack on Mlle Roux?*

A: It was about a year after M. Durand left off coming to see me. I was working late one night, on some costumes for a big film with complicated ornaments – the last people had left the building hours ago. I remember because it was the start of the summer and you could just hear, if you strained your ears, the birds on the roof of the building, cooing like they do on warm evenings. I was hurrying to finish so I could get outside.

Then I heard footsteps, the costumery door opened and M. Durand was there. I could see straight away that he was not himself. His shirt was unbuttoned down to three buttons and he smelled of alcohol and something else, something sharper.

He came into the room and stood in front of my sewing machine. 'Whatever is the matter?' I asked. He half-fell into the chair I offered to him.

He sat there and he just stared at me. 'Whatever is it?' I asked. I suppose I was fussing because he frightened me, just looking and looking like that.

He tried to say something then, but it was too garbled for me to make out. His breath reeked of wine; I thought he might be sick, and moved the costumes out of the way of him; he laughed to see me taking such care of my work.

'You are a good employee, Elodie,' he said. He reached out to touch my cheek but he missed, and his hand fell away.

'I don't know what you mean, sir,' I told him; he was already looking around the room as if he wanted to speak, but had forgotten what he wanted to say.

'Terrible things happen in the world every day,' he said.

'Yes, sir,' I said. I started to pack up my desk. I thought I had the measure of him then: an argument with his wife, and he wanted a listening ear and a woman to tell him he was worth something. Well, I wasn't employed for that; I wanted to go home.

He mumbled some other things then which I couldn't hear,

and went suddenly to sleep, or seemed to, his chin on his chest.

So I packed up my belongings and put my coat on, wondering whether to leave him there. Finally there was nothing for it but to go to the door and stand by the light switch ready to extinguish it.

'Are you going to be all right?' I asked him, trying to get him awake. On the one hand, I didn't like to leave him; but the rest of me wanted to get clear.

He half-woke up. He said, quite distinctly: 'Unless the summer is a dry one.'

I thought I'd misheard. 'Whatever can you mean, sir?' I asked him.

At that he seemed to come to. He looked just like his old self: that brazen stare, undressing you, if I may be bold. Then he laughed at me and said, 'You're a good girl, Elodie.'

I gave up trying to understand it. I shook my head at him and smiled back, and then I left. When I got to the courtyard I took a deep breath. I remember thinking how good it was to be there, in the fresh weather, with the evening ahead of me.

Q: And then?

A: Shortly after, the gifts began to arrive. A bunch of flowers, first, from him; but there was nothing between us any more – at work we avoided each other.

I then came home to find a fine necklace in a box pushed under my door, and his signature on the card. After that, a box of exotic fruit; a hat from Mme Chanel in the wrong size.

The kind of gifts men think women like. And never anything written on the card apart from his capital A.

You don't want a powerful man to feel he owes you something.

I began to think back to that evening in the costumery. And I started to wonder, what was it they would find, if the summer was a dry one?

Juliette and Adèle
1967

'And then?'

'And then. Inspector Japy got up from the front row of the gallery, where he had sat throughout the trial, and made a case that the trial should be halted whilst an investigation was made of the lake at the rear of the Durand property.'

She sips her coffee. 'The courtroom was cleared, the police marshalled, the Durand house emptied of servants, and the special department set up camp in the grounds.'

'What did you do in the meantime? Were you free to go?'

'Denis and I waited in his apartment, in cafés, in the Jardin du Luxembourg. We enjoyed the sun.

'On the eighth day we were sitting on a bench in the Jardin des Plantes, admiring the panthers prowling round and round their cage. A sergeant came running to where we were, and asked whether I could follow him please.

'We were taken in a police cab. We arrived at the woods just as it was starting to be twilight: pale air, fluttering things in the bushes. The police experts were still working all around the lake. They had arranged on the ground all the objects they had found: coins, old strips of fabric, a couple of wedge-shaped pieces of blue-and-white china. Relics of picnics past.

'They led me to a shelter by the far bank and drew back the curtain and showed me a set of bones, laid out on a soggy tartan blanket, with dead leaves still underneath. They had not cleaned the whole skeleton yet, only the femurs – bleached yellow, like a museum exhibit. I remember how long they seemed in comparison to the rest of her body.

'I told them to cover her up. The policeman was surprised. He said: "We are not the malefactors." I told him I didn't care, and I pulled the blanket over her.'

She holds her hands out on the table in front of us.

'How did you feel?'

She considers this. 'The policemen took me out onto the bank and asked me, *Is this where what happened to you, happened?* I said yes and showed them where it was I woke up after the attack, on the west side, by the trailing willow. They wouldn't look at me; they kept their eyes on their work.'

She smiles faintly. 'I was glad to see that they had to look down.'

Luce and André, ii.

And suddenly there is just this girl, standing in the hallway with enormous eyes taking in all the things she can't be used to seeing. And André standing behind her, watching her look; and she, Luce, says nothing because she doesn't want to break up the tableau.

André says: 'I want you to meet Mlle Doulay, from the costumery, who is here to look through your wardrobe and alter the things that need altering.'

Luce says: 'How nice to meet you, Mlle Doulay,' and the girl positively gapes, then a smile breaks out all over her pretty face. She has extremely good teeth but doesn't smile as if she knows it.

André says: 'I've had the spare room made up for an overnight stay, since your wardrobe is extensive.'

They all laugh, and go their separate ways – the girl escorted upstairs by Thomas, and André, over his shoulder, gives Luce a white-toothed challenge of a grin.

That night, over dinner, the girl doesn't know what cutlery she should use; she plunges in, and then waits, confusion puckering her brow, looking to her hosts for help.

She is breathlessly enthusiastic; answers questions about Pathé ('It is the finest, most splendid place in the entire world, probably, so vast and so rich') and the costumery ('We are a sort of band of sisters, all working to help each other, and the materials are so fine'), wide-eyed and serious, so that Luce has to try not to catch André's eye. But after every answer there is a pause where it is impossible not to just look at her: at the cream of her skin and the freckles on the backs of her hands.

Towards the end of the meal, emboldened by the wine, which she can't be used to, Mlle Doulay starts to ask questions. *Have they enjoyed the state of wedded bliss long?* She talks like an etiquette manual from the 1890s. André says, frowning to hide his smirk, *just under six years*, pretending not to remember the precise date.

And has your union been blessed with fruit?

Even the girl senses it was not the right question, and colours, but does not know how to get back. André does well: he says, a little coyly, *Not yet: but we hope*, and snaps his fingers for Thomas to bring the wine.

As the last plates are cleared away Mlle Doulay does not realise she is supposed to excuse herself before the hosts; her face reddens as the silence grows, and she finally palms-up from the table and says goodnight. Luce listens to her light footsteps ascending the stairs.

They are left alone together in the dining room; things unsaid flutter around the candlelight.

The following morning, Mlle Doulay sits on the salon floor surrounded by taffeta, tulle and organdy, scissors snip-snipping gently along a seam. Always the frown of concentration: everything is to be taken seriously, but not just in a general sense – each thing she comes across, Luce thinks, is a new thing.

The girl holds aloft a gown whose bodice has been ruffled to hide the fact that it has been let out and let out again around the waist, and says: 'Are you sure this must be altered? The silk ruching is very fine and we won't be able to save it.'

'Yes,' Luce says. 'Put it on the mending pile. I have lost so much weight recently.'

Mlle Doulay lifts the dress and looks past it to Luce's thin waist, and nods, understandingly but without understanding. Anyone else would have arched an eyebrow, asked the question: but facts roll off Mlle Doulay like water, and she bends her head obediently and goes on snipping.

'I have been unwell,' Luce tells her, 'and have only been back on my feet a few months. Flat on my back for almost a year!'

Nothing.

Later, Mlle Doulay spreads the dressmakers' thin paper onto the parquet and draws arcs in pencil on it; her hair snakes loose and falls over her eyes but she doesn't notice this, either. Luce watches one tendril fall, then the next, until more hair is out of the chignon than in it; then watches as the girl sighs and sweeps it off her face and behind her ears.

That evening, the girl drinks more than is good for her. Perhaps she isn't sure what is the polite formula to refuse wine; or perhaps she doesn't want to. What she wants is to hang on André's every word, nodding rapidly, and making little observations not to the point, just for the sake of saying something to him.

At the end of the meal she excuses herself – placing a hand on the table to steady herself – and bobs a curtsy to Luce as she leaves. Her steps scurry up the stairs.

A moment later, hurriedly, André pushes back his chair, mopping his lips with his napkin.

At the door he says: 'You only have to tell me not to.'

Luce thinks about it, shrugs, and smiles. He hovers, momentarily uncertain, wanting something more from her, and then ducks his head and exits the room; his footsteps jog up the stairs after the girl's.

Luce lets a few minutes pass and then she follows, her hand crabbing up the banister into the darkness of the stairwell.

She reaches the third-floor landing and listens, unsure which room has been given to the girl; aware, in her tingling hands and feet, of the attic and what the doctors said she must try not to remember. But there is no need to be anxious: it is very obvious which room contains Mlle Doulay, from the breathy, rhythmic 'oh' coming from behind the door closest to the stairs.

Luce shuffles closer and lays her ear to the cold wood panels, and now it is possible to hear André's grunts, the creaking of the bed; even the rustling movement of the sheets tangled around their legs.

She always wondered what she would feel if this were to happen and now she knows.

Jealousy and distress, it turns out, are born of surprise; therefore she isn't jealous or distressed. She only feels – and this is not a surprise either – a hollowing-out of the loneliness that has become habit over the short time she has been well again, making it deeper.

She tries to understand why it should be so, and realises that by this act of being with Mlle Doulay, André has taken action where she has not. He has chosen to cast out his solitude behind him, like a medieval devil. Sure enough, there it is, coming out: a hoarse, protracted cry from him, overlaid by the girl's fluting moans.

The next morning, the girl sits on her salon floor, cutting out paper patterns, and they have a pleasant conversation. Luce recounts amusing stories of her friend Aurélie's exploits being married to the Minister of the Interior; the girl listens, wide-eyed.

Even over dinner the conversation flows between the three of them. She watches the not-so-subtle glances Mlle Doulay shoots André over the top of her wine glass quite calmly, and when André hesitates at the door, she waves him away.

She doesn't mean to go upstairs after them; she intends to turn off at her own floor, but finds that she has climbed the next two flights almost without thinking.

This time there is more noise: André is being rougher. The girl sounds almost distressed, her breathing reduced to thin wisps and then a strangled whimper.

Luce hesitates, her palm flat on the door. Then she turns and walks down the stairs to her own room and gets undressed for bed as usual. Her hand, when she reaches up to unhook her necklace, has a fine tremor in it. She looks at the tremor in the mirror, holding her hand level and watching it vibrate against thin air.

The next morning, the girl says: 'You look pale, Madame,' and Luce is so surprised that she answers, 'I am always pale.'

'I suppose that must be an advantage, in your career,' the girl says. She is sitting on the salon floor with her patterns arranged around her: a child at play. 'They say that Madame Sarah Bernhardt envies you your complexion, I read that in a magazine, is it true?'

Her neck droops as she leans to pick up a far-flung fragment of chiffon.

'Yes,' Luce says, 'it's true.'

The girl looks up, her mouth a perfect oval. Then she does another unexpected thing: she blushes. The colour creeps up her neck and over her cheeks until she is the colour of a radish. 'Imagine,' she says, 'having Sarah Bernhardt be envious of you.'

Imagine that.

Luce asks the girl questions, not vague conversational ones without issue, but listening to the answers with a kind of hunger in herself that she did not anticipate.

Mlle Doulay vouchsafes she has two brothers, both of whom are a little rough, and that she wanted to better herself. She considers working in the costumery to have bettered herself; she will be quite happy one day to become chief costumière, if she works hard enough.

Luce finds herself saying: 'You could aspire to more.'

The girl bends her head. 'I could never be like you,' she says, and bites her lip. 'The things you've done, the people you have met. And living in a house like this!' She looks up and around, her face shining with happiness. Then she blows the hair out of her eyes and continues her work.

It has been months, it may have been years, since anyone has told Luce they wanted to be like her. She looks down at her hands: the tremor is still there, but the skin on the backs is flushed and healthy-looking. Come to think of it, she is warm, not uncomfortably so, but in the pit of her stomach, a slight fluttering. Something tethered about to take flight.

That night, she puts her cheek to the cold door as well as both hands.

You! André shouts inside the room, then says over and over, *you, you.*

The girl moans. She sounds nothing like herself. She sounds older.

Luce shuts her eyes.

Days grow into weeks. Luce's clothes are cut to pieces and reassembled under her fascinated gaze: the cloth supple and refined in Mlle Doulay's hands. Nobody speaks of her leaving. The household seems better. André laughs like he used to laugh when they were first married: full-throated, teeth on show.

They talk about everything. Mlle Doulay seems to like to listen to her talk. Luce tells her anecdotes of her time at the studio; which directors are pleasant to work with, which less so; tittle-tattle about the other stars in the Pathé portfolio. The girl frowns as she stitches, sitting with Luce's dresses draped across her lap, listening and asking the odd question.

Occasionally she sighs. 'It must be wonderful,' she says, 'it must be just wonderful.'

Luce says: 'You could act, if you chose to. I could get you a role.'

'Oh, not me, Madame,' the girl says, holding a needle to the light to thread it.

One night, Luce lays her cheek to the door as usual. She hears Mlle Doulay's breathing become rapid; the jerking of the bedstead, and André's heaving groans.

Faster, closer. Then Mlle Doulay's voice. Louder than normal, saying an intelligible word for the first time, not her usual vixen sounds: the word she is saying is a name, which is André's.

She sighs it out, familiarly. Luce imagines her smoothing the curly hair from André's brow, looking at him with tenderness.

She listens, to hear if perhaps she was mistaken. Then André says, low, as if giving in to something, another name: the girl's, it must be. *Victoire*, he says, over and over. *Victoire*.

Luce turns and makes for the banister, and goes down the stairs as fast as she can. Undresses, tearing at the newly mended nightgown, and lies in the dark, her chest heaving but unable to get in enough breath.

In the morning she does not remember going to sleep. She remembers the dream she has had: the girl bending over her, smoothing the hair from her brow. In the dream Luce has mumbled something, and pulled the girl down beside her. Startled eyes clouding over; they reach for each other. When she wakes up she thinks for a moment the dream was real: perhaps it was.

She goes to the salon to wait for Mlle Doulay. The clock strikes nine; then ten past. At a quarter past the door opens. The girl comes in with head held low, and says: 'I am very sorry. I overslept.'

She does look sorry. She looks strained.

'You are pale,' Luce says.

'No more than usual, Madame.'

'Yes, you are very pale.'

There is a pause. The girl sits in her accustomed chair, face down, reaching for her sewing. 'You are kind to look out for me, Madame.' Then she blushes, holding up a dress, and says: 'This is ready to try on.'

Luce looks at the girl. Then she goes to her, takes the dress and makes a play of rubbing the fabric between her fingers. 'Very good,' she says, 'very fine.'

Then she starts to change in front of her, slipping out of her day-gown.

The girl looks away, in a panic.

'Let us see it with the petticoat you fixed the other day instead of this one,' Luce says, and removes her under-things.

The girl won't look at her. The autumn light slants through the window panes and illuminates her feet, which are the object of her special focus. She goes to fetch the petticoat without turning to face Luce, and when she hands it over, her fingers tremble.

'Now help me into the dress,' Luce says gently.

Where the girl puts her hands on her waist to help her, Luce feels how hot is the contact of their skin: it takes two attempts to fasten each button.

When it is over, Luce crosses to look at herself in the full-length mirror. As if she has been given a licence, Mlle Doulay's face hovers over one shoulder, now looking and looking and blushing and blushing.

'It fits,' Luce says, smoothing the material over her hips.

The girl turns quickly away and busies herself collecting up Luce's clothes.

'What is your name?' Luce asks. 'I mean, your given name?'

'I thought you knew. Victoire,' she says. 'It's Victoire. I thought you knew.'

She straightens. She holds an armful of garments, flushed from the effort.

Luce smiles.

~

The girl spends all her days in the salon now. When she runs out of mending, she comes to sit on the floor by Luce's feet, and reads.

One day, Luce reaches down and twirls a tendril of her hair around her finger. The girl says nothing. After a moment she inclines her head forward to give Luce better access to the nape of her neck. Her neck, her shoulders and cheeks are a warm pink. Neither of them speak. After a while the girl forgets to turn pages.

The dinner bell makes them both start. The girl gets to her feet hurriedly, smoothes her skirts and almost runs from the room.

Luce sits thinking, her eyes gleaming in the firelight.

The following night, September 25th, is a wild one: trees rock outside the windows, and the light goes quickly, leached from the sky in a single swoop.

'We'll sleep well tonight,' André says over supper, rubbing his hands idiotically. Mlle Doulay looks down at her plate. Luce wants to reach for her hand: can it be the girl is afraid of storms?

They finish the meal in silence; just the rain bursting across the dining-room windows in great spatters. André gets to his feet, mopping his mouth and smiling at them.

The girl still won't look at Luce until the last moment; and then it seems she cannot tear her eyes away.

'Goodnight,' she says.

'Goodnight,' Luce replies, and, as an afterthought: 'Sleep well.'

'Yes,' the girl says, distracted.

Luce doesn't go to listen that night. Nor does she undress.

Instead she waits in her bedroom, reading *Thérèse Raquin,* for half an hour; then shuts the book and pads to the door, opens it and goes to the stairs.

She has guessed correctly. From the floor above comes the soft closing of André's door; his footsteps across his bedroom floor.

She mounts the stairs; one flight; two; until she is standing outside Victoire's door.

She lays her cheek to the panels. No human noise: just the wind that is everything, going through the house.

Softly she turns the handle and pushes the door inwards, waiting at the threshold until her eyes have adjusted.

Blackness turns to grey; then the soft shape of Victoire's bare shoulders. She is turned on her side away from the door, but there's no sound of breathing, just a sound of listening. In the room is the sharp smell of sex.

Luce crosses to the bed and stands there, with her arms folded.

The waiting is terrible, but also pleasurable.

Victoire doesn't move.

Luce puts a hand on the girl's shoulder to half-turn her – no resistance. So she stoops, her hair trailing over the girl's face and exposed collarbone, and presses their lips together.

Nothing. Then the girl makes an indeterminate sound; after a moment her mouth starts to move under Luce's.

Luce can smell André's cologne on her.

The girl's eyes half open – shining slits in the grey light – she reaches her arms up and loops them around Luce's neck.

Lower in the bed there is an indeterminate shifting and straining under the covers; Luce reaches a hand down and begins to rub over the sheets, at the fork of the girl's legs.

'Victoire,' Luce says. The girl sighs Luce's name. Sighs again. But then jerks: starts to struggle and push the hand off, and sit upright.

Now she looks startled, half-mad, her breath heaving.

'No,' she says.

Luce bends closer to calm her, placing a cool palm on the girl's forehead: this time the girl shrieks in alarm, tries to bat the hands away, and when it doesn't work, shouts out, a loud, inarticulate sound. Luce releases her; the girl pulls the covers close up under her chin.

'What is this?' André says, standing on the threshold in his nightgown, hunting rifle in one hand, lamp in the other. 'I thought we were being broken into.'

'I was asleep!' Victoire says.

'You were not asleep,' Luce says.

André puts the lamp on the bedside table, takes in Victoire's expression, and looks at Luce. He is looking hard at her now, trying to see under her skin.

'What is this?' he says again.

Victoire says, clutching at the sheets, colouring: 'She is a madwoman, she tried to kiss me, and come to me in my bed.'

'Hypocrite,' Luce says.

André looks at her as if he is seeing someone new.

'Why should you always have what you want, and I never?' Luce says.

'I will go to the police,' Victoire says. 'I will go to the police and tell them Luce Durand is a monster!' She hops down from the bed, all white-eyed, and runs across the room to the door.

André catches her in mid-flight and holds her firm; now he has her by the waist, turns his face to whisper calming words in her ear; she stands transfixed, listening to him.

André places the point of his chin on the girl's head: over the top he looks at Luce, and his lips curl upwards.

It is very simple for Luce to cross and close her hands around the stock of the hunting rifle in his hand, without really knowing what the gun is for and what she would do with it, and silently André's hand tightens on the barrel, and they struggle, while Victoire buries her head in his neck and sobs and does not see.

Then plaster is flaking from the wall by the door and her ears are ringing, and the girl is no longer standing but lying on the parquet, dark red spreading over the sheet still wrapped round her. André is looking down at the gun in his hands, at his finger still wrapped around the trigger. He drops it. It clatters to the floor and falls next to the girl.

André is the faster thinker. He ushers Luce out – closes the door and when the servants come running, tells them it was just the sound of the storm, a tree falling, a natural occurrence.

When the sun comes up he goes to the servants' quarters and gives them an unexpected day off.

They walk out to the lake, sure of being unobserved, with the bundle slung over André's shoulder in a fireman's lift, Luce walking behind.

At the lake he wraps Victoire in the canvas covering. Luce has a last glimpse of the girl's face. She looks very young, almost a child; but the beauty makes Luce feel nothing; or rather, it only makes her feel cold.

André slips stones inside the canvas wrapper and heaves her off from the bank at the point where he knows the water is deepest.

He goes to Luce and slaps her twice; once across each cheek.

Back at the house, with the servants starting to return, cheer and cooking smells, Luce shakes and begins to vomit. She makes no move to get to the commode.

'I can't stay here tonight,' André tells her, but she doesn't answer. The servants have come to hover in the doorway, afraid; André considers what is best and telephones Aurélie Vercors, who arrives just as he is leaving.

Aurélie crosses to where Luce is and puts her hands to her face. 'Tell me everything,' she says.

After that, she and André will not have anyone in the house but themselves and their long-term domestic staff. They never host a dinner or a salon; they make excuses not to invite guests in. There is no need, anyway: they are more in demand than ever, every night a new party to attend in Paris, arm on arm, smile on smile.

Luce is enraged by the stupidity of the ordinary maids, but neither of them suggests an alternative.

One evening, at the very start of 1913, the front door opens and another girl stands there, and André behind her.

'This is Huguette,' he says, 'from Pathé. She has agreed to be your new helper.'

After the shock, Luce sees that Huguette is very plain – almost comically so. Her hair hangs like spaniels' ears down her neck; her face has a sharp quality, as if she is inclined to be pettish.

André says to Luce, in the flat voice he uses when he does not want to show emotion: 'I can't watch you in difficulties over simple things.'

The girl watches the two of them, a private tennis match. Inside herself, Luce hunts for alarm, for some sort of echo, and feels nothing.

Perhaps she was right: perhaps all that really did happen to someone else.

'Yes,' she says, 'Why not? Yes.'

Juliette, x.

The archivist snaps the switch for the fluorescent tubes and they click on, one by one, keeping pace with us down the narrow aisle between the shelves, finger to her lips as she counts her way along.

'P for Peyssac,' she says, lifting down a large cardboard box. 'This is everything that was left to the archive in his estate.'

We lift the lid.

A mushroom cloud of dust clears. The box is only a third full, its paper cargo yellowed and crumbling.

The archivist lifts the topmost layer of paper away. 'Do you want me to read through these?' she asks.

I shake my head, scanning the contents of the box. 'We're looking for a container. Something airtight, ideally – where he could put a strip of film.'

The first object to surface is a slim metal case, its hinges rusted.

The archivist looks at me; I snap it open. Inside the case is frayed blue velvet, in which a slender medal is nesting.

'Croix de Guerre,' the archivist says, turning the silver cross over. 'From 1915. It must have been awarded to him just before he died.'

There is nothing behind the velvet and the back of the case.

The next thing is a set of fountain pens, their barrels dark with age; the archivist crouches, her elbows tucked into her body, and unscrews the barrels one by one.

The only other thing left in the box, aside from the letters, is a photo-frame, which I take out. I unclip the frame and lift off the wooden back; take out the photograph and check between the picture and the frame. Gently shake the ensemble.

There is nothing. I hold the photo for a minute, staring at the space between the frame and the back of the picture, then put it back on the desk.

We look at the empty box.

'I'm sorry,' says the archivist. 'There's nothing else.' She smiles. 'I suppose it's lost for ever,' she says.

'I suppose,' I say.

'Maybe he destroyed it.'

'Maybe,' I say. 'But why go to the trouble of cutting it out in the first place? If it meant so much to him. If he wanted his work to be preserved for all time. This was the place to do it, wasn't it? Temperature-controlled, safe. It doesn't make sense.'

Something is fighting for attention: a tune I cannot identify. Something Rinaldi said.

I reach for the photograph again. Turning it over, I see Peyssac paterfamilias. His worried face set in a stern frown, he stands with one hand on the shoulders of each of his daughters; his wife hovering behind and to the left, her face a pale smudge. The little girls stare solemnly at the camera, their expressions blank. The taller is wearing a white dress, shoes and veil, posed in an attitude of piety. Just some spidery writing on the reverse of the picture. *On the occasion of Micheline's first communion; to my dear wife. Your Robert.*

I'm still for so long that the archivist's hand reaches out, and she gives my shoulder a gentle squeeze; I jump; we stand, confused, looking at each other.

'Are you all right?' she says.

'It's nothing,' I say. Then: 'People keep mementos of people, don't they? Not of things. Images of loved ones. Like this photograph.'

The archivist shrugs. 'I suppose so. Why?'

Juliette and Adèle
1967

'And then?'

Adèle spreads her hands. 'The trial, in the form it was, ceased. The charge against Luce and André was now murder on top of the attempt on my life, and as it was a capital charge, they were tried for it first. Victoire Doulay's parents were the pursuers-in-justice, and it was their lawyers who led, not Denis. The police took a month to assemble the burden of proof. The Doulay family hired an office for them to prepare the case. Although, as it turned out, there was no need.'

'Why not?'

'The judge asked her if it was she who had shot the girl, or whether it was her husband who had done it. He was giving her a chance to claim her innocence. I remember she waited, and she looked all over the courtroom, up to the ceiling and over to the windows as if someone passing outside would tell her what to say; and then she came to where I was sitting, at the table next to Denis.

'"Yes," she said, "I decided to shoot her."'

I say: 'Just like that?'

Adèle sighs. 'Just like that. The easiest thing in the world.'

'But why? Why did she confess?'

Adèle smiles. 'Why? Because she was guilty.'

'And then they questioned André?'

'Yes. He did his best to pretend that she had implicated him maliciously, but her account of the shooting had been so clear that it was believed. Besides which, there were practicalities: it would have been difficult for her to have carried Victoire to the lake without help.'

'They were shipped out to Guyana on the morning of the ninth of June.'
'And what did you feel when you knew she had been transported?'
'Some parts of me felt heavier, others lighter.'
'And when you heard about André?'
'I was surprised. I had not thought he would become involved in petty squabbles; certainly not before the prison transport even touched land. I had thought he would demonstrate more *nous*. The article said he was thrown overboard with the shank still in his guts.'

'Then?'
'I worked hard, and got promoted. I moved to Vincennes, to my apartment, and have been here ever since.'
'Have you been happy?'
She takes a moment to think about this.
Then she says: 'It has always been surprising. Aurélie Vercors came to visit me, after her divorce. She was with a woman about my age, who looked at her as though she was the beginning of everything.'

'And Luce?'
Adèle says: 'I read about it in the newspaper. There was a little article to say that she'd been released after five years at the work camp and lived in anonymity nearby for five more years. That it was only discovered who she really was when she died.'
'And how did you feel when you heard?'
'I had the impression that the walls of my apartment were made of a thick, viscous liquid: that I could put my hand through

them if I wanted. Everything was fragile and surrounded by a radiant glow: if I tried to go to the door, the door would bend away from me. I thought I was in another room: the salon at the house. The quiet of the silk sofa and the spirals of mica in the sunlight from the window. *I am a speck of dust. I am dancing for you.* Except she was not in any room any more.'

The door to the café opens; someone comes in, orders coffee. The waiters' voices laughing with the new customer.

Adèle is looking at me with a wide, blank smile.

I say: 'And in that time, the time she was free, she never tried to get in touch with you? And you never tried to look for her?'

A shrug. 'Everything we had to say had been said.'

Seeing my face, the smile twitches down at one corner. 'What is it, Juliette?'

'Nothing,' I say. 'Just cold.'

Juliette, xi.

Rinaldi opens the door on the second ring, his face showing perfect surprise, then awkwardness.

'What can I do for you?' he asks. 'Is everything all right?'

'I need to ask you about the photograph of the Pathé workers.'

He smiles warily. Then he relents. 'Very well,' he says, and turns to shuffle away down the corridor towards the salon.

'I'm not sure how I can help you, really,' he says.

'I don't think Peyssac took the film,' I say. 'I think it was someone else. Someone who had the opportunity, who was there on that day, but with a different motive.' I take out the photograph. 'I think it might have been this man.'

Rinaldi sighs. 'Paul Leclerc?'

I run my fingernail over Paul's eager eyes and hairless chin. 'The security guard. The one Adèle Roux told me about. You said he tried to kill himself over a girl who worked at the factory.'

'That's right. In late 1914, I think. He almost hanged himself in the Bois de Vincennes. Very sad.'

'Who was she? This love of his life?'

'He never told me her name.'

I drum my fingers on the photo.

'What happened to him?'

Rinaldi says: 'He left the factory. He'd hurt his back; he wasn't able to work afterwards. He did marry someone else eventually; he ended up living with his daughter on the outskirts of Paris.

She and her husband looked after him. I had a card from her when he died.'

I lean forward. 'What was the daughter's name?'

'Anne something. Something beginning with R.'

It is dark by the time I arrive at the house in Vincennes.

I hammer on the door for a full minute until there is the shuffle of footsteps coming down the hall corridor and stopping just on the other side.

'Your father was a security guard at Pathé. He was the one who stole the film.'

The door stays shut. Inside the house, the dog begins to bark frantically.

'Let me in. I could call the police.'

Silence.

One. Two. Three. Four. Five. Six. Seven. Eight—

Anne Ruillaux opens the door.

She crosses her arms across her chest and suddenly begins to cry: child-like, her fists in her eyes. 'He made me do it,' she says. 'He said, *When I'm gone, take this to the archive, and say you don't know how you got it. Don't tell them I worked at the studio.* We never had much because of looking after him. He said I was due some money. He said it wasn't wrong because the real wrong had been done by the man who made the film. He said we were helping to make everything right.'

In the back, the dog howls its distress, flinging itself at the inside of the closed door in a scrabble of nails.

'Why couldn't you leave me in peace?' she asks.

I say: 'Was it because of the girl that he stole it? The one he was in love with and tried to kill himself over? Was it so he could have something to remember her by?'

She watches me.

'It's because she died, isn't it?' I say. 'He wanted a memento?'

Silence. She shakes her head.

I stare at her, thrown. 'What do you mean?'

Anne says: 'She asked him to destroy the film completely. It would be dangerous to her if anyone saw it.'

'Dangerous?'

'Yes. She could get in trouble with the law.'

Somewhere in the distance an express train passes, on its way south; and when the sound is over, I find everything is clear.

The enormity of it: bile rising into my mouth.

'But he didn't destroy all the film,' I say. 'Your father cut out a scene and kept it separately. That part really was a memento, wasn't it? It was the only scene she was in. That's why he bothered to cut it out, instead of just keeping the whole film.'

A nod.

Silence. Then I say: 'Do you know where he kept it?'

She says grudgingly, as if it's of no consequence: 'He asked to be buried with a cigarette case I hadn't seen before.'

Juliette, xii.

You're walking along the *quais*, between the Pont-Neuf and the Ile St Louis. Long, slanted light; breeze in your hair like someone running their fingers through it. The trees beside Notre Dame are shaking themselves free of their leaves.

You've come here because it's where you go to make decisions, with the city around you like a blanket. The late-lunch cooking smells. Near here a girl walked and bought a postcard of Max Linder; over there, a car rattled home from a party at the Ex-Minister's apartment; the statue of St Jeanne d'Arc was lit up underneath the moon.

Of course there is a bruise: the burning sensation of being tricked, because she has been lying to you since you met. But underneath, what you feel is surprise. Surprise, because now that you're here, there isn't a decision to make.

To come to the end, and find you are not the person you thought you were.

Wind on the surface of the river. On the parapet above a tourist points his camera at you: *click.*

You lift your hand and wave.

WHO DOESN'T COME THROUGH THE DOOR TO GET HOME?

Juliette and Adèle
1967

She frowns as if she hasn't understood. 'You're leaving Paris?' she says. 'A holiday? Where will you go?'

'I haven't decided,' I say. 'Somewhere new.'

She smiles at me. 'Then this is our last meeting,' she says. 'And you've brought some chapters of the book for me?'

'No. That's not what it is.'

'What, then?'

'It's a silent filmscript, of a kind. I think you'll find it interesting reading.'

The café door opens and closes – and that's when she guesses, now, before I have even spoken.

She folds her hands over each other. 'Tell me it instead,' she says.

'We open on the silhouette of a man, hanging from the branches of a skeletal tree. He rotates, as if on a thread; we think he's gone, but then three men rush into the frame and support his legs. One climbs up to cut him down and we see that the man is alive, after all. He clutches his throat and gasps for air. His friends gather round.

'The intertitle: WHAT COULD DRIVE YOU TO THIS HATEFUL CRIME OF SELF-DESTRUCTION?

'Then I think we cut to a close-up of Paul Leclerc's face as he begins to tell his story.'

She doesn't flinch when I say his name. 'Continue,' she says.

'Then we have another intertitle. YOUNG LOVE IN SUMMER.

'We watch a younger, happier-looking Paul walking in the same woods with a pretty girl. She has long, dark hair, she's in her late teens. They exit the woods, holding hands, and go through the Pathé factory gates, where with much blowing of kisses, they part ways, each to their separate section.

'A montage follows. Paul and the girl in a café, flirting; Paul and the girl strolling on the riverside. Paul walking her back to her apartment. He stands mooning in the street while she leans out of the window and waves to him. Next to her, at the window, a fat woman with eyes like currants smokes a cigarette.'

She puts her hand to her mouth: as if she's suppressing a smile.

'Then we cut back to Paul's mournful face. He says *I would have done anything for her. But nothing stays the same for ever...* and we fade to the next scene, in a Pathé studio, empty apart from a few people. A cameraman is filming a young girl, Adèle, who looks startlingly like Paul's girlfriend. She is standing on a stage with various mirrors arranged on it. A director walks around and around the set, agitated, waving his arms and shaking his head. Suddenly he stops. Points. Paul's girlfriend is sitting beside the set, holding a make-up box on her lap. She lifts her head, places her palm on her chest – *Me?* – and allows herself to be beckoned forward. The director snaps his fingers – *You, Camille!* – and someone brings an empty mirror-frame forward and places it on the set. Paul's girlfriend goes to stand on one side and the girl stands on the other side. The director claps his hands in joy and tells the cameraman to start filming. Paul watches from the doorway to the room, a dreamy expression of pride on his face.

'Cut back to the group of friends surrounding Paul by the tree. One of them has a knowing expression on his face. *So her head was turned by the chance of fame?* he says. Paul shakes his head. *No. This was different.*

'Now we go to a dark and stormy night. An exterior of

Camille's apartment, rain spattering its windows. Camille's sister, Adèle, runs to the front door and opens it. She vanishes inside.

'Cut to Camille asleep in her room. The door bursts open and Adèle rushes in. An older, stringy woman hovers in the doorway, her hand over her mouth; behind her the fat woman we saw at the window before. We now see that Adèle is bleeding and clutching her arm.

'Camille says: *Who has done this to you? Why? Is it your employers?*

'Adèle nods. *They have killed me.*

'Camille rushes Adèle towards the bed and leans tenderly over her.

'Adèle's lips move as she tells Camille the story; Camille nods, listening. She gets up. *I'll fetch the doctor.*

'Adèle says, *Don't leave me...*

'Then we see Camille exiting the block and hurrying down the street. As she leaves, a pair of men carrying a gun creep down the street to the apartment block's front door. With exaggerated caution, they sneak inside. Lights go on in the hallway of each floor as they ascend. We see, in silhouette, the thin woman, Camille's landlady, throw up her arms in panic and fall down; in the next window, the fat woman is felled; in the final, Adèle too crumples to the floor.

'The criminals make their escape into the night. A second later, Camille hurries back. We see her ascend the staircase, silhouetted in the windows of the apartment. She stands for a moment and then turns and walks away. She exits the apartment block, just before the police arrive, in a pantomime of whistle-blowing and truncheon-waving. Nobody notices Camille slip away.

'Now we're getting close to the end. In the next scene, Camille stands opposite Paul Leclerc in a different apartment.

'Close-up of Paul's agonised face. He shouts *There must be another way.*

'Camille says: *If you love me, help me avenge my sister.*

'She is holding a gun. She passes it to him and spreads her arms.

'Covering his face with his hands, he shoots her. She clutches her shoulder but remains standing.

'She says: *And now you must see to the other thing.*

'Paul nods, weeping, and exits.

'In the next scene, he arrives at the factory. He removes a set of keys from his pocket and unlocks a shed. He goes to a cupboard in the corner and picks out a film canister. The title says *PETITE MORT*. A DRAMA OF A HAUNTING. WITH DOPPELGÄNGER SCENE.

'He shoulders the canister and produces a matchbook from his pocket; strikes a match and, coughing as the first smoke starts to show, exits the shed.

'He appears, triumphant, back at his apartment, with the canister. The room is empty. His face falls. He searches frantically for Camille but she has disappeared.

'Cut to a police station. Camille, clutching her arm, walks towards the entrance and disappears inside.

'Now we cut back to the present-day scene in the woods. Paul's friends' faces are now alive with interest, whereas Paul's face is written on with misery. She is gone. *The only fragment of her I have is kept here.* He fishes a cigarette case from his pocket.

'His friends look at each other and shrug, thinking he may have lost his reason. They pick up Paul and carry him off-screen, leaving just the solitary tree with the noose hanging from it.'

Camille Roux and I look at each other for a long time.

She says: 'Why, according to your theory, did Paul Leclerc steal the film?'

I say: 'Imagine if it had been distributed. People would have flocked to see it. Looked closely at the person in the mirror. Perhaps they would have realised the substitution that had been made.'

She purses her lips. 'Wouldn't the murderous employers immediately recognise that the girl on the witness stand was an impostor?'

'How could they reveal that the real Adèle was dead without telling the Court how they knew it for sure?'

'And what happens to the girl? The impostor?'

I say: 'Oh, she lives on into old age. At first she wears a veil around the city; and then, when she feels safer, and when she ages, she takes it off. She congratulates herself on getting away with it. Until, one day, it turns out her lover disobeyed her: he kept the stolen film in her memory. It's a lucky escape – he's excised the only scene with her in it. But what if the missing scene comes to light? She decides the time is right to impose her version of events on the world.'

A pause.

'You hired me because I was inexperienced,' I say. 'It suited you to have someone young, who wouldn't ask awkward questions.'

There is a glint in her smile. I think for a moment it's anger: then I realise it's pride.

'But you did,' she says.

We sit together, not speaking, for another minute.

Then she says: 'I made a misstep. With Luce, not contacting me after she was released. You suspected something.'

I say: 'She knew you weren't Adèle, didn't she? She knew that day in the car, outside the courtroom. That was why she never came back. I knew it felt wrong.'

Camille nods.

'In hindsight, there were other things,' I say. 'The way you described the Durands' house. It didn't feel like you'd lived there. And of course, you didn't. You only knew about it from reading Adèle's letters.'

Another nod.

'You must have loved her very much,' I say. 'To give up everything to avenge her. To live as someone else for fifty years. Did loving make-up make it easier? Did you see it as a kind of film trick to end all film tricks?'

A final nod. The point of the chin lifting. Water trembling in her eyes.

The waiter brings us another coffee. She smiles up at him and says thank you.

When he's gone she says: 'What happens now?'

I say: 'The past is another country. Peyssac stole the film. Your memoirs will end with me failing to find the missing scene in his archive box.'

She digests this. Her hands, linked together on the table, are perfectly still.

I say: 'There is just one thing I want to know. Was it worth it?'

She laughs. In the laugh is the laugh of a much younger woman.

Camille, i.

I often go to the cinema.

Tonight, the film is an antique, and the audience is made up of older people, like me, and earnest young ones: boys with their arms slung round girls; girls with long hair and intelligent faces.

Velvet drapes open, and behind this curtain, a screen; and behind its façade are things we cannot see – the toe of the black-clad stagehand whisking out of frame, the tick of the camera, the tension in the director's face – an army of ghosts. So we sit numbly in our seats and soak up the tricks and the story, and on the edge of the frame it takes immeasurable work to create it: ropes hauled, hands chafed, a spark in the writer which becomes a germ which becomes a script. We have paid for our tickets, and we think we own this. And the film humours us, because it's an illusion that is created with love.

I turn my head – certain, from the brush of air, that someone has just taken the seat next to me. The light from the screen flickers over her face.

It took me years to find you, she says sadly. *I don't know how long I can stay.*

It doesn't matter, I tell her. *Flesh of my flesh.* Does anyone ever have enough time?

Louise Walters was born in Oxfordshire and now lives in Northamptonshire with her husband and five children. She graduated from the Open University in 2010. *Mrs Sinclair's Suitcase* is her first novel.

MRS SINCLAIR'S SUITCASE

Forgive me, Dorothea, for I cannot forgive you. What you do, to this child, to this child's mother, it is wrong . . . Roberta likes to collect the letters and postcards she finds in second-hand books. When her father gives her some of her grandmother's belongings, she finds a baffling letter from the grandfather she never knew — dated after he supposedly died in the war . . . Dorothy is unhappily married to Albert, who is away at war. When an aeroplane crashes in the field behind her house she meets Squadron Leader Jan Pietrykowski, and as their bond deepens she dares to hope she might find happiness. But fate has other plans for them both, and soon she is hiding a secret so momentous that its shockwaves will touch her granddaughter many years later . . .

LOUISE WALTERS

MRS SINCLAIR'S SUITCASE

Complete and Unabridged

CHARNWOOD
Leicester

First published in Great Britain in 2014 by
Hodder & Stoughton
London

First Charnwood Edition
published 2015
by arrangement with
Hodder & Stoughton
An Hachette UK company
London

The moral right of the author has been asserted

A catalogue record for this book is available
from the British Library.

ISBN 978–1–4448–2425–4

Published by
F. A. Thorpe (Publishing)
Anstey, Leicestershire

Set by Words & Graphics Ltd.
Anstey, Leicestershire
Printed and bound in Great Britain by
T. J. International Ltd., Padstow, Cornwall

This book is printed on acid-free paper

For Ian, Oliver, Emily, Jude,
Finn and Stanley, with love

1

My dear Dorothea,

In wartime, people become desperate. We
step outside ourselves. The truth is, I love
you and I am sorry that only now do I own
it. You love me. I will not forget the touch of
your hand on my head and on my neck
when you thought I slept. The touch of love,
no longer imagined. Nobody will touch me
like that again. This I know. This is my loss.

Forgive me, Dorothea, for I cannot forgive
you. What you do, to this child, to this
child's mother, it is wrong. It is misplaced,
like me, forced out of my homeland, perhaps
never to return. You too will never return, if
you persist in this scheme. You will persist.
Yet even now it can be undone. But I know
you will not undo. Your soul will not return
from this that you do. Please believe me. In
welcoming the one into your arms, you must
lose another. I cannot withstand. You know
why.

I do not enjoy writing these words to you.
Actually, I cry. Once this war is finished
— and it must finish — we could have made
a life together. To spend my life with you
has become my only great dream and desire.
After our first meeting, as I rode away on my
bicycle, I knew you were as important to me

as water. I knew you were for all time, even as there is no time. I thought of marriage within minutes of meeting you. But it cannot be. You are an honourable woman, but this thing that you do is beyond honour. You do so much to be good, yet you go back on yourself, you invite dishonour. I cannot write clearly, but you will understand. My truly beautiful Dorothea, despite everything, our friendship must here end. I wish you all joy of this world.

Yours,
Jan Pietrykowski

(I found this letter in a 1910 edition of *The Infant's Progress: From the Valley of Destruction to Everlasting Glory*. I placed the book on Philip's desk for pricing, and it went into the antiquarian books cabinet, priced at a modest £15.)

★ ★ ★

I clean books. I dust their spines, their pages, sometimes one at a time; painstaking, throat-catching work. I find things hidden in books: dried flowers, locks of hair, tickets, labels, receipts, invoices, photographs, postcards, all manner of cards. I find letters, unpublished works by the ordinary, the anguished, the illiterate. Clumsily written or eloquent, they are love letters, everyday letters, secret letters and mundane letters talking about fruit and babies and tennis matches, from people signing themselves as Marjorie or Jean. My boss, Philip, long used to such finds, is blasé and

2

whatever he finds, he places aside for me to look at. You can't keep everything, he reminds me. And, of course, he is right. But I can't bring myself to dispose of these snippets and snapshots of lives that once meant (or still do mean) so much.

I walked into the Old and New Bookshop as a customer eleven years ago, and returned the following day as its first employee. Quietly impetuous, owner-manager Philip asked me to work with him. As he said, we were soon to enter a new millennium, so it was time to change; time to take stock, literally. He appreciated my way of loving books and my ability to get on with others. He claimed he found people 'difficult'.

'They're generally pretty rotten, aren't they?' he said, and I half agreed.

He also once declared, 'Books tell many stories besides those printed on the pages.'

Did I know that? I did. Books smell, they creak, they talk. You hold in your hand now a living, breathing, whispering thing, a book.

Philip told me, on the day I started work in his bookshop, 'Study books, smell them, hear them. You will be rewarded.'

★ ★ ★

I tidy shelves. I make sure they are not too tightly packed. I take stock each year, in May, with the blossom trees discarding their petals, the sun shining through the French windows in the large room at the back of the shop, where we keep the second-hand non-fiction and hardback fiction, the sun's vernal warmth thrown over my back

3

like a huge comforting arm and the swallows swooping over the garden, shrieking and feasting on flies. I make coffee in the mornings, tea in the afternoons. I help interview new staff: eighteen-year-old gap year student Sophie, who is still with us, enjoying a gap of indeterminate length; and more recently Jenna, who became Philip's lover within two weeks of starting her job. Jenna was never exactly interviewed. Like me, she walked into the Old and New as a customer; like me, she was engaged in conversation, and offered a job.

There is nobody more passionate about books, the printed word, than my boss, Philip Old. He is driven by his love of books, of the book for its own sake, its smell, feel, age, its provenance. His shop is large, with high ceilings, tip-tappy flagstone floors and a warren of rooms — six in total, plus storage on the first floor. All is spacious and light. We sell new books, old books, antiquarian books, children's books, shelf upon shelf upon shelf of books, lining the numerous walls of this large, luminous cathedral. The building is set back from the busy Market Square, with a neat, pretty garden, lavender and rosemary bordering the stone path that leads to the large oak door at the front of the shop. In the summer we have strings of bunting along the wrought-iron fence, kindly made for us by a customer, and a small hand-painted sign that reads:

Welcome to
The Old and New Bookshop
Open today from 9 until 5
You are warmly invited to browse

4

As a business, the Old and New cannot be making a profit. We have a band of loyal customers, of course — such establishments always do — but a small band. So there must be money somewhere, keeping this business afloat, kitting out Philip's flat on the second floor so tastefully. I have not enquired. Philip never talks about money, as he never talks about his private life.

I have had my share of romance, if I can call it that. At least, offers of romance. One young man, younger than me, part of the regular geeky Saturday afternoon crowd (and seemingly living in a world at least a decade behind everybody else — he always wears a black and purple shell suit) has proffered me his fax number on more than one occasion. Another, recently (red-faced, not entirely unattractive) told me I was the 'best-looking' woman he had seen 'in months'. Patently untrue, and the genuinely beautiful Jenna nearby, pretending to tidy shelves, giggling. I threw her a look. She threw it back. And a year ago, a head teacher at a local primary school (our town has three), a regular customer with a habit of putting all and sundry on the school account. Hovering after I had served him, after I had handed him his stylish Old and New paper carrier bag, lingering. Clearing his throat, asking me out for dinner on Thursday night, if I could make it. If I was available. He had a charming smile, and thick black hair I suspected was dyed.

* * *

5

My father brought in some books this morning, old books belonging to my babunia; my grandmother. She has been in a care home for two years now, but it's taken us a long time to sort through her belongings. There aren't even that many things. Babunia, thank goodness, is not a great hoarder. But my father cannot work quickly these days. I have already been through her books, of course, keeping back a few for myself that I recall from my childhood. When she agreed to live in the home, she said I must keep whatever of hers I wanted. She had no use for reading now, she said, no use for sewing. It was an inexpressibly sad moment. Yet there was no option for any of us. Dad just could not take care of her any more. I offered to cut my hours at the Old and New, but neither of them would hear of it.

I saw my father wandering along the path and I waved, but he didn't spot me. I ran to the heavy front door and pulled it open for him.

He explained he had around twenty books. He had packed them into a battered old suitcase.

'This was hers too,' said Dad. 'Keep it if you like, Roberta.'

I would keep it. I love old suitcases. And already I could think of a use for it.

'How are you feeling today?' I asked, searching his face for clues.

He had been, for some time, habitually pale, a ghastly creamy-grey colour. But he never let on how he was feeling. So he shrugged, his catch-all gesture, meaning, 'Well . . . you know.' He had been in remission a few weeks ago. Now, he

6

wasn't. Quite a sudden change this time, and frightening for both of us.

Philip came through from his office and shook my father's hand. They had met before — twice — and both had confided in me that they found the other to be a 'gentleman'. Philip insisted on paying my father for the books; my father wanted to give them to him. In the end, Dad accepted twenty quid, a compromise sum. He stayed for a cup of tea, sitting out in the back garden in the pale spring sunshine. Then he shuffled away, his bold, rangy walk vanquished. I tried not to notice.

I emptied the suitcase. There was a tatty old label on the inside that read 'Mrs D. Sinclair'. Idly, as I sorted and cleaned the books, I wondered who she was. Dad said this was Babunia's suitcase, but it must have belonged to this Mrs Sinclair first. My grandmother has always had a thrifty, make-do-and-mend mentality, happy to utilise the secondhand, the new-to-you. Dad says she learned the habit during and after the war, 'because everyone did'. It wasn't just a fashionable notion in those days.

I cleaned the dust from *The Infant's Progress: From the Valley of Destruction to Everlasting Glory* (a book I didn't recall ever seeing in my grandmother's house) and two neatly folded sheets of paper fluttered out. A letter! There was no envelope, always a pity. I unfolded the sheets. The letter, addressed to Dorothea, my grandmother, was written in anaemic blue ink, the writing small and neat; the paper was an even paler blue, brittle and dry as a long-dead insect's

7

wing, yellowing around the edges, with little holes creeping along the fold. Of course, I wondered if I should read it. But my curiosity got the better of me. I couldn't not.

I have since read this letter again and again, and I still can't make sense of it. At first I experienced the strange sensation of needing to sit down. So I did, on the squeaky footstool, and my hand trembled as I read slowly, trying to take in every word.

Dorothea Pietrykowski is my grandmother. Jan Pietrykowski was my grandfather, never known to me, never even known to my father. These are incontrovertible facts.

But this letter makes no sense.

Firstly, my grandparents were happily, if briefly, married, but in this letter he seems to declare that he cannot marry her. Secondly, it is dated 1941. Polish Squadron Leader Jan Pietrykowski, my grandfather, died defending London in the Blitz, in November 1940.

2

Dorothy Sinclair sweated in her wash house, where the air was clammy with steam. Moisture clung to her face as she wiped her forehead repeatedly with the back of her hand. Her headscarf had long ago slipped off and she hadn't bothered stopping her work to re-knot it, so her hair stuck to her face like the predatory tentacles of some lurking, living creature. It was important to keep busy on this day.

The copper in the dark, far corner hissed and bubbled like a cauldron, boiling Aggie and Nina's clothes. Their uniforms, on a meagre ration, were muddied and stained almost daily. But Dorothy knew that presenting her girls with a pile of clean, starched and ironed laundry once a week was the least she could do. And despite the discomforts, she loved the work, in her own way. Washing frocks, stockings, undies, cardigans, the girls' breeches and shirts and knickers, and all the laundry from up at the house, was more than just a household chore: it was now her living. Scrubbing, dipping, sweating, stirring, all of these had a rhythm of their own and gave meaning to her day. Turning the mangle over and over, as she did now, wringing the life out of clothes and sheets and tablecloths. And the ultimate pleasure, Dorothy's favourite part of the day: pegging the clothes and linens out on the lines, and watching the sheets and cloths and pillowcases billowing and flapping like triumphant angel wings.

It was important to keep busy on this day. On . . . this . . . day.

She mustn't think. About anything. Since *that* day, she had become adept at not thinking. Oftentimes now she thought in images. Language was partisan, ambiguous. She no longer trusted words. Yet she could not turn her back on them completely. She liked to write, so she tried to write. She wrote furtively, alone, in her notebook. She could not draw, so it had to be words. She hoped she was fashioning her ramblings into something like poetry. But it was hard to make sense, hard to sound pleasing.

She looked up from her laundry. She listened, and stared at the open door through which so little steam seemed to escape. Something was wrong. Since losing . . . since Sidney . . . she had developed a sixth sense, almost akin to smell. She 'sniffed' the air now. Letting Nina's breeches hang loose and bedraggled either side of the mangle, she wiped her hands on her pinny and went to the door of her wash house. She looked up, but was dazzled by the sun, by the rows of white sheets and pillowcases and glittering tablecloths. She squinted up into the innocent blue sky. Small clouds sprinted across it, forgetful children racing home for tea.

Then she heard a drone, a low hum mixed with splutters and growls, like those of a threatened dog. Almost immediately she saw it, a Hurricane, weaving through the air. Surely descending too fast? She had never seen one

10

coming in to land this quickly. Her heart began to thump, the blood thickened in her head, a tightness grabbed her around the throat. Was the pilot playing a game? Dorothy stared. No. This was not a game. The pilot was in trouble, and he was not the only one.

'Please no,' she said aloud, as she ran along the red-brick path. Hens scattered before her, cross and fussing and stupidly unaware of the new catastrophe looming above them. Dorothy reached her back gate, opened it and stepped out into the Long Acre, a field she liked to imagine was as immense as an Arabian desert. She had feared something like this would happen. She had seen the pilots, such young men and so reckless, looping the loop, showing off. It was only a matter of time, she always thought, and now that time had surely arrived. Why didn't he bail out? The stricken Hurricane lurched towards her, listing wildly, like a broken pendulum. Dorothy looked back at her cottage in horror. She turned once more to the Hurricane and, with relief, she saw it veer away from her and her home, heading instead for the emptiness of the huge field. She walked mesmerised through the swaying ears of barley, scratchy-soft and clinging to her bare legs. It was a sensation she loved, usually, and felt herself in tune with.

The aeroplane was close now, close to its inevitable, barely controlled landing, close to the earth and to her and the swaying barley. It swooped over her head like a giant bird, its shadow providing her with momentary relief from the sun.

'Dorothy!'

It was Aggie calling, from a long way away, Dorothy thought. She saw two fawn shirts quivering far across the Long Acre. The girls were running. Dorothy ignored Aggie's shrill calls.

It was good. It was fitting, one year to the day since Sidney. Her poor lost Sidney. She should join him, really she should, and she could, and for a moment she marvelled that she had not thought of this before. She waded through the barley, determined. She marched towards the Hurricane as it gave itself up to the earth. A noise like thunder, a billow of choking black smoke, a sickening thud and the sound of all things smashing.

★   ★   ★

'Dorothy? Pass the teacup to Mrs Lane, please. Dorothy, pass this one to Mrs Hubbard. And Dorothy? Hand round the plate of Genoa cake. Dorothy, do stand up straight. Goodness gracious, child.'

Dorothy hated the feel of her new white frock, stiffly starched and rubbing at her neck. Her mother, Mrs Ruth Honour, looked at her with her usual mixture of pride and disgust while Dorothy dutifully did as she was told and handed round the cake. Mrs Lane and Mrs Hubbard smiled kindly at her but Dorothy refused to look at them, knowing she would meet pity in their eyes. Pity she did not want, ever. She wondered, why did they pity her? It must have something to do with Mummy. Or, most probably, the death of her father. Mourning was over now, and mother and daughter were no

12

longer in black. But Mummy was supposed to be lonely, wasn't she?

Dorothy stood still, watching her mother and her mother's gossiping friends nibble at their cake and sip their tea. The day was hot and her frock so uncomfortable; she longed to be outside, at the far end of the garden, under the gnarled apple tree, barefoot in the grass, singing songs to herself or writing in her head her great poetry, and dreaming about the past, the present and the future. In her imagination she had six siblings named Alice, Sarah, Peter, Gilbert, Henry and Victoria. She knew her brothers and sisters would be waiting for her now, in the cool grass, sitting in the tree, idly talking, teasing one another.

Watching the cake disappear into the garrulous mouths of the three women, Dorothy began to sway. Her throat tightened, her heart raced. She became aware of falling, falling, letting go and landing with a thud on the tea tray, rosebud cups and saucers smashing, tea spilling all over her new, stiff, white frock and all over the rug.

'Dorothy? Dorothy? Oh, you clumsy girl!'

★   ★   ★

She felt something hot and sharp hit her in her stomach. Something else, hot and soft and wet, slapped her face. All around was choking smoke, black and thunderous.

'Dorothy! Get back!' Aggie's voice was closer now.

Dorothy saw the girls floating on the other

side of the burning wreckage, bright beacons in treacherous fog. 'I want to join him,' said Dorothy, but nobody heard her. She rubbed her neck. The new, white frock was too stiff, too rough.

Her mother stared at her.

Dorothy swayed. She fell, slowly, her white frock splattered with blood, her head spinning in a vortex of shame, and the sea of barley cushioning her fall.

* * *

It would always be said that Dorothy Sinclair was a heroine, trying to rescue the young Hurricane pilot who came down to meet his death in the Long Acre field on that hot afternoon in late May, 1940. A brave and courageous woman, never sparing a thought for her own safety. A woman to be held up as an example to others, the kind of woman Britain needed in those bleak and fearful times.

Dorothy knew better.

Still, she let people believe it of her, as it did no harm.

Mrs Compton came to visit her later that afternoon, after Dr Soames had been and dressed Dorothy's wounds, which were sore but superficial: a cut across her stomach, and burns to her face. Fainting and falling down into the barley had doubtlessly saved her from worse injuries. She was a plucky lady, the doctor pronounced.

Mrs Compton had the unnerving ability to

14

make Dorothy feel ashamed of herself. Did she somehow *know?* Dorothy thought that she might. Mrs Compton was a witch, Dorothy understood. She smiled weakly at the older woman and noticed a fine white hair protruding from a mole on her left cheek. Or thought she noticed. Perhaps there wasn't even a mole? It was difficult for Dorothy to see people clearly, to see solidity, reality.

'I don't know,' said Mrs Compton, 'what a state to get in!'

'I just thought . . . '

'I know, love. I know. Such a shame.'

'They've been cleaning up out there all afternoon.' Dorothy indicated the Long Acre and its swaying barley with a nod of her head.

'They're nearly finished now, though, I think. Don't you worry about it. You did what you could. You did more than you should, perhaps.'

'It was nothing.'

They sat in silence, sipping tea. The clock ticked on the range mantelpiece. Distant male voices drifted in through the open window, the voices of men clearing up the flesh and metal in the Long Acre. Had Mrs Compton remembered the part she played in the drama of a year ago? Was she aware of this saddest of anniversaries? Dorothy suspected not. Even more reason to distrust the woman. Even more reason to imagine her prone, with her head on a bloodied block, her ugly face contorted in fear, pleading for her life as Dorothy raised a huge axe, told her to —

'He was Polish,' said Mrs Compton.

15

'I heard they had arrived. A couple of weeks ago, wasn't it?'

'It was. They do say the Poles hate the Nazis more than we do.' Mrs Compton finished her tea with a small slurp. She put the cup and saucer on the table carefully and, folding her hands in her lap, she gazed at Dorothy. Dorothy shifted her own gaze to the window, watching male heads bob up and down, the hawthorn hedge obscuring their bodies. Dorothy thought about the Polish pilot, dead, burned and disembodied. Part of him had hit her in the face. She touched her cheek, and felt the dressing. She must look frightful.

'And how are you keeping, nowadays?' asked Mrs Compton, leaning forward.

'I'm well,' said Dorothy, standing to look out of the kitchen window, watching a hen scratch at the earth and pluck a worm from it. Dorothy, rational, contemplated the worm's futile struggle.

'Good. That's good.'

Mrs Compton sounded doubtful. She glanced at the clock. She must go, she said. A young woman down at the next village was expecting her first baby and had been labouring since half past four that morning. Mrs Compton's services may be needed by now.

Dorothy stared at her.

Mrs Compton moved towards the door and lifted the latch. She turned back to Dorothy, who remained motionless, her back to the window.

'I'm sorry, Dorothy. I should have remembered. It takes time, you know. It *was* around this time last year, wasn't it? If I remember rightly?

Anytime you need to talk about it, I'll be happy to listen. You don't have to ignore it. I know we soldier on with life, but things can haunt us, Dorothy.'

Mrs Compton left then, closing the door, and Dorothy stared after her.

How dare that woman!

She picked up the teacup Mrs Compton had drained so unceremoniously and threw it at the door, hard and fast, before she even knew what she was doing, so that the noise of it shattering surprised her. In pain where the hot metal had ripped through her skin, she swept up the mess.

* * *

Alice, Sarah, Peter, Gilbert, Henry and Victoria lived and moved and breathed in Dorothy's lonesome imaginings. The trouble was, she never really knew where she, Dorothy, belonged in this family of girls with flowing fair hair, strong sturdy boys playing with catapults and hoops, all six children with bright blue eyes and long lashes. They were blessed, she fantasised, with perfectly perfect childhoods. Was she the eldest sister? Austere, serious, strong, bossy? Or was she somewhere in the middle, forgotten, ignored and unimportant? Perhaps she was the baby, the odd one out among the girls with her long straggling brown hair, her green eyes. A cherub with thick little legs. Oh no, that would never do. Little Victoria was the youngest — she was the angel, with pink cheeks and fair curls and big blue eyes. Perhaps Dorothy was the second youngest? She was allowed to play with Victoria's dolls, and the tiny black perambulator. Yes, that was where she fitted, with two big sisters to hug her when she fell, to pick her up and dust her down. Her brothers were of indeterminate age, but all were tall and raucous. They took no notice of Dorothy.

The first male who did take notice of her — many years after her imaginary brothers and sisters had slipped off the slope of her longing — married her. It was a short courtship; her disapproving mother had proclaimed, 'If you marry that . . . man . . . I shall never speak to you again.'

Dorothy met him at a funeral in 1934. Her aunt Jane, an impressive eighty-two, had died during the summer. Dorothy had rarely met Aunt Jane, and not at all since childhood, knowing her only as her mother's rebellious elder sister who had married beneath her and moved away from home, in Oxford, to the distant north which was Lincolnshire. Dorothy's mother, on receiving the news of her sister's death, had puckered her lips and frowned.

'We must visit that fearful county. Please be sure to pack my fur, Dorothy. I do not intend catching my death in a Lincolnshire churchyard, for the sake of my sister or anybody else.'

'Mother, it is August, and it is quite warm. Even in Lincolnshire.'

Of course, Dorothy did pack the fur — along with many other items — and together they travelled by train, Dorothy gazing out of the window for much of the journey, trying to ignore

18

her mother's constant demands. The fields were golden, this glowing August, and she saw men working in them; she saw tractors and wagons and horses and harvesting. It looked like an enviable life, out in the open air, working on the land, in golden fields, in golden sun, with golden skin.

When she met Albert Sinclair, handsome and bucolic, and he told her all about his life on the farm, she was an attentive listener. Why was he at the funeral?

'My sister was Miss Jane's charlady, and I did odd jobs for her, cleaning the gutters or raking leaves. Very nice lady, was Miss Jane. A gentlewoman. Not liked by her family, they say. But goodness knows why, because you couldn't hope to find a nicer person.'

' "Her family" was my mother and I.'

'I'm sorry. I didn't — '

'Don't be sorry. My mother did disown her. She disowns everybody sooner or later.'

Two weeks later, back in Oxford, Ruth disowned her only daughter upon hearing that she was intending to marry this Albert — 'Bert?' — Sinclair. Dorothy was glad. And if it meant she would end up just like her Aunt Jane — that is to say, forsaken and forgotten — she was even gladder. She left Oxford by train, alone this time, with a carpet bag of 'belongings' and her mother's final admonitions ringing in her ears: 'You will regret this! It will come to nothing! He's not good enough for you!' In this way, Dorothy burst free of her extended and regretful childhood.

Dorothy remained a virgin until her wedding night, on 12th November 1934. It was her thirty-fourth birthday. Albert, still very much a stranger to her, tried to be gentle and kind, but he was so very eager, and so virile, that he did hurt her a little. Dorothy tried not to show it, but he knew, because he wasn't entirely stupid. He apologised. She accepted his apology. It got better, of course. He was a big man, strong and muscular and leathery-skinned, and Dorothy grew to love the feel of his arms around her, his warmth and strength. Pregnancy followed within four months of their wedding, but it was doomed to early failure.

Then another, and yet another.

Eventually, after nearly four years of marriage and five miscarriages, Dorothy gave up, her longing for a child replaced by impossible, unbearable dreams and a sad resignation. She became a farmhand's wife, adept at baking and washing and sewing and tending a small vegetable patch, looking after a small brood of hens. She heard nothing from her mother, and after a few stilted letters in which Dorothy talked of her husband, her new life, her pregnancies, she gave up on the relationship. It may as well have been her mother, and not Aunt Jane, lying dead in the ground in Lodderston churchyard.

★ ★ ★

In August 1938, Dorothy fell pregnant for the sixth time, and it was at this point that she began to write poetry 'properly'. Falteringly, at first, unsure of how to put down any words that could mean something. But she tried, and she wrote, alone during the day, while eating her dinner or sipping her afternoon tea. She hid her notebook behind the pots and pans, at the back of the cabinet. She hid it in the table drawer, or under the bed. She hid it in places where Albert would not find it.

This pregnancy lasted beyond the first two months. She felt sick, and was sick, indiscriminately, at any time of day. Her breasts were sore and she burst into tears without warning. Mrs Compton, layer-out of corpses and local midwife, visited when Dorothy was four months pregnant, and looked quizzically at her burgeoning belly.

'Is it a boy, do you think?' she asked.

'I have no idea,' said Dorothy.

Already, the woman was insufferable.

'And how are you feeling?'

'Better, thank you. Now that I'm not vomiting any more.'

Mrs Compton nodded in what she must have imagined to be a sage manner. Dorothy looked away from the older woman. She hated her. She could not stand the gaze that seemed to mock even while it cared. Mrs Compton, somewhere in her late fifties, perhaps sixty, had given birth to six children of her own, five of whom had made it to adulthood. Her eldest grown son had died in the Great War. Her three daughters, fat and fecund, and her younger son all lived in the village, had all married other villagers, and all of them contributed at regular intervals to Mrs

Compton's growing army of grandchildren.

Dorothy did, in fact, think her baby might be a boy. She had a name for him already: Sidney. But she did not share this with Mrs Compton. Albert — hard-working and, by now, hard-drinking, losing his looks — had already said she could call the child anything she liked so long as it wasn't 'daft'. Sidney he approved of. Sidney it was to be. Albert was relieved that his wife was to bear him a child at last. Men on the farm, in the village, in the pub, had made barbed remarks about his childless marriage. He couldn't be doing it right. Did he know where to put it? The taunts had got under his skin, and made him turn against his wife; a hard face, a solid back, a shrug, a look of scorn. But at last Albert was proud of his wife's round, hard belly, her wide smile. To him she became beautiful; she became the wife he wanted her to be.

When she was five months pregnant, Dorothy caught the bus into Lincoln to buy things for the baby, feeling like a prodigal daughter returning home. She bought a suitcase, for storing all the things she was planning to sew and knit. The suitcase was compact, eighteen inches wide, eight inches deep, a mere thirteen inches from front to back. It was a rusty brown colour, with a dark brown Bakelite handle, two small catches and a toylike key. Inside, the suitcase was lined with paper in a pale tartan print, and there was a small gummed label upon which she could write her name, so she wrote

Mrs D. Sinclair

in her large, looping hand. She licked the label and stuck it to the inside of the suitcase.

While in town she also bought fabric and wool, and refreshed her stocks of threads and needles. Now was the time to make. The talk of impending war was, to her, as insubstantial as the first wash a watercolour artist applies to the naked canvas. War was obscure, it was obscured, and perhaps it was happening a long way off, and perhaps it was not even happening at all. She was pregnant, she no longer felt sick, and she had her energy back. This was all she knew. The baby would need cardigans, gowns, jackets, bootees, blankets, shawls. The baby would need a happy glowing mother, a capable and creative and provident mother.

The suitcase slid perfectly under the bed, and Dorothy set to work on filling it straight away. Within a few delirious weeks she had made two gowns in a soft cotton lawn, three knitted matinee jackets with hats and bootees to match, a knitted blanket in soft pale lamb's wool, and a white christening robe. She showed nobody the fruits of her labours, not even Albert, who was aware of her industriously clicking knitting needles, her frowns and sighs and occasional exasperations, her satisfied smiles when the work was going well. She sewed and knitted in near silence each evening by the light of the oil lamp, while he read the newspaper and told her about the war that he said was certainly coming. She barely listened, so involved was she in the approaching birth, the motherhood that was within her grasp at last. Each stitch brought her closer to that moment, that new and mysterious state of being. Each stitch confirmed the reality of the baby in her womb. Each stitch brought her closer to the day when she would leave behind, at last and forever, irrevocably, her girlhood. Every hope she had ever had was invested in each click of the needles, in each pinprick to her fingers. The mother-to-be was satiated with life and vigour.

Upon completion, each garment was laundered and, if necessary, starched and pressed. One by one, she laid her handmade treasures in the suitcase, with great care, as though each item were the baby himself. She retrieved her notebook from the cabinet in the kitchen, and hid it under the baby clothes at the bottom of the suitcase. This was her new hiding place, her domain — secret, private, inviolable. She sprinkled in dried lavender she had saved from her garden, ostensibly to keep the moths from feasting on the wool, but really because she loved the no-nonsense, vinegary-sweet scent of lavender, the safest scent in the world. By the time she was ready to give birth, the layette was complete, and generosity had entered her marriage. Albert saved for and bought a perambulator, huge and black. He fashioned a crib, working in his shed after his long days on the farm. He insisted his wife put her feet up in the evenings and he brought her tea, which he prepared himself.

And the suitcase sat under the bed, waiting to be emptied of its treasures, waiting for its lid to be thrown open and its contents grasped by eager, trembling hands. If she reached out, she could touch it, this dream which was no longer a dream. This time, it was solid and large and inexhaustible. If any apprehension entered her heart, Dorothy could not recall it afterwards. She could only remember the anticipation, the exasperating, cloying, heavy desire for the mystery of motherhood to begin.

For surely now it would begin.

3

Silver Cross perambulator: £150.00
Set waffle pram blankets: *£5.50*
Set pastel pram sheets: *£5.00*
Total: *£160.50*
PAID WITH THANKS

(Handwritten receipt from the now defunct second-hand baby supplies shop Bibs 'n' Blankets, found inside a Dean edition of *Little Women* by Louisa M. Alcott, with an intact dust jacket depicting Jo March as a beauty. But a nice enough copy, to be found on the second-hand shelves in the children's book room, priced at £2.50.)

★ ★ ★

Philip lives in the flat above the Old and New, and today is my third foray into his home in eleven years of employment. The first time had been to help prepare a small party we threw when launching the large new books room. Philip had bought ready-made food from Waitrose: canapés, dips, cheese, biscuits, grapes, wine. He needed help taking it downstairs into the shop, where we laid it all out on the large round oak display table in the foyer. On that day, we threw open the French windows and invited customers to sit outside in the garden. That was my idea, and although Philip was doubtful at first, he was prepared to give it a try. It is now something of a tradition that our customers enjoy.

The second time I entered his flat was to check that Philip was well after being struck down by flu, last winter. He was perfectly well, really, but feeling 'shitty'. Coughing, red-faced, curled up on his cherry-red leather sofa under a blanket and clutching a hot whisky, watching Judge Judy. He said he was too ill to be bored by daytime television, too ill to change channels. And — the worst thing — he couldn't read because his eyes were 'melting in their sockets'. Anyway, he quite liked Judge Judy. A guilty pleasure, he said. Tell nobody. And then he said something quite odd.

'Do you know, Roberta, I only took you on here because you genuinely agreed with me when I said most people were utter and complete rotters. Do you remember?'

Despite the hyperbole, I did remember. I remembered thinking, here was a person I could work with. But when he was crashed out on the sofa, clutching his hot whisky, obviously feeling hellish, I was surprised that he remembered our 'interview' as clearly as I did.

Jenna. She is . . . unexpected. Sophie and I watch the lovers with a mixture of amusement and amazement. Philip? Jenna? Philip and Jenna? Customers join us in our bafflement. It will never last, some whisper. She's not his type. He's not in her league. She's not in *his* league. Some say.

27

Philip is not just a bespectacled, bookish type of man, you must understand. He's scruffy, fond of jeans and loose shirt tails, mousy brown hair curling around his neck. He's surprisingly handsome, when you look close enough. And Jenna is sweet, and very pretty, undeniably. I can certainly see the attraction, on both sides. Six months on from their first meeting and they are still together, against all expectations, holed up in Philip's tasteful flat.

Jenna has stylishly blonde wavy curls, blue eyes. She is the type of woman all heterosexual males between the ages of twelve and a hundred and twelve would stare at in the street, anywhere, everywhere. And here she is, hiding away from the world in the Old and New Bookshop, the girlfriend of its sardonic, forty-something owner. Sophie and I suspect they hold little trysts in the shop. Working together, perhaps hiding away in the back room among the second-hand fiction, the two seem to whirl away from each other if I enter, causing me to stammer an apology, my cheeks burning with consternation. Jenna gives me one of her looks — half amused, half reproachful. I retreat, not daring to look at Philip. I'm never entirely sure which one of the three of us should feel the most embarrassed.

Jenna reads more now, at least. I can't imagine that she read a great deal before commencing her employment at the Old and New. She is just not the bookish type, whatever that is. She unpacks our daily deliveries, biting her bottom lip, ticking off books on the delivery note, making sure they are all there, placing them

28

carefully on the shelves, stacking books ordered for customers under the counter. She concentrates like a little girl learning a new trick on her skipping rope. She asks for help quite often, and Sophie and I go to her aid, patiently. We all have to learn, and we're forming a good team. I know Philip is proud of us all.

Today, Philip's flat is dark and silent. And it is Jenna who ushers me in, not quite touching me, but propelling me nonetheless. She switches on a large Tiffany lamp next to the cherry-red leather sofa. She asks me if I want a drink. I don't. She pours herself a gin and tonic. She has not been at work today: she is unwell. I notice the familiar manner in which she moves around the flat, handling Philip's things, pouring his gin. In these placid surroundings, Jenna is as jumpy as a wren, and I am sorry for her, without understanding why.

There's something amiss.

I feel like a trespasser in Philip's domain. He is at a book fair — he's been away all day — and he warned Jenna not to expect him back until around half past eight that evening. The curtains are still tightly drawn at two o'clock, an empty coffee cup and a plate littered with crumbs still malingering on the coffee table. There's an air of the slovenly, which Philip normally does not tolerate.

'Bottoms up,' Jenna says, and she drinks, quickly. I smile at her, not knowing what to say, not knowing what this is about.

'Roberta, I'm in trouble,' she announces.

'What kind of trouble?'

29

'Of the old-fashioned kind. You know. 'In trouble'.'

And now she cries, shielding her face with her hand and her empty glass. I move to stand next to her, and I rub her arm, making noises of consolation. I'm not sure what to say.

In the end, her tears subside. A box of tissues is extracted from the shelf under the large, round smoky-glass coffee table.

'What do you make of me now?' Jenna asks, pouring another drink and sipping more sedately. Her white hands shake, just a little.

'I'm not going to judge you, Jenna,' I say. 'For heaven's sake, you're a grown woman, and Philip's a grown man. It's not unheard of, is it? It might be . . . unexpected, maybe . . . but you'll work it out. How does Philip feel about it?'

She looks at me, aghast.

'Oh,' I say, looking at the floor, at the curtained window, at the large gilt mirror above the fireplace.

'I found out a week ago. I felt tired. My period was late. I did a test. It's been hell, Roberta, it really has. I don't want children, you see. I never have wanted children. I never will want children. I've always been so careful, but now this . . . catastrophe.'

'I think you should be having this conversation with Philip,' I say, and I curse myself for sounding so prim.

'What the bloody hell for?'

'Because . . . it's nothing to do with me. It's Philip's baby.'

'No. I don't think so . . . I mean, I'm not sure.'

Instantly, guiltily, confusedly, I feel a rush of relief. It's not his baby. It might not be his baby. *It's all right*. It's somebody else's baby. But then, whose baby is it? Has she . . . ?

I am not a courageous person. I shun conflict of any kind. So I sit in silence, not knowing what to say to the trembling woman before me. I cannot think about Philip — the last person in the world, by my reckoning, who would deal in duplicity. Oh, poor Jenna. I can't imagine how she must be feeling . . . what a mess.

She is incredibly pretty, really. A beauty. And like everybody else, including Philip, I'm a sucker for beauty. So you get drawn in, you don't see. And I can't blame Philip for . . . it's understandable. He's not a monk, and he shouldn't have to live like one. And none of it is any of my business, of course. I'm just an employee, nothing more, though I like to think Philip might loosely describe me as a 'friend'.

Jenna sighs, and puts down her empty glass. 'What are you thinking?' she says.

'Oh, nothing much,' I say. I'm so useless, especially at wobbly moments, and this is one of those.

This is a crisis.

Jenna falls back into the sofa, and she cries, for perhaps a minute, then blows her nose dramatically. I sidle along the cherry-red cushions to sit alongside her, and she leans on my shoulder.

I tap her knee, rub her back. 'It'll be all right, Jenna,' I say.

There's a clinic. A friend of hers . . . anyway, there's a clinic. She has an appointment tomorrow morning and will get it all seen to. She'll clear up this mess. Philip will never know. Thank God he's at the book fair again tomorrow. He must never know anything about this, ever. She loves him. She truly does. She made a mistake. Don't we all, Roberta? An old boyfriend, he wants her back, she broke his heart . . . she felt sorry for him, momentarily. Stupid.

'Have you ever had a termination?' she asks me.

'No,' I say, after the briefest of pauses.

'I don't want to go alone. To the clinic, I mean.'

'I understand.'

'Will you come with me? Please.'

'Yes. Of course I will.'

'Because I can't ask anybody else. There is nobody else.'

'I'll go with you,' I say.

'I don't want to ask Sophie.'

'I know.'

Similar ages, twenty-something, both are straight-up, no arguments, nine-and-a-half-out-of-ten women, at least. Sophie has chestnut-brown hair, with chocolate-dream eyes, she is toned and tanned and quite beautiful. There's competition, whispered jealousies — nothing overt, nothing nasty, but it's there. I enjoy watching their rivalry from the sidelines, safely out of the fray, me, a good ten years older, and a solid seven. On a good day. On a very good day. No competition at all, no need for these girls to feel threatened by me as well as each other, and I can just enjoy the disinterest of the casual observer. Well, not quite.

Both of these women are my friends now. And one of them needs me.

'It has to be somebody I can totally trust,' says Jenna. 'I'm not going to tell anybody else and Philip must never, ever know. I can't do this on my own. Please. You're so sensible and discreet.'

'I'll go with you, I mean it. Don't fret. But what about the father?'

Jenna laughs a desperate, queer laugh.

'Oh my God,' she says. 'Roberta, you really are hopelessly naive at times.'

She will tell Philip she is meeting a friend for the day — shopping and lunch — and I will phone in sick. Headache, period pains, whatever comes to mind, whatever sounds plausible. It will be a nuisance for Sophie to be on her own all day. But never mind, says Jenna. She'll cope. We're not busy at the moment, anyway.

I listen in silence as she makes her plans. I recall my last birthday, my thirty-fourth. I brought in cakes, split doughnuts oozing with soft artificial cream, with sweet red syrup described as 'jam', fresh from the bakery next door to the shop. Jenna declined my offer of a cake, stating weight-watching as a reason. I shrugged and told her I would take it home for my cat, who likes cakes — especially on birthdays. I recall Jenna's face, her crushed expression, the redness. She muttered an embarrassed 'sorry', and took a cake. Of course, I felt dreadful; I didn't mean to humiliate her. I later found the doughnut in the kitchen bin, a token nibble missing. I realised then that Jenna is used to being disliked. I don't believe her circle of friends is particularly wide. I resolved to try harder. I'm not the jealous type. And we have become friends, a slow trust growing between us.

So now I must agree to help her. What else am I to do?

'You're a good person,' says Jenna. She blows her nose, and smiles at me bleakly.

And my thoughts wander, as they are apt to do at stressful times, moments of drama. I want to talk to Babunia. I want to ask her about the letter that is even now whispering its strange words, tucked away in my handbag, calling to me. I can almost remember the letter by heart now. I shall visit her soon; I'm due for a visit, anyway. But can I ask her anything about this letter? I can't bear the thought of upsetting her, of trying to uncover secrets she does not want uncovered.

And Jenna is here now, white-faced and scared. I must deal with her first.

4

Agatha Mabel Fisher and Nina Margaret Mullens descended upon Dorothy in March 1940. They were both London girls, fresh from their six weeks of training with the Women's Land Army. They were employed by those up at the hall as farmhands; they were in need of a billet, and Dorothy lived alone in the cottage. She was fortunate, she knew, to be allowed to continue living in the cottage at all. Albert had left to join up, to do his bit, he said, everybody said, but Dorothy knew, as they all knew, that Albert had left to get away from her, to leave behind his disappointment and grief. He wanted other women too, because Dorothy would no longer sleep with him, and she was wise enough to know this, even to understand it. He was only thirty-three. Let him go, she told herself. She did not miss him.

She had started to hear that some at the hall, and in the village, were questioning her right to stay. Albert should not have left, they said. He was a skilled and experienced farmhand, and could have waited for his call-up, which may never have come. It left his wife in a difficult position. Eventually, they put it to her: stay, and be useful. No rent and a small stipend in return for taking in laundry — all the hall laundry. They installed the latest model of boiler and a mangle in the wash house. There was even talk of one of the new washing machines. They strung up yards and yards of washing lines, criss-crossing the garden. And now she was glad she hadn't taken on goats, as much as she had wanted them, when Mrs Twoomey had offered her a pair of kids in the spring. They were such little darlings, but too fond of chewing on fresh laundry.

Then the girls, Aggie and Nina. They were always laughing at goodness knows what, they were cheerful and chaotic. Dorothy took pride in working hard for her girls, even in boiling Aggie's bloodied undies, and the sanitary pads that Dorothy had hastily sewn when the young women first arrived at the farm. The pads were made from a peach-coloured damask tablecloth she had damaged by catching it irretrievably in the mangle. Poor Aggie, she was so slight and fragile-looking, with her blonde curls, her perfect skin, her silvery laugh, and such a pretty little thing, yet she suffered such heavy blood loss, cruel, regular and punctual. In contrast, Nina, who was taller than Aggie, and plump, with a deep smoker's voice, had scant bleeds, irregular and short-lived. She was a girl who sailed gaily through life with all the finesse of an ocean liner. The girls had not been with Dorothy for long — a matter of weeks, really — but already she felt she knew them, she felt she had the measure of them. She would almost say that she loved them.

Dorothy put them in her own room. It was the room she had vacated after Sidney, leaving Albert alone and bewildered in the large brass bed. Dorothy had set up house in the tiny bedroom, overlooking the back garden, the Long Acre field and, beyond, the distant elm trees and Lodderston aerodrome. The small bed, narrow and in need of a new mattress, suited her perfectly. She liked to lie on it with her notebook, writing. Rarely did she recognise the words on the page, when she read them back, as her own.

She made up a new quilt for her little bed, using anything she could find — large patches, small patches, squares, triangles, indescribable shapes — a crazy quilt. She hung her few clothes in the tiny wardrobe, arranged her undies in the top drawer of the dressing table and put a vase of wild flowers on the table next to her bed. Every night, when she retired, she shut the door firmly behind her. Albert didn't knock, not once, and Dorothy was grateful for that. Then he was gone. In August 1939, he simply fled. She didn't know exactly where he was or what he was doing. She heard nothing from him at all. He sent no money. This is divorce, she thought, and her solitary life began in earnest. She became self-sufficient, baking her own bread, keeping back a few eggs each week from her hens; she made new clothes from old clothes, became a truly accomplished seamstress, and learned to use the old Singer sewing machine that Albert said had been his mother's. This year, she had cultivated all her own fruit and vegetables, with varying success, but she ate so little that it barely mattered. Eating became something she did to survive; there was no pleasure in it. Food tasted vile to her, and the act of chewing and swallowing made her feel sick. She began to hate her body, its thinness, its strange and disgusting needs, its inability to be a normal woman's body, the fact that it could not do that which it was designed to do. Whether that design fault came from God, or Nature, she no longer knew or cared.

Then, the billeting of these girls: loud cockneys, their laughter and energy and bad language filling the house, Dorothy cooking for them, cleaning their clothes and bedlinen, mending for them, tending to their comforts after a long and hard day's work. And there were many of those; she had never known anyone to work so hard. Albert had found it easy, with his strength. But these girls fought hard to get the work done, they sweated and cried and kept going, kept going, they blistered, they chafed, they sustained bruises and cuts and calluses. But they never gave up. They inspired Dorothy; they refreshed her life with a new flood of hope and purpose.

★   ★   ★

Three days after the Hurricane crashed in the Long Acre, Dorothy — in some pain, still wearing her dressings, but still trying to be useful, still managing to cook for the girls, managing a fraction of the growing mountain of laundry she was tasked with — had a visitor.

She heard the front gate latch being lifted and the gate being shut, and quickly hid her notebook in the cutlery drawer. She was working on a new poem. It felt like a breakthrough, at last, a couple of sentences with direction. A novelty. Annoyed, she steeled herself for a visit from Mrs Compton. To appear calm, she hummed a tune. She did not want Mrs Compton to get even an inkling of how she was feeling; there was no need. In fact, there was danger in the older woman knowing anything.

But the knock was not Mrs Compton's. It was brisk. Unmistakeably, it was a man's knock. Wiping her hands on her pinny, Dorothy approached the door and opened it.

'Mrs Sinclair?' said the man standing there, in an indeterminate foreign accent that Dorothy guessed was Polish. He held behind his legs a large bunch of hedgerow flowers, trying to hide it.

'Yes?' said Dorothy. She sounded stiff and formal — like her mother, she realised with horror.

'I am Squadron Leader Jan Pietrykowski,' he said, as though Dorothy should recognise his name. Then, in a deft series of movements, he took her hand, kissed it, released it and, with a flourish, he offered her the flowers.

She blushed. 'Oh! Thank you,' said Dorothy, recovering herself, no longer impersonating her mother. She took the flowers and smelled them, as a matter of politeness rather than curiosity. She could think of nothing further to say. Like all men in uniform, this man looked handsome and smart. Her first impression was of dark hair, slicked across from a side parting, and clear tanned skin. He was clean-shaven, his eyes bright blue. A very bright blue. He had a direct and unflustered gaze that both alarmed and intrigued her. He seemed to be two or three inches taller than Dorothy. Not a tall man, not a short man. But younger — perhaps four, five, six years younger. Too young. Like Albert. It was impossible. And all of this shot through her like a sudden onset of fever.

'I have come to thank you for your brave efforts to save my compatriot on Tuesday,' the squadron leader announced. Dorothy thought him grandiose, but she was prepared to overlook it.

'Save?' she said.

'My pilot. On Tuesday. We have heard of your courage. I am here to thank you,' and Squadron Leader Jan Pietrykowski bowed.

Dorothy stared at him in shock, amusement. Something else. Something she did not care to pinpoint.

'I see you have a bandage,' he said. 'I hope your face is not too sore?'

And damn that woman, damn her to hell. The tittle-tattling — ! Dorothy, essentially kind, could not bring herself to even think the word 'cow', let alone 'bitch'. Too cruel, these words, too impolite. And, she was generous enough to entertain, possibly not even true.

'I see,' said Dorothy. 'I didn't exactly try to save him. Everybody seems to think . . . never mind. But thank you. My face is not too sore. It will be better soon, I'm sure. Won't you come in?'

The squadron leader stepped over the

threshold into Dorothy's kitchen and immediately it struck her that this man's presence was a comfort, even a sudden joy. This house had been empty of menfolk for nine months; it had become a feminine enclave, and even more so since the arrival of the girls. She indicated a seat at the table, and he sat. He looked around, and Dorothy noticed he took a long time looking at the mantelpiece with its candlesticks, its clock, its thin layer of coal dust.

'This reminds me of my mother's kitchen,' he said, sweeping his arm around as if sharing with her a vast panorama, 'back at home where I come from.'

'Where is that?' asked Dorothy, preparing teacups, milk, sugar. Her hands shook.

'*Polska.*'

'Poland?'

'Yes. Poland.'

Jan Pietrykowski smiled at her, a wide grin that Dorothy found herself staring at despite all her decorous intentions. She had to stop being so . . . silly. She lost herself in tea preparations. Her hands shook even more. She bit her lip. She repressed an urge to giggle. Had her knees been *punched?* Surely, they had been.

'I know, I know,' she said, trying to steady her voice, which was becoming high-pitched. 'We are all so damned imperialistic. Aren't we?' She cleared her throat. What exactly was the matter with her? Surely, she should know.

If he was taken aback by the coarse language, Squadron Leader Jan Pietrykowski failed to show it. Perhaps he didn't know the word? But

41

his English was pretty good. Dorothy couldn't believe he hadn't heard such words and understood their meaning. Still, she sensed that here was a man she could swear around without incurring judgement.

'My girls taught me that word,' she said. It sounded to her like a boast.

' 'Imperialistic'?' he said.

' 'Damned'. They taught me 'bloody' too.'

'Your girls . . . ?'

'Two young ladies from London. They work here on the farm. Since so many of the men have . . . ' She tried not to sound bitter as she thought of her husband's abandonment of her. 'Since so many of them have gone away.'

'You are an angry woman, Mrs Sinclair.'

She chose to ignore the remark. She made tea, busying herself with the strainer, then pouring in milk — but no milk for him, thank you. Stirring in sugar, one for him, one for her. She was on guard, warned off by this man's perception. Angry? Yes, she was angry. Of course. But was it so obvious?

And she was listening to this man, this strange man — who did not take milk in his tea (extraordinary!) — an unexpected guest in her home, a guest in her country, telling her about his life. He was an only child, he said, brought up by his mother alone, his father not known to him. His mother had been strong, independent, left to fend for herself in a small Polish village near a town he called 'Krakoof'. Dorothy didn't know where 'Krakoof' was, let alone its surrounding villages. The squadron leader's mother was an intelligent woman, he said, and loved to learn

42

languages, and she taught him English from an early age. Thank God for that, he said, because it was making a terrific difference now that he found himself in England, helping, at least, hoping, to set up a Polish squadron. One day soon, he hoped, he would return to his home, perhaps his mother's home, perhaps not, but he would resume his life, go back to a reinstated Polish Air Force, be normal again. Damn the Nazis. Damn the Russians.

He does know those kinds of words, Dorothy thought. 'Yes,' she said. How old was he?

'I am thirty years old,' he said.

Did she actually ask *aloud*? Voices then — hers, her voice, hers aloud, in her head — all were blurring, converging in a confusing mix of anger, revelation and, above all, she realised with horror, titillation. Nine years. *Nine* years? Oh! Oh no.

'And you are a . . . pilot?'

'Yes. A squadron leader.'

'Ah yes, you said. I'm sorry. You must think me terribly stupid. It's just that I am tired, rather.'

'Of course,' he said, and he stood, gulping back his tea.

'I didn't mean that you had to leave. I'm sorry. Please tell me more . . . are there many Polish pilots at Lodderston now?'

'Many, enough to form a squadron. But we are not believed in, our talents it seems are not obvious. We are told to do exercises. But all of us have already fought the Germans, in our own country and in France. We are not novices. We are forced to have English lessons! But I explain I can translate, teach my men myself. We are frustrated. So some of my men play the fool in the air, and now one of them dies without need. But I can see that you must rest. Thank you for what you did. I will myself inform the pilot's family of your brave actions,' and the squadron leader made for the door, opening it.

'Oh no, please don't. Please. It was not . . . it was nothing. It was stupid, in fact.'

Please don't, oh, no, no, please don't go. He was such an *interesting* person.

'Brave,' the man repeated, firmly.

'I'm an only child too,' blurted Dorothy.

'I thought that was so,' he said, stepping through the door, out into the bright afternoon sunshine, obviously determined to escape.

She knew she was being ridiculous. But she liked the way the sun shone on his black hair. Again, he took her hand and kissed it. He nodded to her, and said goodbye. He left. She crept through to the lounge and watched him through the lace curtains, the lace curtains that had become yellowed by the girls' cigarette smoke, and needed laundering. The man had climbed on to a bicycle, and he rode off in the direction of Lodderston and was gone, swallowed by the May blossom, the blue sky, the thick green hedges, the heat haze rising from the road.

Dorothy wandered back into the kitchen. She picked up the wild flowers, she smelled them again, she filled her best enamel jug with water and arranged the flowers, lingering over the task. She placed the jug artfully on the mantelpiece. She stood a while, looking at the flowers. She took out her notebook and wrote feverishly for minutes, perhaps half an hour. She felt she had something to write about. Finally. She smelled the back of her hand where he had twice kissed it. She breathed in, long and deep. Nothing. She picked up the teacup that he had drunk from, and held it to her nose. She smelled the rim, the handle, examined it closely. Impetuously, without any thought of guilt or disgust, she ran her tongue around the rim of the cup, but it tasted only of tea.

★ ★ ★

He cycled away. He'd wanted to stay longer, of course. He wanted to look back at this Englishwoman, who he knew was watching him through the lace curtains. He wanted to wave. But he thought he had better not. He couldn't explain, even to himself, how he had felt, sitting in the woman's kitchen, drinking her sweet strong tea, listening to her gentle voice. He could have listened to her for the rest of his days.

It was odd how a person of significance could just appear in your life, unexpectedly. He had not known what to expect, knocking on her door. He was there to thank her, as he thought he ought to do. He was carrying out just another of his many duties. And when the door opened, there she stood, instant, charming.

He would see her again. He knew this. He had to see her again. He knew. He would return as soon as he could. And he felt — he was certain — she would want that, and there would be no need for a pretext.

5

A photograph: black and white, a man, perhaps in his late thirties, handsome, with a moustache, his arm around a woman. She is short, with obviously blonde hair, a little younger than him, and she smiles broadly into the camera. On the back of the photo it reads: Harry and Nora, Minehead, August 1958. And under that, in a round teenage hand, it says: Nanna and Grandpa Lomax.

(Found inside a paperback edition of *A Bouquet of Barbed Wire* by Andrea Newman. It's an old copy, but in good condition, so I placed it on the general fiction shelves priced at £1.00.)

* * *

I drive to the clinic. Jenna sits resolute alongside me, staring at the people and buildings and trees and vehicles that we pass on our journey. Apart from giving me terse directions, she says nothing. I try to make conversation, but now is not the time, and so I silence myself. We listen to Radio 4 until the building looms before us. A small ignominious brass plaque on the stone gatepost announces that this is the Evergreen Clinic. Evergreen is, I think, a strange choice of name for such a place. I know how Jenna must feel, sitting so still alongside me; yet she appears to be unmoved. I swing the car up the gravelled drive, and park in a marked space. As if on cue, heavy drops of rain falling on to the roof of the car break the silence.

'Will you come in with me? Please,' says Jenna.

'Yes. I thought that was the plan.'

'Oh, thank you. I'm grateful. But I'm scared.'

Of course she is.

'You don't have to go in,' I offer.

'Yes, I do.'

And I know she does. There is no point in prolonging the inevitable, no point in trying to dissuade Jenna. It's a one-woman show.

We walk across a neat lawn where a single magnolia stands alone in the centre — white, pretty, hopeful. We slowly ascend the imperious steps leading to the door marked 'Entrance'. Inside is dark, oaky, leathery. A lady with long, long blonde hair and a name badge stating 'Rita' sits primly at a tacky, veneered desk. I don't believe that Rita is her actual name. She invites us to take a seat in the waiting room, which was obviously once the large sitting room of a grand house. Daytime television blasts out from what appears to be a 1980s set. There are many women here, nervous, waiting, like Jenna, waiting to do something hellishly profound. Right or wrong. It isn't my place to judge. Of course. Yet I feel vaguely nauseous, clammy. Some of the women are young, just girls, with mothers chaperoning them, mothers as nervous as their daughters. But, like Jenna, they look resolute. There are one or two couples, the men holding the women's hands, stroking their arms.

Why are they here? What events have led up to this day, this place, this decision? I shall never know. It isn't my destiny to know.

After an interminable half-hour, Jenna is called and she disappears like a ghost into an unseen room, the door closing quietly behind her. I watch the television and learn how to make triple-glazed chicken in honey, or some such concoction. I clamp my mind off from where I am, what I am doing, what is going on behind the door, the conversation that will be taking place.

Jenna emerges after fifteen minutes or so, white-faced. She beckons me and I follow her outside, where the sun is shining and the birds are busying themselves in the trees, in defiance of this place. Jenna sits on the bottom step and lights a cigarette, which shocks me greatly. Her hand is trembling, cigarette smoke curling around her slender beringed fingers. I didn't know she was a smoker.

'I can have a tablet,' Jenna says. 'Today, once I've seen a doctor.'

'A tablet?'

'It will make the pregnancy come away and I'll bleed. Like a period.'

'You're definitely pregnant, then?' I say, disappointed. How lovely if she had been mistaken, there had been no baby to . . . deal with.

'Oh yes. I could see it. A little flake. On the screen. It was like watching a film, but there wasn't much to see. Just shadows and . . . pulses. Five and a half weeks gone. It's a good job I'm on the ball, eh?'

'Do you still want to do this?' I ask, my voice

48

high-pitched and laboured. 'Are you going to go ahead?'

'I am. Absolutely. This is just a mistake, a great big one. It's not a baby, not yet. It's just a blob of cells and matter. No eyes yet, no mouth or even a proper brain. No skin. There's no crime here, Roberta. Don't go all holier than thou on me. I'm within my rights to do this. It's all perfectly legal.'

'I know that. I wasn't trying to . . . it's okay.' I have nothing else to say.

Jenna obviously does not have a working knowledge of regret. Not yet, anyway. I don't want to cry, so I think hard about triple-glazed chicken in honey, about driving home, being there, safe and alone. I have a sudden yearning to eat hot buttered crumpets dripping with gooseberry jam, the delicious jam Babunia made each year until she was too old to manage it. I recall the bottles lined up on the highest shelf in her pantry.

Jenna drags heavily on her cigarette. This secret between us is already forcing an intimacy that feels too intense. I wish she hadn't asked me to help. And I wish I hadn't agreed to. Sophie would have done a better job; she has common sense and compassion in bucketfuls. I hold back too much. It's something of a problem in my life.

What is it my grandfather said to my grandmother, apparently from beyond the grave? *Your soul will not return from this that you do.*

And as Jenna prepares to return to the trammelled darkness of the Evergreen Clinic to be 'seen' by a doctor, she suggests I wait for her

49

in the car. She'll be all right now. The worst is over, she says. I sit cocooned in the magnified silence of a car when the engine isn't running and I think of Philip, about him never knowing of the events of this day. And thank God for that, because I understand my boss enough by now to know that he would be appalled and hurt, ashamed of this young woman, ashamed of me. And it wouldn't be the abortion itself, nor even the fact that the . . . baby may not be his. It would be the lies and the deceit. Oh, how I want Jenna to cry and deliberate and to change her mind, run out of this building. I want the door to open and Jenna to charge out, clutching her belly, protecting her baby, embracing the instincts that she must be working so hard to suppress. I want to greet her with a huge smile of relief, strap her in the car myself and speed out of the gate, never to return.

But I know it won't happen.

I have a vision of Philip at the book fair, being charming, being affable — his great skill, considering his indifference to just about everybody — and I wonder what is going on at the bookshop, with poor Sophie, alone all day, stacking shelves, serving customers, probably harassed. I cannot wait to get out of here and back into the world I love so much.

My grandfather's letter is still in my handbag so I can read it whenever I need to. I read it now, while I wait for Jenna. I wish I could ask my father about it, but I can't bear the thought of upsetting him. He has so much to deal with already. Does Dad know that his father was, in fact, alive and probably well — at least, well enough to write a Dear John letter to his mother — in February 1941? And that it looks like his parents may not have been married after all? And that his mother did something unforgivable — at least, as far as my grandfather was concerned — to a child.

Did she have a termination? I wonder.

Was abortion legal in 1941? I think not.

What did my grandmother do to 'this child's mother'? Did he actually mean my grandmother? English was not his first language. Perhaps something was lost in the translation of his Polish thoughts into his written English? I wish I could ask my own mother about it; but that's out of the question. That leaves my grandmother, my beloved babunia.

She's 109 years old.

I look up from the letter to see Jenna emerging from the building. I watch her trip lightly down the steps and across the lawn — past the 'Keep off the grass' sign — to my car. We can go home. She has taken the tablet, she tells me, and she smiles like she has just bagged a bargain in the sales. It's a smile I recognise.

6

'To Marcus, 4eva, luv 'n' stuff, Natalie': The card consists of a pink felt heart on a red card background. Handmade, I think. The dot of the 'i' is fashioned into a heart shape. I think at first how frivolous it is, but it's not at all frivolous. It's simple and eloquent and heartbreaking, so I keep it. I believe it was 'Marcus' who brought in the boxes of paperbacks; I watched as he came staggering up the path with his girlfriend, both of them struggling with two boxes each. He addressed her as 'Kim'.

(Card found in the Harper Perennial edition of *The God of Small Things* by Arundhati Roy. Reading copy only, so I popped it into the 30p bargain basket under the window, alongside the front door.)

★ ★ ★

My cat, Tara, and I lived a cosy life for many years. She greeted me with good grace every day when I returned from work, and curled up on my lap on Sunday afternoons while I read or watched the occasional film. She was faithful and devoted, unlike most cats, and I almost believed she loved me as much as I loved her. But last Saturday, I arrived home to find Tara stiff and

52

cold on the doormat. I had to pick her up before I could get in the door.

After dark, when nobody could see me, I buried her under the plum tree in my tiny back garden.

★ ★ ★

It was with a large measure of serendipity that I stumbled upon the vacancy in the Old and New Bookshop. Philip had plans to open up a further room of the shop, to sell a decent range of new books. He needed somebody to manage that side of the business, as well as helping him with the secondhand books. I like to think my newly acquired degree in English Literature helped me to land the job. Philip tells me he liked my friendly, non-pretentious manner and my willingness to clean. He felt I would slot very nicely into his bookshop.

We were a small, tight-knit team, Philip and I, in those early days. Just the two of us, in the shop from nine to five (often much later in his case), both of us for six days a week, most weeks. I have not minded giving up my Saturdays. My social life is sparse. But Philip has always been good company, funny and witty, and observant of his fellow man, if a little too critical. I have enjoyed his company since day one.

As the shop grew, the need for another member of staff became apparent, and Sophie became the third employee. A lovely girl, inside and out — intelligent and kind — perfect for the shop. I think I resented her, at first. I wanted the shop, and Philip — I wanted it all to myself. Sophie was new and pretty and I was jealous, of all things, which was utterly ridiculous. I got over it.

Sophie's boyfriend, Matt, collects her from work on Saturday evenings, and they often ask me to 'hang out' with them. They are getting a Chinese, or a pizza, they're watching a film. I'm welcome to join them. I always decline.

'Oh, come on, Roberta. It'll do you good,' says Sophie.

'No,' I always say. 'Tara needs feeding.'

A soft shake of Sophie's head. 'You need to get over it! Go home and feed her, then pop round to ours. Stay the night. It's just a cat, not a child. You should live a little. For God's sake.'

Philip and I have a professional relationship, but we can laugh and joke together, and often we do. We rarely talk about our lives away from the shop. Philip bought the eighteenth-century build-ing housing the Old and New twelve, thirteen years ago. I believe, I get the feeling, there is no mortgage, there are no loans to repay. Sophie and I speculate that he may have won the lottery. Or inherited money from a dead relative. Of course, we never ask. Some months, I know the Old and New is lucky to break even. It often makes a loss, and usually only makes a profit in December — and even then, only in good years. Yet Philip continues to run his independent bookshop as a going concern, and he has converted the upper-most floor into his comfortable and handsome flat. He is simple in his tastes. Books, obviously, lots of books in his personal collections. And

54

paintings, mostly prints, but I suspect a few originals too, all nicely framed. Plants, lots of houseplants — unusually, for a man, I think. That lovely sofa in the roomy lounge, an old rocking chair. A small television in the corner. No game stations, no Xboxes or whatever they're called, just a handful of well-chosen DVDs. A clean kitchen, small and functional. All is simple and old-fashioned — or, at least, pretending to be simple and old-fashioned.

One of Sophie's recent ideas (Philip values her 'fresh' input) was for one of the book rooms to be given over to a coffee shop. Philip vetoed this immediately. I am secretly thankful for this. But bless Sophie. She is so . . . modern.

'We're not bloody Borders!' spluttered Philip. 'There's a reason they went to the wall, you know!'

And Sophie poked out her tongue at him.

Of course, he was joking. But he's right. We are small, independent. We are unique. We deal in books. We deal in the written word.

★ ★ ★

I'm preparing a simple dinner to share with . . . who? My boyfriend? Lover? The man I sleep with?

We are having triple-glazed chicken in honey, with salad and herby potato wedges. I am not a great cook, finding the whole process rather tedious. A bottle of Pinot Grigio is cooling in the fridge. There is a lemon sorbet in the freezer. Wine is unusual for us because his wife mustn't smell it when he gets home. She thinks that every other Thursday he attends a yoga class, straight after a staff meeting. This blatant lie, so bare and transparent, frightens me a little. Subterfuge I abhor, although sometimes it is necessary. But I do wish his ideas were a little more inventive.

Of course, I feel awful. I never thought — or planned, or expected — to end up in a relationship with a man already married. I think I suffered a moment of weakness, a lapse in my normally quite good judgement. And now I seem to be living with the consequences. He's not happy with his wife, he says, and hasn't been for some time. She's 'difficult', whatever that means. I don't press him on this or anything else. I wouldn't blame his wife for being angry with me if she were to find out, truly I wouldn't. And maybe she would expel him from their home and he would turn up on my doorstep, bedraggled and tearful.

Would he expect to move in with me? Would I owe him that?

I think not. I certainly wouldn't *want* him to move in with me. And I know I shouldn't be carrying on with a married man twenty-two years my senior. It isn't nice and it isn't fair and it will all come to nothing. I know this.

His name is Charles. Old-fashioned, but that's the kind of woman I am, attracted to older men with older-men names. I find them comforting, with none of the rawness and threats of a younger man. They are civilised.

And you don't have to love them, if you don't

want to. They are flattered enough if you like them, invite them into your home and listen sympathetically to their woes. That's the drawback of older men: the woes are endless.

My older man — who, of course, isn't mine at all but belongs to her, his wife, the woman whose name is Francesca and who, he tells me, smells like Febreze — has bought me a cat. She's a replacement for Tara. He knows, as all the regular customers of the Old and New know, that I lost Tara. Their sympathy is enormous, and I believe it is genuine. The death of my cat is a subject up for discussion.

Our first date was, of necessity, some way off from our hometown. He could not afford for anybody to see him on a clandestine date with that woman from the bookshop. (What's her name? The plain one. Rebecca?) Mr Charles Dearhead, Head Teacher at Northfield Primary School. He had too much to lose. And so did I, only I wasn't as scared of losing it as he was. 'We' are a secret, and he trusts that I will always, always keep our little secret.

But I haven't kept it, not completely.

'Are you seeing somebody?' asked Sophie.

It was a quiet Saturday afternoon, a week or two ago. Fax-man had been in, and out, once again reminding me of the ongoing offer of a date. I politely laughed him off, as usual, and continued to look up the difference between swallows and swifts in *Birds of Britain: An Illustrated Guide*. Sophie asked her question, turning to me hastily before another customer arrived at the till.

'Why are you asking?' I said, grinning at her. I wasn't exactly bursting to tell anybody about my fling. But it would be quite nice, I thought, to tell somebody, if only to get another perspective. I realised that we had swifts swooping around the Old and New in the summer. Not swallows. And definitely not house martins.

'You are,' she said, triumphantly. 'Aren't you?'

'I might be,' I replied, and winked at her.

'Who? Who? Who is it?'

'He's married,' I warned. I had hoped it would sound sophisticated, but it didn't.

'Really? Oh! Well, that doesn't necessarily . . . who is it? Does he come in here?'

'Yes.'

A pause. A customer inconveniently filled it, and Sophie hastily, politely served her.

'Who is it?' Sophie hissed at me as soon as the customer was out of earshot.

'Charles Dearhead.'

There was no mistaking Sophie's disappointment. I wanted to reach out and gently swipe it away, as I might a stray strand of hair from her face. I hold a great deal of tenderness for Sophie.

'It's all right,' I said, and shrugged.

Of course it wasn't all right. But it was better than nothing. I'd had rather too much of nothing, and Charles had become my 'something'.

I didn't love him. I would never love him. Sophie and I both knew it. And all this passed between us in those few seconds, telepathically, a silent conversation in which nothing was said but everything was communicated.

'He's a lot older than you,' said Sophie, breaking our spell.

'Twenty-two years older.'

'Too old?' she asked.

She made me think. But not for long.

'Maybe. But he's nice. I like him. He's kind to me. And he is handsome, for his age,' I said, my vanity coming to my defence.

'He's married to his wife,' said Sophie, and our eyes widened and we giggled.

'I know what you mean, though,' I said, and I whispered, 'Mrs Francesca Dearhead, no less. Have you ever seen her?'

'No, I don't think so.'

'He says she's difficult.'

'Aren't you worried that you'll be found out? Philip might sack you. Scandal at the Old and New?'

'Philip wouldn't sack me. And he'll never find out. Nobody will. I don't make a song and dance of it, and neither does he. It's all okay, Sophie. Okay?'

Jenna emerged from the children's book room, where she had been busy putting out the new books delivered that morning. She is a neat person, when she tries, and putting out new stock, arranging shelves, especially in the children's section, has become one of her particular duties. She smiled at us as we cut short our conversation. I don't think she heard any of it; perhaps she thought we were talking about her.

Jenna offered to make coffee. As the kettle boiled loudly in the kitchen, and we could hear her clattering around with cups and saucers,

59

Sophie said my affair with 'the Dearhead', as she called him, was okay, if I said it was. And it was none of her business, which was obviously true.

But I care for her opinions. I know she knows I cannot be truly happy with a man like Charles Dearhead, even if he is handsome. She thinks I deserve better, and maybe that is so. But, living as I do, alone, Charles feels right for me, and he is a sweet man in his own way. And I quite like his way, the fact that he never really wants to speak about me. I can lose myself in his life, and it means I don't have to think too much about my own, which, I convince myself, is infinitely better than his.

Ah, but here he is now. Hassled. Frowning. I've put my Billie Holiday CD on for him. He likes jazz, and so do I. It's good to have that in common. If I sit him down in my small but comfortable lounge, massage his shoulders, pour him a glass of wine . . . there. That's better. Is he? Yes, he is, he is actually smiling now. And asking me what is for dinner because it smells delicious and he can't really believe that he will be able to stay here for the night, our first night together. He sips wine and looks smug. He parked his car two streets along. You never know who might be prying, he says.

Her mother is ill, you see. Francesca's. She's knocking on, he told me, and keeps falling over. She hurts herself, breaks her bones. This latest issue is nothing serious but she needs an operation, he thinks. And there's talk of a home, but she won't go into one. Which isn't really terribly fair on Francesca, who has her own life down here and can't keep dashing up to the Dales every time her mother sneezes.

'Anyway, stroke of good luck, eh?' he said when he telephoned me with the news.

I don't like him to telephone me at work. He rings my mobile, never the shop telephone. On my mobile I have him listed under the name of Ashley.

I leave 'Ashley' in the lounge. In the kitchen I cook, and sip my own glass of wine. I consider showing him my grandfather's letter. But I decide against it. The Dearhead would probably not be interested, and I would feel I was somehow betraying both my grandparents. Especially Babunia. It's private.

I'm luxuriating in fine silk underwear, purchased only yesterday for the big occasion. In a dark red colour, like blood from a deep cut. It looks pretty, but it's all rather uncomfortable; I'm ignoring that, and projecting ahead to his delight later when he removes my clothes to reveal the lingerie. I hope it's his thing. I hope we have a wild . . . no, not wild — what am I thinking? — a nice time.

We deserve it.

* * *

We do have a nice time. Charles is good in bed, and I may as well be honest about that. It's a very major part of his charm, and one of the reasons I remain his . . . other woman. But, somehow, there's a cynical emptiness to it all.

There's something missing.

61

‘What do you expect?’ Sophie, hands on hips, irate, hearing my tale.

‘I don’t know.’

‘Come off it.’

‘I thought . . . I don’t know what I thought. It’s good to have a lover, for want of a better word. Actually, it’s fun.’

‘Yes, of course it is, and you deserve some fun. But you won’t get it from him, not long term. Being involved with a married man is rubbish, constantly looking over your shoulder. You can’t relax, you can’t hold hands in public unless you’re, I don’t know, three hundred miles away, and you can’t be normal. There’s more to a good relationship than just sex, you know?’

‘I know. I do know that. It’s all a bit . . . soulless, I think.’

‘Whatever. If I were you, I’d drop him. Get your life back. That’s the way forward.’

⋆ ⋆ ⋆

And I think. I hear and rehear Sophie’s words, and I end my relationship with the Dearhead. Two days later, over the telephone. Like this.

‘Charles? I’m sorry to ring you at work. But it’s important. Look, Charles, I don’t think we should see each other any more. It’s got to end. I think things have . . . have fizzled out, rather.’

Of course, he is excessively polite. And after pondering for several moments upon his own shortcomings, he apologises for screwing my life up.

I tell him my life is not remotely screwed up. I'm just uncomfortable with the whole thing; he's a married man, after all. And I'm a little bored, if I'm honest.

He's less polite now and says he's boring, is he?

I say no, he is not boring. But the relationship is, frankly. It's getting tiresome. And it's hardly right, is it?

He says I'm not very sensitive, and he always thought that of me. I'm brusque.

I apologise. I try again. The thing is, Charles . . .

The conversation ends with a promise from him not to attempt any further meetings. Of course, we will both be cordial and professional within the confines of the Old and New. And thank God, that is the only place we are likely to encounter each other.

So now the relationship is over. I can keep the cat. He hates cats, anyway. Bloody butchers.

And we shall be happy together, she and I. Of course, I won't miss Charles at all, not even on alternate Thursday nights. I shall, instead, make myself useful. I'll catch up with housework. I'll tackle that ironing pile before I really do run out of things to wear. I'll decorate my flat. I'll take my new cat to the vet. I know I'll miss Charles Dearhead, despite the shortcomings. I'll miss his urbane presence. But I won't feel sorry for myself, I won't allow my essential aloneness to bring me down. Aloneness is the shell in which I gratefully hide. And it's not the same thing as loneliness. Aloneness is what I've always felt I deserved; I choose it, prefer it and want it. You can't be hurt if you are alone. Perhaps that was how my mother felt the day she decided enough was enough. I'll probably never know. But I wonder how alike we might be. I wonder what she is doing, I wonder how she lives her life; how she lives with herself. Guilt is a terrible burden. So, I'm Doing The Right Thing. All is well.

I wish him all joy of this world, as my grandfather might have said.

★ ★ ★

And I so want to talk to my father about the letter.

I'm visiting him. It's a Sunday afternoon, it's pouring with rain — the heavy type that clashes on to windows and roofs like stones thrown by children. My grandfather's letter is nestled snug and dry in my handbag, and Dad and I are drinking tea.

'Have you visited Babunia recently?' I ask my father.

It's a start, an innocuous enough question.

'No. I haven't felt up to it much,' says Dad.

He looks wan today. Tired. I want to ask him about his pain management, I want to hear about the outcome of his last visit to the hospital. We have rarely talked about his illness. He broke the news to me several years ago, but he insisted that we shouldn't discuss it any more, unless it was 'absolutely necessary'. He vaguely

64

refers to visits to the hospital. He mentions a Dr Moore, but it's pretty much a closed subject and one he usually forbids me to even try to discuss with him. So I don't. Of course, he's known for many years, but being the stoic he is, he was determined to keep it from me. Babunia still doesn't know about it. He doesn't want to burden her.

'I'm thinking of visiting her tomorrow,' I say. 'I haven't been for a month or so. I really should go.'

'Good. I'm sure she'd be pleased to see you. I can't go at the moment. She'll know straight away . . .'

'I know, Dad. I'll tell her you're busy. Actually, I might have a couple of questions I'd like to ask her.'

'What sort of questions?'

'Well, I'm thinking of doing a family tree thing.' I'm pretty good at thinking on my feet. 'Everyone else seems to do one, so I thought I'd give it a go.'

'Oh. I see.'

'I'd like to ask Babunia about your father.'

'Well, we don't know much about him, do we? He died during the war, before I was born. You know that, love. I don't know much else about him. He was Polish, that's about it. Your grandmother likes to remind us that he was a squadron leader in the Battle of Britain, God bless her. But you know that already.'

'Do you know exactly when he died? The date, I mean? It might help me to trace him.'

'Mum always said in November 1940. She was

expecting me. Hard to believe, isn't it?'

'What?'

'That I was ever a baby. And so long ago.'

'Oh, I see. I thought you meant . . . never mind. Does Babunia have her marriage certificate?'

'She told me she thought it was lost years ago, I think.'

'But I could look that up, couldn't I? In a register?'

'I . . . well. Yes. I suppose you could.'

'Do you have your birth certificate?'

'Oh, somewhere. Although I rather think that might have gone missing too. I haven't seen it in years.'

We drink our tea and nibble on a digestive biscuit each.

'Your grandmother might have it,' says Dad. 'She likes to keep things safe for me. I haven't seen it since I started claiming my pension, I think. And that's longer ago than I'd like it to be.' Dad winks at me.

'Do you recall ever seeing their marriage certificate?' And now I am beginning to press, just the thing I must not do.

'No, love. I don't think so.'

'But you think Babunia *might* have it? She probably keeps such things all in one place, doesn't she? She's pretty methodical.'

'You'll have to ask her.'

'Is there a death certificate? For your dad?'

'I don't know, Rob. If there is, I've not seen it. At least, I don't think I have. You'll have to ask your grandmother about it all. But, darling?'

'Yes?'

'Don't let on to her. About me, I mean.'

'I won't, Dad.'

'It would break her heart. Always assuming she'd be with it enough to understand.'

'I know.'

'You're a good girl.'

'Maybe.'

'Do you fancy staying for your tea? We could watch *Antiques Roadshow*. I've got crumpets.'

'And gooseberry jam?'

'Sadly not your grandmother's. But I've got Tesco's mixed fruit jam, if that's any good. There might be gooseberries in it.'

And now I feel deflected, stalled; I know my father well, and I think he's hiding something.

Should I show him the letter? No. I'll keep it to myself for now. I don't want to upset him, any more than I want to upset Babunia.

We eat our crumpets and jam, and nothing further is said.

7

Nina eyed the bunch of wild flowers on the mantelpiece. Following her gaze, Dorothy noticed how they burst forth from the enamel jug, a little vulgar, a little showy. She watched her girls as they swiftly ate fried potatoes, fried eggs and broad beans — small, soft and sweet, early beans picked that afternoon by Dorothy under the unblinking sun. Far too early, of course, but there wasn't much else to choose from, yet.

Nina nudged Aggie, and raised her eyebrows.

'You been picking flowers, Dot?' said Aggie, winking at her friend.

'No.'

'Someone picked them for you, then?' said Nina.

'Yes.'

'A bloke?' said Aggie.

'A bloke. Yes.'

'Which bloke?' said Nina, through a full mouth.

Oh, how genteel, thought Dorothy. And: which bloke? Did Nina know all the 'blokes' in the world? Actually, Dorothy thought, there was quite a good chance of that.

'Squadron Leader Jan Pietrykowski, no less. He flies a Hurricane,' said Dorothy, more to herself than to the girls.

'Squadron leader, eh?'

68

'Is he a dish?' asked Aggie, gleefully.

'I don't know. I haven't really considered. A dish? Yes, possibly. Probably.'

'Well, if he is, you would have noticed, wouldn't you?' said Nina. 'You're not that bloody old. What's he like? Where did you meet him?'

'I met him today, here, in this kitchen.' Dorothy surprised herself. Was it really only this day and in this kitchen? 'And he's very nice, very polite. Foreign, of course.'

'What did he want?' said Nina. 'Apart from the bleeding obvious.' Aggie kicked her, and she squealed. 'I'm only asking, aren't I? You don't mind, do you, Dot? It's just, you've got to watch them Polish ones, they've got hands like octopuses. We had fun with them, though, didn't we, Aggie? Blimey, you'd think they'd never seen a girl before. They've got girls in Poland, though, haven't they?'

'Yes. Of course. But these men, you must understand. They've had a difficult time. They're in need of . . . diversion. The squadron leader had to flee his country in pretty ghastly circumstances. They all did. But I'll remember that warning, Nina. Thank you.' Dorothy hid a small smile behind her teacup. It was the cup that the squadron leader had drunk from, and she hadn't yet been able to wash it.

'Well?' said Nina.

'Well, what?'

'Do you fancy him?'

'Of course not.'

'Liar,' they chorused, delighted.

69

The squadron leader returned the following day, in the heat of the afternoon. The first day of June and, this year, flaming. Dorothy heard his confident, sharp rap on the kitchen door.

She had hoped he might return, yet she couldn't imagine why he would. She smoothed her pinny, tucked loose hair behind her ear, cleared her throat. She stood still for a few seconds, breathing in and out, a mechanical effort, consciously performed. She felt a crippling tightness in her throat. Yet she had to be a picture of composure. It didn't do to be anything else. And her knees almost buckled beneath her. She breathed, deep and loud, she tucked more hair behind her ears. She hummed a tune she had heard on the wireless. She would appear normal. On no account could she . . . she yanked open the door.

The squadron leader pushed past her, grinning, carrying a box, bulky and heavy-looking.

'What on earth is this?' said Dorothy, hands on hips, head on one side, while Jan Pietrykowski placed the box on the kitchen table. Her curiosity emboldened her, if only temporarily, and she forgot the tight throat, the quick breathing, the sweat pooling like oil slicks behind her knees.

'A gift for you. For you, Mrs Sinclair.'

'Oh. Why, thank you. What on earth is it?'

'A gramophone.'

'Oh.'

'You like music, no? I think so, because you always hum. At least, these two times we have met you have been humming as I walk down your path. So I bring you music.'

She did like to hum — just simple tunes, half heard, half remembered — and perhaps she liked to dance too, in her mind, humming her tunes, performing her duties, trying not to think about war and absconded husbands, dead babies and dead pilots. It was only natural.

Jan carried the gramophone through to the parlour, at Dorothy's request. She cleared the sideboard and blew off its thin layer of dust. He returned to his car — 'Not my car, our squadron car' — and came back in with a box of records, which he placed alongside the gramophone.

'I can't accept all this, Squadron Leader,' said Dorothy, collecting herself. 'I'm afraid you can't leave this here.' She hated to sound disapproving.

'Then it is a borrowing, from me to you, and you will return it to me when I have to depart, when I return home, whenever that shall be.'

'A borrowing?'

'Yes. Actually, it is not mine. It belonged to another man, a good pilot, an Englishman. I met him when I first arrived in your country. A generous man, of good spirit. He told me if anything were to happen to him, I must make sure his gramophone is looked after and is enjoyed. So I think of you, in this quiet cottage, and your girls who you tell me about. Girls, they love to dance, I think. And you too?'

'Dance? Me? No.'

'Yes.'

'No.'

'We shall see. Anyway, this is yours for as long

71

as you want it, and to enjoy and to use.'

'Don't your men want it? For entertainment?'

'We have wirelesses. We have dances. In fact, next Saturday. I invite you and your girls to the dance, as my guests.'

'But I don't dance. Especially at dances.'

'No need to dance. We can sit and talk. Be like friends.'

'That sounds very nice. I'm sure Aggie and Nina would be thrilled. They so enjoyed the last one.'

'We must have fun when we can get it, in times like these. If my men can't fly yet, we can drink, eat, make joke, no? No need for guilt.' And the squadron leader smiled at Dorothy. 'I shall collect you next Saturday, at seven o'clock,' he announced.

'All right,' said Dorothy, smiling broadly despite her misgivings. 'I'll go, as you have been so kind as to ask. But I shall not dance.'

★ ★ ★

The girls, tired and grubby, arrived back at the cottage around half past five. They took one look at the gramophone and the records, and it seemed their world was complete. They searched eagerly through the stack of records, digging out their favourites. Aggie was delighted to find some Billie Holiday songs — 'You must listen to her, Dot!' — and that odd, brittle-strong voice was now flowing through the house, the jaunty music restoring something to them all. Dorothy immediately liked the joyful-joyless sound of the

72

American woman's voice. And, for an evening, they forgot about the war. There was none of their usual talk: In a year it could all be over, in six months it could all be over, six weeks even, and Hitler will be here, and we'll have no freedoms, and Churchill will be strung up, and . . .

'Dance, Nina!' cried Aggie, pulling the heftier girl to her feet, and spinning her around, laughing, red-faced.

Dorothy sewed and watched. She smiled. It was an inspired idea of the squadron leader's, she thought. Of course, young women like to dance. They like music. Why wouldn't they?

'There's more,' said Dorothy, remembering the invitation. 'We are invited to the dance next Saturday night. Special guests of the squadron leader.'

'Oh, we know all about that,' said Nina, throwing herself down on to the settee, still red-faced, her mousy hair clinging to her face. 'Already invited, we are. All the Land Girls are going.'

'What are you going to wear, though?' said Aggie. 'I've got my blue frock.'

'I don't know. Don't much care either. Might just wear my uniform. All that lovely food up there too! They put on such a spread last time, Dot. You should've seen it. Cakes. Jellies. All sorts of sandwiches. Lovely, it was.'

'Yes, but that's why your dress won't fit you any more!' said Aggie, moving rhythmically around the room, arms held out as though dancing with a partner, her blonde curls flying behind her.

'It's all right for you. Just I've got a healthy

appetite, haven't I, Dot?'

'Indeed you have. Why don't you bring me your dress, and we'll see if I can let it out for you?' said Dorothy.

The dress was a pale green lawn, with a matching fabric belt. Rather old, and in need of a darn or two, as well as letting out. Dorothy examined the seams, which were mercifully generous. After suggesting Nina try it on, she unpicked and pinned it, and managed to let it out to the required size. Nina looked well in it. Green suited her nondescript, pale brown hair, her country-tanned face and arms. Not exactly pretty — and, frankly, fat — but Dorothy still felt something akin to a mother's pride looking at the smiling girl wearing her newly altered frock.

★　★　★

The day before the dance, Dorothy examined her own wardrobe and pondered what to wear. She had three 'special occasion' frocks. The first was red, woollen, with long sleeves, more of a winter frock. It was a little close-fitting, but not too tight. She had never regained the weight she'd lost in the weeks after giving birth to Sidney. The red dress was of a pleasing length, just below the knee, and would show off her calves to advantage if she were to wear her black court shoes. She still had reasonable-looking calves. This she allowed.

She also had a green and blue patterned dress in a crisp cotton, which creased easily and was, besides, too young for her now. She would see if

74

Aggie might like it. And lastly she had her summer frock, with a tiny flower print in pink, black, white and orange. It was undoubtedly her favourite with its summery, short puffed sleeves and its comfy, faded feel. It was perfect for a June dance. She had her pink cardigan she could wear with it, and her brown shoes looked smart with it too. Understated and admirably appropriate for a woman approaching forty, childless, and, for all she knew, widowed.

Her dressings had been removed, and the skin on her face was pink, no longer red and angry. It was still slightly sore to the touch when she covered it as best she could with her powder, just to see how it might look the following evening. It looked acceptable, she thought. She considered her frocks, hanging over her wardrobe door, draped across her bed. She liked them all, but at the same time she couldn't care less if she never wore any of them again. It was indifference, she knew — a horrible, blank feeling that she had become accustomed to over the past year. But still, she would have to choose.

Three dresses. One dance. One decision. There really was only one contender.

★ ★ ★

Nina had been right about the food. Trestle tables were loaded with plates of sandwiches, jellies, trifles, sausages, even cakes. There were large tea urns. And there was mild, if you wanted it, and cider. Some folk even had bottles of wine on their tables, Dorothy noticed. She took a cup of tea and a modest plate of food, and found a chair in a corner. Music erupted all around, loud and insistent. British and Polish airmen and their guests were dancing and laughing. Swing, Dorothy thought the music was called. She liked it, the soaring movement of it, the brashness. She watched the young people dancing, keeping a distant eye on her girls, who were oblivious of her — at least, for now — as they danced and laughed, cheeks rosy, freshly curled hair bouncing on their firm young shoulders. Dorothy felt weak as she compared herself to all these young people; she felt inconsequential. How glad she was to be sitting in the corner.

Dorothy liked to sit in the corner at parties. There was nothing worse than sitting with a large group of people, feeling left out. Or, even worse, trapped. Stupid people, asking stupid questions, interfering. Laughing at jokes that she was not privy to. No, she would take her own company any day. She nibbled at a fish paste sandwich, and wondered why on earth she had agreed to come to this dance. Squadron Leader Pietrykowski had duly arrived at the cottage at seven o'clock, driving the squadron car. He had smiled broadly at her, told her he liked very much her dress. Dorothy felt both elated and shameful. The girls, dolled up and excited, giggled and chatted in the back seat. Nina had her eye on a chap who she hoped to 'talk to' at the dance. The interior of the squadron car smelled of straw and leather and cigarettes, and Dorothy felt dizzy as they flew along the lanes, the hedges and trees and flowers, the cottages, people and bicycles all flashing by them.

The room swam with pulses and energies and jealousies, with chatter and spite and laughter. Dorothy, from her seat in the corner, continued to watch Aggie and Nina, and the other young women and men dancing, laughing, flirting. The squadron leader moved around the room, talking to people, ensuring the music was loud enough but not too loud, chatting with his fellow pilots, with the British pilots. There was talk of the Polish squadron being formed soon. And Dorothy thought yes, how useful it was that he could speak and understand English so well. It seemed that everybody wanted to speak to Jan Pietrykowski. He had that magic, that allure. So whatever she felt — what she thought she might have begun to feel — was nothing, was of no import. Dorothy watched him, her eyes roaming inconspicuously from her girls to him, and back again, and again. She watched as he spoke to the ladies of the village, who were eating greedily, nodding and smiling and gushing.

A couple of them, vaguely known to Dorothy as Marjorie and Susan, marched over to her corner. Dorothy smiled at them as they sat either side of her.

How was she? Everybody was talking about her recent escapade, did she know that? Her heroics?

'It was nothing,' said Dorothy.

'Nonsense!'

'Really — '

'And you seem to have made quite an impression on the Polish squadron leader!'

'I —'

'He is a very handsome man, isn't he? And such a gentleman.'

'Yes, if you say so.'

'And he speaks such good English!'

They smelled of mild and wine. And were far too loud, even for them, she thought, although she barely knew them and had no desire to know them better or speak to either of them. She thought they were friends of Mrs Compton, if Mrs Compton had any friends.

'Marvellous English, yes.'

'And, Dorothy, how are you keeping these days?'

'I'm fine, thank you. The girls keep me busy,' said Dorothy, pleased to come up with a change of subject.

'We always meant to say — didn't we, Susan? — how sorry we were to hear about —'

'These things happen. Don't they?' said Dorothy. She wasn't certain if they were about to talk about the loss of Sidney, or Albert's desertion of her. But she would not talk about any of it with these women. She would not.

'But you must miss him,' said Marjorie. 'And we never see you any more. You do keep yourself to yourself, Dorothy, don't you?'

'I think it's best.'

Susan, more astute than her friend — and bored, or uncomfortable, or both — murmured that Mrs Sanderson had arrived and she should very much like to talk to her, and she and Marjorie excused themselves and returned to their side of the room. They whispered to their friends, among them the newly arrived Mrs Sanderson,

78

Mrs Pritchard, Mrs Twoomey. Perhaps Mrs Compton was with them? But Dorothy had not noticed her. The women looked over at Dorothy from time to time, turning away hastily if she caught their eye. She was being talked about, she knew, but it didn't matter. Let them talk.

Perhaps she should give them something to talk about?

Scanning the room, she smiled brightly at Jan Pietrykowski. He joined her, pulling out the chair recently vacated by Marjorie, and smiled back.

'You are enjoying, no?'

'No. Not much.'

'I'm sorry. You are tired?'

'It's those women. Nosy things. I don't like them.'

'I shall sit with you now. And we shall eat. Can I get you some more food? Your plate is empty.'

They ate. He asked her who various people were. That ugly woman in the grey dress? The group of girls looking daggers at Nina and Aggie and the other Land Girls?

'The fat woman with . . . what you call? . . . jewels?'

'Nearly. Jowls. She is not very nice. Another nosy parker, I'm afraid. The world's full of them.'

'You like very few people, Mrs Sinclair?' said Jan.

'Is it so obvious?'

'Yes, I think so. Some of these people are probably very nice, if you give them a chance.'

'I'll reserve judgement on that, thank you. It's not that I dislike people. You must not . . . please don't think that of me. I'm just tired of it all.'

79

'Yet I hate to see you so lonely,' he said.

She blushed and looked down at her hands. They lay twisted in her lap, fingers intertwined. The squadron leader apologised. He changed the subject, to music, to the dancing. They ignored the quizzical, envious looks from the villagers. Dorothy reflected, as he left her for a moment to replenish their teacups and choose a cake for each of them, that she was getting almost as many disapproving looks as the Land Girls. It didn't do, she understood. A married woman, of a certain age, wearing a figure-skimming red dress (so *obvious*), and hogging the handsome Polish pilot to herself all evening. No. It didn't do at all.

. . . and her husband, poor Bert Sinclair, you couldn't blame him for running off like that, could you? She couldn't furnish him with a child, and no man deserves that. She couldn't even furnish him with a smile, in the end. And she never joined in, did she? She was a loner, she was snooty. Not much company for any husband. Too wrapped up in herself, that one. Not one for friends. A cut above, she fancies herself. Jane Frankman's niece, wasn't she? That's how she met poor Bert. They say her mother hasn't spoken to her since she married him. Lives in the south, the mother, doesn't she? Reading? London? Oxford? Must be lonely for Mrs Sinclair, in that cottage, and all that laundry to do. Doesn't seem right, a woman like that taking in laundry. Still, it keeps a roof over her head. Goodness knows what might happen if Bert were to be reported missing. They'll turf

her out. Then where'll she go? She has no friends round here. Is the mother still alive? Goodness knows. We're not allowed to know anything, are we . . .

This is what Jan Pietrykowski heard as he made his way to the trestle tables loaded with food, negotiating ladies with jowls (an amusing word, new to him, that he would try to remember), ladies wearing austere dresses, ladies who were determined to engage him in conversation.

But he escaped from the attention, and he returned to Dorothy.

Before she knew what was happening, before she could protest, before they could even eat their cakes, Dorothy was steered towards the dance floor and the Polish man's arms were around her, on her, gripping her waist, her shoulder, lightly at first, then more firmly. Around they went, locked together, and they moved in secrecy and silence as if nobody was watching. And yet to Dorothy it seemed that the whole world was judging, but she did not mind. The world could go to hell. She was without a care, for the first time in a long year. And the music seemed to go on forever — in her heart, this music would play forever — and when she looked at the man and he smiled and squeezed her waist in affection and understanding, she let her head fall on to his shoulder and she let herself be danced. And the nervous stirrings in her stomach, her bowel, her groin, the unfurling going on inside her, she accepted with a tacit grace. She was an adult, after all.

Too soon the lights were up, people were

standing and shaking hands, couples were linking arms and preparing to leave, some drunk, others yawning and tired. Cigarette smoke hung over the room like a coarse blanket. There was a babble of goodbyes, and the squadron leader stood aside to allow Dorothy to collect her bag, and to see how Aggie and Nina were to go home.

'We'll walk, Dot!' shouted Nina, as a Polish airman — very young, perhaps eighteen — grabbed her face and kissed her, then released her with loud laughter. She hit him on the back of his head. Dorothy wondered if this was the young man she'd had her eye on.

Aggie agreed, yes, they would walk, and she too was with a young man, who whispered to her. Aggie giggled.

And the group of village girls, one of whom Dorothy recognised as Mrs Compton's oldest granddaughter, called out, 'Tarts!'

Dorothy looked at Jan. 'Do you think they will be all right?' she asked.

'They are not children,' he said, and shrugged.

Dorothy hesitated and he waited, politely.

'All right, then,' she said. And she advised the girls to be home within the hour, as she would wait up for them with a pot of cocoa.

The squadron leader was silent, lost in calm concentration, during the twenty-minute journey back to the cottage. There was a strong moon, and the evening was warm, and the moonlight was enough to see by, if he drove slowly. Dorothy too was silent. The road looked like a slick oily river. She watched him drive, confidently, safely. He was a man accustomed to being in control.

'Thank you, Squadron Leader,' said Dorothy, as he opened the passenger door.

As she got out of the car, he kept his hand on the door and blocked her way. But Dorothy did not feel threatened.

'You use my title all of the time,' he said. 'But my name is Jan. I lead a squadron, yes, and I am a member of the Polish Air Force and that is my job, that is my role, but I am Jan. That is my name. That is the name I wish to hear you call me. I make a point. That is all.'

'I see. Jan. Thank you, then, Jan, for a pleasant evening.'

'Merely pleasant?'

'Enjoyable. Hot and noisy, but fun. Actually, I had a marvellous time with you.'

'That is better. Thank you for being my guest. I am sorry you were so uncomfortable. Those gossiping ladies do not like you, I see. But I do.'

'Thank you. I don't mind being not liked. I prefer it.'

'Why?'

'Because I don't have to spend time with those gossiping women. My life is my own. Do you see? I don't want them to befriend me. I like my quiet life in this cottage, with just the girls for company.'

'You are like a mother for them?'

'Perhaps.'

'They are very fond of you.'

'Well, they give me a reason to get out of bed in the morning.'

'Then it's what I say. For them, you are a mother.'

'Jan, I don't wish to appear rude, but . . . '

'You are tired?'

'Yes. Rather.'

Jan released his hold on the car and walked Dorothy to the cottage door, and he waited while she struggled to unlock it. The lock had been stiff for months, she explained. He said he would bring oil for it on his next visit. The kitchen was dark and warm and smelled of bread, fresh laundry and, faintly, of fish. Dorothy was struck by the smell, as if it were new to her, and she realised suddenly how much this cottage *was* her — not just her home, but her life. Solidly built of red bricks, with square rooms, neatly plastered walls, high ceilings. She felt as though she had betrayed the cottage by staying away for so many hours. She felt like a stranger standing in her own kitchen, listening to her clock on the mantelpiece — tick, tick, tick — and she resolved to reacquaint herself with her home.

As soon as the squadron lead —

As soon as *Jan* had left.

He didn't want to, she could tell. Probably he wanted a kiss. Possibly he wanted more. But she wouldn't, and she couldn't, do any of those things. He was a man whom she could imagine herself kissing and touching, enjoying his body. And the thought of doing that did not make her blush or feel ashamed. But she would not do any of it. And she could not tell herself why, because she didn't know. It was certainly not a moral objection. It was not mere rectitude.

'Goodnight, Mrs Sinclair,' said Jan. 'I will leave you now. I may visit again?'

'Oh, please do. But my name is Dorothy. That is the name I would like you to call me. Now that we are on a more . . . friendly footing.'

'Dorothy,' he repeated slowly.

'It's such an awful name. I absolutely loathe it.'

'No. A good name, very English, I think.'

'Goodnight, Jan. Thank you for a lovely evening.'

'It's true. The British are so polite!'

'Come for tea? Tomorrow, at four o'clock? I can't promise a big spread, but . . . tea and sandwiches. Perhaps cake.'

'English afternoon tea? Yes, I will be here. Thank you.'

Jan stared at Dorothy, and she smiled at him, fixed, obtuse. He smiled back at her — resigned, she guessed — and he took his leave with a slight, stiff bow.

After watching the car drive away, Dorothy roamed through her house, ignoring the marital bedroom, now the girls' room, where her only child had been conceived and born. She entered her own small bedroom under the eaves and removed her red dress, her shoes, her stockings, corset, knickers and bra. She put on her nightdress and dressing gown, and with her cold cream she scrubbed her face free of its lipstick and powder.

She returned to the kitchen and made cocoa, stirring the milk slowly, and then she sat and waited for the girls, who returned two hours later, breathless, dishevelled and drunk.

8

'Dorothea, your tea is different.'

Jan had arrived at exactly four o'clock, on his bicycle. Despite the heat, he was unflushed, not even sweating. True to his word, he'd brought an oil can, and he oiled the lock, catch and hinges on the kitchen door. In preparation for their tea together, Dorothy had placed her wooden table and chairs under the shade of the silver birch trees in her back garden. The trees rattled and whispered in the warm breeze. She'd invited him to sit under them after his handiwork, while she prepared the tea and brought it out into the garden.

'How is my tea different?' she asked, sitting down at last.

'It is very tea-like. Very refreshing. And you have a pretty . . . what is it?' He gestured at the tea-strainer.

'Oh, the tea-strainer? It belonged to my mother.'

'She is dead?'

'No. I took it when I left to marry Albert. I'm afraid I took some rather odd things from my mother's house. It was rather sudden, you see. I thought certain items might come in useful. And some of them have.'

'And some of them have not?'

'Quite.'

'Why did you marry him?'

86

'Why?' She laughed, a little flustered. 'Because I wanted to.'

'And why did you want to?' Jan stirred sugar into his tea, slowly, looking at Dorothy.

'Well, I suppose the right answer would be that I loved him dearly, I simply had to be his wife, he could offer me a wonderful life and eternal happiness. That I fell in love.'

'And the actual answer?'

'Oh, I don't know. Escape, I think. I wanted to escape from my mother. I wanted to strike out on my own and I had no means of doing so, other than marrying. I thought his life sounded interesting, and he was kind to me. There.'

'A sad tale, Dorothea.'

'Dorothea' watched Jan take a bite from a sandwich. His teeth were small, even and white. She noticed the way his fingers curved lightly around the sandwich. He was an elegant man.

'Perhaps it is sad,' she replied.

'Were you ever happy?'

'Oh. What a question. Perhaps I was happy when I was very young.'

'Not since then? I am sorry to hear it. You deserve happiness.'

'I'm not sure what happiness would mean to me, anyway.'

'Perhaps a child?'

'Yes. Oh yes!' Dorothy realised she was leaning eagerly on the table — brazenly, she thought — squaring up to this man, engaging with him in a way that could be considered literally 'forward'. She checked herself, sat back in her chair, and sipped her tea.

'You have regrets, no?' said Jan. He raised his eyebrows at her encouragingly.

'I have regrets, you could say, about certain things,' said Dorothy.

'I have heard talk of it.'

'I expect you have.'

'You lost a baby?'

'I lost more than one.'

'But you gave birth to a child?'

'You are very full of questions!' Dorothy picked up the plate of cakes and offered it to Jan.

She watched him eat, and he seemed unabashed, eating under her scrutiny. She, for her part, always ate guardedly. She hated the way eating contorted her face, and it made her feel exposed.

'I ask too much,' said Jan, wiping his mouth with a serviette. 'Forgive me, I am sorry. I like to know, that is all. You are an interesting lady and I would like to hear more about you. Sadness turns us into people, surely you understand? People with hearts that thump in our chests, and souls that dream. You see?'

It was becoming increasingly difficult to hold off from Jan.

She took a deep breath. 'Sidney. That was his name. A dear little boy. He was taken away. They — Mrs Compton and Dr Soames — thought it best. But I didn't want them to take him away. I wanted him to stay with me. I wanted to hold him and comfort him and tell him how sorry I was to have let him down.' She was breathless and close to tears, but it felt right to have said such things — things that she needed to say.

Things she had never said.

'The child was born dead?' Jan asked. The birch trees swayed softly around them, gently rattling their silvery leaves.

'A stillbirth, yes. He was silent, no crying, you understand? There was just this dreadful quietness. The stillness was terrifying. He was blue, I shall always remember that. Translucent.'

'Trans . . . ?'

' . . . lucent. As if I could almost see through him.'

'Ah.'

'Not like a little human being at all.'

'I wish it had not been so.'

'Thank you.'

'And now I have upset you.'

'No, no. Truly. I think I need to talk about it with somebody, from time to time. It doesn't help to bottle it all up and try to pretend it didn't happen. It did happen. And it's with me all the time, I can't stop thinking about my little Sidney . . . his little body . . . what became of him? He was a person, you see. A dead person, but he had been alive, kicking inside me, I felt him kicking every day. I so wanted to be his mother.'

Jan said nothing, but he passed her a serviette. Dorothy took it, wiped her tears and blew her nose, then apologised.

'Fate played a cruel trick on you, Dorothea. Or God did.'

'God?' said Dorothy.

'You believe in God?'

'No. I do not.'

89

'You never pray?'

'I have done.'

'But you prayed to an empty sky, no?'

'Of course.'

'So for what did you pray?'

'For my babies. For Sidney, in the last few days before he was born. I thought it might make a difference. I thought prayers might keep him safe.'

'But the prayers did not work.'

'No.'

'There are no gods. This I know. There is no sense to this life, what we call life. All around is madness and cruelty and things that are unfair. That which pleases one person dismays another. Nothing is personal, no great being is up there or down here, plotting against us. Everything that happens, happens because it can. There is no meaning beyond life itself, the breathing and sleeping and eating and talking and loving and hating, all of this. And the losses, we lose from the minute we are born, or whenever life begins. I do not know when life begins. Does anybody know? But life, it is hard. It will always be hard. This I believe, Dorothea.'

'I see.'

'You do not like?'

'I think I do. It makes far more sense.'

'More sense than what?'

'Oh, Sunday sermons. The bleatings in church.'

'You go to church?'

'No. Not now. It's ghastly. I was forced to attend every Sunday as a child. Jan? Do you mind if I ask why you are calling me Dorothea?'

'Because it is an even prettier name than Dorothy. You are a Dorothea.'

'I think I like it. Say something to me in Polish. Please.'

'*Ty jesteś piękną kobietą.*'

'Such a strange language!'

'No, simple. Much simpler than yours.'

'You think so?'

'Of course.'

'So what did you say?'

'I said this is a beautiful garden, this is a beautiful afternoon, and all is perfect here and now.'

'I'm not sure I believe that.'

'Well. You will have to wonder, then.'

'I shall.'

'My wife was always 'wondering'. I think I am not easy to understand. Not translucent perhaps?'

Wife? But she thought . . . You ridiculous woman. Oh, goodness, had she — ?

'Jan, I . . . I'm sorry. You are married.'

Dorothy berated herself. Of course, but of course. Did she really think a man like Jan wouldn't be spoken for? Oh, how awful — !

'I am not married,' he said. 'I *was* married.'

'Your wife died?'

'No. She was young — a beautiful, young woman. We married when we were both eighteen. My mother said no, not to marry, but we didn't listen, we married, we were in love.'

'What happened?' She barely dared to ask, so her words were whispered, and were lost in the swaying of the trees.

'We lived happy, for a few months only, we

made a pretty home. But I was not enough for her. She was restless. She wanted more. Other men. She took other men. I angered, I shouted. I was betrayed and I made her out of the house. And I was lonely. So I too left the house. I joined the Air Force and I have not seen her since. She returned to the house of her father. We have divorce.'

'I'm sorry, Jan. It must have been difficult for you. I know how fragile a man's pride can be.'

'A woman's love. That is the fragile thing.'

'All love, surely?'

'No. Some love is solid and is not breaking.'

'Does not break,' she corrected, and immediately wished she hadn't. 'But you have been disappointed in love?'

'As you have.'

'Yes, and everything can be broken, Jan. I've accepted that in my life. You cannot trust anyone or anything, it just doesn't do.'

'You think not?'

'Why don't we talk about something more cheery? I know, your music box. The girls are enjoying it so much! They love to sing and dance and they whirl around in the parlour of an evening, so lost in themselves and the music. It's priceless.'

'And what do you do while they dance?'

'I sew. Mending, of course, and alterations. Nina, the bigger girl, she eats like a horse and her clothes need letting out constantly, it seems. She can't have had much to eat back in London. She's from quite a poor family, I think.'

'Yes. She is one of many children?'

'She has two elder brothers, I think, and a little sister and brother — twins, I believe. I so envy her! The twins have been evacuated from London, to Wales. She tries to write letters to them, but I have to help her. She's hopeless, she can barely read or write. She says she misses London, but I rather think she should be glad to be away from it. Why volunteer for the Women's Land Army if you would prefer to stay in the city?' She stopped abruptly, aware that she was talking rather rapidly, and not making much sense. 'But perhaps you like city living?'

'I have not lived in a city. You have?'

'I lived in Oxford, as a child. It was too noisy and crowded and busy for my liking. And that was in the days before there were so many motor cars.'

'How old are you, Dorothea?'

'Why, I . . . well, since you have asked, and you did tell me how old you are, I shall tell you. I'm thirty-nine years old. I shall be forty in November.'

'A young woman.'

'Nonsense. Too old. Too old for babies, anyway. Perhaps that was my mistake with Sidney. Trying for too long, allowing myself to fall pregnant so late in my life. It was stupid of me. So I was punished.'

'Punished by whom?' His clear blue eyes were fixed on her.

'I don't know. My mother? She may have cast a spell on me.'

Now his eyes crinkled with mirth. 'You are not serious?'

'I suppose I'm not. But she is a witch.'

'Why do you say such a thing?'

'Because she had no right to motherhood,' said Dorothy, standing and beginning to clear the table.

Jan sprang up to help her.

'She was hopeless, just utterly hopeless. It's been five, six years now, since I heard from her. She was furious with me, you see.'

'Because you married Albert.'

'Yes. I left her home, my home, to marry a man 'beneath me'. She couldn't stand it. She thinks we still live in Victorian times. Well, we don't. It's the thirties now. Actually, it's the forties already, isn't it? Modern times, modern women. Look how they go on these days! Look at my girls. They're shameless at times. But I don't blame them. I really don't. You only get one life. And times are hard, they're frightening. God only knows how this will all end.' Dorothy turned towards the cottage, holding the tray. 'Would you like more tea?'

She insisted that Jan stay where he was, and enjoy the afternoon's peace while it lasted. She replenished the tray with a fresh pot of tea and clean cups and saucers, and topped up the milk jug and sugar bowl. Today she would not spare the sugar. Then she popped upstairs to look at herself in her dressing-table mirror. She was tempted to apply lipstick, but she resisted.

On her return to the garden, she found Jan recumbent on the ground, his legs crossed, one hand behind his head, the other holding a blade of grass that he chewed. He smiled broadly at her as she placed the tea things on the table.

'Are you all right down there?' she asked. She felt bemused, but she could not say why. Perhaps because Albert had not been one for lying around chewing grass. Albert had been anything but nonchalant.

'I am perfectly all right. Dorothea, do you fear this war?' he said.

'I hoped there wouldn't be another one. We all did, surely?'

'Of course. But it was always coming, I think. It was going to happen sooner or later. And now it has, and we must fight again for the good.'

'I hope we'll win. All of us. Somehow! It's really starting now, isn't it? Churchill in charge at last . . . it makes it all seem more real somehow. You feel that something will *happen* now. And you Polish chaps arriving. But we need a miracle. Don't we?'

'We need a miracle. And yes, the war it is coming. Hitler will not stop short.'

'Will there be one, do you think? A miracle?'

'I don't know,' said Jan, and for the first time he sounded sad.

'Are you afraid?' she asked him.

'In my heart lies hatred. I want to kill these Nazis. The biggest pleasure, no, the next biggest pleasure in my life is killing Nazis.'

'Have you killed any yet?'

'Yes.'

'Really? Is that murder?'

'No. It is justice. Those monsters have destroyed my country. They kill children, they kill women, like you, women in their gardens, in

95

the fields, they shoot down, there and then. They forced me to flee my homeland and so they should expect me to kill them. They destroy my country. I have no mercy.'

'I see. I'm sorry, Jan. It's all so bleak. And all these soldiers returning from France. The newspapers can dress it up how they like, but it's a defeat, surely?'

'Defeat? No. A tactical withdrawal, I have heard it said. Many are rescued, don't forget. They can gather themselves, rearm themselves, start again. Like me, leaving *Polska*, getting here eventually, my men and I, all of us with one aim, to kill the bastards that took over our country. Dorothea, has my fighting talk alarmed you?' He sat up, discarding his blade of grass.

'No, I'm not scared. I've given up being scared. I've feared so much in my life, and my worst fears came true. The spell of fear has been broken somewhat. There's no fear left in me.'

'That is hard talk for a woman.'

'I am weary, but that's all.'

'World-weary?'

'Yes, I suppose so. Nothing much shocks or surprises or delights me any more.'

'Nothing?' He moved closer to her, and perched at her feet like a dog seeking affection.

'Don't you know that feeling?' said Dorothy.

'I think I do. But I don't like it.' He frowned when she shrugged. 'You do like it? You like being, in Polish is *cynik*. Is it the same in English?'

'It is. But I'm not a cynic.'

'But yes, you are *cyniczny*. It's understandable. Hard times bring hard reactions. This is war. This is life, all our wars and battles. Nobody will blame you.'

'Blame me?'

'For feeling as you do. You are not alone, Dorothea. Not you.' He put an odd emphasis on the last word.

'You say that . . . are you alone?'

'In my thoughts and my heart, yes. But I am surrounded by men, some of them boys, who look to me, who listen to me, who rely on me. In that way I am not alone.'

Dorothy was suddenly very aware that Jan was a mere inch or two from her knees, which were bare and quivering. Really, it was . . . inappropriate. Why on earth had she not put stockings on? She tried to pull her skirt down a little, but Jan appeared not to notice her discomfiture.

'But you are lonely?' she asked.

'As you are,' he replied.

'Loneliness can be a good thing. Sometimes.'

'How is this?'

'It makes one think properly, and understand things. When you have time to be alone, to think, to just cogitate.'

'Cogitate?'

'Cogitate . . . um . . . mull things over. No, that's no good . . . consider? Anyway, I think we are all essentially lonely, don't you? Nobody can really understand another's mind. We're all inside our own heads and minds and hearts. But that's how it has to be. We can only reach out so far to others. Maybe our fingertips will meet somebody else's, and that will be a beautiful moment. But it can never be more than fingertips.'

The squadron leader was examining his hands. Dorothy felt as if she had stopped breathing. She inhaled deeply, and sighed.

'You are a philosopher,' he said at length.

'Goodness me, no. I'm just a woman with time to think. Mundane tasks lend themselves well to thinking. Washing, ironing, mending.'

'You are 'just a woman'?'

'Yes.'

'But a thoughtful woman. A woman of intelligence. You see in clearness where others do not.'

'No.'

'I think so.'

They lapsed into silence, Jan resuming his prostration at her feet. He took up another blade of grass.

★   ★   ★

'This is nice, Jan. To sit quietly and not have to talk.'

The sun was beginning to sink, casting a golden glow over the Long Acre, over Dorothy's garden, over Jan as he lay now on his stomach, examining the earth beneath him. He looks like a child, she thought.

'I dislike too much talk,' said Jan. 'Too much of talk is nonsense. With you there is exception. But almost always I prefer my own company.'

'Yes. I understand. Where did you grow up?'

'In a small village. Near Krakow.'

'Yes, of course. You told me on the day we met. I'd not heard of it before.'

'As I had not heard of Lincoln before arriving here.'

'You lived with your parents?'

'I lived with my mother. The woman I called mother. I had no father. He was never known to me.'

'Ah, you said. Forgive me. But what do you mean, you *called* her your mother?'

'And so we get to it.' Jan shook his head. 'She took me as her own child. My true mother was young when she became pregnant. Young and not married. I don't know too much about what happened. I was lucky, I have been told, to have been born. If you understand. I was brought up by my aunt, my mother's elder sister, a widow. My mother left the village, she never returned. I have not heard from her.'

'My goodness. But your aunt? Was she good to you?'

'Of course. Yes. She loved me. I called her *matka*. Mother. I was safe, I was fed and clothed and educated. I was bright. She had more children, after me. Two girls. But I do not regard them as my sisters.'

'Why ever not?'

'Because they were not the children of my mother. You understand? She left me, my mother, it doesn't matter who with. She did not want me. I was a shame. I am a person with no roots.' He sat up, stretched and stood.

She looked up at him. 'But she was your real mother's sister, you said, the woman who brought you up? Not so far removed from your roots.'

99

'But still removed. That is enough. I wanted to be with my mother. Ever since I can remember, since I could understand. If I was naughty, I would hear, 'You are like your mother!' It was not said in cruelty, you understand. But it was said. My mother was not loved, you see, she was not respected for having a baby outside of marriage. I think she had to leave. But she should have taken me with her. She chose not to.' He sat in the wooden chair opposite Dorothy, sighed and looked deeply into her eyes.

'Thank you for sharing these things with me, Jan,' she said.

'We all need a friend, no?'

* * *

It felt as though the night would never fall, and Dorothy didn't want it to, but the sun finally dropped all the way below the horizon, and stars and planets announced themselves one by one, prompting her to rummage around in her kitchen for a candle. She brought it outside in tremulous hands. As soon as Jan had lit it with his cigarette lighter, moths and indeterminate insects busied themselves flying into the flame, their tiny bodies fizzling and dropping beside the candle. Dorothy and Jan looked on in speechless fascination, powerless to prevent the deaths. They heard owls in the distant woods, small scurryings in the hedges, and the eerie night-time rustle of the birch trees.

Jan rose to leave at thirty-two minutes past ten, and she rose with him, mirroring his movement. He did not say when he would return, but he held Dorothy's hands in his and kissed them, first one, then the other. She stared at him. His kiss on her mouth, when it came, was the most alive thing she had ever known. His lips moved soft and hard on hers and she felt a rush of white heat, like nothing she had ever imagined. His teeth were like tight, hard pearls. She found herself, against all her sense of propriety, running the tip of her tongue over them. And as if waking from a stupefied and tropical dream, she stiffened, she became aware of the facts. Her hands rose up and she pushed at his chest, unsure, panic rising in her like vomit. He drew back, took her hands in his again and smiled at her. He said he was sorry. Mute, Dorothy shook her head. But she tried to smile at him, until her lips trembled and her cheeks stiffened. She felt like a young girl, sickened by the shock of her very first kiss.

They walked together to her front gate, and he took her hand in his as though they were taking a lovers' stroll past a duck pond. He whispered goodnight and rubbed her arm reassuringly. She thought he winked at her, but in the failing light it was hard to tell. She watched the Polish man and his bicycle disappear into the darkening night, slipping away from her like an apparition.

She stood alone for many minutes, staring after him into the gloom.

9

13th September 1947
Dear Marion,

I write to thank you for your visit last week, it was lovely to spend time with you and Lionel again. Peter had a marvellous time too. So nice to play tennis once more. We made a grand set, didn't we? Since your departure I have been bottling and jamming fruit, we have a bumper crop this year. And the weather has been so hot! I think of Denis always at this time of year, how he loved his fruit! And his tennis, of course. Peter played terribly well, didn't he? He grows more and more like Denis with each day that passes. Very soon he will be off to university, and I don't mind admitting, dear Marion, that I shall miss him dreadfully.

Do visit us again, dear, any time you can manage it, and please give my love to Lionel. I hope his tooth has stopped playing him up? And that your headaches are subsiding? Headaches are such a trial.

Yours, with love,
Hilda

(The first letter I found at the Old and New, and I can't remember in which book I found it. It's not the most fascinating of letters, but it has a sweet poignancy, and I took it home to begin my collection, which is now housed in Mrs Sinclair's suitcase. I have formed a mental picture of Hilda, her teenage son Peter, her dead husband Denis. I see her with her hair scraped back in a bun, I see her face hot and red as she throws herself into jam-making. But I don't think it helps.)

* * *

There are changes in Jenna, changes only I notice. Hair not brushed so well, make-up clumsily applied, or missing altogether — something I thought I would never see. Her clothes are creased, her skin is dry and flaky across her nose. Her cheeks are hollowing, and she has shadows under her eyes, grey-purple shadows that speak silently, I think, of guilt. Of regret. Sleep-dust litters the corners of her eyes. These changes are subtle, you understand. She has hitherto been impeccably presented, and now she is less than impeccable. Now she is more like me. She is a seven out of ten.

I know exactly how she feels, and I know how much it hurts, though the circumstances were different.

It was at university. I hooked up with a student who was good-looking, clever and funny. I'll spare his blushes and keep his name to myself. I felt flattered by his attentions, and I fell in love, I thought. It was fun. It was bloody brilliant, in fact. Until my period was two weeks late. Panic. A solitary late-afternoon trip to Boots. A long wait overnight (because in those days you needed to test your first urine of the day). Two

103

pink stripes. Not one, which is what I wanted, but two, very clearly, very pinkly. There was little discussion between myself and the handsome student. Just a conviction that it 'might be best to terminate'. 'We' were too young. 'We' were career minded. 'We' had no intention of . . . so I visited the GP, then the clinic, discreetly, swiftly, alone. Handsome Student said he was 'grateful'. I broke up with him.

I've never told anybody else about my termination. I've never felt the need to.

Does Philip notice the differences in Jenna? Surely he must. Does he *know?* Perhaps Jenna bled for days, prompting concern, which led to a confession? Perhaps she is still in pain? I hope not. And yet I feel hardened, somehow. Something has changed between Jenna and me.

I shouldn't have helped her. It was a mistake. It was all too raw, too close to my own experience. I could have told her it was something I had been through too; I could have told her in the car as I drove her to the clinic, or even on the way home. I understand, I could have said. It will be all right in the end. She would have nodded, maybe smiled. Instead, she smoked a cigarette, holding it outside the car window, and we spoke barely at all.

I can see that Jenna now wishes she had confided in anybody else but me. She's done her best to avoid me since the very day after the clinic. I try to be kind; I make her tea, take it to her wherever she is in the shop; I once went to hug her, because she looked so very sad. But there was no hug. Now, we speak only when we have to, in clipped, purposeful sentences. Neither of us alludes to that day. She doesn't look at me. I want to help, but I'm not sure how to, I'm not sure what to say. It is so much simpler to do these things alone.

★ ★ ★

Babunia's care home is serene and hushed. There are pretty gardens behind the building, and the house itself is reassuringly small. It smells nice. The nurses and carers are uniformly professional and kind. Dad and I, and Babunia, chose the home together, and I know we chose the right one. It's a pity it's not a little closer, but a thirty-minute drive is not such a big deal.

I have telephoned ahead, and I am met in the entrance hall by a woman who introduces herself as Suzanne. I don't remember meeting her on my previous visits.

'I'm the new Entertainments Manager,' she explains, 'but I do all sorts, really. I wanted to meet you. Your grandmother and I have formed something of a rapport.' Suzanne tells me what I already know — Babunia is the 'darling' of the home. She is no trouble, and not even incontinent yet. Probably she never will be. Dignity, that's what she has kept hold of, Suzanne tells me, glowing with pride, as though she is talking about a high-achieving niece.

'Can I see her?'

'Yes, come on, I'll take you down to her room.'

I follow Suzanne, who is slim and wears a purple dress with purple high-heeled shoes. She

has masses of thick red hair, walks with a feminine wiggle, and it's impossible to guess her age.
We reach my grandmother's room and Suzanne
knocks. When there is no reply, she slowly opens
the door.

'Dorothea?' she calls.

Babunia is sitting in her armchair, her back
to the door, facing the large bay window. The
garden is filled with flower beds, which look
pretty in the height of summer, but are fading a
little now that it's August. There are small fruit
trees, a bird table, wooden seats. I look at her.
She does not turn round. She is so still, she may
be asleep. She may be dead.

Suzanne stands back to let me pass into the
room.

But I hesitate.

'Go ahead,' Suzanne says, smiling at me
kindly.

'I don't want to upset her,' I whisper. 'She's so
. . . vulnerable.'

'Why would you upset her? She'll be delighted
to see you.'

I slowly walk towards my grandmother and
stop beside her chair, looking down at her grey
hair, which is in her habitual neat chignon. She
slowly inclines her head towards me and I smile
at her. She opens her mouth and struggles to
speak, tears pooling in her green eyes as she
searches my face. She looks utterly dismayed.

I had not expected this. I've stayed away too
long, a month is too long. I should come every
week, as I used to do.

'Who are you?' she says.

106

* * *

Despite our reassurances that I am her granddaughter, Babunia continues to ask me who I am. She wants to know what I am doing here. It feels like an accusation. I can see real fear in her eyes, which is horrible.

Suzanne and I sit either side of her, holding a hand each.

'It's me, Roberta. I . . . I love you.' It seems an odd thing to say in the circumstances; but it's the right thing to say, all the same.

She shakes her head, and Suzanne tries to explain. But Babunia, panicked and tearful, is not listening. So we sit, the three of us, in silence.

When, eventually, Babunia dozes off, Suzanne and I converse in whispers.

'She's not always like this,' I tell her.

'I know,' says Suzanne. 'Only yesterday we were doing a crossword together and she got some of the answers.'

'Why doesn't she know me?' I ask.

Suzanne shrugs. 'I don't know. She gets easily confused some days,' she says. 'You must try not to worry.'

* * *

I am at work when I get one of the calls I have been dreading.

'Is that Miss Pietrykowski?' says a female voice, navigating my surname with some difficulty.

107

'Yes.'

'Oh, hello, I'm a staff nurse from the ward where your father . . . Mr — '

'Yes? Is he all right? What's happened?'

Philip, talking to a female customer, looks over her shoulder at me and raises his eyebrows enquiringly.

'He's okay, Miss Pietry — '

'Look, I know it's a bloody mouthful. Why don't you just call me Roberta?'

'It is rather, Roberta, yes. Thank you. Your dad had to come into hospital, an ambulance brought him in an hour or so ago. He's all right, a little uncomfortable, but stable.'

'But what's the matter?'

'Breathing problems. He's on oxygen. The doctors are hoping to change his medication and send him home again, but not today. I know his wish is to be at home as much as possible.'

Dad made me swear he will be allowed to die at home, and I have promised him. But I don't think he's going to be dying any time soon, as I frequently remind him.

I thank the nurse, finish the phone call, and tell Sophie I must go. I grab my bag and jacket and, as I hurry to the door, Philip calls after me to take all the time I need.

10

Mrs Compton smiled at Dorothy as they sipped tea and avoided, as usual, talk of any importance. Dorothy — also as usual — had not actually invited her visitor, and she wished the older woman gone. She was trying not to look at her, not to gaze too long into those eyes that were as cold and hard as a bathroom in winter. Perhaps if she stayed silent long enough, Mrs Compton might take the hint, and go away. How Dorothy wished now for the simple presence of her two girls, with their loud, frank talk, their apparent lack of fear, and their no-nonsense attitude to life. Dorothy was 'too nice', they often told her. You just have to stick up for yourself from time to time. It won't do you no harm. But the girls were across the fields, at the North Barn, up to their elbows in cow shit, straw, milk, calves, cauls, blood. And Dorothy wasn't sure what 'sticking up' for oneself could really mean.

She had no idea why Mrs Compton had called round again so soon after her last visit. The woman was asking her inane questions. Was she coping? How was the wound on her tummy? Healing up by now? Her face was certainly looking better, and she would not scar, anybody could see that. Such a relief, wasn't it?

Dorothy gave perfunctory, correct answers, and drank her tea.

'And how are you keeping, nowadays?' said

Mrs Compton, with crushing predictability.

Dorothy gave whatever answer was expected, barely registering the words. She had not seen Jan for three days. Something was happening, there were aeroplanes coming and going. There were rumours that the Germans were poised to attack, they were going to gas the entire country, they were going to invade any day, and soon. They were slaughtering people on the streets of Warsaw. They were 'rounding up' the Jewish people. Perhaps in Krakow too?

Dorothy didn't join in with the rumours. She laundered, she sewed, she cooked, she tended her hens, she thought about how much she wanted to see Jan, she wished for him to appear in her wash-house doorway, solid and strong, looming through the moisture like a saviour.

'The war news isn't good,' announced Mrs Compton.

Dorothy made no reply. She could think of none.

'I reckon we're for it,' the older woman went on, leaning forward, inviting Dorothy to speak, to open up, to smile at her.

Sullen, rude, stand-offish, Dorothy didn't care. She knew she would be described as all these and more later, in the village, Mrs Compton shaking her head, gossiping with the other women. Dorothy knew she was something of a mystery, and therefore unlikeable. She knew she was without friends.

Eventually, Mrs Compton rose to leave, promising to return the following week.

'There's really no need,' said Dorothy in what

she hoped was a determined, assured tone.

'Oh, I like to keep up with all my ladies!'

'But I am not one of your ladies. I am my own lady. Now please go, and don't bother to return. Ever. You nosy old witch. You baby-stealer.'

Of course, Dorothy didn't say these things. She only smiled a dry, scornful smile. And said over and over to herself, in her head, her head that seemed to be stuffed with cotton wool, with wood shavings, with pure white flour: Leave me, woman, leave me alone.

★   ★   ★

A further week passed with still no word from Jan. Dorothy, resigned, deduced that she had put him off forever with her reaction to their kiss. Perhaps he thought her immature, or neurotic. Perhaps he thought she did not like him and no longer wished to see him. Perhaps he had simply not enjoyed kissing her as much as he hoped he would.

Oh, it was disappointing, and she berated herself, over and over. What else did she expect? What else did she deserve?

But in the end, he came. There was the confident knock at the door, another bunch of wild flowers, another smile that seemed to welcome her, even though he was the guest. He entered the kitchen, he put down his hat, he loosened the top button on his tunic as he took the chair she offered him at the table. She wanted to ask him why he had not visited for almost a whole fortnight. But she could not. It was not her business. It was not important. So she made tea, while he watched her wordlessly. She wished he would speak, though she half enjoyed the intensity of the silence between them. It was another hot day and he rolled up the sleeves on his tunic, revealing brown, lean, strong forearms.

Dorothy tried not to notice. Really! It was all so inappropriate but . . . oh, heavens. It was out of her control, and she had not admitted to herself, despite her longings, what had happened to her. She had not yet accepted the state she was in.

His arms were poetry.

'I bring news,' said Jan, eventually, after clearing his throat and taking a cup and saucer from Dorothy's hands. 'Thank you.' He sipped.

'Good or bad news?' said Dorothy.

Now they were talking, it was all right again. She could now be the polite, interested, middle-aged, educated woman, befriending the foreigner who could speak her language so well, and was a long way from home. Propriety came rushing through her door.

'Ah. That is for your own interpretation.'

'It's not good so far. Go on.'

'I am leaving Lodderston. Not just me. The men. My men. We have formed a proper squadron.'

'Where are you going?'

'Kent. Closer to the fighting.'

'It makes sense.'

'It makes perfect sense, dear lady, no?'

'Would you like a biscuit? I made them this

112

morning. A little lacking in sugar, but they're perfectly acceptable. At least, Nina always says so.' She slid the plate across the table.

'Thank you.' Jan took a biscuit, ate it quickly and took another.

'When do you leave?' Dorothy asked, not wanting to hear the answer.

'Today.'

'Today! Oh. I see. Things happen so suddenly these days, don't they?'

'I apologise. I should have let you know this was likely. But we have been busy, training, flying, negotiating with the RAF.'

'No, no, please don't apologise. You owe me nothing, Jan. And I did think something like this would happen.'

'It's going to get worse before it gets better. You do realise that, Dorothea?'

'Of course. I'm not a fool.'

'No. You are not a fool.'

There was a pause.

'I hope not,' she said, to fill the silence.

'So I must take my leave. But I vow to return, whenever I can. I will return to visit my friend in her little house made of bricks.'

'You make me sound like a character from a fairy tale.'

'You are.'

Dorothy felt herself redden, all over, a strange, hot, thrilling rash seeping over her body. Her spine tingled.

'I see,' she said. 'Well, I'll certainly be here. I hope.'

'That is good, as it should be. Now I must go.

Thank you for your tea.'

'You have to go right now?'

'Yes. I'm sorry.'

'But you'll be safe, won't you?'

Jan leaned across the table, took Dorothy's face in both hands and looked into her eyes. She dared not blink.

'I give you my word,' he said, and let her go.

So he would not kiss her again.

He stood up and put his hat back on. Dorothy walked once again to the front gate with him, and watched him mount his bicycle.

'But shall you truly be safe?' she said.

She put her hand on his arm. She wondered at his bodily strength, his solidity. She fantasised their skin might meld together and they could disappear into the red and bloody safety of each other's bodies. But she had no right to think about this man in such crude terms. She was a married woman.

'But yes,' he said, 'I have told you. I have good luck, always. Polish luck. Can I write to you? Please?' And at last he sounded not like the confident 30-year-old man he always projected, but like a young boy. He placed his other hand over hers.

'Yes, of course. But I don't write letters,' she replied, blushing again; he was rather too good at embarrassing her.

'Why do you not write letters?'

'I don't like the way I write them.'

'You are a strange lady. Now is a good time to make an exception, no?'

'Perhaps.'

He removed his hand and looked down at hers

where it still rested on his arm. Hastily, she used it to tuck a stray hair behind her ear, flushing even more fiercely. He seemed not to notice.

'We leave in two hours, three at most. We shall fight, eventually, when your compatriots wake up and see what we can achieve. Perhaps in France, perhaps in England. So I must return and prepare. I got away, to say goodbye to you, my new friend. But I must now return quickly. Look out for me. We will fly over. You must wave to me. I will be in front.'

Jan started to ride off. He looked back and waved, which made him wobble. 'Mrs Sinclair?' he shouted over his shoulder. 'Your biscuits definitely need more sugar!'

Dorothy laughed.

But when he was gone, the laughter drained from her throat, tears gathered in her eyes, and real fear crept into her blood, despite her claim to no longer feel it — an idle boast, of course. And so already she was no longer Dorothea to him. Their fledgling intimacy had taken a step backwards, and it was her fault. She was his 'new friend'. She was Mrs Sinclair again. Fear she would conquer. Because if he could, she could. He had good luck, he claimed. Was there such a thing as Polish luck? Such a notion! But it was something to cling to. He would be safe. There was no room for fear.

She returned to her kitchen and, against all her thrifty impulses, she broke up the remaining biscuits, carried them on the rosebud serving plate out into the garden, and scattered what remained on to the ground for her hens.

Dorothy lingered in the garden, slowly gathering in her laundry. It was stale-dry and stiffened by the sun. The sky was pure blue, and the sun beat down on her like a public flogging, so she stripped down to her blouse and skirt, and undid her two top buttons, confident that she would not be visited again today. She removed her stockings — something she had done often this summer — and she felt the sun's fierce heat on her bare legs, like the caress of a giant.

She admitted to herself that she was enraptured. Alone in her garden, unwatched, unshackled, she could open up to herself, and she did. She wanted to kiss Jan, hold Jan, she wanted Jan to —

She just wanted Jan.

And then, hearing the distant roar as the squadron of Hurricanes started its engines, Dorothy ceased her work and looked towards Lodderston. She left her laundry and the sanctity of her garden and wandered out into the Long Acre, where she watched as the Hurricanes appeared from beyond the elm trees on the far side of the field, one by one, and fell into formation. She shielded her eyes from the sun, and within seconds the large formation was heading her way. The Hurricane in front suddenly dropped, low, lower, flying towards her as though to crash, and for one awful moment it seemed to Dorothy that he *was* going to crash, and suddenly it was that day in May all over again, only this time Dorothy felt no need to end her life. And of

116

course it was Jan — in absolute control, as one would expect — and he waved, he actually waved to her, and he was so low that she could even see his large grin, his gloved hand waving to and fro like a mechanical puppet.

This was their time, theirs alone, and she felt this moment could never be taken from her. This smiling, gentle man, flying over her, was preparing to kill other smiling, gentle men, to actually kill and maim and injure other men. And he was looking forward to it, she knew. He had already killed.

It was all so peculiar. He was brave, or he was evil, or perhaps he was both — one doesn't necessarily preclude the other, she thought, does it? — and Jan was gone, off ahead like the lead in a skein of geese. And Dorothy waited and watched until the whole growling squadron had flown over. And soon it was out of earshot, it had flown beyond the horizon, and she knew that she might never see the squadron leader again. He could be gone forever, snatched out of her life, out of their burgeoning friendship, after such a short beginning — like Sidney, her darling little purple-blue-dead Sidney. Jan could be plucked from the sky by a capricious quirk of fate, or more likely just a belligerent German. Things happen because they can, he had said, and although this idea should have been a comfort, it truly wasn't.

Fighting her tears, she took down the remaining rows of laundry and folded it, pressed it, aired it, and while performing these familiar tasks she trawled through each and every moment of her time with Jan — their conversing, their kissing, their dancing. She vowed to pray for him every day, to pray to that wide, empty sky that Jan occupied, even if God did not.

★ ★ ★

Jan saw her, a small figure, not among the white sheets and pillowcases and tablecloths billowing in the breeze in her garden like gigantic white flags, but standing starkly in the field like a lonely scarecrow. He had wanted her to surrender, this strange Englishwoman he might never see again. He had forewarned his men that he would be flying down towards her garden to keep a promise, and he ignored the smiles, nudges and winks that this prompted. It was an open secret that their leader had fallen in love with this (widowed?) Englishwoman, for he was a soft bastard, despite being a hard bastard. They indulged him, and made jokes over their radios as he swooped down, ahead of the rest of the squadron. He turned off his set, because this was his moment and hers. He wanted to be alone with her. He saw her face turned up like a child's as she stood, minute and alone, in the field, looking at the sky, expectant and awed. He smiled and waved, and he was convinced she had clearly seen him and waved back.

Once past her, past her garden and the surrounding fields, he allowed himself a sob, two sobs, strangling a third before switching back on his radio and telling his men to be vigilant, to be safe; they would all be needed in the coming days, weeks, possibly months. God forbid, but yes, perhaps even for years to come. If they were to spot any Luftwaffe aircraft on this journey — which was unlikely, but possible — they were to shoot the Germans down; they were to show no mercy.

He knew it hardly needed saying, but still he rallied his men. 'Remember,' he said in his native tongue, 'the Nazi bastards deserve everything they get.'

11

24th June 1940

Dear Dorothea,

So this is the first of the letters I am to
write to you. I hope there will be many more
— although, of course, that means we shall
be apart. But better that than dead, no? Did
you see me wave to you last Tuesday? You
looked so sad. I hope you are happier now. I
would have written sooner to you, but every
day there is something to do.

Do not fear for me. I have not yet met
danger. My men and I are taking part in
exercises, always we are asked to do that
which we can do already. It is frustrating!
And we are humiliated. But we are not
allowed to argue. But I do argue, because I
speak English. I reason, but to no good yet. I
do not give up. Already they are sick of my
pestering. Some of these people, they are
arrogant. Only English people can fly, they
think. Oh, forgive me, but I am cross. But
we shall succeed in the end.

We live in nice quarters here. Food is
good, lots of it, beds comfortable. I have my
own room, of course, quiet, at the end of a
corridor. I can shut the door and shut out
the world, and write to you. I wait for your
letter,
Jan

2nd July 1940

My dear Dorothea,

I have had no word from you, but I trust you received my letter. I now send another. Badly written, I expect, but I am tired. I argue still. Sometimes I wonder if I should have bothered coming to England. But I had nowhere else to go. Still it is disappointing. My men are in fury. But what to do? The wheels of English minds turn slowly, it seems. They do not trust us, but I think they should be glad of our help, our experience, our skills. They now talk of giving my squadron an English leader. So it seems even my English is not good enough.

But what of you, dear friend? What is happening? My guess is that you carry on as you were? And the girls? They still work hard, still amuse you? They are good young women, good company for my friend, lonely in her red house, hiding in the Lincolnshire fields. I think about you often. I do not know when I shall return to see you, but I hope it will be soon.

I miss you. Please write to me.
Jan

6th August 1940

Dear Dorothea,

Sometimes it is easier to write down on paper our deep thoughts and feelings than it is to speak of them. I have to tell you that the few weeks we enjoyed were the best of my life. Despite everything that has happened, is

121

happening, and will happen, whatever it is that brought me to England and to you is something I will always be grateful for. I have had no time to write. Every day it seems we must practise, practise, practise. And for why? The British officers, they do not like me, I know. My men are desperate to fly, to fight the Germans. We need combat. I think soon we will, they will see they are wasting our talents. The days are long and most are warm and sunny, so there are many battles. The Luftwaffe gives the RAF no peace. But today has been quieter and all have had opportunity for rest.

I am scared, Dorothea. For when you have found the one great joy and comfort in your life, it is hard to say goodbye. So there will be no goodbyes for us. I will return, my death only can prevent it. Can you write? Often? As often as you can? Until I can visit again?

I do not want to say goodbye, so I will not. This is temporary. We shall sit and talk in your garden, we will talk again of this God we do not believe and we will drink your nice tea.

Until then, think of me often, as I will think of you.

Your Jan

12th August 1940

Dear Dorothea,

I hope you received my last letter? Finally, we are in operation, in real combat! Our squadron has been recognised and we fly

122

every day. *My men are happy at last. And I am in charge. Remember I told you they wanted an English leader? Other Polish squadrons have a Smith or a Jones, but ours has Jan Pietrykowski. I am trusted! Already we have shot down Germans. I shot down a Stuka myself, I chased it from the sky. It was a moment of pure joy for me. The RAF has suffered great losses, no doubt you have heard the news. Each day we trust we will survive, but for many, they wake to their last day. I cannot see how this can end well. Yet we must believe. The Luftwaffe is strong and persistent and we cannot easily match it. What this will develop for my men I dare not think, nor do I want to think. We can but fight, and hope, and at last we do, and it is so much better than those stupid exercises. Yet already I write too many letters to mothers and fathers of dead sons.*

I tell you a little of my day. This is what we must do. Awake and out of bed at four o'clock, half past four. Early, but necessary. We eat breakfast, good bacon, eggs. Sometimes kippers. Always toast with butter, and lots of tea, only not as nice as yours. We go to the dispersal hut and we wait here, we wait for the telephone to ring. The call can come at any time. Sometimes we are waiting for hours, on bad weather days. I play poker with the men, I win often. But play only with matchsticks. We play chess. We lay on the grass, we have deckchairs, we read newspapers, books. Rainy days, clouded days are the best, we get rest, perhaps we do not fly at all. But mostly the weather is fine and we go out early, often twice, three, four times, any time. My men are exhausted, they sleep when they can, if on leave, they sleep, all day, all night. But there is little leave. Sleep has become a luxury. Some men cry at night, I hear them. I try to comfort, but the fear and despair are too strong and not until morning can they again take hold of their courage and eat, and fly, and fight. When we scramble, some men are sick. We all leap from our skin when the telephone rings. The little click before the ring begins, it is a bad sound. All are nervous, waiting is horrible. You must imagine this.

Yet we get good hits. Yesterday my squadron shot down two Stukas. A good day. One of them was mine, as I told you. Yet I find myself sad at causing death. I don't know why. The Stuka crashed into the sea. Nothing left of the German crew who I thought I hated. Do I hate? Am I a murderer? I do not know. I can only say I am a fighter.

How is life with you? And the skies above you? Has harvesting begun yet? Aggie and Nina, they continue as normal? They still enjoy the music box?

I must finish now, Dorothea. There is much to do and so little time to do it. I have reports to write. I keep the squadron diary too, which needs to be written while the day is fresh in my memory. It is half past one in the morning. I am tired, but I am alive. Do not fear.

Until next time,
Your Jan

19th August 1940

Dear Jan,

You may not believe me, but it is so. This is the first letter I have written, aside from the three or four I sent to my mother after my marriage. I don't count those. I apologise for not writing to you sooner. I have no excuses other than my own stupidity and reticence. Things that are written down are so permanent and that always frightens me somehow. But I write to you now in friendship and trust.

Thank you for all your kind words to me in your letters, which come thick and fast and are a joy to receive. The last few weeks have been a special time that I shall always remember. You are a good man, Jan, far too good for a woman like me. Please don't trouble yourself with thoughts of me while you are down there in the thick of things. You have more than enough on your plate. I am absolutely not worthy of the depth of feeling you express. I am conscious of your feelings and I should like to return them. But it is hopeless.

I trust that you will remain safe. I hope and believe that you will. Any time you can, if you get enough leave, please visit. The girls and I will be pleased to see you.

Dorothy

25th August 1940

My dear Dorothea,

Your letter was a joy to receive, all 225 words of it. But you are wrong. You are worthy. And there is always hope. Hope is all we have now — everyone, all of us. I fear your cities will be next, of that I am certain. Did you not say that your girls are from London? They have families living there? The Luftwaffe bombed London last night. I hope that it will not happen again. Our losses continue, but I think we are still enough, with the RAF, to fight. And your Winston Churchill says such good things about the pilots (the Polish ones too). You may have heard him on the wireless? We are become heroes! Not murderers at all. Our mood is high, despite death all around us. And it is a miracle that we seem to be holding on. But, of course, everything has its price.

What of you? Do you continue with your laundry, your sewing? You are a woman of industry. I think if you don't work, if you are not busy, you will allow yourself to think too much, and fret?

Now I must write to a mother in Polska. Her son died yesterday, lost in the sea. I do not know if my letters arrive. But I must send. I wish for courage to do a good job and be a small comfort to the boy's mother.

Your Jan

16th September 1940

My dear Dorothea,

So autumn arrives, and with it a change of
tactic, as I thought. Do you recall I said this
would happen?

Are you safe and well? I doubt very much
the Luftwaffe is interested in bombing Mrs
Dorothea Sinclair in her little cottage, lost
among the fields of Lincolnshire. But you
must be vigilant, being so close to the aerodrome, as the Germans will attack anyone
— women, children, it means nothing to
them. I told you of that. It has happened.
These Nazis, these Germans, are cowards.
But they are dangerous cowards. Yesterday,
we are told, was a good day for the RAF, we
fight on, we score hits. The Luftwaffe are not
having it easy.

I hope to get some leave in the next few
weeks, perhaps in October. If that is so,
could I visit you? To sit with you again in
your cottage is a dream I hold dear.

Until then,
Your Jan

20th September 1940

Dear Jan,

Poor Aggie has had word that her fiancé
has been killed. His name was Roger and he
was a pilot in a Spitfire squadron. I didn't
even know she was engaged to be married.
She met her young man shortly before leaving London, and she was in love, she tells
me. She is desolate. Nina and I try to cheer

her up, but she talks of going home to London — a thought to make one shudder in light of all that is happening there. She will be far better off staying here and enjoying the relative safety of the country. She still goes to the dances and the pub regularly.

Aggie's news made me think about Albert, my husband, and whether the same will happen to him. Although, of course, he is in the army. As we are still married, I suppose I would receive a telegram? I think of you, every day. I must confess, I've started to pray for you, prayers of a sort. Is that silly?

The weather grows colder, and I can smell winter. The trees are becoming bare and such a wind blows, howling around the house at night. Please visit in October. I can make up the bed in the spare room, it is rather small but comfortable enough. Do let me know in advance, if that is possible? So I can make all the preparations. Do you think you may have leave over Christmas time? A long way off, I know, but we need to look forward to things.

Nina is well, although she took a funny turn yesterday evening. She was trying to cheer Aggie up by getting her to dance — you know how those girls love to dance — well, Nina keeled over, out cold for a minute or two. We put her head between her legs, and later we got her to bed and I made her drink a hot toddy. Aggie tells me she slept well. And this morning, when they both went off to work, Nina was cheery enough. She works too hard, I think.

Bombs fell on Lodderston aerodrome last week. Nothing much — some damage, we hear — and two ground crew were killed. The noise was indescribable, so how it must be in London or Liverpool, I cannot imagine.

I have no other news. Mostly day follows night here, and things go on in the old familiar pattern. I suppose there's a comfort in that.

Dorothy

12

For my best friend, Charlotte, on her 30th birthday, because she also loves to shop!

(Inscription found on flyleaf of Penguin Classics edition of *Madame Bovary* by Gustave Flaubert. Evidently, Charlotte does not love to read. Inscription aside, as new copy. Placed on classic fiction shelf in entrance lobby, price £2.50. I bought it myself after a few weeks and have since read it twice.)

★   ★   ★

Dad was okay in the end, thank God. After three days in hospital, during which his breathing stabilised, he was allowed home. I visit him each day after work. He needs rest, and plenty of it, but he won't let me 'do' for him. He never will. We chat, drink tea, eat crumpets or muffins — 'There's only so much brown rice even a gravely ill man can eat!' — we watch the news, we watch *Pointless* and he always beats me. But I know that I cannot ask my dad any questions about the letter. It isn't fair to bother him, and it would be nothing short of cruel to potentially turn his already troubled world on its head. Yet I wonder . . . I wonder if his world *would* be turned upside down? Or would it be mine?

And my visit to my grandmother, although it

was a pleasure to see her once her initial confusion had passed, was unproductive. In the end, Suzanne left us to ourselves, and I simply sat with Babunia, holding her hand, commenting on the garden. I'm still not sure that she realised who I was.

But in subsequent visits Babunia recognises me, and smiles, and asks me when that son of hers is going to deign to visit. I am going every week, as I resolved, and it's a joy to meet up first with Suzanne, who tells me about how Babunia is getting on, the things she says, her preoccupations: these are often unfathomable, Suzanne explains, and I nod in understanding. She's always been like that, I say. I tell her I'm immensely grateful that she has taken the time to befriend my grandmother; it's a relief to have somebody looking out for her, somebody we can all trust. Suzanne says it's a pleasure. Of course, Dad wants to go — and will go with me, when he's up to it — but it's hard to think up excuses. Babunia is not a stupid woman. She might guess straight away that something is wrong; he has changed so much, and for the worse.

I have not mentioned Jan's letter, not yet, to either of them. I need to find the right time.

★   ★   ★

I am in the Old and New, the place where I am always to be found. Philip and I are undertaking the task of rearranging some of the shelves in the large old books room. He also wants the French windows to the patio to be polished, closed and locked, as it is late September, and so we are closing up the garden for winter. Jenna is not at work today. Philip explains to me she is unwell, and in bed with a whisky and hot water — a cure-all his mother always swore by. I have my own thoughts regarding this illness, but I say nothing. I hope she is okay. But she will not let me know. Our friendship, I fear, is finished, turned in on itself.

At the desk, which is manned by Sophie, a woman is asking for me. She has a cultured voice, educated, confident. I know who she is instantly. I freeze. A surge of bad adrenaline flows through my veins, the dread-rush of certainty. I look at Philip, who looks back at me quizzically. A roar starts up in my ears, a cacophony of cursed voices. This cannot be happening. Oh no, no, no, not this, not now.

'Roberta?' calls Sophie.

'Don't worry, I'll find her,' says Francesca Dearhead.

Slow, deliberate footsteps in high-heeled shoes become more pronounced as they tick through into the back room. She has come in search of me, as I knew she would one day. And now she stands in the doorway.

Like a child, I hope that if I close my eyes this will stop. If I concentrate hard enough this won't be happening, the roaring in my body will end, here and now. But nothing stops. The roaring becomes louder.

Mrs Dearhead's scent floats around her, and it is not Febreze at all, but something expensive, and tasteful. And as I open my eyes again she is upon me, slender hands on slender hips, a queasily triumphant smile revealing even, white teeth. She seems taller than me, although she is probably around my height, elegantly dressed in a cream wool coat, her black hair immaculately styled. She is invading my personal space and I take a step backwards, intimidated.

'You . . . *shameful* little woman,' she whispers, staring at me as though I were a tarantula.

'Hang on a minute,' says Philip. He puts down his pile of books on a footstool, takes off his spectacles and glares at her. Almost imperceptibly, he moves an inch or two closer to me.

'Are you aware that this . . . employee of yours . . . has been carrying on with my husband?' says Mrs Dearhead. 'Do you know who my husband is?'

'Vaguely,' says Philip as he wipes his spectacles and puts them back on. 'Are *you* aware that this is my bookshop, and are you further aware that I do not tolerate any form of abuse, physical or verbal, towards myself or any member of my staff? Is that clear? Nor do I listen to . . . loathsome tittle-tattle.'

The few customers, formerly leafing through books, chattering, murmuring, are inexplicably quiet. There is a marked silence in the Old and New. Somebody coughs. I even think I hear a muffled 'Shh!'

'This woman deserves to be sacked!' she shouts, her composure finally slipping a little as she indicates me with a dismissive wave of her slender hand.

I find myself wondering whether she has recently touched her husband with those hands. She's a lot more attractive than I had imagined, and younger. Did they still . . . ? Of course. Don't be so naive, Roberta. My God, Jenna had a point.

'I do the hiring and firing around here,' says Philip, flustered, and both myself and Francesca Dearhead stare at him, wrong-footed. Did he really say that?

She turns back to me. 'Do you have anything to say?'

'I think I do, actually.'

'Then please say it. I am all ears.'

'I am not carrying on with your husband.'

'Of course, you would deny it. But I know you are.'

'But I'm not. Whoever told you such a thing?' I know, absolutely and certainly, that my former lover would not reveal our affair to anybody, least of all to his wife. It would make no sense for him to do so. Especially now that it was over, and I had been the one to finish it.

'That's my business,' says Mrs Dearhead.

I take a deep breath. I can see she has the bit between her teeth and she's not going to give it up. I don't have much choice if I am to salvage anything even resembling dignity. 'I *was* seeing your husband. For a while. But it's over now. It's been over for some time. I can assure you that is the truth.'

'I see. Is there anything else?'

'Only that I'm sorry. I am truly very sorry. I'm not sure what happened, really. To me, I mean. It was a mistake.'

I am aware that Sophie and Jenna are in the doorway, watching us, Jenna obviously roused from her sick bed by the commotion. There's a look of fascinated, intrigued horror on their beautiful young faces. I look at Sophie. She grimaces. Jenna avoids meeting my gaze. Behind them, dear little Mrs Lucas — a regular customer with an inexhaustible appetite for second-hand Mills and Boon — is peering over their shoulders, aghast.

And Francesca Dearhead's face is calm again, her smooth, tanned skin unpuckered. She studies me, her curled lip betraying her thoughts before she voices them.

'Well. You're not quite as I pictured you. You are younger, I suppose, just about. But what else? I can't see it.'

'That's enough!' says Philip.

Jenna reddens, glaring at Philip. Sophie looks at me, raising her eyebrows.

'I really am very sorry,' I say, 'but it truly is over. And not much happened, anyway, if I'm perfectly honest. Your husband is in love with you. Not me. I'm too shallow for him. I'm no good for a man like him, not good enough, as you seem to be suggesting, and you're absolutely right about that. And if it took a stupid . . . pseudo-affair for your husband to find out where his true affections lie, and to appreciate what he already has, that's not such a bad thing. Now, if you don't mind, Mrs Dearhead, I'd like to get on with my work.'

Francesca Dearhead turns and pushes past Sophie and Jenna and Mrs Lucas, all of whom gape after her, open-mouthed. I hear her high heels tap-tap-tapping on the flagstones in the foyer; I hear the front door open and close. A

135

pause; then the silence breaks, customers murmur again, there are sniggers; a throat clears. Sophie and Jenna recede like discreet angels. Mrs Lucas stays a moment or two longer, then she too evaporates, and only Philip and I remain.

I can't look at him.

'Put the books down, Roberta,' he says.

And I realise I have been clinging on to a large pile throughout the whole episode, hiding behind them, barricading myself in. I am trembling, so Philip takes the books from me, and sets them on the floor. He leans towards me and suddenly he gently moves aside a stray strand of hair from my face. He looks at me warily, as one would stare at a troublesome wasp, deliberating whether to kill or rescue it. Our heads have never been so close. But I won't look away from him, I will not twist my eyes to the side like a person ashamed. Even though I *am* ashamed, horribly so, and my face must be reddened and anguished.

'Go upstairs and get a drink,' he says, looking away from me at last. 'Tell Jenna to leave you in peace.'

★ ★ ★

'Good for you,' Jenna says, handing me the brandy I have requested.

I take it, gratefully, with a shaking hand. The brandy is hot and angry in my mouth, in my throat, belly, legs.

'Good?' I say, between mouthfuls.

'You told that silly cow where to get off. That's exactly what I would have done.'

136

'I've been seeing her husband. She has every right to be angry.'

'But causing a scene in public like that! I'd be ashamed to make such a fool of myself. Wouldn't you?'

'Yes, of course, but she's upset, isn't she? She's half Italian, and you know what they say about Mediterranean temperaments . . . I thought she was rather cool about the whole thing, really. She just wanted to have it out with her rival. And when she discovered I'm not actually much of a rival . . . I don't know. I got the impression she was relieved, more than anything. It could have been worse.'

'Have you really been seeing him?' Jenna asks. 'Was it all true, what you said? What she said?'

'I was seeing him, kind of. But it wasn't a grand passion by any means. If that's what you're getting at.'

'He's a bit old for you, isn't he?'

'Yes. But it's over now, anyway.'

'God, it was funny. I heard her shout. I should think the whole bloody town heard it! And I just had to come down and see what all the fuss was about. You've caused quite a scandal, Roberta P.'

'Jenna?'

'Yes?'

'I wonder if I could be left alone for a few minutes. I just need to recover myself here. You know?'

Jenna looks like a child scolded in public for picking her nose, but she shrugs her shoulders nonchalantly enough. 'Of course,' she says.

And leaves me.

13

12th November 1940

My dear Dorothea,

I find myself realising today that I have not heard from you for a while. And I remember that today is your birthday. I send you many greetings. I trust all is well with you? I am satisfactory. We are kept busy trying to defend London, but it does not always go well. We are helpless at night-time, the frustration is unbearable.

I hope to be visiting you soon, perhaps the first week in December? A day, maybe two, no longer. I had no leave in October — disappointing for me, and for you, I have to hope. I am tired and I need the rest. I need time to be relaxing and spending time with my friend with her good food and tea and conversations. The room with the little bed, it sounds like a wonderful place to be. I need peace, Dorothea.

Until December,
Your Jan

★　★　★

The evenings were drawing in, and Dorothy was finding it difficult to sew without the aid of sunlight. She huddled under her oil lamp, she lit extra candles and she peered more closely at her work, frowning, pins in her mouth, her familiar tarnished thimble a comfortable fit on her middle finger. She listened to Billie Holiday, she listened to the chatter of the girls, she thought about Jan, away from her, in danger, all his strength and maleness no protection against the vulnerability that threatened to take him — at any moment, day or night — one bullet, one destroyed engine, one plunge into the cold, dark sea. The possibilities haunted her.

She was making a set of antimacassars, using an old linen tablecloth with a stubborn stain she hadn't managed to wash out. She was embroidering on each one a circular rosebud pattern, using green and pink threads. This was the third; the first two were already adorning the settee. It was satisfying work. It kept her busy, and it allowed her to climb into herself, to lose herself in thoughts of Jan. For he was all she wanted to think about. The black hair, the blue eyes, the smile, the near-perfect English, the clear-thinking ideas so similar to her own. His hard-soft face, his foreign accent, faltering, polite. His mile-high laugh.

She read and reread his letters. She was keeping them in a small bundle, one on top of the other in the order she had received them, tied together with a dark blue ribbon; they nestled among Sidney's clothes in the suitcase. She had a dozen or more letters, all on pale blue paper of an ethereal thinness, all written in a neat hand, recognisably *his*, smudged here and there, all in blue ink. To see the postman open her gate, stride down the path whistling, and then laugh when she rushed to the door to relieve him of his delivery, was the highlight of her week.

'You've got it bad, love!' he would say. But there was a shrewd look behind his twinkling eyes that spoke of gossip and suspicion. Goodness only knew what tales he told of her in the village, in the pub, everybody mocking her — 'Falls over herself, she does, for letters from her Polish lover boy!' She knew she was the subject of talk among people who were friends of her husband, people who had known Bert Sinclair all his life.

What a fool she must appear to everybody.

Yet the letters arrived. She snatched them from the postman, she read them eagerly, once, twice, three times. And then the unbearable wait for the next one, occasionally punctuated by her own inadequate replies — short, but not succinct, not interesting or funny, not even particularly informative. The immense disappointment on the days when the postman failed to arrive. These were long days.

Thank God, she thought many times, for the girls. Like birds of paradise, they coloured her life. True, Aggie was more sombre these days, but she tried hard to be cheerful, and sometimes succeeded. Nina and Dorothy tried hard to rouse her, talk to her, and console her when the tears flowed. Both girls lived in daily fear of bad news from home. The bombings were continuing, and the news was no comfort. All three women listened in respectful silence to the wireless each evening. Both girls talked of visiting their families in London, but the estate could not spare them, and Dorothy was secretly glad.

Another washday, a dull mid-November morning, winter hanging over the world's window like a threadbare curtain. The girls were long gone, hiking off across the fields wrapped up in their coats, hats, scarves, gloves, boots, each with a bag of lunch prepared by Dorothy — sandwiches with fish paste, a boiled egg, slices of pickled beetroot, a Thermos of tea and, for a treat, a home-baked biscuit. It was the least Dorothy could do. She had eggs — plenty of eggs compared to most — flour, some butter. Even sugar. She always made sure now to put enough in her biscuits.

There was a breeze, cold, but strong enough for drying, if only partially. Sheets flapped and slapped on the lines, gulls and rooks circling, cawing and fighting, the clouds racing by as though late for an appointment. Hens, earth-bound like Dorothy, clucked and pecked at the hardening ground. And Dorothy, alone, was lost in hot water, in soda crystals and soap, lost in her longings. So many longings that she couldn't tell them apart, couldn't separate them any more.

Suddenly aware of a presence, she turned from the copper, wiping her hair back from her face, and there he was, a man in the doorway, a heavy-looking kitbag slung across his shoulder. He was leaning against the door frame, a cigarette protruding from his lips and the smell of the smoke breaking through the steam.

She stared.

'Hello, Dot.'

'Albert.'

★ ★ ★

Aggie and Nina returned at dusk and seemed surprised to see this man, Albert, sitting at the table drinking tea. He was brawny, muscled, yet his eyes were pale and insipid, and appeared not to focus on anything. Even so, he looked the girls up and down, lingering on Aggie.

The evening meal was a stilted affair, punctuated by awkward conversation and long, impenetrable pauses. Under Albert's unnerving scrutiny, the young women ate their dinner slowly, propriety replacing their usual abandon and appetite. Even Nina, perennially hungry, finished second. They all listened politely as he told jokes and stories none of them wanted to laugh at.

After the meal, after their tea and the daily dose of news on the wireless, the girls yawned and said an early night would be just the ticket. And Dorothy and her husband were alone in the lounge. If he noticed the changes she had made — the rearranged furniture, the crazy-patchwork cushions she had made last winter, the antimacassars — he didn't comment.

'You got a gramophone?' he said.

'Yes.'

'Where d'you get that, then?'

'A friend gave it to me. It's a . . . borrowing.'

'What friend?'

142

'You don't know him.'

'Oh, it's like that, is it?'

'No. It's not 'like that', not at all.' Keeping her voice light and steady, Dorothy explained the events of May and June, and the respect and friendship she had earned from the squadron leader. She did not mention the letters. She did not mention the kiss, or how much she missed him, or his lean, strong, brown arms.

'Well. That's all right, then,' said Albert, leaning back on the settee with his hands behind his head, his legs stretched out in front of him.

'Can I ask, Albert? What . . . why are you here?'

'A man can come home, can't he?'

'I suppose so. But you have been gone for over a year with no word. I had no idea if you were alive or dead. And I am your wife.'

'I'm not dead, am I?'

'No.'

'Those girls give you the runaround?'

'No.

'Just make sure they don't. You're not their bloody mother, are you? Don't worry, Dot, I'm not hanging around for long. I've got four days' leave. Then I'm back to it. But I want to come home after the war, if it ever bloody ends. I want to come back and . . . I was unfair, a bit. But I want to make it up afterwards, when we get back to normal. Perhaps we could try again? Have a baby?'

Her stomach roiled. 'Albert.'

'Yes?'

'I'm forty years old now.'

He waved a dismissive hand. 'My Aunty Lou had her last when she was forty-two, or forty-three. Can't remember which. But she was an old bird. And I've been thinking, I should send money — for your keep, like.'

'No.' Her voice was tight and clenched. She would not take money from him, not now.

'A man should support his missus.'

'I have all the money I need, thank you, Albert. I launder for the estate and get paid by them. I'm independent now.'

'Oh. I see. Doesn't seem right, though.'

Dorothy allowed herself a smile. Albert wasn't a malicious man. He was just a man. Simple. There was no hatred here, on either side. Yes, she had been bewildered and disappointed when he had abandoned her. But all was well. Because she had found her life after he had gone. She was his wife, but in name only.

Albert seemed disappointed but resigned when she firmly showed him to the small bedroom with the single bed. The bed was made up with brisk cotton sheets, two woollen blankets and her favourite quilt. Albert, who had no reason not to imagine the room was made up in readiness for his anticipated return, made no comment. He sat on the small bed, looking up at her, as she stood in the doorway. His eyes were dispassionate. He never had been able to read her. They were, and always had been, utter strangers.

'Goodnight, Albert.'

'Goodnight, Dot.'

14

Albert kept out of her way for much of the following day. She made him breakfast, which he praised highly. He spent the morning pottering around in the garden and the shed, tinkering with his bicycle. After lunch, he slept. And when he awoke at around five, he said he would go down to the pub. She made some sandwiches, and watched him eat his before he went.

He left, negotiating the November fog and the blackout on his bicycle; with relief, she made herself a fresh pot of tea and ate her own sandwich alone in the parlour as the girls had not yet returned from their day of work. She listened to the wireless while the fire crackled in the grate, warm and glowing and safe. Yet she felt uneasy. What if there were *talk*, in the pub? From Albert's friends — those still there, at least? He would hear things.

. . . your wife and the squadron leader, the Polish one. Friends, eh? Come off it, Bert. Very friendly, they are. Postman says she fair climbs the wall waiting for letters from him.

She's head over heels. Got the goat of girls around here, set their cap at him some of them had, but he didn't seem to notice. You missed the boat, mate. Bad luck . . .

Albert would drink his mild. He would listen. He would say little.

The girls returned, tired, cold and hungry, putting an end to Dorothy's uneasy thoughts. They ate their evening meal in the kitchen, and then the three women retired to the lounge with their cups of tea and listened to the wireless. The girls seemed as relieved as Dorothy that Albert had gone to the pub. They stayed home and kept her company while she sewed, and later they listened to the gramophone, and none of them mentioned him.

Albert reeked of alcohol, the mild he had always favoured. It was late, and there was an edgy new rawness about him that Dorothy didn't like, a flaming in his face that spoke of anger. It spoke of danger, and she was on her guard. She had hated those nights, which became more frequent as their marriage went on, when he returned from the pub drunk and stinking, loud and often obnoxious. It looked as though those nights had returned.

The girls were in bed. Dorothy was in her seat by the window, sewing by the light of the oil lamp, peering from behind the wire-rimmed glasses that she wore only for close work, only at home. For Dorothy was still vain, in her own quiet way.

Albert threw himself into the settee and sat wordlessly for a few minutes, crossing his legs, uncrossing them, sighing, clearing his throat.

146

Dorothy continued to sew. Perhaps he would fall asleep, and wake up in the morning hung-over and forgetful. She would say nothing to him.

He glowered, shifted and cleared his throat again.

Still Dorothy did not speak. If he had something to say, he would just have to come out with it. He was a grown man. He must act like one. She would say noth —

'You going to tell me what's been going on with this Polish cunt?'

Dorothy continued to sew, not daring to look at the man who was her husband, but not her husband. She wasn't even sure she had heard him correctly. Albert was an earthy man, she knew, but he had never sworn around her (apart from the occasional 'bloody'), not once. He had never said anything so crude.

'Well? You not going to tell me about your fancy man?' Albert sneered.

'My what?' she said. She glared back at him.

'I've been hearing all about it. Seems that everyone knew but me. Flowers, letters, this fucking gramophone!' Albert sprang up and made a lunge for the music box.

But Dorothy was there first. 'No, Albert. Leave it alone. If not for me, then for Aggie and Nina. It's not yours. It's ours. Your argument with me has nothing to do with those girls. It gives them such pleasure. The music — '

'And how much pleasure does your fancy piece give you, eh?'

'I will not be drawn into this nonsense, Albert.

147

I will not. You're drunk. Please go to bed.'

'Don't tell me what to do in my own home, woman.'

'This is not your home. You haven't lived here for months. This is my home.'

The slap came hot and sharp and hard, and it knocked her off her feet. She staggered, righted herself, and put her hand to her cheek. The blow had awakened the pain from the May day — was it really that long ago? — when she had tried to 'save' the young Polish pilot. Everybody had made her into a heroine. But her husband now, slapping her in the face, drunk and panting, had no respect for her. He stood before her, his eyes as wide and empty as the Lincolnshire sky. And when he grabbed at her and ripped her blouse open it came as no great surprise. And his mouth pushing on to hers, his breath sweet and sickly and acrid with tobacco, and their teeth clashing as she tried to twist away from him. He gripped her face with one hand, and pulled her skirt up over her hips with the other. He was strong and relentless, and in another era, an earlier life, Dorothy would almost have been thrilled. His fingers dug into her cheek.

'No, Albert. Please!' she gasped, before his hand covered her mouth.

He didn't hear, or didn't listen, she was unsure which. He spun her round and pressed her face into the settee, his large rough hand pushing her neck down. She could barely breathe, let alone cry out, as he knelt behind her, thrust aside her knickers with his bullet-like fingers and, after a few misdirected thrusts,

148

broke into her body, piercing her. He released her neck and she suppressed the urge to cry out in pain. She would keep still, she must not move, let it be over with, let him do this thing he was determined to do. Please don't let this wake the girls, it mustn't, it mustn't. Be quiet, Albert, please, for God's sake. If the girls were to hear and come down the stairs . . . she must make no noise. She bit her lip so hard she tasted the brutal tang of blood. Albert grasped her hips and held them firm, and his movements slowed and became rhythmical, as though they were actually making love. He was pulling her on to him, harder, slower, but he was mercifully quiet, and each thrust told her: *You are mine, not his, not that Polish bastard's. My wife. You are my wife.*

And when it was over, he crept away from her and she remained on the settee, face down, frozen. She could not think, or move, or absorb what had happened to her. After a few minutes, she pulled her skirt down. She stayed on the settee until she heard his breathing become slow and gruff, like a heavyset dog's. Turning her head, she saw he was in her chair by the window, legs and arms at strange contorted angles, his bullish head lolling to one side.

Dorothy slowly twisted herself round so that she was sitting on the floor, and leaned back on the settee. She had married this man. She had *loved* him, once. She stayed motionless and without further thought for an hour, perhaps two, eyes wide open, until she became too cold, until the need for sleep became apparent. She raised herself from the floor and, without a glance at

149

the man snoring in her chair by the window, she quietly left the parlour. Closing the door behind her, she dragged herself to her room, not bothering to visit the privy first, nor wash or brush her teeth. She climbed into her narrow bed, wrapping herself up under the sheets and the blankets and the quilt. It was a freezing, foggy night, but she must have fallen asleep and dreamed, because in the morning she sprang awake with a bright sun streaming through her window. She remembered her dream and in it she had held a young baby, she had kissed a baby's soft head, and he smelled of musk, of lavender, oranges, honey.

★   ★   ★

Albert was gone.

Nothing of him remained. Nobody would know that Albert Sinclair had returned to his abandoned wife, accused her of adultery, and assaulted her in a few unremarkable moments of rage and jealousy, a common fit of pique. To the world — that is, to her girls and her hens — Dorothy presented her usual face, free of make-up and pretensions, and followed her usual habits, making tea and breakfast, packing lunches, scattering grain for the hens, setting the fire under the copper and watching the girls set off for the North Barn. She found herself thinking about the possibility of a baby who may even now exist in what remained of the red, lush warmth in her womb.

She found herself also thinking about Jan.

Jan so far away, in all ways, always.

150

Day piled upon day, heavy, grey, those bedraggled days of winter. She was afraid to find blood with each visit to the privy, frequent fevered interruptions to her days. In the two weeks since Albert had left she'd felt no cramping pains, no tension, no anger or clumsiness or weepiness, all of which regularly accompanied the machinations of her monthly cycle. Hope was once again looming in front of her, large and fat, obvious as a prostitute and just as mysterious. She told herself it was almost worth it, those few minutes of Albert's rage and aggression, the few minutes of pain and humiliation, his lust — as greedy and short-lived as a child let loose in a sweet shop — her shock, and her dread not of what was happening to her, but of being discovered. The hideous thought of Aggie and Nina flinging open the door, their shocked faces, Dorothy, despite herself, crying *Help me!* And sometimes it seemed to Dorothy as though these things had actually happened; she thought she could remember the girls' faces, their shock and disgust. And sometimes, while feeding the hens, while darning stockings, she would shudder at these quasi-memories, sick at the thought of being caught.

Was she caught? No! No. But if she had been . . . and the possibility now opening up in front of her, despite everything, was thrilling. But she tried to remain unaware, to ignore the secret drama that could, *could*, be blooming inside her. She tried not to think too much, yet it was

151

impossible not to think about it, and not to dream.

She tried not to be intimidated by fears, real fears, the fear of blood and failure and of life being washed away along with the precious egg, the lush preparations of her womb, the spring of life itself. The life-spring was in her, on her, around her. It was her, but she had no power over it, she had no control, only hope.

15

Jan flew steady, keeping his course, waiting for the enemy. Yesterday, he'd picked one off, a Dornier. He'd fired at it repeatedly, trying to kill the gunner first, as you should. He'd strafed the aircraft and with sweet satisfaction he'd watched as it spiralled towards the ground, caught in the earth's inexorable pull. There was nothing like it, he thought, nothing as satisfying as killing your enemies. He thought the crew had stayed in the Dornier, he had not seen any of them escaping. Perhaps he had shot them all. That was a small justice. The only good German was a dead German. And one way or another he'd killed four in one attack.

The day was bright, and so cold that there was no need to climb to any sort of height before the frozen air gripped him. But cold was the least of his worries. The squadron was flying day and night, supposedly protecting the city of London from the German bombs that continued to fall, relentlessly. Sometimes he and his men did all right, sometimes not. Men were lost almost daily, good Polish men. Somehow, today, he was alive. And today, he knew, he would kill again. But he himself would not be killed. It was a matter of faith.

His gaze flicked around: here, there, above and below. He always used his eyes, his own perceptions. He could not bring himself to trust this new 'radio direction finder', nor did he enjoy giving trite, dry orders to other men — even though that was his job, even though they were his subordinates. In the air, in battle, after his initial instructions, it was every man for himself. On the ground, he could be the boss, but not up here, in this diaphanous space that belonged to nobody. Up here was chaos, flight, adrenaline.

He saw them, a skein of bombers, the hated Dorniers, ugly, elongated, with death written all over them. He pulled his Hurricane round swiftly and gained as much height as he could. Up . . . up . . . he wanted the sun behind him, always it was best to have that advantage. It was impossible to get to the bombers this time, he realised, flanked as they were by wearisome Messerschmitts, vicious little aeroplanes, quick, deft, deadly. Admirable too, Jan had to concede. A formation of Spitfires flew in under him, picking off the 109s. But two were on him, he knew it, breaking off from the main group and heading for him, escaping the Spitfires. The 109s split. He could only keep one in his sights.

Swinging round, he steadied his Hurricane, aimed, fired his guns for two seconds. Missed. Where was the other? Was somebody on him? He thought so. Two seconds again. Missed, missed, *damn*! His guns pummelled nothing but sky, and the 109 flew on towards him, firing back.

Had he been hit? The smell of hot oil swamped his cockpit, and all was clatter and panic. He worked always within panic's stabbing confines and the fear, he knew, kept him alive. He banked right, gained height, pulled round, levelled, aimed, fired, fired, running out. And yes, as he predicted, the familiar scene of smoke, death, and the welcome sight of the enemy aircraft twisting towards the earth. The pilot bailed out, his parachute opened like a huge silk moth breaking out of its cocoon, and Jan, grimly enraptured by such a perfect target, took his time, slowly flying lower towards the German pilot dangling helplessly in the sky under his huge parachute.

Jan's flight officer (English, as the Poles were not entirely trusted to manage their own squadron effectively) shouted over the radio: Where the bloody hell was he? They'd lost one, bloody hell, they'd lost him and the rest of them needed orders. Now!

Jan carried on, barely listening to the pompous and panicked Englishman. He had the parachute in his sights. He knew he was acting against the Geneva Convention. Would he be court-martialled? Perhaps. But he knew of at least two other Poles in his own squadron who had performed this act, and countless more Germans. Everybody seemed to get away with it. So would he. The British didn't seem to approve. But so what? And the Nazis had trampled over the Geneva Convention every day of this war. Rumours out of Krakow spoke of them shooting hospital patients as they lay in their beds and forcing men to dig their own graves at gunpoint — and not only men. They were throwing sweets on to the ground, and as the children scrambled for them, the Nazis laughed and kicked them to death. Jan doubted none of these rumours.

Nazi bastards get all they deserve.

Jan fired. His last ammo, he knew. And no real need to waste it in this fashion.

The parachute shut up on itself, disappearing into a thin silver column, lethal as a blade. What did the British call it — the Roman candle? And the German who had been dangling aimlessly beneath it suddenly shot earthwards to his death. His name was Hans, or Dieter; he had a sweetheart in Berlin, or in Munich; he had a mother, a father. For just a few more seconds, they had a son. It was a cruel death, Jan knew — but was not all death cruel?

And what would the Englishwoman say? He could imagine her, if he allowed himself to, her stray hair being pushed back off her face, but he did not allow himself to think of her while he was flying. But the killing — murder? — of this young German, it stuck in his throat, it stalled him, just for a moment, and he feared her reproach more than anything, this woman who had lost her own precious son. And he understood what her son had meant to her. He should have told her how he —

And for a moment, two moments, he lost concentration, he didn't look.

Jan felt an explosion in his arm. He caught the stench of pumping blood, of something else, something chemical. God, not the cooling fluid? He felt a torturous, burning sensation, although he felt — he knew — there was no fire. He had to fight the fog that threatened to close in on him, and he struggled to pull his Hurricane round, one-handed and bellowing in pain. He

156

radioed he'd been hit, and then he remembered there had, of course, been two 109s. He'd made the indelible mistake of focusing on the one, one he had already rendered harmless. And where now were the bombers? They were gone, they had got through, and they were going to release their terror, as Jan had released his.

He looked around for the other 109 and he saw him in his mirror, on his tail, so close, so fast, he swore he could see the whiskers on the German pilot's face. Jan dropped his aircraft — a useless manoeuvre, he knew, but at least it brought him closer to the earth. He was determined he would land this stricken aircraft. The RAF could not afford to lose it for no good reason, and pain was not a reason. He was damned if he was going to simply sit there and die. He could barely breathe. And suddenly he saw the 109 aflame, black smoke, a shrill whine, a twist, a turn, and it was gone.

And Jan's flight officer gloated over the radio that he'd got the bastard, and for Christ's sake get down, Pietrykowski. Now, if you can. Get back, man.

16

3rd October 2010

Dear Philip,

I hereby give you one week's notice of my intention to leave my employment at the Old and New Bookshop. I have enjoyed the past eleven years in so many ways, but now I feel it is time to move on.

Yours,
Roberta

(Letter written and waiting in my handbag to give to Philip tomorrow.)

★ ★ ★

At least now the customers have got over The Scene. The gossip has subsided, nobody is talking about me any more. For a while there I was a scarlet woman, but my infamy has been short-lived and now I am plain old Roberta ('Rebecca?') again, Philip's right-hand woman and stalwart of the Old and New. It's a good place to be.

But Philip has not forgotten. He is keeping his distance and avoiding any mention of The Scene. I don't blame him, of course, but I do wish he would forget about it — like everybody else seems to have done — and I wish he would forgive me. I apologised, of course, the same day.

Fuelled by my hastily downed brandy, I sailed back down the stairs to the shop, and found Philip continuing with the rearrangements in the back room, pencil in mouth, frowning, his hair perhaps a little more dishevelled than it had been, his cheeks a little pinker. He looked at me, as I stood in the doorway.

'I'm sorry, Philip. I never thought . . . I didn't think she would ever . . . but she has. I don't know what else I can say. Really. I am so very sorry.'

He looked at me with what I can only describe as dissatisfaction. He didn't seem to hear my apology. He sighed, he looked away, he scribbled a price inside a book cover with his characteristic flourish. I have never seen anybody look more disappointed.

'Perhaps you could take over here while I grab some lunch?' he said wearily. 'These need pricing, those over there need dusting, and these need putting on the lower shelf, as we discussed this morning. Oh, and could you remember to clean the windows too, please? Or get Sophie to do them. Thank you.'

He hasn't spoken to me since.

Getting home from the Old and New, to my flat, to my cat bought for me by Charles Dearhead — the cat I call Portia — is a relief. I tell Portia all that happens each day, and she listens and asks for her supper, and I cook mine, or more often I butter some bread, splash milk over cornflakes, nibble on chocolate digestives and sip coffee. I'm not sleeping, I'm tired, I look washed-out and lank-haired, and I'm so sorry all this has happened.

I'm lonely.

That's the bottom line. Lonely and, I believe in my heart, a little messed up. Charles Dearhead meant nothing to me. In fact, I didn't even like him. Boring. Self-centred. Urbane? Did I ever truly believe that? I put his poor wife through a terrible time, their marriage perhaps irreparably damaged. And that was a matter of choice, my choice. I shall not do that again, I promise myself.

And now my friend — the only person, I have realised, whose opinion is essential — appears to despise me. I have been thinking, and thinking, I can't stop thinking, and I have to leave the Old and New. Philip does not want me there, he has made that clear. I shall write a letter of resignation tonight. I think he will be shocked, though probably relieved, and will thank me for my integrity. Except I have none. This I have proved to myself, to Philip, to Sophie and Jenna, to various intrigued and scandalised customers. Thank God my father hasn't got wind of it.

Did I 'invite dishonour', like my grandmother before me? Yes. Of course. And I have brought dishonour to the shores of Philip's life too. Oh, I should live a little! Not hide away in a bookshop all my life, dipping my toes into the murky waters of sex with a man so much older and so much more married than me. Sophie was right.

I am not scared to hand in my notice tomorrow. I'll find another job. I have savings, I am frugal with clothes and food, I run an economical car. The Old and New is more of a home to me than anywhere else on earth, but I am resolved now to leave that place of warmth and humour because that is what must be done.

But it will kill me.

★ ★ ★

In the morning, I ask to speak to Philip. He is accommodating, as usual, and we go to his small office at the back of the shop. I take my time in closing the door. When I turn, I see that he has retreated behind his desk, the expansive but cluttered desk that he was sitting on, relaxed and interested, on the day he 'interviewed' me for the job.

'Philip,' I begin, not looking at him, 'I want to give you this.'

'What is it?'

'It's my notice.'

He takes it from me. He eyes me, opens the envelope, reads the note, rips it in two, and throws it into the bin. 'Let's start again, shall we?' he says.

'What do you mean?'

'Do you love him?'

'I'm not sure what love is.'

'Don't be ridiculous. Do you love him?'

'Charles Dearhead?'

'Are there others?'

'No! And no. I don't love him. Why would I?'

'That's precisely what I've been pondering. So what on earth are you playing at?'

'I'm not playing at anything. It's finished. I . . . I stepped outside myself. That's all.'

'Yes. I think you did, rather. You see, I keep

asking myself . . . I keep asking why a woman like you . . . why are you wasting your life on a man like him? I mean, come on. He's a complete twat. Sorry.'

'You think so?'

'Yes, I do. Frankly.'

'Whatever you think, it's none of your business.'

'Oh, but it is.'

'It isn't.'

We stand, facing each other across the huge walnut desk, this gigantic obstacle it seems we shall never be able to surmount, in a pantomime of our own making. But neither of us is laughing. Philip removes his glasses, cleans them awkwardly on his shirt front, puts them back on and clears his throat. It is a familiar routine. His face twitches with a strange kind of pleading innocence, willing me to do what he wants me to do. Philip's eyes are fixed on me, and my heart —

Oh, but surely. Surely? No. I'm crazy to even think it.

What is it that holds me back? Am I shy? I'm not *shy*. Am I not good enough for him? Whatever, none of it matters any more. It's over. And it didn't even begin.

'Look,' he says. 'You can't leave.'

'I can.'

'Yes, yes, of course, you can, what I mean is . . . I don't want you to.'

'Why on earth not? I've embarrassed you horribly.'

'You've embarrassed yourself, that's all. But

nobody cares. This sort of thing always blows over. I forbid you to leave, actually. You do remember that I defended you? Utterly?'

Of course I remember. 'Philip — ' And to my surprise I start sobbing, loudly. I didn't want to cry. I hate to cry.

'Oh no,' he says. 'For God's sake, here, take my hanky.'

Only a man like Philip would have a clean hanky in his pocket. I blow my nose. Pull yourself together, Roberta, I tell myself. Sort this out. 'I thought you would be used to crying women. With Jenna around, I mean.'

Not for the first time, I regret my thoughtless words. Philip stares at me, he feels the need to remove his glasses again, he runs his hand through his hair. He puts his glasses on the desk. I hope he doesn't sit on them in that absent-minded way of his. It wouldn't be the first time.

'Jenna and I are none of your business.'

I know this is true. I hate myself. And I am wrong, of course, quite wrong. Philip regards me as an employee, and only an employee. He is in love with Jenna, not me, and I cannot believe I even framed such thoughts, admitted such hopes to myself.

'I'm sorry,' I say, blotting out my dreams. 'I didn't mean to intrude.'

'Forget it, Roberta. I understand. And you shall stay. I absolutely depend upon you. This place would fall apart but for you.'

'What about Sophie?'

'She's capable, a sweet girl, she knows well enough what to do. But you . . . you lend this place some gravitas. You *are* the Old and New. Don't you get it?'

'Gravitas? Me? Causing scenes like last week's? Come off it, Philip. You are the Old and New. It's your shop.'

'Then, *we* are the Old and New. One of us can't operate without the other. And you didn't cause a scene, that ghastly woman did. So I ask respectfully and in all sincerity, please will you reconsider, and please will you stay? Please, Roberta.'

The fact that we are even having this conversation is enough to convince me. I have to leave. I have to leave now. Sod the notice period. If I don't leave now . . .

'I am leaving, Philip. I'm so sorry. I'll go now.'

'Right now?'

'Yes.'

If I think Philip is about to clamber over the desk, grab me, kiss me on the lips, shake me by the shoulders and beg me even further to stay, I am mistaken. He holds out his hand and I shake it. It is warm, his grip is firm, yet his touch feels somehow fragile. His eyes are vague, as though he is peering into a murky and troubled future, and I fear he is close to tears. And I fear my rising desire to comfort him, so I release my hand and leave the office.

I'm aware of him, standing alone, receding from me as I leave, watching me go in silence.

17

7th December 1940

Dear Jan,

I am sorry not to have written to you recently. But as you know, I don't like writing letters. And I have been so busy with one thing and another. The war and its ruination of this world may as well be happening on another planet. We see and hear so little of it now that the squadron has gone. Of course, there is still activity on the aerodrome, just not as much as before. But no more bombs. No more Hurricanes landing just a whisker from my house! Thank goodness for that. You know, I still think of that young pilot and I feel sorry that he died in that way.

Well, December has arrived. I do hope you can make it up here to see us, I'm sure Aggie and Nina would be pleased to see you again. Aggie goes on all right, missing her chap and dreadfully sad, but she soldiers on. Nina and I both do our bit to cheer her up. I hope Christmas will restore her spirits and despite all that is going on in this world, I shall do my best to make the day a happy one for her.

As for your needing peace, Jan, I am possibly the last person who can offer you such a thing.

Yet, I am your
Dorothea

Two weeks and five days after Albert raped her, the familiar cramps began. For a day she managed to ignore them. But the following morning, the blood began to flow, and she had no choice but to acknowledge once again the bitter disappointment that blighted her life.

She knew he would never return, and that was one small consolation. She hoped he would be killed, really, to make everything easier. And because he deserved to die after what he had done to her.

He had abandoned her, knowing how much she wanted another child, knowing full well that if he went away there could be no further children. But hadn't she abandoned him too, setting herself up in the tiny bedroom at the back of the house, shutting the door on him night after night? There could be no child if she didn't —

It was hard to believe that she once fancied herself in love with the man. He could offer her nothing. But she had not thought him a bully. Had he done this to other women? She thought not. No, it was just her, his wife. His anger was directed at her, nobody else. She could imagine him, in a different home, with a different woman; she would be younger, simpler, they would be happy together, and he would even be loving, in his own way.

But still the thought nagged at her, should she report him? What exactly would she report? A soldier returning home on leave and having relations with his wife? Who would believe there had been any wrongdoing? And now it was surely too late. Perhaps he didn't even understand that he'd done anything wrong, although he had gone a day earlier than he'd said he would. Out of guilt? Perhaps he had learned his lesson.

And what if she *had* fallen pregnant? How on earth could she have begun to explain to Jan? Because she knew — yes, she was absolutely certain about this — Jan would come back, she would see him again. She could have told him the truth, but would he have believed her? Perhaps he would think it only natural. After all, Albert was her husband.

But no matter. There was no baby. There was just her — empty, hurt and bloodied. Nothing to tell, no confessions to make.

⋆   ⋆   ⋆

Try as she might, Dorothy could not get her words to rhyme. So she ceased trying and she let her words take shape on the page as they would, as they seemed to want to do, with a life of their own. And at last this small collection of words seemed to her a poem. She felt that she had written her first, perhaps her only, poetry. And she would be the sole judge, she knew that she would never share her writing with another.

But her words, as she shaped them, read them, over and over, in snatched moments, late at night, early in the morning, startled her, gave her a strange unearthly sensation of power, like running along a wide, empty beach on soft-firm sand with youthful and boundless energy. It was a small liberation, but from what, she could not comprehend.

18

Such lurid dreams!

The woman was on her hands and knees before him, her eyes closed — this, the most ladylike of the women he had loved, the most demure. He cried out — he must have cried out often — and one of the nurses would be by his bedside, as suddenly and silently as an apparition. Oftentimes it was the nurse named Sylvia, nineteen years old, he guessed, pure-skinned, angel-white, soothing him with a quiet word, a soft murmur, a cool hand on his brow. She would check his pulse, holding his left wrist, checking his dogged heartbeats against the little watch strapped like an amulet to her breast pocket.

Was he in pain?

Yes, but not the kind she talked of, not the kind she even knew of, he thought.

The pain in his arm was nothing to the pain in his heart, and that in turn was nothing compared with his physical desire. Love, at this stage, was secondary. He acknowledged to himself that he was once again in the grip of pure lust, the most vulgar emotion. Sylvia and the other nurses must have noticed. They bathed him and dressed him, they were familiar with his body. But it mattered not. Where was the shame, in truth? He was born a man.

He longed to clamber back into his Hurricane,

to be back among his men. He wanted to kill more Germans. And that was a lust too, and sometimes it was difficult to define where each lust began and ended. He even wondered, in tortured lucid moments, if his aroused state was entirely due to thoughts of the Englishwoman.

Dorothy. Dorothea. Hardly could he bring himself to think her name.

Mrs Dorothy Sinclair.

The hospital bed was comfortable enough — white and firm. His sore, aching arm was broken. Smashed in several places, the doctor said. It would give him 'gyp' for the rest of his life, and by that Jan inferred it would give him pain, irritation. But he was alive, he was well. And he would return to flying, he proclaimed to the doctor, within the next week.

It was his right arm, which was unfortunate. He couldn't write. He had thought of asking a nurse to help him, but no, he did not want his words to one woman shared with another. The nurses were pretty, young, confident and — with him, at least — flirtatious. He flirted back too, a little, if he wasn't too tired, but only to be polite. They were gentle girls doing a difficult job. He did not desire them.

A new doctor came. He sat on the bed, introduced himself as Dr Burton. He wanted to talk, if that was all right. Jan was no fool, he knew he was a head doctor immediately. He told him so, and Dr Burton smiled. So, then. They could be frank.

It was not a good idea to return to flying too soon.

'We fear you are fragile, mentally. Exhausted. You need to rest longer,' he said.

'That cannot be done. I am needed,' said Jan.

It was a fine winter's day with pale diluted sunshine, small puffs of cloud skittering across the blue sky. Out of the window he could see other wounded men sitting in wheelchairs with blankets on their laps, being wheeled around by the pretty nurses, or sitting and smoking, contemplating the views across the hospital gardens to the fields beyond.

He had no idea, he suddenly realised, exactly where he was. Which hospital was he in? It appeared to have been converted from a grand house. But he did not know its name. He thought he was still in Kent, but perhaps he wasn't. Somehow he hadn't ever thought to ask.

'If you return so soon,' said Dr Burton, 'have you considered that you may be a liability? Your judgement impaired? Not to mention your injuries, which will not have healed fully.'

Jan found the young doctor smug, like most doctors. This Burton thought he was God, obviously. He looked dapper in a grey flannel suit. But he was not God, and Jan was determined to keep this young man in his place.

'I am not 'impaired',' he told him. 'I shall return today, if you like. No? So I give myself three, no, two more days, and I return. I flew back to my aerodrome with one arm. Two weeks ago, I think? It is healed. I feel it is healed. It is very near to healing. I will remove this plaster myself if you do not do it for me. I will do this.' He made a violent tearing action at his injured arm.

Dr Burton shook his head. He asked Jan questions: Where did he come from in Poland? Where did he learn his English?

Jan, bored, defensive, said as little as possible.

The doctor reiterated his warning not to be foolish, to consider his squadron — its safety, his own safety.

Jan kept up his stubborn silence. He was behaving, he knew, like a spoiled brat. But he would not be bossed around by a doctor who looked as though he had never killed a rabbit, let alone a fellow human being. Jan could not communicate with such a man.

Dr Burton gave up, thanked Jan for his time and left him.

19

Dorothy smiled to herself as she basted the chicken, slaughtered just the day before by Nina. Dorothy could not bring herself to perform the task, and Albert had always been the one to snap the birds' thin tremulous necks. Last Christmas, alone, she had not bothered with Christmas lunch, but this year she had plucked, gutted and now cooked the bird with great pleasure. The smell was divine, she thought, the house was warm, the frost outside clinging to the world like washed lace, and she and the girls were cosy and contented. Dorothy was determined to make Christmas Day a good one for all three of them. Besides the chicken, there were roasted potatoes, Yorkshire puddings, parsnips from the garden. And port, a bottle hidden away by Dorothy for years, taken from her mother's house. Why she had taken it, Dorothy couldn't fathom; it was just another item in her strange and ill-considered trousseau. Perhaps, she mused, today was why: Christmas Day 1940, cold, but calm. And safe, for now.

The girls had sipped two small glasses each already and were lounging, listening to their favourite Billie Holiday songs. They had loved the presents Dorothy had made for each of them: simple linen handkerchiefs she had dug out from the bottom of her rag bag and which she had embroidered with their initials, pressed and then scented with a handful of lavender; a silk scarf for Aggie that Dorothy no longer wore; a red lipstick, barely used, for Nina. Not astounding gifts, but something sitting under the small Christmas tree for the girls to open, wrapped simply with brown paper and kitchen string.

Dorothy was glad there were no presents for her. She had never liked them. She would be expected to smile and say thank you; she felt obliged to be thrilled. Her mother's idea of presents had been *The Infant's Progress: From the Valley of Destruction to Everlasting Glory*, and other hideous books that Dorothy had never read but had hidden away under her bed. They were probably still there, she thought, as she took a modest sip of her own glass of port. The thrill of alcohol, its exuberance, was a sensation Dorothy rarely allowed herself. She loved too much the hot, glowing feel of it in her mouth, her throat, her gullet, through her stomach, down deep into her legs. She loved too much the feeling of losing oneself, of being buoyed up, and the opportunity it afforded for blurring and forgetting. But she could not forget the way in which Albert had acted towards her after he had taken too much drink. She would never allow herself to get into that state, to lose her mind completely to drink's calamitous charms. But today, this Christmas Day, she was allowing herself the pleasure of alcohol. December had been a month of further disappointments, and she needed to forget.

Despite his promises, his hints and suggestions, Squadron Leader Jan Pietrykowski had not visited. Indeed, he had not written for over a month. Was he dead? Dorothy thought not. She *knew* not. Was he injured? It was possible. It was probable. Perhaps the squadron had been moved again? Perhaps he was cross with her? Did he know, somehow, about Albert and her brief, shameful, blameless relations with him? Such a shrewd man, she would not have been surprised if he had guessed from the tone of her last letter, from her careful choice of words. But, of course, it was impossible. Wasn't it? Nobody was that intuitive.

'What's up, then, Dot?' Nina said. She was languishing on the settee, her port glass glowing in her plump hand, the glass rimmed by the red lipstick she had been unable to resist trying on.

Dinner was nearly ready, and Dorothy had emerged from the kitchen to take a short rest. 'Nothing at all, Nina,' she said. 'Dinner will be ready in ten minutes. I'm just letting the chicken stand.' Dorothy sank into her chair by the window.

'You're the best ever cook,' said Aggie.

'Oh no, but it's good to feel useful. You both looked so cold this morning.'

'It's bloody freezing out there,' said Nina. She shifted on the settee, wincing as she did so.

'Are you quite well?' said Dorothy.

'Yeah. Course I am. Just feel a bit funny. Can't get comfy. I'm ever so hungry. Can't wait for that dinner.'

Dorothy turned to the window. Slowly, she rose from her chair, transfixed, wide-eyed.

'What is it, Dot?' said Aggie, coming to stand

175

beside her. She flicked the yellowed lace curtains to one side. 'Oh!'

Squadron Leader Jan Pietrykowski was opening the gate. He was carrying a bottle-shaped brown package and a kitbag. A small open-topped car was parked half on the road, half on the verge, crimson and bright as a brand-new toy. Dorothy wondered that they hadn't heard the car arrive. But, of course, the music was loud.

'You've been pining for months, and now he's here. And you're just going to stand there?' said Aggie, taking her glass from her.

As if in a dream, Dorothy made to go back into the kitchen, to open the door and let him in. But her knees, disobedient, would not budge.

'I can't,' she whispered.

'I'll go!' said Aggie brightly, handing Dorothy's glass back, and she half ran, half skipped through to the kitchen.

Dorothy looked aghast at Nina, who grinned in her disingenuous manner, took a large mouthful of port and shrugged. Dorothy groped behind her for her chair and sat down. She stood again immediately as Aggie entered the lounge, followed by the unmistakeable smell of uniform, of hair grease, of kindness. And the man, more handsome than she remembered, the man she had longed for, stood once more in her parlour, smiling, unwrapping a bottle of champagne, no less, and looking at Dorothy as though she were Elizabeth Bowes-Lyon herself.

'I apologise for arriving without asking,' he said. 'I had a last-minute pass. Twenty-four hours only. Tomorrow, I must return to Kent.'

'I see,' said Dorothy. Her throat was so tight she felt she might suffocate. He was extraordinarily handsome. Had she not noticed this before? She thought she had. But there was something wrong, something amiss with the way he held himself, the way he moved. And it was still a shock to her that she cared so much.

'But for now, today, Christmas. Good times, good wine. Good company.' He looked at her, and smiled.

She smiled back.

Suddenly, it was Christmas.

Jan followed her into the kitchen where she helped him remove his greatcoat, which was wet and cold, and laid it over the clothes horse in front of the range to dry. Gentle plumes of steam filled the room. He opened and poured the champagne, with his left hand, holding the bottle awkwardly against his body. Goodness knows how he had come by champagne. But who cared? It was champagne! And Dorothy could see he was in pain. He held his right arm at a curious angle. Nevertheless, he helped her to dish up the dinner, putting the heavy plates on to the table one at a time, using his good arm.

'I'll call the girls through,' she said.

But Jan put a finger to his lips and shook his head. He gently took hold of Dorothy's waist with both hands. She looked away, embarrassed. He took her chin in his good hand and softly tilted her head towards his. He kissed her, soft and light. She did not want the kiss to end.

'You have lost weight, no?' he said, releasing her.

She opened her eyes.

Had she? Perhaps. Since Albert's visit she had certainly lost her appetite.

'I've been pining for you,' said Dorothy, and she smiled shyly at him.

He laughed his big, hearty laugh — the laugh of one who doesn't laugh as often as he should — and she blushed and pulled away from him, calling to the girls that dinner was on the table.

They ate the food and washed it down with the champagne and more port. Jan said he was hopeful that all was not lost; the death all around was not in vain. There had been a victory, of sorts, despite the bombings, and the war could and would be won. There had been no invasion, and there was no sign of one coming any time soon. They could all take heart from that.

'But I have no idea when the war will end,' he said, pouring himself another glass of port. The last glass. The women had insisted.

'Years?' said Dorothy.

'I hope not, but I suspect so. I do not expect to return to my homeland for a long time.'

After dinner, they listened to the King's speech, and then the girls made space in the lounge and insisted on dancing, giddying themselves until Nina, red-faced and full, plonked herself on the settee, laughing. Drunk and tired, she soon slept, and Aggie left the cottage to milk the cows alone. It would take three times as long, she said, but Nina was all in. Let her sleep. She deserved some time off. She worked like a bloody packhorse.

Alone in the house, apart from the sleeping girl, Dorothy and Jan cleared the dishes and washed up. Jan, ever mindful of his arm, winced once or twice.

'May I have a look at your arm?' she asked him as she put away the last of the dishes.

'It's nothing,' he said.

'But it looks as though you're in a lot of pain.'

He shook his head and changed the subject. 'May I stay tonight? On the settee will be all right, I have my kit. Only it is so cold, and colder still now it is almost dark. And I am not expected back until ten o'clock tomorrow morning.'

'Yes. Of course you can stay. You must. But in the spare room. I prepared it for you weeks ago.'

After Albert's departure, Dorothy had stripped the bed, turned the mattress, scrubbed the floor. She had remade the bed and scrubbed the settee, over and over.

Aggie returned, and Dorothy made sandwiches and tea. One of the cows had mastitis, Aggie thought. Nina, awake now and slothful, announced herself to be 'full to the bloody brim' but happy to accompany Aggie to The Crown, to 'see who was about'. The girls disappeared upstairs and returned, a few minutes later, changed and lipsticked. Jan offered them a ride, one at a time, in the little red sports car. It was an MG, loaned to him that morning by his English flight officer. 'Take care of her, Pietrykowski,' he had said. Jan wasn't certain that he had meant the car.

Dorothy watched and waved from the parlour window as each girl was whisked away. And while Jan was ferrying for the second time, Dorothy made up a fresh tea tray and set it out on the low table in the lounge.

'Thank you for giving the girls a trip in that car,' she said. 'I'm sure they think it very glamorous.'

'It is glamorous, isn't it? And fast too. And red! But so cold, like flying. So I got here in time, in time for your delicious dinner.'

'You didn't write.'

'I'm sorry. I hoped a surprise would do. Besides, I could not write,' and he raised his arm.

'It's incredible to see you again,' said Dorothy. 'Please may I have a look at your injury?'

'There is no need.'

'What happened to you?'

'Nothing. Nothing to speak of. A small injury, a scratch. No need for any worry.'

Dorothy said nothing. She slowly sipped her tea, and concentrated on the tick, tick, tick of the clock, the crackling of the fire. She felt the man's gaze on her, unwavering. He perched on the edge of the settee, drinking his tea in long gulps. She had hoped he might be more comfortable with her. But, of course, she could not expect too much.

Truly, they barely knew each other.

★ ★ ★

He recalled these cups from their first meeting, when they had tea in her kitchen, all those months ago, in May, months that could just as easily be years. And yes, she had aged — imperceptibly to others, perhaps, but he noticed one or two new lines around her mouth, her eyes. She was definitely thinner. He noticed these things, because he looked. He looked at Mrs Dorothy Sinclair as only a man in love can look, with attention to detail.

There had been few women in Jan Pietrykowski's life: his young bride, lost to him after just months of marriage, followed by an intense but short-lived fling with a young woman who had bewitched him for a while; and once, once only, but shamefully, the wife of a colleague. Dorothy seemed to him, now he was in her presence again, to fill the world with womanhood. And he had missed her presence, reading over and over again the odd, stilted letters that had occasionally arrived from her. She was no writer, as she was quite possibly no lover. And if he found that out — if he pushed this woman beyond her endurance, if he tried to 'get into her knickers' (a peculiar phrase he had heard often since being in England) — then the spell between them would be broken, irretrievably and forever. At this moment he hated being a man, the ludicrous physical reaction that accompanied thoughts of her. And he had thought of her often, before and after his injury, alone, at night, in bed (and sometimes not alone, not at night, not in bed), imagined pleasure overtaking all sense, all reason. He imagined Dorothy above him, wide-eyed, sweating, hair crumpled, face flushed, breasts swollen.

And now, to be here with this woman, in her warm and safe home, was almost more than he could bear. The fear and exhaustion he had so long fought finally beat him, and his face caved in like a bullied child's. Rising from the settee, he stumbled towards her, knocking into the tea tray as he did so, and the tray swayed on the edge of the low table, and he waited for it to fall, but it righted itself.

Jan fell to his knees and Dorothy stroked his hair, cradling his head in her lap. And he was glad to feel her compassion, to know that hers was intact while his had been blown apart.

'Hush, Jan. Come now, it's all right,' she whispered as she tentatively stroked his glossy black hair.

He cried. Her hand found his neck and stroked back and forth, back and forth, a hypnotic movement that had the desired effect. She repeated her request to see his arm, and this time he allowed her to remove his tunic and roll up his shirt sleeve. The arm was reddish-purple and swollen, but surely less so than it had been. Still, it saddened her.

Even injured his arm was a work of art, and she could not stop looking at it. Gradually, his sobs lessened. The clock ticked, and the fire crackled. His head was heavy in her lap, he was perfectly still, barely breathing; she thought he slept. She looked down at his hair, the curve of his ear, the tiny birthmark shaped like Italy just beneath it, his cheek and his solid jaw. Dorothy ran her hand over the stubble that was beginning to shoot forth like small black arrows, then turned her hand over and stroked his face with the back of her fingers. She gazed down at the closed eyes of this man who was also still a boy, at the tear tracks crusting like fresh ice on his cheeks; she gazed at his strong neck, stretched across her lap as though on the executioner's block. His surrender, she realised, was complete. This was Jan, the person, the man. She kept perfectly still, save for her stroking hand.

He could be, she dared to imagine, her happiness.

And later, after an hour, perhaps longer, Jan raised his head to look at her. 'I'm sorry, Dorothea.'

'No.'

'I am a coward. You see, I am.'

'No.'

'I cry like a baby and sleep in your lap.'

'I like babies.'

'I know.'

She held his shoulders. The male strength flowed from him into her hands and up to her arms and flooded through her body, to her lungs, her heart, her stomach. She gritted her teeth and held him firmer still, and for a moment there was panic in his eyes.

'Jan.'

It was not a question.

He raised himself, balancing on his haunches, reached for her hair and loosened it from its chignon. He curled it around his fingers and smelled it, and then she was on him, her mouth grasped his, and she kissed him, she took control. He seemed stunned, and for a moment he did nothing, nothing at all, until he stood, pulling her up with him, and with one movement he gathered her up in his arms, wincing again, just for a moment, and then they were through the door, and he was carrying her upstairs, and grappling to open the door of a bedroom, any bedroom. The one he found was the little spare room made up for him, and he threw her on to the bed and kicked the door shut behind them.

20

17th November 1944

Dearest Eliza and Bert,

Just a note to let you know I had the baby at last! Four nights ago, just after midnight, so she shares her birthday with me. I have named her Diana. My mother has been helping with the housework while I rest and nurse Diana and try to sleep. I read too, such a luxury to lie in bed all day. Thank you for the Agatha Christie books you sent for my birthday. I am enjoying them, and quite see now why you are such admirers. Diana is a wakeful baby and very hungry, which is not always comfortable for me. I love her dearly and shall feel like this for always. Is there a mother who doesn't? If only Bob were around to meet his little girl. My heart breaks each time I think of it and I cry often. Mother calls it the baby blues, and perhaps it is, even though I think I have reason enough to be crying. Wish me strength, dear friends, to be both mother and father to this baby girl. Do visit when you get the opportunity. You are much missed down here,

Jean

(I found this letter inside a first edition of Agatha Christie's The Moving Finger. Philip asked me to check the book over and wrap the almost pristine dust jacket in protective cellophane. It was later placed in the locked antiquarian cabinet priced at £230, and it sold shortly thereafter.)

★ ★ ★

The day is bleak but the care home is warm and sheltered. Suzanne is there, greeting me with a smile.

'How are things?' she says.

I tell her almost everything. I like talking to strangers, or near strangers. They don't judge. I don't tell her about Babunia's letter from my grandfather, even though I can sense it burning a hole in my handbag, demanding to be set free. I do tell her a little about my stupid affair with Charles Dearhead, his wife's confrontation with me, my leaving the Old and New. I tell her about my father's illness. I tell her how Philip defended me.

Suzanne is a good listener. She says she likes the sound of Philip.

I ask her how my grandmother is.

'Not so well,' says Suzanne. 'Dorothea is confused more often than not. But I don't feel that it's senility, not as such. I feel that she has something on her mind, some burden, as old people often do. It's probably nothing at all, just something she has kept within her all these years and has now blown out of proportion.'

I don't know what to say. I'm not about to betray Babunia's secrets, even if I knew what they were.

'The name you call her, Babunia, where does it come from?' asks Suzanne.

'It's Polish for 'Grandma'.'

'I thought it probably was. Your grandfather was Polish, wasn't he?'

'Yes. I think she likes me to call her that in memory of him. He died when she was expecting my dad, you see. It was a wartime romance. They weren't married for long before he died.'

'Married?'

'Yes.'

'But Dorothea was never married to your grandfather.'

'They were married in 1940.'

'Oh. I'm sorry, Roberta. I thought you knew. It's just . . . she told me she never married him. She was married, but to somebody else. She changed her name to your grandfather's, though. I expect she was ashamed — in those days, it was a big deal to have a child outside of wedlock. And by another man. That could be what's troubling her . . . Oh. Now I've upset you. I'm sorry.'

'She just took his name, you mean?'

'It looks that way, yes.'

'Is there a deed poll certificate?'

'Yes. She showed it to me not long after I first started here.'

'May I see it?'

'Of course.'

★   ★   ★

Later, my mobile rings. It's Sophie. She telephoned me at home the day I walked out of the Old and New, in tears.

She couldn't believe I had left. When was I coming back? Couldn't I patch it up with Philip?

I told her no, I could not.

Now she is calling to tell me that Philip has been interviewing. 'There's a woman called Patricia, very tall, taller even than you, with very short grey hair, lots of beads and bracelets. Philip asked me what I thought of her after she left. I said she was nothing like you. And I'm sure he was going to cry, Roberta, I swear. He moped off into the office and I didn't see him for two hours.'

'What can I do about it?' I ask, crossly. None of this is my concern.

'Nothing, I suppose. He's interviewing again tomorrow. Jenna's helping — but to be honest, she's more of a hindrance. And she's acting weird. I'll let you know how it goes.'

'If you want to, that's fine.'

'You do know you could come back right now. I mean, you could walk into the shop this morning and he'd take you back like a shot.'

'I don't know that.'

'I think you do.'

★　★　★

I hate the word 'orphan'. I'm not an orphan, of course, not yet. And can adults be described as orphans, anyway? I sit alone in my flat, sipping a glass of Pinot Grigio, not getting drunk exactly but feeling sorry for myself, going over my pathetic life, hating myself. And, of course, regretting my hasty departure from the Old and New. I'm hoping to get a call from Philip, begging me to return. But the telephone in my hallway sits stubbornly silent, cold and inanimate, and the mobile phone in my handbag has nothing to say either.

I consider ringing Dad. I want to talk to him. Suzanne showed me the certificate from 1941, which proved to me that my grandmother changed her name by deed poll from Mrs Dorothy Sinclair to Mrs Dorothea Pietrykowski. So at least now I know the suitcase was hers, and hers all along, and now it's mine. And so what if Babunia had an affair and fell pregnant? It must have happened so much during the war. I wonder who her husband was? Did he die in the war? Is that why she changed her name? But why did she lie to us about it, to Dad and me? I don't care if she was married, or had an affair, or had a dozen affairs. I'm pretty sure my dad wouldn't give a fig either, he's pretty laid-back about most things. But of course, Suzanne was right, things were different back then. I understand that my grandmother is very much a product of her time.

And does Dad know any of this? My dear father, gradually dying from this hideous disease, refusing to fully accept his limitations. He has an aversion to hospitals, and I can't blame him for that. My mother, Anna, Dad's former wife — they are long divorced — is unavailable to me, for reasons entirely of her own making. My grandmother is confused and old, possibly weeks from death — even though we have been fearful of that for a decade, probably longer. It seems to me she has always been weeks from death. I've broken off my only proper adult romance (I don't count the unfortunate episode at university), which in itself isn't a tragedy, but it feels like one. I've been exposed in public as a home-wrecker (although the Dearhead marriage, from what I've heard, appears to be intact). I've cut myself off from the person who is surely my best and most reliable friend. And this letter, this stupid letter that I wish had not fallen out of *The Infant's Progress*, seems to refute all that my grandmother has told me about her early life.

I sip my wine. I read the letter again, although I know it by heart now, but I read to search for clues and answers that I will not find. I can't think ahead. I can't think sideways. All I can think about is the past, which is unravelling slowly. All I can do, it seems, is wait for it to reveal itself to me.

21

Dorothy awoke and realised it was snowing. The bedroom was too light, the world too still. It was but five o'clock, and she guessed she had slept for three hours, perhaps less. She sat up and pulled back the curtains. It was cold and white, so she lay down again and snuggled into the arms that had held her through the short night, and the owner of those arms stirred, and kissed her head, and told her to go back to sleep.

'It's snowing, Jan.'

He sat up then, leaned over her and looked out of the window. He exclaimed in Polish. 'I have to get up. The car . . . before there is too much snow. I'm sorry, my darling.'

'It's perfectly all right. I know you have to leave early.'

She watched as he climbed out of bed, and marvelled that he was not at all abashed by his own nakedness. It was funny to think how familiar she had become in one short night with his body, when this man was really still a stranger to her. She could not recall all that they had enjoyed together; it was as though she had been drunk, which she certainly had not been. Were they lovers? Yes. Of course. He was her lover. All the rumours were true.

He dressed, and left the bedroom to use the privy. She climbed out of the bed, and tiptoed through to her own bedroom where she watched him walk along the path to the outhouse, his breath billowing in the morning snow-light. She roused herself then, dressed, and in the kitchen she cleaned out the range, reset and lit it and boiled the kettle for tea. She set out some bread, some butter, some gooseberry jam. Jan must eat before his long journey. She boiled more water so he could wash. He performed his ablutions and dressed himself properly in the spare bedroom while Dorothy sat in the kitchen and sewed the buttons back on to his shirt.

If the girls knew that Dorothy and Jan had spent the night together — and, of course, they must know — they said nothing. Dorothy had heard them come in the night before, late. This morning they were preparing for a long day of work, all the more arduous after the previous day's festivities. As she sewed, Dorothy listened to them all as they ate bread and jam, drank tea, exchanged subdued niceties and talked about the day's work ahead. She knew Aggie and Nina were watching her mend Jan's shirt, and she could feel the weight of their intrigue.

'Christ, my belly hurts,' announced Nina, rubbing her stomach and waving away a second slice of bread and jam.

'I'm sorry to hear that,' said Dorothy. She looked over at Jan. He was about to leave. She was dreading the separation, trying to spin out these remaining moments left to them. Yet she could think of little to say.

Nina rushed to the privy, looking wan and cold on her return.

'So did you girls have fun last night?' asked

Dorothy, to break the unusual silence.

'Not as much as — ' began Nina.

But Aggie shook her head.

Dorothy smiled sweetly and avoided the cool gaze of the squadron leader who, she could see, had finished his breakfast. She glanced at the clock. It was very nearly six o'clock. He must leave. She could not contemplate how she would bear this. Five minutes of separation would be too long, she thought, and she suppressed tears.

He put on his greatcoat, scarf, hat and gloves and picked up the kitbag he had packed before breakfast. He cleared his throat. Taking the hint, Aggie harried Nina to get ready, and the older pair watched as the girls trudged out into the snow and moved off for the North Barn, across the Long Acre field. They made slow progress in the falling snow.

'I don't want to go, my darling,' said Jan, finally. 'But I must.'

'I know. I understand. But you will come back to me? As soon as you can?'

'Of course I will. And you will write to me? Properly?'

'Yes. I will. My letter will reach Kent before you do. How's that?'

'I am likely to have a new address soon. But write anyway, letters are sent forward. I'll let you know my new posting as soon as I can.'

They hugged, and Dorothy cried. And they prepared to part, Dorothy slinging her coat over her shoulders to walk down the garden path and watch Jan roar off in the car. He would ignore the snow, he said. It was nothing compared to the snowfalls at home. A last kiss, a wave, the cold engine growling and the crackle of snow as he drove through it, and he was gone.

Once again, she stood alone.

She waved until he had rounded the corner and was out of sight. Conceitedly, part of her had hoped he would stay, claim illness, incapacity. But she knew him better than that. The snow drove her back inside to her hearth, to her empty house. She cleared away some of the breakfast things. She found his shirt, on her chair where she had left it when she got up to prepare for the big goodbye. She had sewn all of the buttons but one back on, and she had forgotten to give it to him. She would have to send it on. She drifted upstairs to the spare bedroom, where the smell of sweat and maleness lingered. The sheets were crumpled. Dorothy lay on the bed and closed her eyes. She wanted to remember last night forever, so she would have to start remembering it now, before the memories began to fade. She luxuriated in the feather pillows, which smelled of him. She thought of his hard warm body, his soft mouth, his tongue on her and in her.

Later, after she had slept a little, she rose from the bed and tidied herself, and resolved to have a bath. But first she must let out the hens, the poor things, and bake bread, and begin preparations for that evening's meal for the girls. The washstand Jan had used that morning needed cleaning, the water disposing of. This she was reluctant to do. Even his dirt was desirable to her, sacred. She smiled to herself. She felt inordinately thrilled.

After tidying away the breakfast things, she set to making the bread. As she kneaded the dough, her mind dwelled on all that had happened in the last day and night. It was momentous, this she understood. To take a man like Jan into her life, into her body, into her very self, allowing him to possess all her emotions, to see her for who she was — it was new. She had not had that completeness with Albert even before the rape, the ugly name for the act she now accepted had been visited on her.

But life had to go on. Jan was gone, back to his work, back to play his role in the game they called war, and she was alone again. She would launder and sew and cook and play mother to the girls. Her life, her tiny life, punctuated at last by love, was not to change, could not really be changed. Perhaps, once the war was over . . . but she dared not think that any happiness of hers could endure. Happiness was an illusion.

She set the bread to rise in the linen cupboard. She would write to Jan, a wild, girlish letter proclaiming her love. He would be surprised to receive it so quickly, but she had promised. And she wanted to make him smile and remember, as much as she did. She would write to him every day!

She went to the small oak writing desk in the parlour and wrote feverishly for half an hour, perhaps an hour. About what? About joy. Between the lines, she wrote of her desire for wifeliness and motherhood. Ah, motherhood. Funny, but Dorothy had not considered the notion of falling pregnant, being pregnant now with Jan's baby. Their coupling had been about them, their love, their lust. She wrote in her letter about her desire only for Jan, her dreams for their future, if they had one. After finishing her letter, reading it, rereading it, she found herself wanting to write it again but knowing it would be ruined if she did. She took an envelope, kissed the letter, tucked it inside, and addressed and stamped it. Pulling on her coat and boots, she ran through the snow, her hair flying behind her, to the postbox at the top of the lane.

Returning to her cottage, slow and deflated, she ambled, enjoying the chill crispness. She felt cleansed. The snow was falling like graceful ballerinas, and the world was silenced.

Until she thought she heard a shout. Again. Her name.

Was it Aggie?

Yes, there she was, holding on to her hat, running across the Long Acre towards the cottage. Dorothy hastened, and made it to her front garden as Aggie came through the rear gate, red-faced, out of breath, eyes wide in panic.

'Aggie?' said Dorothy. 'What's the matter?'

'It's Nina. I think she's dying!'

'Dying?'

'She's up the North Barn. Can you come?'

'What's wrong with her?'

'She said she felt bad this morning. She feels sick, and she's getting awful pains. Shrieking her head off, she is. Please hurry, Dot.'

'My God, is she poisoned?'

'I don't know.'

Dorothy locked the kitchen door, and the two set off. The snow was thickening. Why hadn't she sent Aggie for Dr Soames? Dorothy wasn't a nurse, she couldn't help Nina. She wasn't even a mother. She had never mopped a sweating brow, spooned broth, or cleaned up vomit other than her own.

Dorothy struggled to keep up with Aggie, who ran ever faster as they approached the barn. The snow was now falling thick and fast. Aggie pulled the barn door open. Entering, panting, Dorothy felt a surge of relief to be out of the cold. Aggie pulled the door to behind them. The barn was dark, and as she waited for her eyes to adjust, she cast around to find Nina. Her gloveless hands were cold. It felt as though her feet were shrinking in her gumboots. She breathed deeply, getting her breath back.

Nina was in the farthest corner, curled up on a pile of straw. She moaned, a strange lowing noise. She was an animal. And she was in pain.

'Nina?' Dorothy knelt beside the stricken girl, and felt her head.

She was neither hot nor cold. Aggie knelt on the other side of Nina, and held her hand.

'Dot? Oh!'

'Where does it hurt?' said Dorothy, removing her coat and placing it over Nina's shoulders. 'Nina, listen to me. Where does it hurt?'

'Oh God, everywhere! So bloody much . . . ' Nina squirmed and rocked, crying out.

Dorothy and Aggie stood up. Aggie looked small and lost.

But Dorothy ignored her childlike trembling. 'Has she eaten anything strange? Anything she shouldn't?' she asked urgently.

'I don't think so. We all ate a lot yesterday — '

'But we all ate the same, and you and I are fine and so was Jan. I don't understand. Nina? Have you . . . you've been sick, yes? Oh yes, a little. No matter. Anything else? Have you . . . soiled yourself?'

'Course she hasn't!' cried Aggie.

'Nina?'

'I had to go to the privy three times this morning but nothing since then. Oh. Oh no. Oh my fucking God.'

'Aggie, run to Dr Soames. If he's not there, try Mrs Compton. She's better than nobody, I think she trained as a nurse once. And she has a telephone. I expect an ambulance will have to come. Something's obviously wrong. Appendix, perhaps?'

'But that can be dangerous, can't it?'

'I think so. She'll be all right. But go for help now, please.'

'You'll stay with her, won't you? Dot? She won't die?'

'Of course I'll stay, and of course she'll not die. The very idea! But I can't help her much. Run, Aggie, now.'

Snow hurled itself through the heavy barn door as Aggie pushed it open. With one last anxious look at Nina, she left the barn and pushed the door shut behind her.

Nina was sweating now, eyes closed, and she lay still and quiet. Dorothy crouched down and touched the girl's face.

'I can't bear it,' said Nina, and she began to cry. 'I'm going to die. I am.'

'Nonsense. Aggie has gone for Dr Soames. You will be perfectly all right, Nina.'

'Oh fuck, fuck, fuck!'

Nina flailed wildly for Dorothy. She pulled the older woman off balance, and Dorothy fell down beside her. Nina would not let go, gripping Dorothy's arm harder, screaming into her ear. Dorothy struggled to free herself of the desperate girl, and sat back on her heels. She swallowed hard. She stared at Nina, writhing in the straw in agony, convinced she was going to die, and understanding dawned on her, fierce as an Egyptian sun.

She ran to the barn door, thoughts piling on thoughts, realisation flooding into her mind and galvanising her like nothing ever before. It was all there, it was all clear, all of a sudden. Oh, but she had been so blind!

'Aggie!' she cried into the blizzard, more loudly than she had thought herself capable of shouting. 'Aggie!'

She waited, but Aggie must have gone out of earshot; her figure failed to reappear through the swirling snow. Dorothy slammed the door and threw herself back down beside Nina. She turned the girl's face towards her own and looked squarely into her wild, frightened eyes.

'Nina, when did you last bleed? You know. Your monthly? Can you remember?'

'Buggered if I can.'

'You've been putting on weight, haven't you?

199

I've had to let out your clothes several times, haven't I?'

'So bloody what?'

'Have you felt any movements inside? In your body? Pokes and prods? Kicks? Somersaults?'

'I've felt lots of wind. Sometimes it hurts.'

'Nina. That's not wind. Well, it's not only wind. I think you have a baby inside you.'

'What?'

'And probably there's not much time. I think we're going to have to do this ourselves. It's all right, Nina, hold my hands, that's it. Hold tight. Bear with this one and we'll get you out of your underclothes. All right, don't panic, that's it. Breathe, Nina.'

Nina, crying, moaning, gripped Dorothy's hands.

'Don't fight it,' said Dorothy, lowering her voice to a whisper as the girl's cries subsided. 'That's it. My God, I can't believe how blind I've been.'

'What are you talking about?'

'You're having a baby.'

'Are you mad? A baby? Inside of me? A baby?'

'Yes. That's it. Hang on to me, there, that's it. Well done. It will pass, all of this.'

Nina screamed, then gradually she calmed, and lay still again. 'I'm expecting?' she said.

'Why didn't you tell us?'

'I didn't realise. I swear.'

'How could you not know you were pregnant?'

'I don't know. I just didn't know. That's all I can say. Are you sure?'

'Nina, you're in labour. I think these are

200

labour pains, coming in waves. It's your body pushing the baby out. You're giving birth!'

'I'm having it now? But I can't. Oh no, it's coming back. Help me, Dot, please!'

Dorothy held the girl, and rocked her through the pain until it subsided.

Nina relaxed again.

'How could you not know?' scolded Dorothy. 'Oh, you silly, blind girl. Didn't you even suspect? Didn't you think this might happen? Listen to me. You're at the end of your pregnancy. You're getting labour pains. They come and they go, and they are very, very strong. Yes? I know. Hold on again. That's right, Nina. Breathe. Breathe. There's a girl. Well done. Now, I want to take off your clothes, just your bottom half, and have a look. Because I have the feeling you may be having your baby quite soon. I . . . I know these things.'

Nina looked wildly at Dorothy, searching her face as if she could not speak Dorothy's language, and did not understand.

'Nina. Can I take off your trousers and your underclothes now, please?'

'I can't,' moaned Nina, the agony seizing her again, and she writhed and thrashed and moaned.

The pains were coming so quickly, one hard on the back of the other, and Dorothy knew birth was imminent. She took off Nina's boots and pulled down her breeches, which were wet. As if in a dream, Dorothy gently parted the girl's thighs. Peering at her, she could see that Nina was, indeed, in the throes of labour.

201

'You're going to have a baby, Nina, that's for sure. I can just see its head. Listen to me now. I know it hurts but you *are* having a baby. You're in the thick of it. And it's supposed to hurt and you are not poorly and you are not dying. I promise you. You must know that. Oh, why on earth didn't you tell us?'

'I didn't know, I swear,' she panted.

'So you keep saying, but . . . Well, never mind now. Keep my coat around you, Nina, if you can. That's it. Hitch up! That'll be nice and warm for your baby when he comes out. We'll have to keep him very warm — as warm as we can manage, at any rate. You'll need something underneath you. Is there anything in here we can use? Anything at all?'

Dorothy looked around and spotted a tarpaulin in the opposite corner. Rushing over to grab it, she saw a line of cows in their pen, ephemeral breath floating out of their nostrils as they lowed softly, nibbling hay, staring as though in fascination at the drama of human birth unfolding before them. So focused on the labouring girl, Dorothy had not noticed them before. But now their presence was an unexpected comfort. Dorothy grabbed the tarpaulin, unfolded it and shook it out. Where on earth was Aggie? Hopefully reaching Dr Soames by now, or Mrs Compton. But even as she thought this, Dorothy shuddered inside. She wanted to do this herself. The intimacy of the barn, the inquisitive cows, the poor hapless labouring girl, and her — and her alone — to help bring this child into the world. And Mrs

Compton . . . the woman was not to be trusted around newborn babies. Mrs Compton would ruin everything.

Dorothy rolled Nina on to her side, spread the tarpaulin out underneath her and rolled her back on to it. She knelt beside Nina, and urged her to hold her hands, to squeeze tightly.

'Nina, listen to me. Next time you get the pains, I think you can push. Push as though you were . . . how can I put it? . . . as though you were in the privy. Do you understand?'

'Shitting, you mean?'

'Exactly that. Don't hold back, Nina. It's all perfectly natural. We're both women here. There's no shame even if you do — '

'But the baby won't come out of that hole, will it?'

'What do you think? Surely you've seen enough cows giving birth? Good God, Nina.'

'Don't half feel like I'm going to shit myself. Oh, Dot. Don't leave me. Oh God, oh God, oh God!'

And Nina pushed — for she was strong, if exhausted. And she was capable, if shocked.

'That's it, Nina, keep going. My goodness, there's not much longer to go now. Try to breathe, breathe now before the next pain. That's it.'

'I can't be having a baby. I'd know, wouldn't I?'

'Never mind about that now. You are having a baby, trust me. Are you ready? Hold my hands, don't let go. See? Aren't they warm and strong? Now gather yourself, breathe deep, and push, Nina, push.'

Nina stared at Dorothy, the girl's wild eyes locking on to Dorothy's. The baby's head began to emerge, and Dorothy removed Nina's hands from her own. She moved to kneel before the labouring girl, hands outstretched, waiting. And it seemed to Dorothy that the sun was about to shine on her, stronger and brighter than ever before, it was going to burst out from behind thick and dark clouds, and her life would become at last a life of illumination and warmth. But she could not truly tell why she felt this.

Nina, red-faced, sweating, threw back her head and bellowed. And from her body erupted a head of dark hair, a pinched-up little red face, shoulders, white-purple arms, belly, legs, twisted slime-grey cord, and blood, mucus, a gelatinous flood of indeterminate fluids. Dorothy gasped, and Nina sagged back on to the tarpaulin, and the baby cried, loudly, and Dorothy saw the baby kick and flail, strong like his mother. Strong like he should be.

'Oh, you're beautiful!' cried Dorothy to the baby, enchanted. She hastily removed her cardigan and wrapped it around the baby, and placed the little boy in his mother's arms. She drew up the mercifully large tarpaulin over the mother and child, and she repositioned her coat over Nina's shoulders. It was as warm as she could make them. It was enough, she reasoned. It would have to be. The baby, cries soon subsiding, lay quiet and calm, and Nina leaned back on the straw, exhausted, eyes closed as though asleep.

'He's truly perfect, Nina,' said Dorothy.

Nina made no reply.

Dorothy, sitting back, breathless, stared at the scene before her. Thoughts fired through her like a speeded-up newsreel. Nina was a mother. She had a baby, red-faced, angry, vigorous. Living. Very much living.

She noticed the girls' packed lunches and Thermos flasks.

'Nina, love, I'll get you some tea in a moment. Come on, sit up a bit, that's it. I need to cut the cord.'

Dorothy pulled the tarpaulin up over Nina's legs. She had no means of cutting the umbilical cord. She looked around the barn, but nothing was to be found. Yet it must be cut; it was bloody, and dirty, and bad luck, she thought, if not cut free of the baby soon. Could it even be dangerous? The thought sickened her, for a moment, and she wanted to cut the cord now before . . . before . . . even though this baby was free. Free of his mother's body, safely. The cord now simply trailed between mother and son like a question mark. She had to be calm. She must look after Nina. If the after-birth would only come away, all would be well, probably. She pressed down on Nina's belly as hard as she dared, and the afterbirth gushed out in a bloody pool. Leaving it lying in the straw between Nina's legs, she pulled the tarpaulin back over the girl and her baby, poured tea from one of the flasks she had made up for the girls only that morning — a mere few hours ago, fresh then from her intimate encounter with the squadron leader, blissful in the short-lived afterglow of a momentous night.

Nina sipped tea, her hand trembling so much that Dorothy had to hold the cup for her. Piling up more straw behind the new mother, Dorothy helped her to sit up, lifted up her jumper and helped her to undo her shirt and bra so she could feed her baby. He suckled immediately, eyes closed, a picture of peace and joy. Nina stared down at him, half in horror, half in wonder. Dorothy wrapped her coat more firmly around Nina's shoulders, covering the baby as much as she could, tied the sleeves of her cardigan together so the baby was swaddled, and finally helped herself to a cup of tea. She realised she was trembling almost as much as Nina.

The barn door creaked open and Aggie, drenched in snow, entered, alone. She closed the door, headed towards Nina and Dorothy and stopped dead.

'What the blazes — ?'

'Nina had a baby. She was in labour. It's a little boy,' said Dorothy, and she could feel a wide and stupid grin slicing her face in two.

'A baby?'

'Yes.'

'A real *baby?*'

'Shut up, you bloody idiot,' said Nina. 'Can't you see it's a real baby?'

'But . . . but you're not . . . I mean, you weren't pregnant.'

'Oh yes, she was,' said Dorothy. She refilled the cup from the Thermos and handed it to Aggie.

Aggie took it, staring at Nina and her baby. 'You kept it a secret, Nina?' she said, breathless.

'I didn't bloody know, did I?' said Nina.

'How could you not know?' said Aggie.

'Aggie, she claims not to have realised. It can happen sometimes. It's not unheard of. Nina's not regular like you. It can happen.'

'I can't believe it,' said Aggie, shaking her head.

'Did you suspect?' said Dorothy.

'No.'

'No more did I. It happens.'

'Let's have a look at him, then,' said Aggie, leaning over her friend to see the baby, who had ceased feeding and was asleep, swaddled tight in Dorothy's gorgeous — and ruined — pink cardigan.

'Oh, Nina. He's beautiful . . . ' and Aggie cried, softly.

The cows shuffled their hooves, and Dorothy sat before them all, surveying this holy tableau. Nina, perennially unmoved, shrugged. The girl was pale, exhausted and in shock.

Dorothy recovered her senses. 'Where's Dr Soames, Aggie? Mrs Compton?'

'I tried both their houses, but nobody was in. Boxing Day, isn't it? They must be visiting.'

'I see.' She said this with a surge of something that felt oddly like relief. 'Look, we need to get Nina and this little chap home and in bed. How on earth are we to do that?'

'The tractor? I can hitch it up to the trailer and they can sit on the back. But shouldn't they go to hospital?'

'What?'

'Shouldn't they go to hospital?'

'No,' said Nina quietly. 'I'm not going nowhere. Get me back home, that's all I want. No one is to know, all right?'

'No one is to *know?*' echoed Aggie.

'Of course not. I'm nineteen, I'm not married. I've just had a baby. I don't hardly know who the father is.'

'Since when do you care about that sort of thing? Mary Knibbs had a baby, don't you remember? When she was only sixteen?'

'I do bloody remember. And her mum and dad booted her out and she went to a home for unmarried mothers. Don't *you* remember? And everyone called her a tart. And all her friends dropped her just like that, including you and me.'

Aggie looked down at her feet, sobered. Dorothy listened intently.

'Nobody is to know!' hissed Nina. 'Nobody.'

'We could ask Mrs Compton?' said Dorothy, wanting to be helpful. She felt she ought to be solicitous.

'That old gossip? Good job she wasn't in,' said Nina.

'But you might need medical help,' protested Aggie.

'No. I won't need help. Tell people I'm ill. That's it. I'm ill. I can't work for a few days. That's all.'

'But what about the baby?' said Aggie, wringing her hands.

Her anguish, Dorothy thought, was understandable.

'Dot will take care of him. You'll take him to

208

the adoption people, won't you, Dot? Nuns? Somewhere?'

'Of course I'll help you, Nina,' said Dorothy. That feeling again — was it exhilaration?

'I can't keep it,' said Nina.

Aggie looked from woman to woman.

'I need to cut the cord,' Dorothy told her. 'Do you have a knife?'

She did. Dorothy held the cord and sawed at it with the knife, and at last it slipped apart, jelly-like, a strangely lifeless amputated limb.

'Aggie, go and get the tractor ready, will you? Aggie? Go on, it's nearly dark now. It must be done. We need to get these two in the warm, in bed.'

'I don't like this. Promise me, when we get back, promise me we'll send for Mrs Compton? If nobody else?'

'First things first,' said Dorothy.

'If she dies or the baby dies, how are you going to feel then?'

'Neither Nina nor her baby are about to die, what a silly notion. You're being melodramatic. He's as vigorous as hell and so is she, despite appearances. But they need to get warm. I'll talk to you later, tomorrow. But now we must act. Please, Aggie.'

Aggie shook her head and left the barn without another word. She returned with the trailer hooked on to the tractor, the cold engine of which grumbled and whined like a child suddenly awakened from a deep sleep. She and Dorothy helped the exhausted new mother on to the trailer, hushing her cries of pain when she

209

stood up, Dorothy murmuring to her that, yes, everything 'down there' would feel bruised, battered, tender, for a few days. But not to worry, soon you will be in bed, and warm, and safe. Dorothy handed the tiny baby to Nina, covered them both in coats and the tarpaulin, gathered up the afterbirth and cord and scattered the bloodied straw around the barn. She climbed up beside the mother and child, placing the detritus of birth at the far end of the trailer. She would hide it under the hedge later.

Aggie drove them home, stealthily and slowly. And God Almighty, Dorothy was cold, perished, she realised, in just her skirt and blouse. But what could be done but get everybody home? Aggie drove on — no headlamps, of course, but the eerie light given off by the snow showed them the way — across fields, down the track, across the Long Acre and back to the cottage. Dorothy took the baby from Nina, and Aggie helped her to clamber down from the trailer. The party made their way gingerly and silently along the frozen back path to the kitchen door, Dorothy and Nina looking around furtively in this strange evening, snow everywhere.

In the dark, empty kitchen Dorothy switched on the electric light. 'Sod the blackout,' she said, but she instructed Aggie to make sure all the curtains in the house were drawn tightly. She lit candles, ready for when she would turn out the light, settled Nina on the settee with her baby, tucked them up in blankets and lit the range in the kitchen.

Aggie returned the tractor and trailer to the

yard. Still Dorothy could not believe it: Nina, expecting all that time, and nobody had known? Nina hadn't known? It seemed impossible — but, of course, there was a new baby boy to prove it.

Nina was a mother!

Dorothy shuddered.

Nina was not a mother. But she would learn, she would have to learn. Nobody is a mother until they have a baby, are they? she reasoned. That little boy, small and helpless, lying against his mother's breast, so peaceful, so oblivious.

Lighting fires, making tea, Dorothy's head pounded with fear, with shock, with unquestionable but baffling delight. She was feverish in her work, and this long night was only just beginning, she knew.

22

Dear, darling Jan,

Oh, my love, life sparkles today! You have been gone for three hours now. It feels like three decades. I hope you are enjoying a safe journey and are not stuck in the snow somewhere between here and Kent. I miss you already. I missed you before you left, before you got out of bed this morning. I even missed you while I slept alongside you last night. I shall never forget. I shall miss you always, while you are not here with me. This cottage felt like a home until you left this morning. I long to share my home with you, to share my life with you, to be all that my womanhood will allow. And dear man, I do not pray, as you know, but if I did I would pray each and every day for you, for God to return you safely to me. And I would pray that I could be here for you and be the woman you deserve. And I would pray for this war to end soon. Darling, I feel alive. Do you remember when I said that falling in love was like touching fingertips? It has happened, for me, and I hope, for you too. I am the most fortunate of women. Please write, and soon.

Yours forever,
Dorothy

★　★　★

Jan drove through the white landscape, faster than he should. He was very cold but he ignored that. It was so early and dark on this 'Boxing Day', as Dorothy called it. She was a beautiful woman, Dorothy Sinclair. Strangely girlish and ripe, and not young. Dorothea. Maybe, he dared to hope, Mrs Dorothea Pietrykowski, because he knew already, he had decided long ago, that she would be his wife — a feeling as immutable as the moon. There was no alternative for them. And she felt it too, he thought. Only a catastrophe could keep them apart. She could do no wrong. And so, he would not return to Poland. He would not, even if he could, which was impossible to foresee. He would stay here in England, this austere country, where people laughed, like his own people, where they had a strong sense of humour, despite all that was threatening them. He liked it here. He could speak the language well enough. And, he thought, this country would owe him after the war. The Polish squadrons were contributing so much at last, it would not be forgotten by this country that did so much 'by the book'. And the Allies would win this war . . . of that, now, he was certain. Hitler was a fool, and fools do not prevail. And Churchill was obviously not a fool. The war would be won. Somehow.

Driving away from Dorothy, he felt more alone with each rotation of the wheels. She was so warm. And he had felt so light and fluid, lucid, in her arms, with her legs wrapped around him, and he longed to be back in her bed. It had cost him so much to get up that morning, to stumble out into the freezing dark morning air, to wash and dress, eat her breakfast. Watching her as she so carefully sewed the buttons back on to his shirt, such a patient woman, how his love had risen for her then, her honey-brown hair shining in the candlelight. He realised she was certainly damaging her eyes while sewing in such dim light in the dark morning. But that was who she was, this most selfless of women.

Would she write to him? A proper letter at last? This time, he thought — he knew — she would write to him freely, with love and abandon. He could not wait.

23

We did Whernside today, Ingleborough tomorrow. Went to Bolton Abbey on Monday. So far weather is sunny and warm, aren't we lucky? We hope to do Penyghent if weather lasts, on Friday. Everything is comfortingly the same up here, just what we all love about it.

(A postcard of Hawes in Wensleydale. Sent to 'Mum and Dad' and signed by their daughter Abigail. This was found inside a 1946 copy of *Jane Eyre* published by the Zodiac Press, and a very good copy, priced at £12 and placed on the hardback fiction shelves in the back room. I was tempted to keep the book, as I had kept the postcard, but it sold quickly.)

* * *

It's a scourging late October day, that day in autumn where you finally understand that summer really is over. The wind is blowing hard, a cold rain is drifting across the churchyard. It's the sort of rain that seeks to slap your face and blind you.

I am standing at my father's grave. It's at the bottom of the churchyard, by the wall, where there had once been stinging nettles and a compost heap. I tiptoe through the graves, some

215

of them familiar from childhood. Mary Sarah Wight, beloved daughter, sister, niece, wife, aunt, mother, grandmother, great-grandmother and friend, 1868 to 1967. That was always my favourite. I always thought, what an amazing life Mary Sarah Wight must have led. To be all those things, to all those people, for all that time.

I stand now, alone in this bleak churchyard, and I feel so small. It frightens me. I had not spoken to my dad about . . . certain things . . . and now we can never speak again. He died a fortnight ago. The decline was sudden and swift. The breathing problem returned, only much worse. He was rushed to hospital. And there he stayed for four days, begging all the while to be allowed home to die. I backed him up, and finally I took him home. A kindly nurse called Lisa came to Dad's house and brought oxygen, showing me how to help him use it. She administered morphine and other drugs. They, all of them — Dr Moore, Lisa, a couple of Dad's friends — wanted him in the hospice, it was 'the best place for him'. But when I discussed it with Dad, while he could still reason and say what he wanted, he refused. So I refused too. And between us, somehow, Lisa the nurse and I looked after Dad. And how strange it was. I became familiar with my father's body, his bodily functions. I washed him, brushed his teeth, combed his hair, washed the bedlinen when it was soiled, dressed him, undressed him. I had to be like a wife to him. Lisa and I were with him when he died. It was swift, in the end, and merciful. Lisa said she had witnessed far worse deaths.

I felt no shock, at first not even any sadness. Then, that night after his death, trying to sleep, I realised I had not phoned anybody to tell them the news. There were a few friends, a few former work colleagues, from his days at Pietrykowski and Wallace, but I would gather myself and ring them in the morning. In fact, I would email most people, which was so much easier and safer. My voice would not hold out, I feared, over the telephone. They were all the sort of people who would not mind my crying, they would come to the funeral and say nice things about my father, and it would be truthfully meant, and it would even be comforting.

* * *

There is one other person to tell, of course. I think, I wonder if . . . I know I should . . . tell Babunia that her only son has died. We have never told her about his illness. Dad and I discussed it after he first told me he had it, years ago. We would not worry her; the chances were that she would die before he did. But she is still alive, and Dad is not. And it will take some thought, and sensitivity, and I seriously doubt I am up to the job. I have put it off so far. The time needs to be right. I need to feel strong first. And right now I feel as weak as a soaked tissue.

I've been going through my father's things and I have found his birth certificate, neatly folded and stored in a Manila envelope along with his decree absolute. And my Polish grandfather was alive, according to the birth certificate, on the day that my grandmother registered my father's birth, which was 13th January 1941. I can only assume my father knew this, as he must have read his own birth certificate. And she was already calling herself Dorothea Pietrykowski, which I think must have been an outright lie — the deed that Suzanne showed me wasn't drawn up until March 1941. Were my father and grandmother in cahoots? Did Dad know the full story? I wish I had pushed him, and got some answers. Because, of course, now, as I feared, it is too late, another piece of the jigsaw is missing and I may never build up the whole picture. Do I want to, though? I don't really know what I want any more. I seem to have become bereft of all my energy, as well as bereft of my father.

I miss him. I loved him so much. He was my friend as well as my father.

And if I expect anybody, anyone at all, to pull up in his car and find me standing alone at my father's grave in this whipping-whispering rain, to stroll over in a nonchalant yet purposeful way, to put his arm around me in friendship, as a colleague might do, and tell me how sorry he is, and offer to buy cakes, and make a sweet, hearty mug of tea, and make me laugh with a pithy and sardonic comment about the inexplicable nature of death, or grief, or of life, I am to be disappointed.

Why do I feel this need to be rescued? I have lived alone, essentially alone, for sixteen years. By alone I suppose I mean without a long-term partner. By alone I suppose I mean without children. For most of my life, I have been without my mother. Now I feel tears blooming, I cannot stop them, and I know I am feeling sorry for myself, that most despicable of emotions. And I need a friend, I know this, I want a friend so badly. And by friend I mean lover, confidant, trusted individual, significant other. Maybe I even mean husband. Maybe all this distils down to that. I have denied myself all of this. I stand still, looking at the sky, the church, feeling the rain mingle with the tears on my face, and I cannot look into my future. I stand alone — for hours, it seems — and finally I recall myself, and I walk back to my car. I climb in, and I am so cold I cannot get the key into the ignition for several pained minutes.

24

Oh, but Nina was so cold. Dorothy put the shivering girl and her baby boy in the girls' double bed, and banished Aggie to the spare room. Initially, Aggie baulked at this — knowing what had only recently occurred in the room, and in particular the bed — but Dorothy told her briskly to help herself to fresh bedding from the linen cupboard and to stop being silly, for heaven's sake. Aggie found the forgotten dough set to rise in the cupboard that morning, and Dorothy told her to throw it away. It was a hell of a waste, but it couldn't be helped. Dorothy delved into the bottom of her wardrobe and retrieved the stack of nappies and pins she had bought two winters ago. They were huge on the tiny newborn, but they would do. She hauled armfuls of logs and a scuttle of coal upstairs and lit the fire in the double bedroom, then she dressed Nina in a flannel nightgown and bed jacket and put fresh warm socks on her poor cold feet. She piled an extra eiderdown over Nina, tore a bed sheet in half and swaddled the baby in it, and instructed Nina to keep him in bed with her that night, but to be careful. Dorothy helped her to arrange pillows and showed her how to wriggle down the bed so her head was level with the baby's head, meaning she would not pull up the covers and suffocate him.

Dorothy took to her own bed, but kept her

door open so she could hear each time the baby woke up. And each time he did, she got up, poked the fire and added more coal. Nina did not want to feed the baby. So Dorothy explained, with patience, that there was no suitable milk available and Nina would have to feed him if she didn't want him to die — at least, until they could get milk for him.

'Might be best if he did die,' said the bewildered girl, holding her baby awkwardly, but trying to feed him.

'Do not talk like that,' said Dorothy as she helped Nina to position him comfortably.

He latched on, squeezing shut his tiny eyes, his little body rigid with the richness of suckling his mother. Dorothy was wakeful, watchful, fearful, all night. She didn't mind the little boy's cries and whimpers. She thought these sounds had been taken from her forever. Nina was clearly exhausted, as all new mothers are, but she rocked him and fed him with Dorothy's help.

By the first light of dawn, as the cockerel announced its arrival, Dorothy was both delighted and dismayed to wake from a fitful doze to find Nina fast asleep, cuddling her little boy, also fast asleep, mother and child breathing in unison, pink-faced and contented. It was a vision Dorothy couldn't tear herself away from, and a rage ballooned inside her, a blind and fierce feeling of hatred and nausea. She was still rational enough to recognise jealousy, although she had never truly felt it until now.

She put on her pinny and made breakfast, and Aggie went off to work with a concocted tale of

221

her friend's illness, her vomiting, her incapacity. The need for recuperation. Poor overworked Nina, it had finally brought her crashing down. If anybody questioned her story, Aggie was to ignore the questions. On no account was she to tie herself up in knots. Nina wanted this baby kept secret, and Nina's wish must be respected. So. There it was.

Dorothy pulled her suitcase from under her bed, blew off the wisps of dust, and with trembling hands unlocked and opened it. Sidney's clothes were pristine and fresh, and the evermore aroma of dried lavender swamped Dorothy with the welcome surprise of a spring heatwave. She took out the bundle of Jan's letters and threw them on to her bed along with her notebook and pen. With care she carried the case across the landing to Nina's room, and showed her all the things she had once made. Nina must use them, of course. There was nothing else. Dorothy gave the baby his first wash — just a lick and a promise, as Dorothy's mother had always called it — with Nina looking on as she gently wiped the baby's face and neck and hands with a flannel. And as she and Nina dressed the baby boy, it seemed to Dorothy that this baby was a charmed imposter, animating the ghost-clothes meant for a different baby. A baby who no longer existed, and who might never have existed, he was so distant from Dorothy now. The clothes were a large fit, but Nina's baby looked well, Dorothy thought, his little legs kicking, his arms quaking up and down as if in joy at the lovely new clothes he was so privileged to be wearing.

Nina was clumsy and still in shock. She was feverish and trembling. Dorothy hoped she would not need to call in the doctor, even though she knew, yes, this should be done, really, both for Nina and for her little boy. It was common sense, it was the responsible thing to do.

She brought the tin bath into the kitchen, boiled water and helped Nina to bathe. 'Let me look after you,' she murmured.

The girl was cold, hot, shivering. But she pronounced herself warmer after the bath, and Dorothy helped her back upstairs and tucked her back into bed.

'You're a good woman, Dot,' said Nina. 'I don't know what the bloody hell I'd do without you.'

'Nonsense. I'll bring you some tea.'

Dorothy threw out Nina's bright red bathwater, rinsed the bath and refilled it for herself. She hadn't washed since the morning of Christmas Day, and part of her didn't want to, but she knew she ought to. She luxuriated in the water, taking time to soap herself and to slowly rinse it off with her flannel. Her towel was stiff and warm, and she allowed herself to stand in it for some time, wrapping it tightly around her body. In time she dressed, threw out the bathwater and replaced the bath on its hook in the wash house. There were chores to attend to, a baby and his weary mother to look after.

Dorothy remained confident. She was vigilant. Nina was hardy. She would pull through. She stoked up the fire in the bedroom. Babies need to be kept very warm, she advised Nina. And you need to be warm too, so stay in bed and look after the baby.

'He was Polish,' said Nina as she watched Dorothy put coal on the fire.

Dorothy smiled a slow, rueful smile of understanding. It might have been compassion. She hoped it was compassion.

'He was funny,' added Nina. 'I liked him. It's wartime, ain't it? I think he's the one that died. In the crash out the back. The one you tried to rescue.'

'Oh.'

'It couldn't have been . . . I don't think it was nobody else. Not at that time anyway. Do you see?'

'Yes, I see.'

'But that's no help to me. My mum and dad . . . I can't tell them. They can't ever know about this baby. Shirley. My brothers. I can't tell none of them.'

'What on earth will you do?'

'Have you spoken to the nuns yet?'

'No, of course not, you ridiculous girl! Oh, I'm sorry, Nina. Forgive me. You gave birth only yesterday. I haven't had time . . . it's . . . I don't actually know of any nuns. Nina. Please understand.'

'You can find out. You're clever, Dot. People listen to you.'

The baby, who Nina had named David, suckled in unknowing peace at the young woman's swollen and cloud-like breast. His hair was dark and sticking to his head, and he was blessed with the tangy, musky, minty, yeasty, orangey, earthy, other-worldly smell of the newborn baby. The smell was a drug to Dorothy, but Nina appeared unmoved.

'Nina, there is no real shame in having a baby, you know. Whatever the circumstances may be. A baby is a gift.'

'I don't care about that,' replied Nina. 'I don't want it. I never even knew I was carrying it. You believe me, don't you?'

Dorothy patted her free hand. 'I do. I truly do. I didn't know you were carrying him either, and I'm much older than you and I should have realised. There were signs that I should have noticed. You've been so hungry! You even fainted, do you remember?'

'I do. Rotten feeling, that was. Like falling off the edge of the world.'

'Just try to get some sleep, will you? If you want to get back to work this week, you must rest.'

'I am going back to work this week.' Nina's jaw was set stubbornly. 'But what about David? How can we hide him?'

'What do you mean, 'hide him'?'

'I don't want anybody knowing about him. Please, Dot. Not anybody.'

'Mrs Compton? She could look at him, make sure he's all right?'

Nina shook her head. 'No. After what happened with your little . . . oh, sorry.'

'That's all right,' said Dorothy. 'We'll keep her out of it, shall we? Dr Soames? But on second thoughts, he's terribly officious. I'm not sure he'd keep your baby a secret.'

'Not him, then. Nuns it is. Nuns know what to do with babies, don't they?'

'There are no nuns!' said Dorothy.

Nina wilted a little. 'Then what the bloody hell am I going to do? I'm not a mother. I don't want a baby. I'll be disowned by my mum. She always said to me and Shirley, if either of us gets into trouble, she'll never see us or the baby. She'll have nothing to do with us. She meant it too, I know my mum. I ain't going into one of those homes for unmarried mothers either. I've heard about them.'

'But you're nineteen, Nina. You're a grown-up young lady. You can do with your life as you choose. Think ahead, think about five, ten, twenty years from now. You'll be your own woman and nobody will necessarily know or care that your son was born illegitimately. People get over things like that. And besides, perhaps your mother will actually love her little grandson. Her first special grandchild.'

'Love him? She don't even love any of us, so why would she love a child born out of wedlock?'

Dorothy frowned. 'Nonsense. Of course she loves you.'

Nina snorted. 'No. She does her duty by us. There ain't much love to spare in our house. She hates Dad, and he hates her. She's always said, if she had her time again, she wouldn't get married and she wouldn't have kids.'

It didn't look good for Nina, Dorothy had to admit to herself. Her mother had not written to her since she had been at the farm — could she even write? Dorothy wondered — nor had her elder brothers. Her father, Dorothy gathered, was often drunk. How would the baby fare in such a family? The thought hung heavy over Dorothy like the snow-laden sky she glimpsed through the lace curtains, the large golden-black clouds once again threatening to disgorge themselves.

It was impossible. What were Nina's options, truly?

'I'll take care of him for you.' Dorothy wasn't sure at first if she had uttered the words aloud. But they resounded around the room, portentous, like a roll of thunder in the mountains.

'You?' said Nina, astonished. 'What, you'll be his mum?'

'If you want.'

The women locked eyes, both desperate, searching. Dorothy felt as if she were finely and perilously balanced on a mountain ledge, and if she were to let go, or stumble, she would fall into a dark and endless oblivion. She breathed hard.

Finally, Nina shook her head.

Dorothy looked at her, trying in vain to silence her heaving heart.

Nina opened her mouth as though to speak, and closed it again. But finally, she spoke. 'You'd be good to him? You'd look after him, properly? And you wouldn't care what people said about you, would you?'

'No.' Dorothy could barely speak, her throat tight with fear and anticipation.

'That's because you ain't afraid to tell people where to get off. Not really. You've got brains.

You can work people out. But I'm scared, I am, underneath it all.' Then, 'You'd really look after him?'

'Yes,' said Dorothy fervently.

'What, as if he was your own? How would you do it? Everyone knows you ain't been carrying. You're thin as a bloody rake. People will know.'

'People around here will, yes.'

'You mean, you'd take him away?'

'I have family in . . . well, miles from here.'

'I see,' said Nina. For the first time since Dorothy had known her, she looked as though she were deep in thought.

'What do you think?' said Dorothy, after a while.

'It sounds all right. Better than nuns. But I can't ask you to do it for me.'

'In that case, ask me to do it for your baby,' said Dorothy, taking Nina's hand now. 'I can't bear the thought of . . . David in a home, with no real mother. It's not what the dear little chap deserves.'

Do it for me too, Nina, damn it. Don't go all doubtful now, you oafish girl, not now it's within my grasp. I wrap my life around this longing.

'And nobody would know?' said Nina. 'That I was his real mum, I mean? You'd not tell?'

'I'd not tell a soul.'

'You'd say he was yours?'

'Yes.'

'You'd love him?'

'Oh yes.'

'You love babies, don't you? You miss yours.'

Dorothy could tell Nina wanted to convince

herself. 'I do. Very much.'

'So David would be the son you didn't have?'

What to say? What was she looking for? What to say now, not to destroy everything, not to ruin this chance, with the wrong words, the wrong tone, the wrong look. The words came to Dorothy, one by one, as if in translation.

'No, Nina, he wouldn't be that. I believe . . . I know that I can give David all the things you can't or won't be allowed to give. I'm fortunate to be able to give him a life you can't even imagine. I mean that in a kind way, Nina. I will have property one day. Money, I hope. There is a nice home for him, a bedroom all of his own. I shall fill it with toys and books. He'll go to a good school. He'll make friends. He'll want for very little. Of course, you can send him to the nuns if you feel that would be better for him . . . '

Nina looked at her baby, fast asleep at her breast, milk glistening on his chin, his breathing soft and calm. Dorothy watched the girl, then looked at the baby — who she knew she would not call David — and she prayed, as hard as she ever had, with all her heart, so hard she almost believed that somebody was actually listening and could help. And when Nina handed her the baby, dressed in Sidney's clothes, Dorothy took him in trembling arms, and held him close to her heart, and kissed his head.

Nina turned away to sleep, and stated that she would not feed him once Dorothy had sorted something else out, because milk leaked on to her clothes and she couldn't have people seeing that. It was embarrassing, and it would give her away, wouldn't it? Dorothy said she understood, and then she carried the baby downstairs and laid him in the big black pram that had been languishing and mouldering out in the shed for two years. She had brought it in, late the night before, scrubbed it clean and aired it by the fire overnight. She covered the baby boy in the blanket she had knitted once in such hope and gladness.

Unaware, the baby slept.

* * *

Practicalities took over. Dorothy would need to procure milk. She had bottles, bought for Sidney — Dorothy had planned to feed him herself, but Mrs Compton had recommended the purchase 'just in case'. She dug out the four bottles, still in their boxes, and washed them, enjoying the sensation of the smooth glass in her hand as she traced the odd bananalike shapes. She inserted the teats into the bottles, in readiness. She had never fed a baby before.

Bottles were easy, milk less so. Dorothy did not want to use the powdered milk she had heard about. It was unnatural. No, real milk it would have to be. But cow's milk was too much for a tiny baby, she knew. It would make him sick, give him stomach ache, or worse. Goat's milk? She knew it was nourishing, good for poorly babies. A wet nurse, even if there were any left these days, was out of the question.

Nina's milk would dry up. In a few days she

could return to work, and Dorothy could make arrangements. In a delirium of joy and fear, she stood, alert, gently rocking the pram. She felt — she knew, intuitively — that from this point on her life would be governed by falsehood. It would be so, and her life, with this baby, no matter what, would prevail above all else. There was no other future for her. It was laid out before her like a map, and she could trace every turn she would have to make.

She rocked the pram, and waited for the baby to wake up. Unbearable hope bloomed again in Dorothy Sinclair's heart. And she knew if her hopes were to come to nothing, yet again, the disappointment would crush her, finally and forever.

★ ★ ★

And Jan. She almost did not want to think about him. He had been but the briefest of interludes. Sweet, welcome and glorious. Just yesterday — *yesterday!* — he had been her great opportunity. Today, he was gone. It was inconceivable, but already she had another, a greater, opportunity.

And Sidney, her precious little boy, what of him? She allowed herself to worry that he might not like this new baby, this other little boy taking his place. But Dorothy knew such thoughts were illogical, irrelevant. Her secret was safe from Sidney.

The baby shuddered, and sighed, and slept.

25

Marshall

I hate you Rachel hates you we all hate
YOU so the best thing you can do is never
get in touch with us again do you hear me
you ugly little man? My sister and me, we're
going to be okay after all but not until you
are history so please leave us in peace to sort
things out we no longer require you do you
get that?

Jacqueline

(Letter found inside John Gray's *Men Are from Mars, Women Are from Venus*, quite a well-read copy, so priced at a reasonable 80p and placed on the self-help shelf in the back room.)

* * *

Portia fails to understand the grief that follows my father's death.

I weep, I rage.

She stares at me, cold and uncomprehending. 'Histrionics!' she seems to say.

I don't think I like cats very much. Why is she even here? Her mission in life, apart from irritating me, seems to be to wilfully destroy delicate life, birds and mice and shrews, such dear little trembling creatures. I make a note to contact the Blue Cross. Let them take her. I don't want her here any more.

I am alone in the world. My father is actually dead, my mother may as well be dead, and I don't even have Charles Dearhead any more to make sterile love to. I miss him, all of a sudden — because, I believe, even sterile love is better than no love at all.

And I no longer remember to eat. My clothes are becoming loose, my hair lank. I can't be bothered to hoover or dust, wash up or shop.

I fret, I sleep.

I dream that I am a little girl again, being bounced on my father's knees, squealing with delight, waving my hands around, too vigorously, scratching his cheek, but I didn't mean to — 'I'm sorry, Daddy' — and he's dabbing at his cheek with his handkerchief, annoyed, but telling me not to worry, little Robbie Roberta, and he tells my mother my nails need cutting, and my mother, sitting in her chair by the fire, her long hair shining in the firelight, ignores us. And now I can no longer decide what is real. She was still with us. Maybe it was the following day that she left? She didn't collect me from school. I waited and waited in Miss Romney's class, and she let me cut paper and card in the guillotine. Miss Romney remained bright and cheerful, but I knew she was worried. Eventually, Dad came into the class-room and picked me up and hugged me. He was crying, which I didn't like. He shook his head at Miss Romney, thanked her and carried me home.

I must be unwell, I have a temperature, I think. I feel aglow. A day in bed. That's what I need.

★ ★ ★

Day one: sleep. Sweat, a lot. The logical part of me that appears still to function underneath the raging tells me I have flu, a fever.

Day two: more fever, more sweating, Portia's endless complaining, my mother's sleek and shiny hair in the firelight. Nothing happens, but I think I feed Portia. I ought to feed Portia. My father has a gravestone, but it's written in a strange script that I cannot read, and it is high summer. The bees are buzzing around the honey-suckle that grows under my kitchen window. The bees are buzzing around me, swarming, hideous and loud. I think my phone is ringing, I think I hear a girlish and familiar voice saying she'll try my mobile. My mobile, plugged into its charger on the bedside table, rings. I can't move. It rings, it stops. I think I sleep.

Day three? Feeling hot and thirsty and weak, and hating Portia. She looks thin too, I think. And then I understand, she would look thin, I'm not feeding her. I ran out of her food, possibly yesterday, possibly the day before. I'm surprised she is still here and has not absconded to the neighbour who, I am fairly certain, feeds her regularly, just as she fed Tara. This could be day three, or day six, or seven. I can't count any more. And the awful truth is that there's nobody to help. I am alone in this world and living now among the fevered and garish rubble that once was strong and good, my life that I had once built for myself.

Day four, I think, or eight? The doorbell

ringing, and my not truly hearing it or connecting with it, and it ringing again.

My mobile rings. I grapple for it as it falls on to the floor. I pick it up, I can't read the name. Was it my father? Surely not my mother?

'Hello?' I think the voice is mine. Or maybe it's Portia's? She has been speaking to me recently. At least she is still here. I am not alone. Oh, she looks hungry.

'Roberta? It's me. Philip. Are you all right? I'm at your flat. But I guess you're not in?'

Philip? He's never been to my flat.

'I am here,' I manage to say. My voice sounds like a squeak. 'Hang on. Please.'

I stumble into the hall and, sure enough, there is the shadow of a real person through the frosted glass of the door. I eventually unlock it, and I stare at a man who looks exactly like my former boss, Philip Old, only more handsome. He stares back at me. The first person I have seen in four days. Or five. Or eight? Is it Friday? Somehow, I think, it must be a Saturday. The sun is shining like it does on Saturdays. It's bright, and shining frostily, like it does in autumn. Is it still autumn? I have been floating through the poetry of summertime. My Dad has a gravestone, but I can't read what it says. The language is foreign, it is gobbledegook. The honeysuckle is in full bloom. The bees torture my head, they crawl inside my ears and into my mind, colouring my world — ugly, visceral colours. My mother is so beautiful.

'Roberta, you — '

I think he gets no further. The world is folding

in on itself, I can't breathe, my throat is tight, I can't think or compute, but I know I'm slumping, and I know there is someone there to catch me, so I must let it happen, I must slip down into the unconsciousness which I know is waiting for me.

I can feel arms, I hear heavy breathing. 'Oh fucking hell!' somebody says. But whether it's Philip or Portia or myself, I don't know.

And I am gone. Into the darkness. And it is heaven.

★ ★ ★

I wake up in my bed. It's been hours, I think, since I faded out. I am in clean pyjamas. It is dark outside. I can smell coffee, cat food, toasting bread. I am not alone. I sit up, fragility keeping my movements slow and pained.

'Hello?' I call. I can hear Radio Four murmuring from my kitchen.

Philip appears in my bedroom doorway. 'Hello,' he says, his head on one side, smiling. He is eating toast.

'I don't really know what's going on,' I say.

'You're ill. You've been ill for days, I suspect. Sophie was worried when she couldn't get a reply on either of your phones. She rang me at home this morning. I came to see if I could help. You fainted on me in your hallway. Nutshell.'

'What day is this?'

'Sunday.'

'What time?'

Philip examines his watch. 'It's twenty-six

minutes past seven.'

'At night?'

'Yes.'

'What time did you get here?'

'Around two this afternoon.'

'I passed out for five and a half hours?'

'No, you were out for a minute or so. Don't you remember? I carried you in here, we changed you into your pyjamas. I tucked you into bed.'

'I don't remember.'

Was I wearing knickers? Unwashed for days? Had Philip removed them? Did Philip see me naked?

I blush.

'Don't worry, Roberta,' he says. 'Your dignity is more than intact. Besides, we've known each other for quite a while now, haven't we? So if I happened upon your underwear while helping you into bed, it's of no great consequence. Is it?'

'No.'

There is a strange silence in the room. Philip stands in the doorway, looking at me. I have not seen this expression before. He looks like he feels sorry for me. I don't like it much. I am relieved when Portia glides into the room and jumps up on to my bed. She purrs as I stroke her and hold her to my face, feeling her soft fur, reacquainting myself with her familiar cat smell.

'Thank you,' I say to Philip, burying my face in Portia.

'For what?' he says.

'For everything. Thank you. For being such a good friend,' and here I am now, crying, tears rolling down my cheeks, the cat leaping away because she has never liked crying. I notice she is no longer speaking to me.

Philip sits on my bed, puts down his toast and takes my hand in both of his. His hands are warm and buttery.

'I'm sorry about your father,' he says.

'I didn't tell you about him.'

'No. But everyone else did. It's a small town, Roberta. You should have told me. Why on earth didn't you ring? I could have helped. And I would have liked to have gone to the funeral. As it was . . . it was difficult. You and I parted on bad terms, I felt.'

'I couldn't . . . I don't expect anything from you.'

'I'd do anything for you, Roberta. Any time you ask. You may have worked that out by now.' He smiles kindly at me.

'No, I haven't worked that out.'

'Then you must be extremely dim.'

I have no reply to this. Philip is sitting on my bed, holding my hand, making what sounds like a declaration of loyalty, if not devotion. And I am scared and sad and feeling rotten and I can't imagine how I must look and smell. I wonder if he has emptied Portia's litter tray. I rather think I was sick in the bathroom at some point in recent days. I don't recall cleaning it up.

'Roberta. Look. We've been beating around the bush for so long now. It's all becoming such a bore. We've already wasted too many years in the sense that we have not been honest with each other. Whether from simple shyness or fear or

238

even compunction, I don't know. What I mean is, I love you like a sister. But that doesn't make me your brother, does it?'

I think Philip just uttered the words 'I love you'. Ambiguously, of course. Typically. But he's right, too many years have been wasted, too much time has passed, and if I were to die now — and, believe me, I feel close to that state — I know what my one overwhelming regret would be. I know this, I have admitted it to myself. I just need to find the guts to admit it to him, and now.

'I don't have a brother,' I say. It's not, of course, quite what I meant to say or wanted to say, but it will have to do. At least it's true.

'Would you have liked one?'

'Yes. Oh yes.'

'Me too. I have a sister. But she doesn't approve of me.'

'Philip?'

'Yes?'

'I love you too,' I mean to say. I am breathing hard and fast, and my heart is thumping like it has to be free of my body. And I'm sweating — but that doesn't matter, because I've been sweating for days. I have to say these words to this man, who is still sitting on my bed holding my hand. I have been quiet for too long, quiet and stupid. I deserve this chance. I'm going to take it.

But all I can manage is, 'Can I come back to work?' It's pathetic.

'I thought you'd never ask,' says Philip. 'Of course. But only when you're up to it.'

'Thank you,' I say. Nothing more.

'No, thank you.'

'Philip, does she make you happy? Jenna?' I feel breathless and charmed. Slowly, slowly I'm building up to it.

'Sometimes. It's . . . difficult.'

'I'm sorry.'

'I'm awfully stupid, Roberta. I'm a man, after all.'

'You're not stupid in the least,' I say.

'I don't find relationships easy.'

'Does anybody?'

'My parents did. I never heard a cross word between them all through my childhood. Mind you, I was away at school much of the time.'

'Boarding school?'

This is the first time he's told me anything about his childhood.

'Boarding school, indeed.'

'I see. You were . . . quite well off, then?'

'I still am, my dear, I still am.' Philip winks at me. He's not done that to me before. 'When one is fortunate enough to go through life with sufficient money . . . it should make life so easy, shouldn't it?'

'Yes, I . . . I suppose so,' I stammer, blushing.

He seems amused. 'Yes, well. Enough of this bullshit. I'm going to get you some toast, you can't have eaten properly for days. Then I'm going to leave you to get more sleep, but I'll bed down on the sofa tonight, if that's okay?'

I nod weakly.

And he carries on. 'I phoned Jenna earlier to fill her in. She's being very understanding, actually, and hopes you feel better soon. And don't worry about anything, I've fed the cat and cleaned up. I'll be here in the morning, and we'll talk properly. You're still feverish, but I need to know you mean what you say about coming back, and I want you to understand that I mean what I say. All you have to do is eat, then sleep. Do you mind if I open that bottle of Pinot Grigio in your fridge?'

I eat two slices of hot buttery toast, then two more. Then I sleep. I dream, drifting in and out of sleep. He loves me, he loves me not. Finally, I lie still, I close my eyes, I go over all that Philip and I have spoken about.

And he's here all night, watching over me, my friend.

26

Dorothy and her boy. He was dark-haired, skinny, alive, and together they were sitting on a riverbank at nearly twilight. The river moved softly, a water vole scurried from the water into his hole in the bank. She heard a noise like a thousand angel wings beating, but it was starlings, a huge flock of them, a murmuration swarming over the treetops, black, moving as one, this way, that, evening sunlight reflecting from a myriad of wings like shimmers of pure gold. Dorothy reached for her son's hand and he smiled as, together, they watched the birds, the mother and her son, hand in hand, contented and joyous. But there were no more starlings. Instead, there were crows, and they were angry. And in front of them, fleeing for its life, was an owl, its wings beating furiously, a fear in its eyes that Dorothy and her son could clearly see. Dorothy clutched her boy to her, cradled his head in her arms and rocked him until the terrible spectacle was over. And like all dreams it was soon over, half remembered.

★ ★ ★

But that day in 1939, the day of Sidney's birth, was never just half remembered, although she tried hard to forget. The pains did not abate.

She couldn't finish her laundry, and had to

leave Albert's Sunday trousers in the mangle, her undies floating in the copper, the soapsuds forming a scum on top. She sent Albert on his bicycle for Mrs Compton, who followed him back on her own bicycle, both arriving red-faced and tired. It was three o'clock in the afternoon, a warm, fresh day in May with a softening breeze. Mrs Compton bustled into the kitchen with a heavy-looking carpet bag, black and worn, which she placed on the table. Dorothy, sitting by the range, looked up at Mrs Compton.

'What do we have here, then?' Mrs Compton asked, hands on hips, looking down on Dorothy malevolently, or so it seemed to the labouring woman.

For surely this *was* labour, the pains coming and fading rhythmically, each one harder and longer than the last? It had been going on for six hours now, more or less, by Dorothy's reckoning. But she couldn't say exactly when they started, those first faint tremors, gradually turning to pain.

'You're quiet enough,' said Mrs Compton. 'The baby isn't on his way just yet. Get a nice cup of tea.' She looked at Albert, indicating the kettle on the range.

Surprised, he shook it to make sure there was water inside. There was.

'And then relax, eat, get to bed early, both of you. I'll come back in the morning. I'll leave my things here.' She indicated her bag with a tap.

Dorothy did, and did not, want Mrs Compton to leave. Fear of what was to come, the task before her, and dismay that the baby wouldn't be born in the next hour or two fuelled her anxiety. 'What if the baby comes in the night and you're not here?' she said.

'He won't, love, trust me, I've seen hundreds of women like you. And it's your first, he'll be a while yet. I'll come back nice and early, I'll come at six. How's that? Try to sleep.'

She left. Albert and Dorothy sipped tea, Dorothy catching her breath with each pain as it surged through her body, stinging the tops of her legs, crashing through her belly like a newly sharpened knife. After a while, they ate and talked a little, Albert eyeing her anxiously. They went to bed at nine o'clock, and he tentatively rubbed her belly until he slept. Dorothy stayed awake and wished forth her baby. The idea of the pains getting any worse was becoming inconceivable.

Dorothy listened to Albert snore for a while, until she got out of bed and walked around the house. She decided to be useful, so she returned to her wash house. In between pains, she finished off the laundry and hung everything out on the line to dry overnight. The night was warm, the breeze still present, it was a perfect night for drying. That task completed, she returned to the house, quietly retrieved the suitcase from under the bed and carried it down to the parlour. She took out all the things she had made for this baby, for Sidney. She was convinced the baby was a boy, so much so that she had not even considered any girls' names this time. She smelled Sidney's clothes, shook them, smoothed them and laid them out on the settee, trying to decide which outfit she would dress her baby in first. Then she packed them all away again and napped on the settee.

Around three o'clock in the morning, she awoke with a strong wave of pain, suddenly stronger, harder, and she doubled over, crying out. She feared something was wrong, some indescribable tragedy was surely unfolding inside her. The pain was unnatural. She woke Albert, sending him for Mrs Compton. Yes, she knew she'd said she would come back early, but she was needed now. It was only just gone three, yes, she knew that, but please, Albert. I'm scared. Albert thought her melodramatic, but Dorothy didn't care. It was happening only to her and so only she knew.

When she was alone again, the pains grew stronger, harder, more frequent and urgent. It seemed that Mrs Compton and Albert would never return, she would have to give birth on her own, it would be bloody, the baby would wail and she wouldn't know what to do. She struggled upstairs between pains, got on to the bed, and rocked on all fours, trying to keep up her breathing. She tried to focus on something else, the day ahead, whether it would be warm and dry. It seemed likely. She got off the bed, as the rocking motion and squeak of the castors were making her feel sick and reminded her of this baby's conception. She knelt on the floor, trying to concentrate, trying to remain alive and sane.

They arrived. Dorothy could hear Mrs Compton heaving up the narrow stairs, calling over her shoulder for Albert to boil the kettle.

'Hush now, Dorothy, all's well!' said Mrs Compton as she entered the room.

Dorothy did not realise she had been making any noise. 'It hurts. I'm scared.'

'I know, it will hurt, you're giving birth. It's all normal, and you will survive.'

'There's something wrong. Wrong here.' Dorothy pointed between her legs and gasped, she grappled for air, a pain sweeping over and through her. Was she being squeezed through her own mangle?

'Nonsense! There's nothing wrong here, nothing at all,' said Mrs Compton. She whisked open the curtains and lit candles, and she told Albert to light the fire.

And he did, glancing anxiously at his labouring wife, worried for her but also wanting to escape the confines of the birthing room as soon as he decently could. It was no place for a man.

Mrs Compton bustled and busied and prepared Dorothy, removing her knickers and making her lie down so she could examine her. Her hand felt huge and rough, without finesse. It wouldn't be long, she announced, washing her hands at the washstand. It was nearly time to push.

'I can't.'

'You can and you will. You want this baby born soon, don't you? Don't you want to hold him?'

Dorothy did. Of course. So when the time finally came, an hour or so later, Dorothy pushed.

She strained she sweated and screamed and cried out that she couldn't go on that it was impossible that something was wrong very badly wrong she knew it the pain was too much she couldn't bear it any more when was this going to end why was she in pain and deep in her mind Dorothy thought of her mother probably asleep now but she would be up later and dressed prim and proper sipping tea from what was left of the rosebud teacups that Dorothy smashed when she fainted and fell on them as a young girl in her stiff starched frock she would never forget that day she thought of Albert downstairs in the kitchen was he pacing was he listening she didn't want him to hear these animal noises she knew now she was making these screams and cries and grunts these desperate noises of a woman who is struggling to enter motherhood while outside her window the swifts were swooping and screeching who knows that despite what she is being told by the woman before her something is wrong very badly wrong and she wanted to kiss Albert suddenly kiss him hard on his mouth on his strong hard stomach because she hadn't done this nearly enough even though it pleased him beyond measure she wanted the pain to stop stop stop stop please stop stop then burning tearing ripping bursting burning burning the worst pain yet everything inside her was being propelled out of her she was on fire burning burning to death and then a gush an outpouring a slither and a small strangled cry that was not the baby and Mrs Compton in her haste knocked her bag and a candle on to the floor and she swore and grabbed the baby who was in fact born and purple and wet and she grabbed him and smacked him hard and a voice screeching

No! and the baby blue blue not purple after all but blue and small so small and black hair and slippery skin and Dorothy reached out for him and blood spurted from somewhere Dorothy thought the cord which was coiled around the darling boy's neck a serpent and Mrs Compton white-faced clutching at the cord, pulling it over the baby's head but it was tight too tight too constricted blowing into his mouth and gasping panicked crying for Albert to fetch Dr Soames immediately now hurry Albert something is wrong with the baby hurry Albert and not a noise from downstairs save the banging of a door and Dorothy lying back exhausted on her pillows all sense of pain all sense gone all hope gone because she knew yes she knew that this would happen it was written in her blood her guts she would not be a mother for long if at all and darling Sidney destined not to live in this world it was in his colour and his stillness the quietness of the baby unnatural and horrible and dead he was dead Dorothy cried out loud she thought and Mrs Compton sitting on the end of the bed holding the bundle blood-soaked and empty of life.

'I told you something was wrong,' said Dorothy.

Mrs Compton stared back at her, formulating a response, Dorothy thought.

'Nobody could know. It's nobody's fault. It happens sometimes like this, and I tried to free him. I did. It was too late. It happened before he . . . he was deprived. I'm sorry.'

The doctor came and examined the baby, then Dorothy. Albert did not enter the room. The doctor turned to Mrs Compton and instructed her to take 'the body' away, to wait outside, and on no account to show it to either of its parents. He would certify the death and take 'the body' to the hospital. He put his hand on Dorothy's shoulder and said he was sorry, my dear, and he instructed her to rest for a few days, and to let the milk dry up and let the blood dry up, let her wounds heal, she had torn a little. He left the room to speak to Albert, and a single anguished cry rang from the kitchen.

Dorothy stared out of the tightly shut window at the May blossom, creamy and curling this morning in the lush hedges, the blue sky looking so cheerful and knowing, but not caring that this happens sometimes, and it was a beautiful warm May morning as all the May mornings had been this year. And Mrs Compton, still clinging to her bundle with one arm, packed away her paraphernalia with the other. She blew out the remaining candles, they weren't needed any more, and she made for the door, bearing the bloodied bundle, not looking at Dorothy, not saying a word. She crept from the room with the bundle that was now hers, stealing away Dorothy's baby.

'Let me see him,' said Dorothy, her voice low and defeated.

Mrs Compton took one step back into the bedroom. 'No, love, it's best if you don't. You heard what Dr Soames said. You have to forget. They do say it's bad luck.'

And Mrs Compton left, cradling her bundle, pulling up the door behind her, dropping the latch with the sound of finality.

27

The baby was hungry. Dorothy arranged with Mrs Twoomey for a large jug of fresh milk from her goats to be brought up to the cottage each morning by her lad. Dorothy would pay a shilling a time, which she felt was a fair price. Could her lad please leave it by the gate? Dorothy was trying to keep the house silent, you see, so as not to disturb Nina. The poor girl needed her sleep, until she was strong again. Oh yes, she was exhausted, she had a terrible cold, headaches, vomiting. Dorothy thought it might be influenza. It was the season. And her nerves! The poor girl. And the coughing. No, no need to see a doctor, a few more days of rest and she would be fine. Thank you. Nina wasn't one for doctors.

Mrs Twoomey thought it odd, at first. But yes, she had heard that one of them girls had fallen ill and was recuperating. Hope she goes on all right. Strapping girl, that one, you wouldn't expect her to go down with any sort of illness. Mrs Twoomey's goats were fine goats, as she always boasted, and their milk was quality. Fed it to her eldest lad, she did, when he was a tiny baby, when he was barely alive. Got him through when she thought he was going to die. And look at him now. Oh! But she forgot. She was sorry.

'That's quite all right, Mrs Twoomey. I'm just grateful you can spare me some milk,' said Dorothy.

Mrs Twoomey told Mrs Sanderson that Dorothy Sinclair had turned up at her house that morning, begging for milk, looking peculiar. Mrs Twoomey had handed some over, and accepted a shilling for it, so where's the harm? But the look in that woman's eyes. She looks right through you. She was desperate for that milk. Always a strange woman, that one. And a little easy (which you wouldn't expect of a woman like her), so they say, especially where the Poles are concerned. All over the village, that story. For a woman of her years! She's still a good-looking woman, of course, to be fair to her. Not pretty, but pleasing on the eye. On men's eyes, at least. She has a sort of nobility. Rumour is she's head over heels, and poor Bert still alive, as far as anyone knows, and him coming back in November to patch things up. He got short shrift, they say. Well. We all know why, don't we? A red sports car was spotted speeding through the village on Christmas Day. Oh yes, Mrs Pritchard saw it, and her husband, he thought it was an MG, and very nice too, and it wasn't seen going back *until the following morning*. Mrs Pritchard doesn't see so well these days, of course, but she swears the Polish squadron leader was driving the car. They say Mrs Sinclair has taken it hard, him being posted down south, and he writes her love letters. And is *he* married? Not a very young man. Funny goings-on up at that cottage over Christmas. Those girls are tight-lipped, though. Worship her, they do. And now one of them is ill. That's why she wanted milk, she said. The big lass. Not the little pretty one. You'd think it would be the other way round, but there you are.

Mrs Compton listened to this gossip, and more, as breathless Mrs Sanderson rattled away, barely drawing breath in her eagerness to pass on any 'news'. And next, Mrs Pritchard, who confirmed the sightings of the red sports car.

Mrs Compton thought it none of her business. Dorothy Sinclair was a law unto herself. But she should pop in, perhaps? It was such a pity she was always made to feel so damned unwelcome. She knew by now that Mrs Sinclair did not want her there, probably because she still blamed her for the loss of her baby the May before last. But the poor thing was dead before it was born. Perhaps it had been dead for several hours, a whole day even. It had happened before, it would happen again. Mrs Compton recalled her own firstborn. A girl. Born dead. And Mrs Compton remembered that feeling of emptiness afterwards. For years afterwards, even with the safe arrival of five consecutive babies, Mrs Compton felt there was a hole in her life that only her first dead child could fill. And, of course, it could never be filled. It was a woman's tragedy. The years had gone by, and Mrs Compton rarely thought of it now. You just had to get on with your life and soldier on with what the good Lord saw fit to grant you. It wasn't your place to question Him. But still, Mrs Compton felt a strong sympathy for the Sinclair woman. It was compassion, she was pleased to realise. Poor Mrs Sinclair had a head on her shoulders. She didn't gossip. There was no malice.

She would go, just this one last time, to see if there was anything she could do. Losing a baby, and such a longed-for baby, that was hard on a woman. It could bring about such low feelings, low thoughts, for years afterwards. Mrs Compton understood this.

Yes. She would go. One last time.

28

Baby John, eight days old, was already chubby and rounded. His dark hair lay flat around his head, his cheeks glowed pink and his big blue eyes seemed to look at everyone and everything in a state of perpetual astonishment. Mostly they locked on to Dorothy, the woman who fed him, clothed him and rocked him. His little fingers splayed out as he waved his arms around in between his swaddlings. She found she was swaddling him less; the poor little boy seemed to prefer being able to move freely. She would not upset him. He slept now in her bedroom, in the crib Albert had made for Sidney. Finally, now, on the eighth day, she was bathing him. His cord stump had shrivelled and dropped off, and the time seemed right now to wash him properly. Dorothy buried her nose in his hair to breathe in his glorious baby smell. A smell that, she had to admit, was beginning to wane. He no longer had the intoxicating scent of the newborn.

She was nervous in case she dropped him, his body was so slippery. But he was still and calm in the crook of her arm as she washed him in the kitchen sink, so she stopped worrying and enjoyed the look of wonder on his face as she trickled water on his belly and head. He squinted as drops of water splashed into his eyes. Afterwards, Dorothy wrapped him tightly in his towel and sat with him in front of the range, cuddling him and humming to him. While he slept, Dorothy began to mentally compose the letter she would later write and post.

Nina was back at work on the farm. Her breasts were drying up, after swelling for a day or two and then subsiding like balloons with a slow puncture. Dorothy made pads for them, just in case, which Nina was careful to place inside her bra each morning. The baby had mercifully taken quickly to the bottles of goat's milk, suckling noisily and frequently, but in such tiny amounts that Dorothy was shocked he was still alive, let alone gaining weight. And so much of the milk was secreted, loudly and triumphantly transformed, into his nappies.

Dorothy made her plans. She would tell nobody. She knew where she would have to go, and what she would have to do. Nina, although exhausted, was relieved to be back at work and had relinquished all responsibility for her baby to Dorothy. The young mother barely glanced at her son.

* * *

Dorothy had overheard, the evening before, Aggie and Nina talking. She hadn't meant to listen. Their bedroom door was ajar, hers wide open. The girls were whispering but, in the silence of the cottage at night, their voices carried.

'Did you really not know you were pregnant?' Aggie could not, it seemed, let sleeping babies lie.

'I said so, didn't I?'

'I know what you said.'

'Why are you asking, then?' said Nina.

'I just don't think I would go through the whole nine months without knowing. I don't see how any woman can.'

'I don't think it was nine months. Thinking back on it. More like eight. That's all I can say.'

'I'm your best chum, Nina Mullens, and I know things about you.'

'You don't, though.'

'You can tell me the truth. Didn't you have even an inkling?'

'No.'

'But you were in labour for bloody hours. Didn't it occur to you?'

'Nope. I just felt poorly. I was scared, I thought I was going to bloody cop it. I was as shocked as Dot when he came out. Honest.'

'Oh, Nina!'

'What?'

'I wish you were keeping him. Can't you think about it?'

'No.'

'You will regret this,' said Aggie, 'one day.'

At this Dorothy sat up in bed, clutching her knees, listening intently. Baby John slumbered in his crib.

'No, I won't.'

'He's your baby. Not hers! It's not right.'

Dorothy winced. But she could not stop listening.

'Why ain't it right?' asked Nina.

'It's not . . . I don't know. Official. She's going

256

to keep your baby and nobody will even . . . what if she treats him badly? You won't know.'

'Do you really believe that Dot is going to treat John badly?'

'David,' corrected Aggie.

'John. David. Don't matter to me.'

'What if her husband comes back? He'll know it isn't his, even if he doesn't know it's not hers.'

'Eh?'

'You know what I mean!'

'None of his business, is it? Besides, he ain't coming back. They fell out, didn't they?'

'But have you thought it through, Nina? I mean, properly?'

'I can't keep the baby. I don't want the baby. We've been over it a dozen times. She does want a baby. She can have mine. It's perfect for everyone, ain't it? Apart from you, it seems.'

'He's not a bloody doll!'

'Ssh! Keep your voice down,' hissed Nina.

'And where's she going? And when? She can't stay here. People will put two and two together. I'm surprised nobody's got wind of this baby already. I don't know. Perhaps they have.'

'Have you said anything to anyone?' said Nina sharply.

Dorothy's heart was jumping and thudding, and she wondered if the girls would hear her breathing, would know they were being spied on. She tried to breathe slowly.

'Of course not. I'm true to my word.'

'I haven't told either. And Dot definitely hasn't. There's nobody else. Nobody knows, do they?'

'I don't see how they can. But one snooping person calling round and it will be all over the village.'

'That's the beauty of it. Nobody comes to her house. Keeps herself to herself, don't she?'

'But what if the postman hears him crying? What then?'

Yes. What if the postman heard him crying? But it was taken care of. Wasn't it? It was seen to. She'd thought of it all. Hadn't she?

'He won't hear. You know she keeps all the windows shut now, and the back door locked. Stop mithering me, Aggie. She keeps him upstairs most of the day, you know she does. Nobody's going to hear. Stop your worrying.'

'What if somebody sees all the nappies and clothes on the washing lines?'

'Don't you notice anything? She puts all that stuff on the horse around the fire overnight. She's not bloody stupid!'

'Ssh!'

'Have a bit of faith. Like I have.'

'She's going to just leave, you know. I know she is. We'll come back one day and . . . she and that little baby, they'll be gone. You'll never see David again.'

'John. I'll never see John again.'

They said no more.

Eventually, Dorothy slept.

3rd January 1941

Dear Mother,

Forgive me for not writing to you for such a long time. Much has happened in my life.

258

Albert is missing. I am a widow, or so I must believe, and I have a child. Mother, the child is not Albert's, and in a way I think you will feel relieved to hear that. I now believe you were right about him. He was not good enough for me. The father of my child is a special man indeed. Cultured, intelligent, courageous. But he is in danger, as so many are in these times. I hope that after the war, if all is well, we shall marry. He is a Polish man, the sweetest, kindest man I have ever met.

Mother, I would like to come home. With John, my baby. He is eight days old today. Please can I ask you to consider taking us in? The estate wants the cottage for others now that Albert is presumed dead. Your grandson is a beautiful baby and I know you will love him as much as I do.

I shall wait for your reply.
Your daughter,
Dorothy

★ ★ ★

John had wetted her lap after his bath, too long had she sat with him by the glowing fire, singing to him. She put him in a clean nappy and dressed him, then she put on a clean skirt and stockings. In a moment or two, John would be asleep. But until then, she was holding him tight, rocking him and singing to him some more. They were sitting in her chair by the window, in the parlour, and his gaze seemed drawn to the bright

259

snow-light streaming in from outside.

These days in January, the coldest and bleakest in the year, the month itself grey and white and interminable, always filled Dorothy with gloom. But not this year. This January, her days were filled with the utmost joy. Blissful in her new life, revelling in the motherhood that had at last revealed itself to her, its glorious sacrificial abundance, she was the happiest she had ever been. She was getting on top of her chores now, catching up with the estate laundry as well as her own. John still slept for much of the day, so she worked quickly while she could. Regretfully, her work was not as thorough as once it had been. But nobody had noticed, she hoped.

She rocked John and sang 'Summertime' to him — badly, she knew, but John seemed to enjoy it. And suddenly he had fallen asleep, as only babies can do. She placed him in the black perambulator and covered him with his soft blanket, positioning him closer to the fire, but not too close.

She knew that soon she would have to leave Lincolnshire, she would have to abscond with this baby. Aggie's overheard warnings from the night before filled Dorothy with apprehension. It was time to take action, to stop revelling in the beauty of the moment. She would not be able to take much with her. She made a mental list. And her biggest worry: How on earth was she to get to Lincoln station unseen? Or, failing that, at least arousing no suspicion?

She needed to get the letter to her mother

posted, but what should she do with John? She did not want to carry him, in case she was spotted, and pushing him in the perambulator was out of the question for the same reason. He was so very fast asleep, breathing quietly and evenly, sighing occasionally. Quickly, she put on her coat and her gumboots. She could get to the postbox and back in perhaps five minutes. She carefully locked the kitchen door behind her and ran, as best she could, through the crisp, cold air, the frozen snow slippery beneath her feet.

★ ★ ★

The ice sleeked itself across the path leading to Mrs Sinclair's kitchen door. Mrs Compton picked her way along it, slowly, slowly. She felt unsteady on ice these days; she wasn't getting any younger and she had a morbid fear of falling and breaking her hip. It happened to older women. Mrs Compton had cycled out to the cottage; it was only a two-mile trip, but it had taken her over an hour. Once or twice, where the roads were particularly slippery, she had pushed her bicycle. It was a relief to reach Mrs Sinclair's cottage and leave the bicycle propped against the hedge.

She reached the kitchen door and pushed it gently, just to see. She tried the handle. Locked. That was unusual. Of course, out of politeness, Mrs Compton always knocked when she visited, but she knew that Mrs Sinclair's door was usually unlocked — or, in the warmer months, ajar. But then Mrs Sinclair was alone all day, with no immediate neighbours. In her position Mrs Compton might have locked her door too.

She knocked again, and waited.

Was nobody home?

She had noticed that the lace curtains were missing from the window in the parlour, so she retraced her steps back round to the front. Gingerly stepping across the frozen grass, she shielded her eyes and peered through the window.

29

A photograph: a little girl in white socks and T-bar shoes, her hair in bunches, wearing with apparent pride a frilly dress whose colour must remain a mystery. A huge smile, with her two front teeth missing. Holding the hand of a woman, but a woman with no face, no head, just legs, a dark skirt, an arm and a hand, holding the little girl's. Nothing written on the reverse.

(Found inside Hilda Boswell's *Treasury of Nursery Rhymes*, very good condition, priced at £15 and placed on the children's collectables shelf. It sold the same day.)

* * *

Philip visited me each day while I regained my strength, staying for many hours, during which he cleaned my floors, cupboards, windows and fridge freezer. I hadn't been aware that my flat was so grubby. He fed me and encouraged me to shower and dress. On the third day, he finally left, telling me his work was done, and he said I could turn up at the bookshop whenever I felt like it, whenever I was ready. I wasn't ready for a while. I still felt feeble. I had weight to gain, skin to bring back to life. I was determined to look like myself before I returned to my old job and faced everybody. I took my time.

But now I am ready. Sophie hugs me, Jenna hugs me and Patricia, our new recruit, shakes my hand. Philip emerges from his office, smiling. I offer to make coffee. After I've handed round the mugs, Philip sets me to work. Today I am to go through the hardback fiction, remove all books that have been on the shelves for a year or more, and make a bargain shelf of them, all at half price. It's the sort of job I adore.

Book dust is a comforting smell, but it's bad for you. And I feel precarious, a little vulnerable. If I look around too much, if I move too much, these walls, these shelves, like living entities, will they turn in on me, will they sneer and jeer, will they see me run home in tears, laughing at how clumsily and slowly I run? Are these books actually alive, whispering about me, hating me?

Get a grip, I tell myself. For God's sake, Roberta. They're just books, and you're better now.

★   ★   ★

I saw Babunia yesterday. I thought it made sense to go to her before returning to work, before December really gets going. I went along with the intention of telling her about Dad, and took her flowers for the birthday I'd missed in November. She liked the flowers, but hadn't realised it was her birthday. Was she 108 now? she asked. Or 107? I said, something like that. And she'd had another telegram from the Queen. But she didn't think the Queen had really signed it.

'You look peaky,' she observed, looking at me closely. This I liked. This awareness, always so comforting.

'I'm fine, Babunia.'

'Have you been ill?'

'No! Just a cold. Nothing to worry about.'

'Even so. You must take care of yourself. You young things don't wear enough.'

'Look at me!' I gave her a twirl.

She eyed my thick polo-neck jumper, cardigan, jeans and boots, and harrumphed.

Aha, defeated!

'How's that son of mine?' she asked.

And I hesitated. What to say? She was so happy and sparkly and bright, like the decorations I was putting up in her room.

'He's fine,' I said eventually. 'A little busy with work.'

'I thought he retired,' she said, pulling a long piece of golden tinsel from the box of decorations, many of which were as old as me, if not older.

I took the tinsel from her and shook it out. 'Oh, he did, but you know Dad. He likes to keep his eye in.'

'I'm proud of him. My son.'

'I know you are. I am too.' To stop my voice from breaking, my face from crumpling and giving it all away, I wrapped the tinsel gently around her shoulders and kissed her forehead.

She laughed.

★　★　★

So I dust, I am happy, I am home again. And each book I examine becomes warmer in my hands, softer somehow, and I am pleased to be hidden away in this back room, with the French windows firmly shut against the gathering gloom of winter, and Sophie on the till, and Jenna and Patricia decorating the foyer with a Christmas tree and holly and ivy, and only the occasional customer finding me as I sit on the squeaky footstool cleaning books, repricing books, repositioning books.

An envelope falls out of a reprint of a 1949 edition of Elizabeth Bowen's *The Death of the Heart*, a novel Philip and I both love. I recall discussing it at length during the early days of my employment here. I pick up the envelope. It looks and smells new; the ivory-coloured paper is thick and watermarked, linen, a high-quality envelope. It is sealed. I turn it over in my hands. It is addressed to 'Roberta'. And, of course, it takes me a few seconds to digest that this letter is for me.

30

Dorothy, running back to the cottage, stopped in her tracks as she reached her front gate. She let out a small involuntary scream, at which Mrs Compton, standing at the parlour window, turned towards her.

John cried out too, short and sharp and clear as the day's crisp air, despite the glass separating him from the two aghast women.

Dorothy stared at Mrs Compton. Mrs Compton stared at Dorothy. Neither woman spoke, nor blinked. Whose move it was, neither knew.

Oh God, no, this could not be, not now. So close now, to John. So close to her plans coming to fruition, so close to fulfilling her long-held dream, so close to the happiness she had stopped believing could ever be hers. And this woman, this awful woman, her own living *nemesis*, staring through the parlour window, the clear window stripped of its smoky-yellow lace early that morning, the curtains drying now on the horse in the kitchen, this odious woman staring at the huge black perambulator in which the baby was now awake and screaming, in innocence and without guile.

What could Dorothy do? Did she have the gumption to tell this woman what she truly wanted to tell her? But what was the use? It was too late. She could see. The woman had eyes

— oh, how she had eyes — and Dorothy closed the gate behind her, marched to the kitchen door and unlocked it. She sensed Mrs Compton following her, and felt as tethered as a dog on a lead.

She slammed the kitchen door behind her and locked it.

'Dorothy?' called Mrs Compton, her voice only slightly muffled by the door. 'Dorothy? Let me in. Please? I'm not going to . . . it's cold out here. I've ridden on my bicycle to see you today. I've been hearing things. Worrying things. I promise I am here to help. Nothing more and nothing less.'

Dorothy ignored Mrs Compton and stumbled into the parlour. She picked John up, and he calmed quickly. She held him tight. Tears rolled down her cheeks as she cursed her own stupid forgetfulness, her carelessness. She stumbled and shuffled back to the kitchen door, slow, slow, trying to put off the inevitable confrontation. She held baby John even more tightly to her.

'Cold!' pronounced Mrs Compton briskly when Dorothy finally opened the door. Dorothy stood back, trembling and clinging to the slumbering baby, pulling his knitted blanket closer to him.

What was cold? Dorothy wondered. The weather? Dorothy's reception? The house? No, not the house. Fires were glowing in all the grates.

Dorothy laid the baby, now sound asleep again, back in his perambulator, and wheeled it into the kitchen where it loomed large and black in the corner. She made tea, hastily, barely giving it time to steep, and poured a cup for each of them with hands still shaking. Mrs Compton affected not to notice, and sipped. The clock ticked. Small talk was made, more observations on the weather. Enquiries after Nina's health. Neither mentioned the sleeping baby, his blissful sighs, his sweet-whispered rumours erupting into the room.

When John cried again, Mrs Compton rose from the table, but Dorothy jumped ahead of her and stood in front of the perambulator, barring the other woman's way.

'No!' cried Dorothy.

'But it's crying.'

'I'll pick him up. You don't touch.'

She picked John up and rocked him, soothing his cries. She took him to the kitchen window and stared out into the whiteness of the day, and again she cried, soft and low. How strange, she thought, how strange that this baby was no longer a secret. His presence was known about — by the last person Dorothy thought entitled to know about him — and John himself was so unaware of the battles ahead. He wanted comfort, and he didn't care who knew about it or who comforted him. The awful truth: anybody would do.

Dorothy whirled round from the window to face Mrs Compton, whose face was a picture of confusion and concern.

'Please leave,' she said.

'Whose is this baby?' replied the older woman.

'It's a baby. Just a baby. I asked you to lea

269

— No. I'm telling you to fuck off. I want you to fuck off out of this house and never come back. Do you understand?' Dorothy could feel her cheeks blazing, both in shame at her language and fury at the thought of losing John.

'There's no such thing as just a baby, Dorothy.'

'He's mine,' she blurted.

'Yours?'

'Yes.'

Mrs Compton looked utterly baffled. 'But you're not . . . you weren't pregnant, were you? I saw you before Christmas. You were thinner than ever.'

'This is my baby,' insisted Dorothy.

'Impossible,' replied Mrs Compton crisply.

If they were stags — or rhinoceroses or even elephants — Dorothy thought they would have locked horns by now, they would have been grappling, fighting to the death. She was breathing hard and fast, and her heart was thumping in her chest like never before, harder even than when Albert had raped her.

Clutching John to her breast, she stroked and kissed his head, and couldn't prevent her tears landing in his soft dark hair. 'You are not taking this one!' she hissed, glaring at the older woman.

'All right, then,' said Mrs Compton. She seemed oddly calm, almost friendly.

'Is that all you have to say?'

'What else can I say?'

'Nothing, I suppose.'

'Please tell me about this little chap. Please. It is a boy?'

'A little boy. Yes,' replied Dorothy, warily.

'And how did you . . . come by him, Dorothy? Did you . . . ? Oh, God forbid. You didn't steal him?'

'Of course not.'

'I know how hard you took the loss of Sidney. It wouldn't be the first time a baby was stolen by a grieving mother. And I would understand, if that is the case. Really, I would. But,' and Dorothy noticed a new authoritarian tone in her voice, 'this baby would need reuniting with his mother. Have you thought of how she must be feeling?'

'Don't presume to talk to me about my Sidney,' snarled Dorothy.

'All right. But I do want to talk about *this* baby.'

'Have you heard of any babies missing?'

'No. I admit, I haven't. But that doesn't mean — '

'This baby is not stolen,' said Dorothy. 'You have my word.'

'So whose is he?'

'He's mine. I told you already.'

'We both know that cannot be. Is he a nephew, then? A friend's baby?' Mrs Compton's brow was furrowed with the effort of trying to understand.

'No.'

'Dorothy. Please tell me.'

'He's Nina's baby!' yelled Dorothy. 'All right? Nina gave birth to him. But she doesn't want him. Nobody is to know. I look after him. She says I can have him, if I want him.'

'Oh my!'

'Indeed.' Dorothy shushed John, who had

woken at her shout and was fretting.

'Nina's?' repeated Mrs Compton.

'We didn't know she was expecting. She claims not to have realised herself.'

'I can scarcely believe it. When was he born?'

'On Boxing Day. I helped deliver him, up at the North Barn.'

'Born in a barn? Like the good Lord himself.'

'If you like,' she replied, wearily.

'Well, I must say, you gave me quite a fright. I feared the worst, I really did. I'll get on to Dr Soames. He'll know what to do. Has Nina seen him?'

'No, of course not!' Dorothy was gripped by a new panic. 'Nobody is to know. Don't you understand?'

'You did say. But is Nina well?'

'I believe so. She's still bleeding, but she has no pains. She tore a little, but she tells me it feels like it's healing. And there's no fever. She's not particularly weak, just rather tired.'

'Why don't I have a look at her?' Mrs Compton spoke softly, a tremor in her voice Dorothy had not heard before. 'I've sewn up many a new mother. It's too late now, really. But I could have a look and make sure all is well?'

'And then what?'

The clock ticked and John began to mewl for milk.

Dorothy waited, her heart thumping and her breath coming in shallow pants.

'That will be between you and Nina,' said the other woman, eventually. 'You have your own arrangements in place, I am sure.'

Dorothy was unsure that she had heard Mrs Compton correctly, but the woman's face was kindly and placid.

'She wanted me to send him to the nuns,' Dorothy told her, stroking John's hair, gently jigging him up and down against her chest. He was becoming more agitated, the hunger of the newborn baby unbearable, edging him towards the point of no return.

'God forbid,' said Mrs Compton with feeling. 'Why don't you warm his milk? And I'll look at him properly. He looks well, I must say, but you never know. Is he drinking goat's milk by any chance?'

* * *

Mrs Compton pronounced the baby to be bonny and in no danger.

The goat's milk was agreeing with him, she could see, and yes, the more she thought about it, the more sense it made to keep all of this quiet. Nina, God bless her, was not the cleverest of girls, not even knowing she was expecting, and she didn't even want the little chap. She was not maternal enough. Some girls weren't. How old was she? Nineteen? Well, quite young still. And fond as she was of the good times . . . and Dorothy, you are, well, you are mature, and capable, and you have had such rotten luck . . . and any fool can see you love him already, with that love only true mothers have, love for a newborn. The ancient desire to protect. Nina could not be relied upon to have the sense

273

. . . she might, in time, find a husband willing to accept her illegitimate child, settle down to motherhood, do all right by her son. But the little darling needs that now, as well as in ten years' time. And Dorothy, you are such an excellent mother. You deserve this stroke of luck, this gift, whatever you want to call it. Just let me know how I can help. I can help.

And the morning gave way to afternoon, and the afternoon wore on, and the fires glowed in the grates and more tea was made; sandwiches were cut. The baby was cuddled, and fed again, and changed. And at three o'clock, Mrs Compton left, to return to the village on her bicycle through the sullen January twilight.

A pact had been made, secrecy assured, an unlikely alliance formed.

★　★　★

Days passed, in which nothing much happened. Each day seemed to remove Nina further from her child, and pull Dorothy closer to him. It was cold, day and night. The winter would last forever, Dorothy felt.

Each day she waited for a letter. They were anxious, long days.

Eventually, the postman came, and a small letter fluttered on to the doormat in the kitchen.

8th January 1941

Dear Dorothy,

I received your letter with surprise and delight. Dearest, of course you and your baby must come home, regardless of all that has passed between us. I find that this war has softened me rather. 'Life is short' is a much-used adage but, nevertheless, it is true. I am alone often these days and I must confess the idea of company, and a grandchild, is appealing. I shall expect you in your own time.

Mother

★   ★   ★

The office was large and austere, with oak-panelled walls and a ceiling like a moonless night. Dorothy hated the feel of the slippery leather seat, fearing it would prove treacherous and precipitate her on to the floor. She was sweating, though the room was by no means warm. The woman opposite her, huddled inside a thick cardigan, smiled at Dorothy.

'Well, I'm ready now. I need a few details.'

Dorothy gave John's name, her own name, her maiden name, her address, the father's name, his address, his occupation. She had written out the night before all that she was going to say this morning. They were newly-weds, she and Jan, she explained. They had rushed to marry before the baby came. It was wartime. People do rash things. Dorothy shrugged.

The registrar — a world-weary woman, by the look of her — did not react. She just wrote everything down, not looking up — except to query the spelling of Pietrykowski, of course. Dorothy had to ask her to spell Jan with a 'J', not a 'Y'. Her jumping bowels were more than ready to propel their contents from her body. She thought, for one awful moment, that she was going to vomit. She breathed deeply, and told the registrar that she had been a little unwell, very tired, since the baby arrived.

'And when was John born?'

'On the twenty-sixth of December.'

'And where was he born?'

'In a barn.'

'Good Lord.' The woman glanced up again at this, sharply, as if suspecting a joke.

'At Lodderston Hall Farm.'

'In that case, I'll put the farm's address as his place of birth. Heavens above, the poor little thing.'

'He caught us . . . he caught me unawares. It was very sudden.'

'I should think it was. But isn't that the best way? My poor sister laboured for hours with her children. I know which I would prefer.'

No further comments were made, and Dorothy left the office clutching John's birth certificate. She ran for her bus, catching it just in time, found a seat at the back, and opened up the certificate. It was there, in front of her, on pink paper, in blue ink. John's mother. John's father.

She had broken the law; the certificate was a work of pure fiction. Yet it was unequivocal. It was surprisingly easy.

And Dorothy felt strangely, truly *alive* for only the second time in her life. She sat on the bus, looking out of the window, knowing she would never make this particular journey again. A new excitement reeled through her, a fear, a huge shudder. She recalled the owl in her dream, fleeing the mobbing crows.

And if thoughts of Jan crept in, she ignored them. She did not want to hear his voice — his wise words, his common sense and, above all, his disapproval. She was going to take this chance, the chance of a lifetime, and nothing anybody could say or do would sway her from the path she alone had chosen.

She would sacrifice anything; she would sacrifice everything. She knew that now. That too was unequivocal.

★ ★ ★

Back at the cottage, John was asleep in Mrs Compton's arms. He'd had milk and two nappy changes, and in between he'd slept like a lamb nearly the whole time. He was no trouble, the little dear. Now. It was done?

Dorothy nodded.

'And tomorrow, you must leave, as we've planned. I'll be here at half past six sharp. Don't worry how I'll manage it, just trust me. You be ready to go. All will be well, Dorothy. You must not look back.'

31

Earlier than usual, Dorothy made sandwiches for Aggie and Nina and filled a Thermos flask. Not one each today, unfortunately, she explained. She had broken one of them; it was smashed to smithereens, what a nuisance. She would have to replace it as soon as she could. She said goodbye to the girls as normal, casually, bidding them to keep warm, checking they had their scarves and gloves. Wiping her hands on her pinny, brushing a strand of hair from her face. It was another day, just another day in this, the new realm of ordinary since Boxing Day.

Mrs Compton and Dorothy had decided it was best to say nothing. What if Nina had a change of heart?

Be careful. Tell a white lie. Tell as many white lies as you need to. Young girls can be so fickle. It would be inconvenient, to say the least. It would break your heart, Dorothy. Say nothing. Act normally.

* * *

Dorothy stood at her kitchen window and watched the girls pick their way across the Long Acre, two forlorn figures becoming smaller and smaller, finally disappearing. She cried, just a tear or two, feeling she would never see either of the girls again. They had been through so much

278

together, these difficult months of war, such hard work, losses and death all around them, bombs and crashes and heartbreak. Dorothy hoped, sincerely, that both girls would fare well. Somehow, in that part of her where sure and secret knowledge lodged, she knew they would be all right.

Dorothy made sandwiches for herself, wrapping them in brown paper, and hurriedly cleaned up the kitchen. She gathered up her essential items. In the suitcase she packed John's birth certificate, his clothes and blankets, and Jan's shirt. (She had sewn the final button on, but as yet she had not laundered or pressed it, wanting to preserve the scent of the man she loved. She could not bring herself to forget him, reject him, swap him completely for the baby who had taken her now for his own. She never would send the shirt to Jan.) She added the bundle of his letters, along with minimal toiletries and a change of outfit for herself. She packed her sandwiches in her shopping basket, along with John's Thermos of warm milk, the one glass bottle she had room for, some bibs, nappies, pins and powder, and his washcloths, wrapped up in a knitted nappy cover. Her purse was in her handbag, and she could at least sling that over her shoulder. She had two pounds, loaned to her by Mrs Compton. Once she was settled, she would repay the older woman. They had discussed money at length, of course.

At least she had no cumbersome gas mask, because she had not gone along to any of the fittings. Regrettably, she could not take the perambulator, impossible on such a journey; it would have to stay where it was. She wondered if she would be able to free up her hands enough to buy, hold and drink a cup of tea at the stations on her journey. It seemed unlikely.

Other worries assailed her: What if her mother had changed her mind? What if she were to turn her away? Dorothy hoped her mother would remain softened, upon seeing her little grandson, and allow her 'widowed' daughter to take up residence once again in the Oxford home Dorothy had been so relieved to escape from seven years before. The whole plan was pinned on this. This was the heart of the matter. Going home. Returning to her mother. A simple plan, an obvious plan. She could but hope that her mother had not reflected too much and had a change of heart. Dorothy knew she would have to tell her mother everything, in all probability, in the end. But she would think about that when the time came.

Mrs Compton, true to her word, arrived at Dorothy's cottage early, carefully timing her arrival to ensure the girls had left for work. She was driving Dr Soames's car. How she had procured it, Dorothy had no idea, and she didn't ask. Mrs Compton and the doctor were pretty thick. Perhaps she had concocted a story about needing to go further afield in all the ice and snow — complaining, perhaps, of the relentless cold of January, and a woman labouring and in need of help.

Before leaving the cottage, Dorothy wandered from room to room for the last time, looking at

all the things she would be l
was almost everything. S
and Nina would contin
at least for a while, perha
of land girls, and wondered
time to cook and clean and la
over the music box, wiping o
dust, lifting and lowering the
borrowing, always that, not a gif
find a way to return it. But she cou
would have to leave it for the girls to ta
And continue to enjoy, she hoped. Unti
be collected by its true owner.

In the feverish days since John's
Dorothy had tried hard to give no thought
Jan. Yet he was there, in her mind, her bod
trying to get her to notice him. He was impossible to forget. She could not conjure up for herself his face, his voice, the feel of his firm brown arms, she could not recall clearly the blueness of his eyes or the blackness of his hair. Already he was a memory from some long-gone era. She was sad for him, this dear man who had given her so much in the brief months of their acquaintance. He was her first and only lover in the true sense of the word. And if the baby had not entered her life in his haphazard, squalling fashion, she would have taken her future with Jan, probably marriage, a life together. There would have been no babies, certainly. She felt her body was now done with trying to bear children. This terrible atrophy would have panicked her just a few days ago. But now she had John, and nothing else mattered.

John. Jan or John.

hoice, if it had to be a choice, had been

★   ★   ★

Compton said little in the car on the way to
oln, concentrating on her driving. She did
unteer that she had taught herself to drive,
any years ago, against her late husband's
dvice. She thought she was a good driver, she
old Dorothy, but she didn't like it, especially in
the winter. Still, it was proving useful now. And
Mrs Compton smiled sidelong at her, a slow
smile of conspiracy.

Dorothy was trying to resist the urge to cry.
Leaving her cottage, her home of six years, was
not easy. It had been the scene of the major
events in her life — in this cottage she had lost
her virginity, conceived several babies, given
birth to one. She had lost her Sidney, fallen in
love with Jan and taught herself to sew and to
cook. Above all, it was the house in which John
had been given to her. She knew she would never
see the house again; she would never even set
foot in the county again.

At the station, both women looked around
nervously before emerging from the car into the
freezing morning fog. Mrs Compton insisted on
carrying the basket and the suitcase to the ticket
office and holding John while Dorothy bought
her ticket. Then Mrs Compton bought her a cup
of tea from the station cafe.

'You may not get another chance,' she said.

'Have one now, for heaven's sake.'

Dorothy thanked her and drank the tea hastily, and soon they were making their way to platform three in silence, the click of Dorothy's heels the only sound. It was early, she was catching the first train out, and there were no other passengers about, mercifully. Yet Dorothy was uneasy, looking around, licking her dry lips, clearing her throat. On the platform, Mrs Compton insisted on waiting with her and stood close to her, too close, like a guard.

'What's going on?'

Dorothy and Mrs Compton started as a slight figure in long coat, hat and gumboots stepped out from the waiting room.

'Aggie,' said Mrs Compton, moving to stand in front of Dorothy and the baby. 'What are you doing here?'

'Getting wise to your game, that's what. What are *you* doing here, anyway? She can't bloody stand you.'

There was silence on the platform for a moment, then Dorothy gently eased round Mrs Compton and said, 'Aggie, can we talk?'

'That's what I'm here for. That, and to stop you stealing Nina's baby.'

'I'm not stealing him,' cried Dorothy, indignant.

'What *are* you doing, then?' Aggie's expression was fierce.

'Giving him an opportunity. Giving him a life.'

'Rubbish. You might be able to fool Nina, but you're not fooling me. This isn't right, and it's probably against the law. I'm going to find out. If you get on this train,' and indeed it was now entering the station, steam and smoke and grit billowing around it, a low whistle announcing its arrival, 'I'm straight off to the police. They'll most probably hook you off at the next stop. Fancy getting arrested, eh, Mrs Sinclair?'

'I'm getting on this train,' said Dorothy stiffly, clutching John tightly.

'Go ahead. But you leave David with me, or just you wait and see what happens. I thought you were a proper person. I really did. But you're not. You're selfish and rotten and I hate you.'

Mrs Compton, who had maintained a fretful silence since the two women began arguing, now hurried to open a carriage door as the train halted in a cloud of steam and a spray of black salty grit. Dorothy shielded baby John, from the steam, from the grit, from Aggie, as Mrs Compton picked up the suitcase and basket and climbed up into the train. Aggie stood in front of the carriage door.

'Come on, Dorothy!' called Mrs Compton. 'Get on the train.'

With surprising speed and strength, Aggie reached out and grabbed the baby from Dorothy's arms.

'No!' cried Dorothy.

Mrs Compton leapt from the train, light on her feet for a woman of her age, and rounded on Aggie. 'You give that baby back.'

'No. I won't. She has no right to do this! It's terrible.' Aggie's jaw was set in defiance, her eyes blazing.

'You stupid girl,' said Mrs Compton. 'What do

you know about 'rights'? What about John's rights?'

'His name is David, and he should be with his mum,' retorted Aggie. 'She's not thinking, she's still in shock. At first, I thought she must have known. But now I reckon she didn't, and it surprised her even more than it did us. But she'll get used to it, being a mum. I'll help her, and so will others. She'll get by. But you, and *you*, both of you, you're taking it all away from her.'

'Please understand,' said Dorothy passionately, 'no harm will ever come to this little boy. I love him as my own child. He *is* my own child, and I will love him to my dying day. I beg you, please, Agatha, please do not go to the police. Think about the consequences. Nina will not bring up this child, you know that. He'll be sent to a home, an institution, at best he will be adopted by strangers. I'm giving him security, and love, a comfortable home. I'll give him an education. Everything.'

Aggie shook her head, looking down at the baby.

He gazed up at them all, eyes wide and unknowing.

The girl's shoulders sagged in defeat. 'What can I do?' she said, tears beginning to trickle down her cheeks. 'Go on, then! Take him. But shame on you, Dorothy Sinclair,' and slowly, sobbing, she handed John back.

Dorothy stepped up on to the train, followed by Mrs Compton. Aggie sank on to a bench, rooting in her pockets for her handkerchief.

'Good luck,' said Dorothy's unlikely ally,

gently stroking John's cheek. 'And good luck to this little man too. I'll take care of her,' she added, indicating Aggie with a wave of her hand. 'Perhaps you could send more money once you're settled?'

'Yes. Of course,' said Dorothy. She felt she ought to sound grateful. She *was* grateful, damn it. 'You've been very kind.'

'Nonsense.'

'Will it be all right, do you think?' cried Dorothy, suddenly gripped by anguish. 'What if Aggie's right?'

'It's going to be fine,' soothed the older woman. 'Think of the future, forget that silly girl out there. She'll not tell a soul. She's not going to the police, I'll see to it. Nobody will ever know.' Mrs Compton leaned in, and lowered her voice even further. 'I will never tell. You have my word. Think ahead, that is what you must do. Don't look back, ever. You have a glorious life as a mother ahead of you. Good luck, Dorothy.'

The whistle blew, so Mrs Compton hopped off the train and slammed the door shut behind her. Dorothy placed the remarkably unruffled baby on the seat, opened the window and leaned out. The two figures receded rapidly as the train pulled away, and she thought how small Mrs Compton was, how small Aggie was. Nobody waved. Then they were gone, swallowed in the steam and the smoke and the January gloom.

Soon Lincoln was gone too, and the train was in the countryside, passing between flat fields. Then came the first small station, with soldiers, aircrew, sailors. But there were no policemen.

She looked around anxiously, sweating, heart thumping. But the train eventually pulled away and on into Nottinghamshire. At each station they passed through, Dorothy braced herself for policemen, but none appeared, just more servicemen. The waits were agonisingly protracted, and she tried to remain patient. Her last train journey, as she had travelled up to Lincolnshire towards Albert and marriage, had been relaxed and easy, and the memory of that long-ago November calmed her, a little. But perhaps the police were waiting at Nottingham, where she would need to change trains.

But no. The change was harried, jostling, chaotic. There were more soldiers, sailors, airmen, an inexhaustible flow of young men, loud and raucous, and some of these young men — young women too — were heading for oblivion and some would still be alive in fifty years, she thought, and it was a horrible, horrible fact but somehow triumphant too, the triumph of life, its rampant arbitrariness. And now there was a lone policeman. As she walked past, carrying her baby, her basket, her suitcase, her handbag, he smiled at her, but that was all, a small sympathetic smile. So Mrs Compton must have 'taken care' of Aggie, as Dorothy would be 'taking care' of Mrs Compton. But she put such bitter thoughts to one side. She needed her mental and physical fortitude to carry her and John through this trial, to endure this long and momentous day. She knew that this was the most significant journey of her life.

But would she always be glancing over her

shoulder, expecting to be caught? Would she be afraid forever? Or would it heal over, this crack, this fear, this irrefutable knowledge that John was not truly her child and the whole world would know it?

⋆　⋆　⋆

John slept, milky and contented. The swaying of the train had lulled him to sleep, and she cradled him on her lap. She was glad, because after a while the earlier train had seemed to unsettle him — or perhaps he had just sensed her own discomfiture — and he had cried so much that Dorothy resorted to walking up and down the corridors with him. She had to push her way past servicemen, who were ever swelling into a large homogeneous group, lounging in corridors, leaning out of windows, sitting on kitbags, smoking, making jokes, nudging each other, one or two of them leering at Dorothy. Some were obviously perturbed by the crying baby. She recognised none of the faces on the train. She was anonymous, a freedom she knew she would seek for the rest of her life.

The last train of the journey, boarded at Birmingham New Street, was just as crowded with servicemen, just as smoky and dark and noisy. In the carriages it was stifling, in the corridors icy. Leaving Birmingham, Dorothy was offered a window seat, and a brash but polite soldier placed her suitcase on the rack above. She settled into the corner as best she could, and fed John his third bottle of goat's milk; the

Thermos had enough milk left for one more feed. Dorothy hoped it would be enough to pacify him for the rest of the journey, and prayed he would not need another change of nappy — having already changed three of them on dirty, rocking, cold corridor floors, she did not relish the thought of changing any more. She would not use the filthy toilets.

But what to do with the soiled nappies? They were in her basket, and they reeked. She wished now she had had the forethought to dispose of them in a rubbish bin on a platform when changing trains. She would have to do something about them now, so she smiled at the servicemen who looked her up and down as she pushed past them into the corridor, carrying John and the basket of dirty nappies. She put down the basket and forced open a window with her free hand. The blackening air whistled past her like a sudden wish for death, and one by one she threw the wet, filthy nappies from the window as the train rattled and swayed through the darkening afternoon.

*   *   *

At three minutes to five, the train at last pulled into Oxford station and Dorothy was able to disembark for the final time, carrying her suitcase, her basket, her handbag and her baby. She felt that now the journey was almost over, now that she and John had reached Oxford and were a long way from Lincolnshire, from Aggie and Nina and Mrs Compton — the people who knew her secret — he *was* finally hers. Trembling with fatigue and anxiety, Dorothy found a seat in the ticket hall, where she sat for a few moments, composing herself. John was asleep, and she held him gently.

A minute or two later, she left the station and entered her home city for the first time in seven years, marvelling at its old familiar grandeur, its air of insistent superiority. It was dark, cold, and the dastardly blackout had settled over the early evening. Dorothy knew she would have to walk home. She estimated it would take an hour or more to get to her mother's house in the north of the city, carrying everything. She was so tired, but she would avoid the buses. She could not bear the thought of another smoky and over-crowded journey. There was less snow here, she noticed with some relief, and the evening was milder than she had been used to in recent days. She walked past the Ritz cinema on George Street, with its queue of cold and war-weary people waiting to get inside its warmth and be transported to an altogether lighter, more sparkling world. She walked past shops, some of them familiar to her, all of them closed now. The shop workers were making their way home, as she was.

She walked. One foot in front of the other, one step at a time.

Be in the moment, she told herself. Be here, and now, and be thankful for it.

★　★　★

The house just off the Woodstock Road still looked the same, as far as Dorothy could tell in the dark. The front door, she thought, was still blue. She stood a minute or two, breathing deeply, preparing herself for this final hurdle, then rang the bell. John began to whimper. Her arms burned with the burden of holding him for so long, one-handed, with the suitcase in the other, and the basket and her handbag hooked over her elbows. It might be nice, Dorothy thought, to lay John down. It would be a relief to have that weight lifted from her, just briefly, to hand him to somebody else. She felt that, any moment now, everything — including John — would tumble from her.

Her mother answered the door. She peered through the gloom at her only daughter, seemingly without recognition. Had Dorothy changed so much? Then, suspicion clouded her mother's face. Yet the bitterness around the mouth was gone, although the lines were deeper. Her mother looked tired. Perhaps lonely. Definitely old.

'Hello, Mother.'

'You came?' gasped Dorothy's mother, a wrinkled hand held to her chest. She stared at the baby, who was mewling like a kitten, his little restless movements becoming stiffer, angrier.

Dorothy knew the mewling would soon become screeching. He needed milk, quickly. They had come so far. And he had been so good.

'This is your grandson, John. Mother, we've come home. Like I said we would.'

Dorothy's mother held out her arms and took

John, and Dorothy slowly lowered the suitcase, bag and basket on to the doorstep. The shock of suddenly empty arms made her feel light and insubstantial, as if her arms were floating, and she found herself in the queerly painful state of emptiness, after hours of burden.

'I'm in the soup, rather,' she began. 'But John's father is a good man. Make no mistake. He flies a Hurricane. He's a squadron leader, like Douglas Bader. Only he's Polish. He had an injury and he carried on flying. He's a brave man and he's very honourable. I was asked to leave the cottage. Like I said in my letter.' She stopped abruptly, aware that she was babbling.

Her mother had been ignoring her, cooing and shushing at the baby. Now she looked up at Dorothy quizzically. 'The house is not, perhaps, as you remember it,' she said slowly. 'Have you really come home? There are no more servants. There is not a great deal of money any more. Your room is as you left it, though possibly a little dusty. But nothing you can't manage.' Then she seemed to realise where they were. 'But what on earth am I doing!' she cried. 'Come in out of this cold, child! Whatever next!'

'Mother — '

'You're exhausted, my dear. The fire is lit and tea is on the hob. Perhaps I was expecting you? That's it, in, in, let's close this door . . . it still sticks, do you see? Oh, Dorothy, let's not mind what has passed between us. Mothers and daughters should never talk over the threshold.'

Dorothy stepped into her mother's house, and her mother shut the door firmly behind her.

32

'Happy Mother's Day to Mummy I love you soo much, love from Bobby': A home-made card with a child's drawing of a mother and a little girl, with a tree, grass and flowers and a huge sun in the corner. The writing inside is wobbly, up and down. It is sweet. I think the creator of this card could be another Roberta and I wonder if her mother regrets losing, or even knows she has lost, this precious card. I keep it safe.

(Found inside a mint 1950 Penguin edition of *Black Narcissus* by Rumer Godden, priced at £5.00 and bought by myself.)

★ ★ ★

I put the letter addressed to me in my handbag. I haven't opened it. It's from Philip — his writing is always recognisable — but I have no idea what the letter says, and I am too scared to find out. Stupid. But I fear I was too honest with him when he came to my rescue and I know, I fully expect, this letter is his way of letting me down gently. I can't bear the embarrassment of reading his rebuke, his explanations, however elegantly put. So, I'm ignoring it and carrying on as normal. As is Philip, it seems. You would almost think there was no letter.

Today is bright and cold. I make coffee for everybody once we have all arrived. Philip has decided he needs me to help him sort out his 'disastrous' office. It hasn't been cleaned 'properly' since 2001, he claims. He may be right.

We work together for an hour or so, diligently and quietly, as usual. There's a good deal of dust and clutter and piles of books, and we uncover many forgotten treasures, books that ought to be out on the shelves.

'Roberta?'

'Hmm?'

I'm dusting books. He's sorting through paperwork.

'Your mother.'

I stiffen. I stop dusting. 'What about her?'

'Did you, I mean, of course, I'm trying to ask, it's not my business but . . . does she know about your father passing away?'

Silence.

Eventually, 'I haven't told her.'

'Do you not think she should be told?' he says quietly, eyeing me over his spectacles. 'Would it not be the right thing to do?'

I look away from him. I do not speak about my mother. Philip has never mentioned her before, and I don't like it. 'I don't have anything to do with my mother,' I say, stiffly, continuing with my dusting. 'I haven't done for years.'

'Why not? Your parents were divorced from each other, you know. Not from you.'

'Is that so?' I say.

Philip looks at me sharply. 'Is it not?' he says.

'No. It's not.'

'So?'

'So what?'

'Would you tell me the truth? About your mother?'

The truth about my mother? What is that? My truth would certainly not be her truth. My truth is actually the frantic ravings of a confused six-year-old. But I'm going to tell him this secret, this thing of which I have always felt ashamed, even though I was, am and always will be entirely innocent of blame. This thing that has cut me in two all my life.

'It's all a bore, as you would say,' I begin.

Philip nods patiently.

'My mother left us when I was six years old, just walked out one day while I was at school. Dad didn't know if she was alive or dead for three days. She rang us after the police tracked her down, and she told Dad she couldn't cope any more with married life or with motherhood . . . with him, she meant, and me. I haven't seen her since then, and from that day my father and my grandmother brought me up. Nutshell.'

Philip is stunned. I can see realisation flood through him. But he has no idea what to say, and now I am crying, though I hate myself for it. So he gets up from his desk, walks round it, stands beside me and puts his arms around me. He whispers my name. He kisses me on my head, I think, I can't be sure. He rubs my back. And at that moment, of all moments, that most innocent of moments — far more innocent than secret (and unread) letters planted in books — Jenna bursts into the office to ask if we would like coffee or tea?

* ★ ★

Later, I show Philip the letter written by my grandfather. Embarrassed, stammering a little at first, I tell him about the parts of it that don't make sense, and about Suzanne's revelation. We are coming to the end of our big clean-up in his office. It's been a long day. I ought to talk to Jenna to explain. My mind is racing.

Philip scrutinises the letter, then hands it back to me. 'Why don't you just discuss it with your grandmother?' he says.

'It would upset her,' I reply.

'Wouldn't it be worth it to discover the truth?'

'Possibly. But I don't want to upset her. Obviously.'

'Did you ever ask your father about it?'

'I tried to once, but I didn't get anywhere. I got the feeling he knew things but didn't want to talk about them.'

'Well, so what if your grandparents weren't married? It's not the end of the world, is it?'

'No, I suppose not. I just hate the idea that her life has been a lie.'

'That's up to her, Roberta. Did she draw a war pension, do you know?'

'I don't think so. I'm not sure. I never heard her talk about one. But then if he was Polish, she perhaps wasn't entitled to one.'

'She wouldn't be entitled if she wasn't married either. It all adds up, rather. But she was married to this other chap, you say? Hmm. It's all quite a mystery, isn't it? Of course, that would appeal to you. But don't eat yourself up over it.' He sips

296

his coffee. 'I'm sure this Suzanne woman is telling you the truth. And you've seen the deed poll, you say? There's your answer.'

'Oh, I don't know what to think any more. It's driving me crazy.'

'It's been a hard few weeks for you,' says Philip, softly.

'You have helped me so much. I'm ever so grateful. Really.'

I wonder if I should bring up the subject of the letter I found and say I don't intend reading it. That actually I understand. And I don't need a letter to let me down gently.

But Philip waves his hand, and moves the moment on. 'Will you tell her about your father?'

'I couldn't bring myself to last week. She's lost her only son.'

'Hmm. Perhaps it would be kinder to say nothing.'

'I think so, but she asks about him every time I visit. I'm running out of excuses for his absence, you know?'

'Poor you. What about your mother?'

'What about her?' I snap, angry that he's brought her up again.

'Couldn't she throw any light on this letter?'

'Oh. I see. Actually, I don't know. I've not considered that.'

'Well, it might be worth trying to make contact with her over this, if nothing else. This business seems to be consuming you, rather,' and a strange look clouds Philip's face.

I'm not sure if it's something he said, or something I said. But he looks pink and flustered. Jenna enters the office and strolls over to Philip, snaking an arm around his waist and declaring herself very, very bored. Can't they call it a day? She'll cook. The office looks immaculate! She beams at me, with a smile that I'm not certain is really a smile.

I must talk to her.

From: Roberta Pietrykowski
Sent: 08 December 2010 20:25
To: Anna Mills
Subject: John Pietrykowski

Anna,
I hope you don't mind my contacting you out of the blue like this. If you are the right Anna Mills, I am your daughter. I thought I should let you know that your former husband, John Pietrykowski, died in October. He had been unwell for many years. He was brave and strong until the very end, avoiding hospital as much as he could. Maybe you can recall how much he hated hospitals? He died at home, and I was with him. I thought it only right to let you know.
Regards,
Roberta Pietrykowski

From: Anna Mills
Sent: 09 December 2010 18.19
To: Roberta Pietrykowski
Subject: RE: John Pietrykowski

Dear Roberta
Thank you for your email. I wonder how you

tracked me down. But, of course, nobody is invisible these days. I have also wondered if I would ever hear from you. I am sorry to hear about your loss, and I am not surprised to hear that your father was stoic in his illness and death. You have not asked me about my life, and that is understandable, so I will not volunteer any information. The people in my life know nothing of you.
Anna

From: Roberta Pietrykowski
Sent: 09 December 2010 19:52
To: Anna Mills
Subject: RE: John Pietrykowski

I have no intention of giving away my existence to the people in your life. Sorry I am such a shameful secret.
Roberta

From: Anna Mills
Sent: 09 December 2010 21.40
To: Roberta Pietrykowski
Subject: RE: John Pietrykowski

You are not shameful, Roberta. I have just moved on with my life in more ways than I ever thought possible and I bear no resemblance, on any level, to the woman that was Mrs Anna Pietrykowski.

From: Roberta Pietrykowski
Sent: 09 December 2010 21:58
To: Anna Mills
Subject: RE: John Pietrykowski

I understand.

From: Roberta Pietrykowski
Sent: 10 December 2010 19.03
To: Anna Mills
Subject: My grandmother

Anna,
Sorry to trouble you again. I still don't want anything from you, apart from some information. I wonder if you know anything about my grandmother, Dorothea, who I am sure you can remember. I have discovered that she was not married to my grandfather. Did she ever speak to you about this? And also, do you have any idea when my grandfather died?
Thank you,
Roberta

From: Anna Mills
Sent: 11 December 2010 09.34
To: Roberta Pietrykowski
Subject: RE: My grandmother

Roberta,
I guessed I had not heard the last from you. Dorothea and I were never on close terms,

sadly, but I do remember her quite clearly. She was a noble woman, which may sound odd, but I can't think of a better word to describe her. She did tell me, while I was expecting you, that your father was a 'miracle' in her life. And that she lost a baby boy before John came along. I have no idea if your grandparents were married or not, but I wouldn't be surprised if they hadn't been. Dorothea didn't discuss him with me, but I always got the sense that John's father was her lover. There was never any husband talk, if that makes sense in this day and age. To be quaint, I suspect your father was a 'love child'. I don't know when your grandfather died. During the war, wasn't it? John never knew him.

If you would like to meet up, somewhere neutral, I am happy to do this. I live in London. I won't blame you if that is not on your agenda, I will understand perfectly. The offer is on the table, that's all.
Anna

From: Roberta Pietrykowski
Sent: 11 December 2010 20.17
To: Anna Mills
Subject: RE: My grandmother

Thank you, Anna. I am researching the family tree so that is why I asked. Ancestry is fascinating, at least to me. I didn't know that my grandmother had an earlier baby. Isn't it odd

how we all keep secrets from those we love, or are supposed to love? She is still alive, by the way. She turned 110 in November. Tomorrow I am going to visit her. I will think about meeting up with you and I'll let you know.
Roberta

From: Anna Mills
Sent: 12 December 2010 12:11
To: Roberta Pietrykowski
Subject: Secrets

Roberta,
Your grandmother was — is — a deep woman. Sometimes secrets are necessary. You will find this out in life, if you haven't already.
Anna

33

Dear Mrs Compton,

I enclose an order for thirteen guineas. It includes the two pounds you kindly lent to me and some extra for A, if you think it will help. I do hope she will see sense over this. At any rate, I was not apprehended on the journey as I feared I would be. J and I arrived safely at my mother's house. The journey was long and arduous, as I expected. My mother is delighted with her grandson. She is less so with me, I think, but I am happy to say we get along well, much better than we ever did before I left. J has broken the ice between us and we are set to make a happy household, I hope.

I have registered for war work and Mother will take care of J while I am out of the house. I hope to be useful. The money I earn will certainly help Mother too, as her own source of income has practically disappeared. I wonder she had enough to lend me to send to you. Of course, I did not tell her what I needed the money for, and I shall work hard to repay her. My father left her money, but she has been using it for living expenses for many years now. I had no idea. I have suggested to Mother that we sell the house and buy something smaller, in which case we may leave Oxford. This would also mean my whereabouts will be less detectable, just in case. I know I shall live in fear of discovery all my life, but all mothers live in daily fear anyway, I have realised, even my own.

Thank you for all your help with J. I do appreciate it. Perhaps it might be prudent if you were to destroy this letter? I think it best if my exact location was to remain unknown. For that reason I am not including my address. I trust you will keep your side of our agreement, as I have kept mine.

Thank you again, and kind regards,
D

26th January 1941
Dear Jan,

Forgive me for not writing to you before now. I hope you received my last letter. It was written in a mad haste after your departure on Boxing Day. Was that really a mere month ago? Four short weeks that seem to me a lifetime — and in a sense, that's exactly what they are.

I expect I made a complete fool of myself writing such silly sentimental things in my last letter, things I can't even recall now. Perhaps you have replied? But I will not get your letter, because I no longer live at the cottage. I have left no forwarding address.

Darling, events took such a turn after you left on Boxing Day. I hardly know where to begin. So I'll just plunge in, as it were, and tell you everything. Nina, poor silly Nina, she had a baby. A darling little boy, on Boxing Day, after you had left. Do you recall she was complaining of feeling unwell that morning? None of us had any idea she was expecting. She claims she didn't know either. Somehow, against my better judgement, I believe her. I thought at first she was fibbing. How could any woman not know she had a baby nestling inside her? But she's not bright, I must be honest. And a large girl, as you know. And, if I can mention such a thing, she was irregular in her monthly cycle. So you can see how she may not have realised.

The little chap was born in the North Barn, among the straw and the hay and the sacks and the cows. It was positively biblical. He is a beautiful boy, born a little small, but in these few short weeks he has become plump and pink and healthy. I helped to deliver him — I was alone with her — and, Jan, it was incredible, and it has changed my life.

So, now to the crux of the matter. Nina doesn't want him. She seems to have no maternal instincts and, Jan, I have. I have them in abundance. You know that about me. I have taken the baby as my own. I have told a lie here and there, I confess. No doubt I shall continue to do so for the rest of my life. But Nina is happy. She would have had him sent to the nuns! I had to step in, don't you see? Her parents would have disowned her, she says, with the baby being born out of wedlock, of course. It doesn't do, as you know. Just think of the poverty this poor boy would have been brought up in. And think of me. I smile now, all the time, I am bursting with joy. Living with my mother again is hard, granted. But she has welcomed her grandson into her home and I believe she has welcomed me.

I have started work, making torpedoes. The day is long and it's hard to leave John, but my mother does a grand job of caring for him. She is a far better grandmother than she was a mother. I am not sure why that should be, but there you are. So you see, we get on all right. And, Jan, do you know, people will never again look upon me with pity in their eyes. I despised those looks people gave me, people who knew about my losing Sidney.

Darling, I know you will react strongly to this news. You will disapprove of what I have done, I know. But please try to understand how I feel. I have a child at last, to love and care for, and motherhood has eluded me for so long, I thought forever. And once upon a time I thought death preferable to life because losing my child was so unbearable to me. Now my life is almost complete.

But I dearly want you to be part of my life too. Dare I hope you had marriage on your mind, as much as I did? I'm sorry for being so forward but, Jan, I can be myself with you, and marriage is something I considered and even hoped for after our very first meeting. I didn't realise at the time, of course, but yes, it felt like you were my husband even then. Can I ask you to please think about it? You must know, and it is only fair that I tell you, that I will not turn back. I cannot. I have named the baby John, for you. I love him as I did my Sidney. He has become my son and you must understand it is impossible for me to give up this child whom I now hold so dear. I have to be honest with you, even though I shall be dishonest with everybody else.

Your music box waits for you at the cottage. I trust the girls will look after it until you are able to collect it one day. Will you? I wonder. It was a marvellous gift, thank you. I shall always love the songs of Billie Holiday, and whenever I hear her sing, for the rest of my life, it will remind me of you, and the time we spent together. It was a marvellous time, my dear.

Yours always and forever in hope,
Dorothea

★　★　★

Jan posted his reply to Dorothea. As he heard it flutter down into the pillar box, so his heart and his hope sank ever further. His life settled back down into its pre-Dorothea state, a state he could only think of now as oblivion.

This woman had soared so high in his imagination. Leaning his head on the cold, hard

pillar box, he closed his eyes, for a second
. . . two . . . three . . . four . . . five.

But no. He could do this. He began a slow
walk back to the squadron car. It was time to get
back.

Everything ached, everything was cold.

34

Dear Helen, How's it going at uni? I kind of wish I'd gone too now, things are a bit boring around here since you left. I went to the wedding of the year, and I have a report for you, as promised.

   It went well, I suppose. Arlene looked a fright in her frock, of course. And Craig looked, well, like Craig, the big-headed arse. Arlene's mother was totally blotto and cried loudly all through the ceremony, and she got even more pissed up in the evening. Darren looked daggers at Craig the whole time, I thought there would be a scrap once the booze started to flow, but he managed to control himself. Don't know what he ever saw in Arlene anyway. I think he had a narrow escape, don't you? She picked the wrong brother to marry, that's for sure. But hey, they deserve each other, I reckon. The disco was shitty, as you'd expect, and the first dance an embarrassment, I thought. But hey, that's weddings for you!

   How's it going with you?

   See you in the holidays, I suppose. Missing you,

   Vanessa

(Letter found inside a book club edition of Maeve Binchy's *Circle of Friends*. A fair copy,

309

priced at £2.50 and placed on the hardback fiction shelves.)

★ ★ ★

I disembark from the train at Marylebone station and bustle through the ticket barriers with everyone else, caught up immediately in the hustle and haste of the city. I pop to the loo, and afterwards I stand and look around me, trying to spot my mother. I have a strong image of her in my head, though I know she must now look quite unlike the slender young woman she had been when I last saw her.

I sweat, a little. My heart beats faster than it normally does. But why? She is the one who should feel nervous, not me.

And then I see a woman, petite, wearing high heels to compensate and wearing them very well, moving serenely through the crowds, smiling at me. She stands before me.

'Roberta.'

'Anna?'

'Yes. I could see you straight away. I knew it was you, I mean.'

We look at each other; I don't know what to say next. I have her eyes. But she is elegant, and I am not. I am tall, a little clumsy, a little bumbling. She is compact, graceful, contained. And I, thankfully, am my father's daughter.

'Would you like to get a drink?' she says.

I nod.

We find a table in the corner of the pub on the station, and she glides to the bar and returns

310

with two glasses of wine. All the while, I can't keep my eyes from her. She is hypnotic. She looks no more than ten years older than me. She is sensual in her movements, attractive and confident. Is this woman really my mother? I imagined her bitter and cruel, wizened, old. Not this. I am having problems recognising her, even though I know, I can tell, I can remember her. Her hair is glossy, an expensive shade of pale caramel brown — not at all mousy, like mine.

'I feel I owe you an explanation, Roberta.'

'Yes, please. I'd . . . like that.'

'But first I want to know how you are, what your life is like.'

'My life is good, usually.'

'I'm sorry your father died. He was a good man.'

'He can't have been that great, surely, if you felt the need to walk out on him,' I say, thrilled to have scored the first hit. She makes me feel like a child, which is not good.

'We'll come to that. I promise. But first, tell me about you. I have often wondered, so much.'

And I tell her, bit by bit, and she asks questions, and I answer them, and we have another glass of wine.

'So,' she says eventually, leaning back in her chair, fiddling with her wine glass. 'Your boss, Philip. He sounds very nice.'

'Yes, he's great.'

'Mm-hmm.'

'Jenna's nice too — his girlfriend I told you about. They make a good couple, I think.'

'Mm-hmm.'

311

I want to change the subject. My . . . Anna is looking at me with some sort of glint in her eye, and I don't like it. What does she know about my life? About my friendship with Philip? Only what I've told her and, well, it's nothing, really. And it's not what I came here today to discuss, anyway. And how can she be so composed? I'm your fucking daughter, I want to shout. Or feel that I should want to shout. But I don't really feel that. I know I'm a bit of a pushover at times, a bit naive, as Jenna said, but my mother is *likeable*. She is confident and poised, and I like having people like that around me. People like Philip.

'Can I have that explanation now, please?' I say, fiddling with my own wine glass. I feel slightly drunk.

She suggests lunch first, and yes, I am hungry, all of a sudden. She orders, pays and returns to our table. 'I'll begin at the beginning, shall I?' she asks.

It sounds light-hearted, but really it isn't. And perhaps, just perhaps, this is harder for her than it is for me.

'All right, then. I was young when I met your dad. Just twenty, and already married, can you believe that? My husband was a brute. A rough man, a bully, he left me scarred in many ways. Your dad was the opposite, so kind and gentle, much older than me. He was already an architect then, getting his career off the ground, and quite lonely, I always felt. I had an affair with him and he encouraged me to leave my husband. It caused something of a scandal in my family.

They seemed to think that Simon — my first husband — was this great guy, a good catch for me. Nobody could see, or they refused to see, what he truly was. I fell out with my family, and moved in with your father, and fell pregnant with you. I divorced my first husband, and John and I were married just before you were born. And you know, your grandmother, Dorothea, was never anything but kind and accepting of me, the situation, all of it. I'll always remember that.'

'So what went wrong?' I ask, so quietly I'm surprised she hears me.

'I went wrong, Roberta.'

'What does that mean?

'I shouldn't have married your father. I shouldn't have had a child. I'm not a natural mother, Roberta.'

'Again, what does that mean?' My voice is angrier than I intended.

We sit in silence for a few moments. I eat my salad, finish my wine and look around the pub, which is louder now, busier. I notice it is gaudy with tinsel and fairy lights. Everybody looks inordinately happy.

'What I mean is, I'm not mother material. I couldn't stand it. I loved you. But that was all. I couldn't bear looking after you all day . . . the boredom . . . no stimulation . . . being at home all day. I know it sounds horribly, horribly selfish.'

'If you hated it so much, why did you have me? You could have got rid of me.'

'I'm so very glad I didn't.'

We talk on.

She thinks I did the right thing to terminate my pregnancy at university. But she thinks I'll be a good mother one day. She says to have one child, maybe two, but not to subsume myself. Be me. Do things I want to do. Get babysitters. Get help. Be an interesting woman for my children to live with. I must inspire them.

'I let you down,' she says. 'As your mother.'

'Actually, the letting down part was when you left. I didn't want you to go. I don't know how you did it. You must be very . . . hard.'

'I am hard.'

'Well, it's not a good way to be. Dad was a nice man, you said so yourself. What did he do wrong?' My voice is wobbling and warbling, and the pain in my throat is proving too much as I fight tears.

'Shall we get coffee?' she says, putting her hand on my arm.

It's good to see there is still a spark of wisdom in my mother.

★ ★ ★

And later, after the tears, after a second coffee, I show Anna the letter from Jan to Dorothea. She reads it once, then a second time, frowning a little.

'What do you know about them?' I ask. 'If anything?'

'A little. I think I told you that Dorothea

314

confided in me once, many years ago, when I was expecting you. We had a little talk. I remember she lent me a dear little old suitcase full of beautiful baby clothes.'

'Really? Did you know Babunia changed her name to Dorothea Pietrykowski?' I say. 'She was really Dorothy Sinclair. The woman at her care home is adamant that my grandparents weren't married.'

'I think she's right. I think your babunia — God, I'd forgotten that name! — I think she had a love affair. I always assumed John was the result of that. Sinclair, you say? That rings a bell for some reason.'

'It's written on a label inside the suitcase, I think it must be the same one. I have it now.'

'Yes! You're right! I thought nothing of it at the time.'

I carefully fold up Jan's letter and put it back in my handbag alongside the unopened letter from Philip that I carry with me too. I should — I must — open it. Soon. I must face the music.

'I have to go now,' I say. 'My train . . . Do you know when he died? My grandfather? Did she ever . . . ?'

Anna shakes her head. She glances at her watch. 'No, I don't know. I think during the war but, well, perhaps not when she liked to claim. When did you last see Dorothea?' Anna stands and puts on her pretty coat.

'Last week. I try to talk to her but she's pretty confused most of the time. She keeps calling me Nina.'

'Nina?'

'Yes.'

'Is there a Nina in the family?'

'No, I don't think so. There is no family other than Babunia and me. You should know that.'

'Of course. She must have been a friend, then. Maybe you look like her. We all have that confusion to look forward to.' She grimaces.

Anna leaves the pub with me. She's going home on the Tube. I realise I know nothing about her life now, the 'people in my life' she referred to.

'Perhaps we could meet again, another time?' I ask.

'Yes. I would like that. In the New Year? Merry Christmas, Roberta. It's been wonderful to meet you.'

I stand and watch her disappear down into the Tube, before heading for my own train home.

35

Mrs D. Sinclair

(Inscription inside my suitcase)

★ ★ ★

When I get home from my trip to London, I retrieve the suitcase from the top of the wardrobe. I use it now to house out-of-season clothing, so it's stuffed with summer tops, shirts, shorts, sunglasses, a floppy floral sunhat, a swimming costume I stubbornly hang on to even though I wore it only once and it's at least one size too small. I take out the summer gear and toss it all on to the bed. Suzanne was right, I think. Babunia must have been married, and my grandfather must have been her lover. I have never seen any marriage certificates, any decrees for divorce or any death certificates. Only the deed poll showing her change of name. No wonder she was so sympathetic towards beautiful, twenty-year-old Anna. I look closely now at the label and, yes, it does look like my grandmother's handwriting — a younger, larger, bolder, firmer version of it. I wonder that I didn't notice on the day Dad gave me the suitcase.

I have so many questions and I cannot articulate them all. Why did she call herself Pietrykowski? To hide her shame? I do know that

317

many a woman has done that — women not actually married to the man they call 'husband' — to save embarrassment, to throw nosy neighbours, colleagues, friends, perhaps even family, off the scent. Did she marry my grandfather at a later date? If she did, why didn't Dad remember him? Did this Sinclair, her actual husband, die in the war? Was *he* really my grandfather? And, finally then, it's an unavoidable question ... who am I? I am called Pietrykowski, but am I really a Pietrykowski?

I notice the name label is peeling off, so I carefully press it back into place, smoothing it down, holding it firmly until the glue takes. I trace over the letters, lingering over them with my index finger, letter by letter.

★   ★   ★

A week before Christmas, and we're throwing a party for our customers. Philip's idea — uncharacteristic, but something he seems excited about. Jenna's gregarious nature must be rubbing off on him, I suggest to Sophie. She shrugs. Upstairs in Philip's flat, Jenna and Patricia are preparing trays of mince pies, bottles of champagne, orange juice, mulled wine, coffee. Nibbles and cheeses. The till will remain open until late into the evening, of course, and I think Philip hopes the whole soirée will generate sales. We could do with them, he says. But he says this every year, and we're still here.

The shop fills with guests, and Jenna looks so pretty in a pink silk frock and heeled shoes, her blonde hair softly curled, and Sophie is laughing, chatting easily with the guests, recommending books. Patricia is mingling, confident, loud-voiced but not jarring, her severely short hairstyle belying her warm nature. I think, yes, Philip must be pleased with the team he has built up here. The team works.

I am standing at the top of the wide stairs that lead to the upper floors. I've just closed the heavy shutters at the large window, and I'm surveying the foyer below, watching the guests circulating and chatting and buying, hearing the cash register ring. Christmas carols are playing softly on the shop sound system. The door behind me marked 'Private' opens, and Philip comes to stand beside me.

He hands me a glass of champagne. 'Cheers!' he says. 'Merry Christmas, Roberta. It's going well, don't you think?'

'Yes. Very well. Everybody seems to be having a good time.'

'And you?'

'Yes. I'm fine. It's a lovely idea of yours, Philip.'

'Actually, I can't take credit for this. It was Jenna's idea.'

We both sip champagne, surveying the scene below. A strange silence descends on us, and I know we are both aware of it.

Philip tuts, sighs and turns to me. 'Thank you,' he says.

There is a look of panic about him.

'What for?' I ask, quietly, scared that my voice will come out too loud and people in the foyer will look up, meaning Philip and I will be required to descend the stairs and be swallowed up in the festive throng.

'For putting up with me,' I think he whispers.

'For what?'

He leans in, I feel the brush of his face on mine.

'For putting up with me.'

And I see Jenna in the foyer, chatting to dear sweet Mrs Lucas. She looks up and meets my eyes as Philip leans in to me and whispers, his cheek brushing against mine.

★ ★ ★

A little later, Philip disappears discreetly into his office, and not long afterwards his girlfriend follows him. Minutes pass, during which I chat and laugh and recommend books, but secretly, truly, all I can think about is Philip. The touch of his face on mine when he whispered to me. How it made me feel. The smell of his freshly shaved skin, his hair, his breathy scent of champagne, and something else. Something new to me, yet unfathomably familiar. Something I know, perhaps from my dreams.

Jenna emerges from the office, flushed, sad-looking. I wonder what —

'Roberta?' she says, stalking past me. 'Would you come upstairs with me, please? Just for a minute.'

I follow her up the stairs, all the way into the hallowed space of Philip's flat. She flicks on a light switch, goes into the bedroom she and

Philip share, takes a suitcase from the top of the wardrobe and starts to throw clothes into it.

I stand in the doorway, watching her. 'What are you doing?' I ask.

'What does it look like?'

'You're packing.'

'I'm leaving.'

'Have you had a row with Philip?' I say.

'No. I've finished with him.'

'Oh, Jenna. Are you sure? I'm so sorry. Can I help?' I step towards her, instinctively.

'Help to get me out from under your feet, you mean? Out of the way?'

I step back again, stung. 'What on earth do you mean?'

'Oh, don't come the innocent with me,' she spits.

'I meant . . . can I help you to patch it up with Philip?'

'I'm not going to be second best. I'm worth more than that.'

'Yes, you are, of course you are. But I don't understand.'

'I have eyes and ears — and, despite appearances, I'm pretty smart.'

'And . . . ?'

I watch her nervously, as she opens and shuts drawers and cupboards, takes off her high-heeled shoes and flings them across the room.

'Maybe I'm not making much sense, Roberta. Let me help you out here. Philip is not in love with me. We don't have a future. I've just had it from the horse's mouth. As if I didn't already know.'

321

'But it's all rather sudden, isn't it?'

'So what? It's true, that's all that matters. He means it. He's in love with somebody else.'

'Did he say that?' I am aghast. I am full of wretched hope.

'He might as well have. I accused him of it, and he didn't deny it. I didn't need to ask who the lucky lady is.' Her voice is high and brittle, full of pain.

I look at the floor, my face burning in shame and anguish, disbelief and dawning hope. Jenna pushes past me and clatters around in the living room before returning to the bedroom and resuming her packing. She opens up a second suitcase.

'It's all right. I saw it coming. I . . . I haven't always behaved well towards you. I was the one who told Francesca Dearhead about you and Charles.'

My mouth drops open. She stops packing for a moment and has the grace to look embarrassed, but when she speaks again there is a defensive, defiant edge to her voice.

'I'm sorry, okay? I'll admit I wanted you out of the way, but I felt guilty as soon as I'd done it, and wished I hadn't. And you were so good to come to the clinic with me.' Her voice wavers on the edge of tears now. 'It's a shame we can never be friends.'

She's right, of course she is, but it's an awful, awkward way to end a friendship.

Her packing completed, she puts on a coat and a pair of boots. 'I'll get Philip to bag up everything else and I'll come back for it another time. After Christmas. Don't look so surprised,' she says, half kindly, half furiously, and she even rubs my arm. 'You'd better go and see him. I think he's waiting for you.'

She leaves the flat, descends the staircases, and — no doubt with a dramatic flourish — she leaves the Old and New behind.

★　★　★

Later — minutes, an hour, I'm not sure how long — I go back downstairs to the shop. Most people have gone. Patricia and Sophie are in a huddle at the till, talking earnestly, and they look up at me as I descend the stairs. I shake my head at them. I go to my handbag, which is hanging on a peg in the corridor where I left it, and take out my two letters.

I put one back, unread on this occasion, and finally open the other.

36

Dearest Roberta,

You have found this letter, obviously. This is something I feel must be left to chance. Of course, I'd probably end up simply writing you another one; better still, I'd be a man about it and ask you in person. But I know how much you like letters, I know you love to stumble across them, read them and keep them. I know how those glimpses into other people's lives fascinate you. So I am writing to you in the hope that you find this. And if this is all too much — or I've made a horrible mistake and you don't, in fact, love me as I love you — well, I'll just tell myself you haven't found the letter. Oh, the games we play.

Jenna and I don't have a future. It's sad, because she is not a bad person, and I haven't been entirely fair to her. But I don't love her, and somehow I need to get up the courage to tell her that. I will do so, in my own time. I hope it will be soon, because I don't want to keep up any pretence for longer than I have to.

Roberta, at some point in the future, when I'm free and you're free, I'd like to take you to dinner. I'd like to take you to several dinners. I'd like us to take a chance and see if

324

*we might not just be right for each other.
I'm in love with you, but I don't know how
you feel about me. You probably think I'm a
middle-aged fool.*

*I don't know when you will read this. But
when you do, come and find me. I'm here.
Philip*

★　★　★

I breathe deeply as I knock on the office door. I
clear my throat.

'Come in.'

I enter the office, close the door behind me.

Philip stands behind his desk. He looks at the
letter in my hand. 'Has she gone?' he says.

'Yes.'

'Is that . . . my letter?'

'Yes.'

'I knew you'd found it. It wasn't where I left it.
I thought — '

'I found it on my first day back,' I interrupt.
His face falls, so I hastily add, 'But I've only just
opened it.'

'Oh. I see.'

'Jenna was rather upset.'

'I know,' he says, sadly. 'I tried to be kind. She
wasn't totally surprised, so my conscience is
soothed a little. And she was sick of me and the
bookshop, she said. I'm dreary, apparently.'

'Do you mean it?' I blurt.

He strides round his desk, stands before me
and places his hands on my shoulders. 'Of
course I mean it. Jenna, she . . . '

'She was nice about it, really. She told me — '

'Listen to me,' he says, cutting me off. 'Jenna was an opportunist. She probably wouldn't see herself in such terms, but she was a gold-digger, I think, to be blunt.'

'God.' I don't know what to say.

He fills the silence. 'I can tell you something Jenna didn't know, though she clearly had some inkling.' He looks rather pained as he says, 'I'm extremely well-off. A millionaire. Several times over, in fact.'

'Oh,' I say. 'Well, thank goodness for that.'

Philip laughs. 'I'm actually the seventh Marquess of Monmouthshire,' he says, grimacing again. 'If I want to be. Which I don't.'

'I see. That makes sense.'

Somehow, none of this is surprising me. It's as though I'd known all along, or half known, half guessed. I have an image of Babunia, sitting alone in her room in the care home, her secrets folded and wrapped deep inside her like layers of sedimentary rock.

'Will nothing impress you, Miss Pietrykowski?' says Philip in mock exasperation. 'And you're quite wrong, it does not 'make sense'. It's bollocks. I don't believe in titles.'

'None of this is really my world, Philip.'

'And you couldn't give a toss, could you?' he asks hopefully.

'Not really.'

'That's what I wanted to hear.'

'Jenna — ' I venture.

'She had the good grace to stand down, as it were. And she had absolutely no idea about me, not truly. Very few people do. So here we are.'

I feel weightless, like I am floating an inch or two above the floor. I don't want to land. 'Indeed. Here we are. What happens next?'

'Let me buy you dinner and let's see how it goes. It's hardly a blind date, so I'm confident it will go swimmingly, but I don't want to stuff it up. Our friendship's a delicate thing.'

'Yes,' I say. 'Dinner would be nice.'

'Tomorrow night? Or whenever you can make it. I don't want to rush you. The new bistro? Candlelight and all that? If it's too much, just say so, and we'll go to the cinema or whatever. I really don't mind.'

'It sounds lovely, Philip. Tomorrow. It's a date.'

37

She is listening to the radio again.

I bought it for her as a Christmas present after Suzanne told me she no longer showed any interest in the television. It's a DAB, but she asks anybody who enters her room to tune in her 'wireless' for her. She has not yet learned to trust herself to use it. She probably never will, Suzanne says. It's asking a lot when you are one hundred and ten years of age.

Suzanne is still spending a lot of time with my grandmother, she tells me, painting her nails, brushing her hair. Talking. In fact, Suzanne has some information for me. Something rather odd that Dorothea told her.

'I think it might be important,' she says to me breathlessly, on my arrival. She has intercepted me in the entrance hall, eager to share her news.

'Really?' I say. 'Can I catch up with you after I've seen Babunia?'

She looks a little crestfallen, but I know she understands. I want to glean information myself, if it's possible, if my grandmother is in the right frame of mind. It wouldn't be right for Suzanne to snoop for me. She will be my last resort. I owe Babunia that.

I close the door of her room quietly behind me and smile at Babunia. She turned when she heard the door opening; she is remarkably alert today, which is lovely to see. A warm spring breeze wafts through her room from the open window. In the garden, children scream and run around. It's another resident's birthday, and her family are all visiting.

I pull up the footstool and sit before my grandmother. 'Good morning,' I say.

'Shh. Please.' She gestures at the radio.

'Shall I brush your hair? No? Shall I paint your nails, then? I've brought you some red polish.'

'If you like. Quietly, though. Please.'

Suzanne has started a vanity box, filled with nail polishes, lipsticks, eye shadows, Olay, cotton wool, cleansing lotion, hand cream . . . no matter her age, she maintains, a woman likes to be pampered. So I thought I'd start 'doing' Babunia's nails too. I set to work. The skin of her large hands is red and wrinkled, the nails yellow and brittle. Years of doing laundry, she always tells me.

'Is your father here?' she says now.

'No, not today. He's busy.'

'Oh, what a pity. He hasn't visited me in such a long time.'

'I know, Babunia. But he sends his love.'

'How's that wife of his?'

'Anna? Oh, you know. Gone. She left years ago, remember? When I was six?'

'That doesn't surprise me. I don't trust her one bit. She's a nice enough young woman, but . . . '

It's a strange kind of lucidity. But I'm getting used to it. As a matter of fact, I know that Anna is well; we met for lunch in London again last week. But I don't tell Babunia that, mainly because I think it will confuse her.

I have completed the nails of one hand. I adjust the stool and take up her other hand. Red suits her, despite her advanced years. The radio programme is about Billie Holiday. I half listen to the story of her infamous life. Insistent jazz music seeps from the radio and dances around the room on the breeze.

'I know this one!' I say. 'Are you still a fan of Bill — Babunia? Oh, what is it?'

Tears roll down her thin, colourless cheeks, and her lips are trembling. I continue to paint her nails, knowing that when you are crying the last thing you want is to be looked at.

'I always think of him,' she says eventually, in a whisper. 'When I hear her sing.'

'Think of who?'

'Him. When I hear her songs.'

'Do you mean John?' I ask.

'John?'

'John. My dad. Your son?'

'No. Not him. Not today. Not even Sidney, today. I do wish my sons would visit me!' she cries, suddenly animated.

Who was Sidney? Was he the lost baby Anna mentioned to me? Anna. The woman who is slowly becoming my mother again. Despite everything, I like her. She's funny and sharp and unconventional. There's a freedom in forgiveness. And she's thrilled for me and Philip.

'You don't have to tell me anything you don't want to, Babunia,' I say, taking a chance, opening the door, inviting her to confide in me. 'But I'm here to listen, if you do want to.'

330

There is a long, dreamy pause during which she seems to drift off from me, arguing with herself, in silence.

She frowns. 'My husband,' she says at last.

'He died in the war, didn't he? A long time ago, wasn't it?'

Silence.

I decide to jump in and say it. 'Jan *wasn't* your husband, Babunia, was he? It's okay, you know. Nobody minds.'

She ignores me. 'I don't think he died at all. Not then.'

'Oh.' I slowly paint the nail on her wedding finger. She wears no ring, and I can't remember there ever being one. Why didn't I notice this before? Widows wear their rings, don't they? 'When do you think he died, then?'

'I don't know, you see. It's not for me to know. But I always felt he was alive, breathing air just like me. It was a comforting thought. I miss him so much. Do you know, I thought I saw him once. But he didn't see me. And goodness knows, it probably wasn't him. He was with a woman with blonde hair. She was much prettier than I ever was.'

Babunia's hand shakes, but I squeeze it gently in reassurance, careful not to smudge the polish. I wonder if she notices. I sense she is somewhere else, a long way from here, and a long way from now.

'He was a good man, Roberta,' says Babunia finally, and she looks out into the garden where the children are frolicking in the sunshine, playing tag. But she does not see them.

331

'Of course he was,' I tell her.

'But proud. Like all men.'

'That's their undoing sometimes, isn't it?' I say, glad to have some common ground at last. 'Pride?'

'Often it is,' she says sadly.

'Do you miss him still?'

'Of course I miss him.'

'You didn't live over the brush, did you?' Sometimes it helps to keep things light, to make little jokes. Despite the endless confusion, she still has her sense of humour, subtle and quiet.

'No. We never lived together. He didn't want me to keep the baby. Was it so wrong of me? I never saw him again . . . but I don't think it was wrong. Do you?'

I feel drained, exhausted. Her words are off-kilter, like discordant music. *He didn't want me to keep the baby.* So she *did* have an abortion. I wonder. Oh, that pivotal, tantalising line in my grandfather's letter! What you do, to this child, to this child's mother, it is wrong.

'Oh. I . . . I'm not sure what to say,' I whisper.

'He wasn't my husband's child. But he wasn't even my child, you see. It was all rather . . . confusing. He was Aggie's. No. Not Aggie's. What am I talking about? Oh dear. Oh. What was her name? Nina! Yes, that was her. Tall girl, fat. Stupid girl, really, and I . . . oh, the poor thing. She was hopeless and helpless. I tried. I did. I told her. I expect she's dead by now. I'll never know if I'm truly wicked or not. I had an accomplice, but she was a witch. But he thought I was. I had to go home. I had to go back to

Mother's house. Do you know what I found under my bed?'

Mute, unsure of what to say, I shake my head. Did she help somebody else to have an abortion? This Nina she keeps talking about, this Nina she has mistaken me for on several occasions?

'*The Infant's Progress*. Of all the things. I'll never forget that wretched book. I put his last letter inside it. He told me off, you see, in his letter. I kept that book for years. I think it's gone now, and the letter with it. And I lost my temper with him and I burned all the other ones. I burned the blue ribbon. I even burned his shirt, Roberta, can you imagine? I had never washed it. All those buttons . . . what a fool I was. I should have kept that, I should have kept everything. I have nothing of his, nothing else at all. I lost him, you see. I was so angry he wasn't going to marry me after all. I was furious with him for years and years. I asked him to be my husband. Can you imagine? I thought he wanted to be my husband. But he wouldn't forgive me. I can't tell you how terrible it made me feel. He broke my heart into so many pieces. So small I couldn't find them and put them back together again. Just as well they're all gone, isn't it, really? But I don't regret what I did. John was worth it. It was right. We don't get everything in life, do we?'

Well, at least that makes sense. My mind is racing as I try to piece together all that she has said.

'Who was Nina?' I ask.

'Nina? I don't know any Ninas! Don't ask

questions. I can't remember everything . . . I'm not going to tell you!' and now the sad, wise old lady is a stroppy child again.

I know I have pushed her too far. So we sit in silence, listening to the radio, and I make tea. She sips hers with a shaking hand. I look at her and wonder if we shall ever talk again. She is barely present now, grey and thin as rainfall on a winter afternoon.

Possibilities present themselves to me. I don't like any of them, so I turn them away, one by one, like tiresome beggars. She was a marvellous mother, both to my father and to me. Nothing else matters. As Philip would say, the rest is all bollocks.

Philip. My fiancé. How grand that sounds, and how strange. I decide to tell her my news.

'Did I tell you? Philip and I are engaged.'

'Philip? I don't think I know a Philip.'

'He's a nice man, the very best, and we are going to be very happy,' I tell her.

She nods, seeming satisfied with that.

'We're getting married in August, and I want you to come.'

She raises her eyebrows and smiles. 'We'll see,' she says, with a flash of that wry humour I have always loved.

The programme about Billie Holiday has finished. I turn the volume down to a soft background murmur, half-hearted waves breaking on a distant shore, but Babunia doesn't seem to notice. Carefully, because I don't want to disturb her, I reach for my handbag. I find Jan's letter, now much creased and crumpled, open out the two fragile pages, smooth them flat and place them on the side table next to Babunia's chair. She has fallen into a childlike doze and, after undoing her chignon, I gently brush her long grey hair, over and over, until it shines.

38

And now that it was over, he had only vague ideas of what to do, or where to go. He was done with flying, and that was his only certainty, apart from knowing he would not return to Poland. Perhaps America? One day, yes, perhaps. But there were things to do first, here in England. There was unfinished business to attend to.

He drove to the cottage in Lincolnshire, and from the road it all seemed much the same. He fancied the same curtains were still hanging at the windows. Yet, on closer inspection, he saw that the garden was not nearly as well kept as it once had been. There were no hens. There was no laundry on the lines, although it was a warm day in May.

He opened the gate and shuffled along the path, and suddenly it was five years ago, and he imagined he could hear the woman's mournful humming. But he could not. He knocked on the kitchen door. It was opened by a young man, who regarded him with suspicion and impatience.

'Yes?'

'I am Squadron Leader Jan Pietrykowski.'

'Do I know you?'

'No, but I knew this cottage. I stayed here. I was a friend to the lady who lived here then. Do you know her, I wonder?'

'Sal might. Sal!'

A young woman, a land girl, came to the door. She was neither Aggie nor Nina.

Jan bowed. 'I am looking for a Mrs Dorothy Sinclair.'

'Oh. I didn't know her. I think Aggie did, though.'

'Is Aggie still here?'

'No. She left in 1942, I think it was. She got moved to a farm in Yorkshire. I heard she's going to marry a GI when he gets demobbed. They're going to Alabama, I think. Or is it Arkansas?'

'And Nina? Do you know the girl named Nina?' Jan tried to suppress his impatience.

'No, but I heard talk of a girl called Nina having a baby.'

'You did?'

'A little girl. She got married, I think. I don't know what became of her, though.'

'Ah.'

'Aggie used to talk about a woman named Dorothy. But I didn't know her.'

'Is there a music box here? A gramophone?'

She looked startled. 'Yes.'

'May I have it, please? I lent it to Dorothy at the start of the war. I have come to reclaim it.'

'It makes no odds to me,' said the girl. 'Bill, what do you think?'

The young man shrugged. 'We're leaving soon to go home, only going to leave it here. Do what you like with it.'

They stood aside to let Jan enter the kitchen, which was no longer Dorothy's kitchen. It was dirty and dark. The parlour beyond was dusty and tatty, with packing boxes jostling for space.

The young woman indicated the gramophone on the sideboard, and Jan, thanking her, lifted it, wincing. The younger man offered to help, and Jan was forced to accept. While Bill took the music box to Jan's car, Jan gathered up the remaining records; some were missing, he thought. He thanked the girl.

She smiled. 'So where you from, then?' she asked.

'Poland.'

'Oh.'

'You going back?' asked Bill, who had come back inside.

'Sadly, no.'

'Don't bloody blame you.'

He thanked them again, and returned slowly to the car.

* * *

And a few weeks later, Oxford. He was feeling better, stronger. The drive to Lincolnshire he should perhaps not have undertaken. Then, he had been weak. But now, all was on the mend. It was summer, and Oxford was a nice city, he thought, grand. And he wandered, marvelling at the colleges, the ivy-clad buildings, unscathed. And he asked people, those he met by chance, in shops, in libraries, in the street. He made himself a nuisance, but a charming one.

'Honour? I am looking for a Mrs Honour?' (For hadn't Dorothy once told him her maiden name was Honour?) 'With a grown-up daughter, Dorothy?'

He was on the point of giving up, tired,

unconvinced, his initial energies and hopes waning, wishing he had kept Dorothy's letter or at least memorised her address before his stupid pride had made him throw it away, when a woman, eager to help a handsome foreigner, brightened and did not shake her head.

'Ruth? Ruth Honour?'

And thus he found himself, tired and shaking, outside a house with a blue door in the north of the city. He breathed hard and knocked. Nobody answered. He peered through a window. The house seemed to be empty, forsaken. He spoke to a neighbour, who was peeping at him over a neatly cut box hedge.

Yes, he'd known the people who had lived there. An old lady and her daughter, both widowed, and the daughter's little boy. Nice family. But they'd gone, oh, three or four years ago? No, he had no forwarding address. The daughter, he thought, had married a Polish man who had died early in the war.

'Do you recall her married name?' Jan asked him.

'Pilkowski? Pentrykowski? Something like that.'

'Thank you,' said Jan, his chest swelling with a feeling he could not put a name to. 'And did she marry again, do you know?'

'I don't think so, no. But as I say, it's been a good while since they moved away. The house has an owner, but nobody lives here. They do collect post periodically, so they may have a forwarding address. Are you Russian?'

'Ah. Of course. Thank you for your time. No, I am not Russian.'

My dear Dorothea,

I have been trying to find you, with no success. I have got as far as your mother's house in Oxford, and there your trail seems to run cold. I write to you there, in the hope my letter can be passed on to you. A vain hope, but all I have. I think, if I try hard enough, I will find you. I suspect you go by my name, and you are most welcome to. In fact, it is my privilege. There can't be too many Pietrykowskis living in England! But at the same time, I do not want to bother you. You may be married again, with new name, and happy, and you no longer think of me. So if this letter reaches you, that is good. If not, so be it. I have a plan for my future, and if I do not hear from you, I will carry it out.

As you can see, I have survived the war, as I told you I would. I fought long and hard, and I became exhausted. As you say here, I ran out of steam. Last few months of war, I am in hospital. My old injury gives me gyp, I tire greatly, in my mind and body, and in the end I suffer a collapse of it all. Terrible. Thoughts of dying, feeling so weak and feeble and sick. But I am better now and all in my life is dancing and singing and light again. Almost all, because you are missing. I let you go and I should not have. It is the worst mistake of my life. I love you more than ever, and I was wrong to judge you so badly about your baby. I want you to forgive me and marry me, as we expected, if you are free to do so, of course, and if you want to. No doubt you are angry with me, disappointed by the letter I sent to you. I regret each and every word of it. I was wrong.

That is all. No more to be said, for now. I am not returning to Polska, to live under Communists, no, and I am bitter about that. But my life will be mine. I have a plan to go to Italy, be with the sun, swim, eat, find work. There will be work. I have a friend who says it is a good place to regain strength. Then, I think of the USA, land of opportunity. Perhaps you and your son could join with me there? This is my most cherished hope.

Jan

39

I'm still here, just. Still breathing and sleeping, waking, watching, thinking.

I remember now, that day we travelled down to London on the train. Just the three of us — me and John and Roberta. It was her tenth birthday, into double figures, so something to be celebrated. John was recovering from the break-up of his friendship with a woman called Kate. It hadn't been a very serious affair, and I had thought all along it had been ill advised. John could be intense when he was younger. And in those days he was, of course, still suffering from the shock of being abandoned by Anna. I'm not surprised Kate broke it off. She understood the heartache both of them laboured under, and she didn't fancy trying, and failing, to fill Anna's shoes. You really cannot blame her.

So, to London. Madame Tussauds first, which Roberta loved. Then, on the Tube to Trafalgar Square. We fed the pigeons, admired the lions — we got Roberta to sit on one for a photograph. She was wearing a striped sweater. It was a chilly day, so we decided to eat lunch indoors. We none of us knew London well enough to have a restaurant in mind, so we wondered what to do and where to go. I was tired.

About to suggest the café in the National Gallery, I turned towards the building and I saw her, a tall woman, somewhere in her sixties, staring at me. She may have been looking at me for some time, I'll never know. She was standing by one of the fountains. With her, a woman, fortyish, and two children, about Roberta's age, a little younger perhaps, both boys. I thought them twins. They were both tall, with mousy hair, and definitely, terrifyingly there was a look of Roberta about them. The younger woman was a feminine version of John. The older woman, Nina — for it was her, unmistakeably — stared at us. She looked at the two young boys, surely her grandsons, and back at John. She was plump, more so than before. She looked tired, grey and careworn. But, I dared to hope, she did not look unhappy. For a second, perhaps two, we looked straight at each other. And in her eyes, behind her eyes, I saw the brash nineteen-year-old, strong, loud, ignorant. All of this in a few seconds. By then my eyesight was failing, of course, but a person's essence never leaves them — especially, you cannot mistake the face of a woman who was once in pain, in need, begging you to help her.

And soon enough she was obscured by other people, with other lives, who had stories of their own, and I realised, with relief, that she was not going to advance upon me. I stopped looking. We found lunch, but I could not eat. My heart would not slow its beating, not for an hour, two hours. Finally, later, as we wandered around the galleries, I found myself thinking about Aggie. Had they kept in touch? And also, thank goodness it had not been Aggie. She might have stormed over, she might have caused a scene.

And soon after that, I found myself wondering about Jan, of course. Always, it was Jan. I don't believe a day of my life has passed since I last saw him when I haven't thought about him, and wondered what became of him. I harboured a hope for many years that I would hear from him, that he would track me down. But he did not. There has been one other man, but he was no more than a minor possibility, five decades ago, divorced, charming. Rich, I think, and rather lonely. We had a love affair that never really ignited. He wanted more from me than I could give. He faded away, or I did.

And now, all of them must be dead, as I should be. Even John is dead. She thinks I don't realise. Roberta, the dear, dear girl, and her with a fiancé now, a very nice man, she tells me. I think I can recall him, bookish and quite funny and charming. They must go on, have children, and build a good, strong life together. I know they will.

I am happy that I can frame these thoughts, happy that this core of me is intact; I can still think clearly in this innermost part, this kernel we all have, that remains undamaged throughout our lives. And I must sleep, of course. I'm so tired. I should have been asleep for years by now. Roberta is brushing my hair, she is so gentle and I am fading, I can feel myself, cell by cell, dropping away. I think it is time. Yes. I will keep my eyes closed now, and not open them again, and I shall go to Jan. If I think it, it will be so.

But — no! Roberta wants something. She wants to know the truth, just like John did. Yes, so simple, in two minutes I can tell all, pull myself together, and put an end to this fretting of hers, so —

'Roberta?'

'Yes?'

★ ★ ★

There. It is done. Confusing at first, but I got there in the end.

And she's shocked, a little, but not very shocked. I rather think she already knew more than she realised. And her hug, so strong, and she meant it, and I'm still her babunia and always will be. And it might have been nice to meet Jan, because he sounded like a wonderful person.

She was proud that I had tried to save the life of her 'real' grandfather. I had to keep that part in; everybody else believed it, so Roberta must too. Perhaps it will become a family legend. That's all right.

She tried to show me something . . . but I couldn't see what it was, I couldn't understand what she was telling me. It's a terrible thing to grow so old, to lose everything you once had, and to find life, the act of living, weaving your way through the day, so impossible.

And now, to Jan I must go. At last, it is his moment and mine. Such a roar, and that sun, my goodness it is hot, and my smooth, strong legs are bare and here comes the squadron, such a roar, and there is Jan's Hurricane, dipping from the sky like a pebble falling through stilled

345

waters, and his face, his beautiful face, his smile, his wave, and I wave back ('Hush, Babunia,' I think I hear Roberta whisper), and stillness now, and heat, all around, and no sound, no sight, and there, it is perfect. And his words, those words at the last, cruel to me then, a comfort now: I knew you were for all time, even as there is no time.

Acknowledgements

I'd like to thank everybody at Hodder and Stoughton, especially my keen-eyed editor Suzie Dooré. Thank you to my agent Hannah Ferguson for taking a chance on me and my work. Also to Debi Alper, Ian Andrews, Victoria Bewley, Sonja Bruendl-Price, Emma Darwin, Katherine Hetzel, Sophie Jonas-Hill and Jody Klaire for the advice, opinions, 'WIP' cracking and all round helpfulness and encouragement. And thanks to Neil Evans and Mark Forster for the technical input. I'd also very much like to thank Susan Davis and all at Cornerstones Literary Consultancy, and Jo Dickinson.

My research led me to three books that were a particular pleasure to read: I forgot I was supposed to be researching! They were *Battle of Britain* by Patrick Bishop, *How We Lived Then: A History of Everyday Life during the Second World War* by Norman Longmate and *For Your Freedom and Ours: The Kościuszko Squadron — Forgotten Heroes of World War II* by Lynne Olsen and Stanley Cloud. Any mistakes are my responsibility.

Thank you to my friends Radosøawa Barnaś-Baniel, for her help with the Polish language, and Tessa Burton, for her delight and encouragement. My mum and dad provided me with the books and the time to read from a young age, thank you to them, and to Pete for being my brother and so much more. Thank you to my children Oliver, Emily, Jude, Finn and Stanley for all the inspiration and excitement; finally, thank you to my generous husband Ian, who makes everything possible.

We do hope that you have enjoyed reading
this large print book.

Did you know that all of our titles
are available for purchase?

We publish a wide range of high quality
large print books including:
Romances, Mysteries, Classics
General Fiction
Non Fiction and Westerns

Special interest titles available in
large print are:
The Little Oxford Dictionary
Music Book
Song Book
Hymn Book
Service Book

Also available from us courtesy of
Oxford University Press:
Young Readers' Dictionary
(large print edition)
Young Readers' Thesaurus
(large print edition)

For further information or a free
brochure, please contact us at:
Ulverscroft Large Print Books Ltd.,
The Green, Bradgate Road, Anstey,
Leicester, LE7 7FU, England.
Tel: (00 44) 0116 236 4325
Fax: (00 44) 0116 234 0205

Other titles published by Ulverscroft:

NORTHANGER ABBEY

Val McDermid

Seventeen-year-old Catherine 'Cat' Morland has led a sheltered existence in rural Dorset, a life entirely bereft of the romance and excitement for which she yearns. So when Cat's wealthy neighbours ask her to accompany them to the Edinburgh Festival, she is sure adventure beckons. Edinburgh initially disappoints, but at a Highland dance class Cat meets Henry Tilney, a pale, dark-haired gentleman whose family home, Northanger Abbey, sounds perfectly thrilling. When Henry's father, the rigidly formal General Tilney, invites Cat to stay at Northanger Abbey with his family, Cat's imagination runs riot: an ancient abbey, crumbling turrets, secret chambers, ghosts . . . and Henry! What could be more deliciously romantic? But Cat gets far more than she bargained for in this isolated corner of the Scottish Borders . . .

BRING ME HOME

Alan Titchmarsh

It seems a perfect afternoon in the Highlands. Standing at the door of the lochside castle that has been his family's home for generations, Charlie Stuart welcomes his guests to the annual summer drinks party. Conversation, laughter and the clinking of glasses soon fill the air as friends and neighbours come together to toast the laird's happiness and prosperity. But Charlie sees the truth behind the facade: the sacrifices made to safeguard the estate; the devastating losses that have haunted him for decades; the guilt that lies at the heart of it all. In a few hours, he knows, the perfect afternoon will come to an end. The past, with its dark secrets of love, death, loyalty and betrayal, is about to catch up with him. And it could finally tear his family apart . . .

MY LIFE IN BLACK AND WHITE

Kim Izzo

Clara Bishop feels life has served her up far too many slaps and not nearly enough kisses — especially when she is suddenly jilted by her philandering husband. But, thanks to a suitcase of vintage clothing inherited from her grandmother, a former film noir actress, Clara discovers that the clothes really do make the woman. Dressed to kill, she adopts a new femme fatale persona: confident, sexy and set on revenge. As her quest unfolds, Clara's life is transported into a living, breathing film noir from the fifties when she finds an unfinished film script. Soon she discovers not only the secrets of her grandmother's past, but the chance to write her own ending too . . .